AFTER THE BREAK

ANDREA JOAN

Copyright © 2016 by Andrea Joan

First Edition, 2016

Cover Design by Mayhem Cover Creations, www.mayhemcovercreations.com
Cover Image ©Scott Hoover
Author photo by Franggy Yanes
Formatting by Stacey Blake at Champagne Formats, www.champagneformats.com
Editor: Kara Malinczak, survivorluvr33@gmail.com
Proofreader: Kimberley Foster Holm, www.facebook.com/kimberley.fosterholm?fref=ts

Publication Date: January 10th, 2017

ISBN 978-0-9982637-1-7
Copyright ©Andrea Joan 2016

DEDICATION

This book is dedicated to me. Because I finished the damn thing. And that is pretty cool.

"Your demons never fully leave. But when you're using them to create something else, it almost gives them a purpose and feels like none of it was in vain. I think that's how I make peace with it."
—Evan Rachel Wood

PROLOGUE

LIAM

Seattle: One Year Ago

Drug of choice; railing lines of coke seems to be on the menu tonight. But I'm not particular I'll shove anything up my nose, down my throat, or into my lungs. Snort, smoke, or swallow. It doesn't matter as long as it gets me so fucking high I can't remember who I am.

Booze of Choice; Jameson. Every. Fucking. Night.

Girl of choice; obviously she has a name, but at the moment I can't fucking remember. I'm sure she told me before we stumbled back to my shitty apartment. I can probably blame this memory loss on the coke, or the booze, or the fact that this chicks' mouth is wrapped so tight around my cock that she is literally sucking the memory out of me, but the truth of it is I have barely listened to a fucking word she has said. I don't care to remember so I can't listen. Blondie probably told me her whole life story when I was serving her drinks tonight, right before she pulled me into the bar's bathroom and let me snort lines off her tits while she shoved my hand up her practically non-existent skirt, but every time she spoke I shut my brain off because I. Don't. Want. To. Remember.

That's the curse of having an eidetic memory. I can't forget anything I hear or see or smell or even fucking taste. Every event, every experience, every single snapshot of my life will burrow its way unrelentingly into my brain like a fucking diseased tick. People think that having a photographic memory is some kind of gift, like a goddamn superpower. Shit, there was a time I believed that. School was a cake walk. Anything I read in a textbook or learned during a lecture was easily categorized and referenced in my mind for future use. I could tell you the ties my Freshman History teacher wore every day of the two-week period he taught the class on the Fall of the Roman Empire. That was almost ten years ago. I can even recollect wall to ceiling to floor what my first girlfriends' bedroom looked like right down to the prayers on all those creepy fucking Precious Moments posters she had plastered over her walls. I was thirteen.

But here is the problem with having every second of my life seared into my memory like a brand. I don't get to pick and choose what is remembered. When something horrible happens to me, something so dark and depraved and painful it would rival my worst nightmare, I will be condemned to remember. Every. Fucking. Detail. In high def. I hear the screaming and the begging, feel the pain of a blade slicing my skin over and over, smell the fear and taste that coppery flavor of blood as real as if it was happening in the present. The memory brutally rapes my mind until there is nothing of substance left and the only escape from the constant punishment of it comes in the form of a powder or a pill or a bottle. Or pussy.

Pussy seems to help drown out the ghosts that haunt me. Temporarily anyway. Which is why I stumbled the two blocks from the bar to my apartment with blondie on my arm. She was more than ready to fuck, she's hot in that fake porn star kind of way, and most importantly she came with snowy white party favors.

"*Fuck* you're good at that, honey," I groan, my large hand grabbing the back of her slender neck pushing my dick deeper down her seemingly endless throat. Bringing the bottle of Jameson to my mouth I take a pull that would put Tommy Lee to shame. The burn hits me quick. I relish the feeling of my eyes rolling back into my head as the effects of the alcohol and coke, mixed with the sensation of a warm tongue licking my cock and taking me deep again cause me to fall back on the mattress, the box springs singing that familiar tune of carnal abuse as I hit it hard.

"You like that, Liam? God you're seriously big," she purrs while her hand takes over where her mouth left off, pumping me up and down.

That should be a huge fucking turn on, but my name on her cigarette laced voice almost causes me to lose my erection, especially when I open my eyes again and find fake violet ones staring back at me, begging for my approval. Approval she will be waiting a long ass time for because the disgust I have for myself in this moment has been reallocated to this chick. Everything about her is phony; colored contacts, cheap blonde extensions attached to her head, and definitely fake tits. Even the scent of her is a fucking turn off; some kind of overly sweet flower smell, but it replaces the odor of death and blood that habitually surrounds me so I acquiesce.

Fuck! Why did I have to open my eyes? Maybe if I get drunk enough and high enough this will never even be a memory.

"Don't talk honey. Just suck."

"Mmmm, I love when you call me honey," she moans, creeping her fingers slowly toward the hem of my shirt, her other hand fisting my dick hard just like I need.

The harder she sucks me off, the harder she works her hand up and down my shaft, the easier it is to push the memory of *that* night further and further away. So I need her to stop fucking talking.

Chuckling, I take her hand off my shirt. "You shouldn't. I only call you honey because I can't remember your name. Now stop talking and suck me off. Or you can leave. I don't really give a shit."

Her faux violet eyes shoot up at me clearly in shock that I would say something so offensive. But I know she won't leave. I clocked her as an insecure bar slut the minute I served her a cosmopolitan and she adjusted her already low cut shirt further down to give me a better view of her tits while constantly brushing her hands over the tats on my arm.

"You're an asshole," she spits out but stays conveniently on her knees in front of me.

It's nothing I haven't heard before, or anything I would argue with. But what the hell did she expect? A few winks in her direction, some shared shots of tequila-which I'm not technically supposed to drink while working- and the mention that I was once an amateur boxer had her panting and guiding my hand under her skirt in the bar bathroom before she even gave her name.

A name I now can't fucking remember for the life of me. Tammy... Taryn...Trisha? Something with a T. Or maybe a P. Nope. Not coming to me.

Goddamn this coke is good. My face is numb, my fucking mind is numb. I need to get the name and number of her dealer before I shove her ass out the door.

"I know I am. But maybe you can help save me. Turn me good again, honey," I say with a cocky smile. I know the effect I have on women without even trying and that little ray of hope should do the trick of getting her gifted little mouth back on my dick.

Christ, I am an asshole.

Blondie smiles big and works her hands back toward my shirt. My entire body tenses at the realization that she is trying to take it off.

"Stop." I snatch her wrist with the hand not attached to my whiskey.

"What? I just wanna see what you're working with under there. I know fighters have cut bodies. It would make me much more eager to suck you off. I may even be willing to swallow," T or P something teases, licking her lips slowly.

Fuck it. What do I care what this chick thinks? Two scenarios could play out. She will either excuse herself as she runs out the door, which is fine by me, or ignore what she sees and continue blowing me. I'm sure my cock would agree that the latter scenario is more favorable.

Normally I try to avoid taking my clothes off altogether, but I know she is not going to let up, and frankly I'm too fucked up right now to put up much of a fight. And I need this. I fucking *need* to get off. I crave the silence in my head, a break from hearing *her* call out for me to help her. To save her. A brief reprieve from seeing and hearing my brother's last fucking breath.

"Go for it, but don't say I didn't warn you." I take another swig of Jameson before lying back on the bed. The ceiling above spins in an endless circular maze, speckles of silver and black dots swirling round and round.

The feel of my shirt gliding up my abs should excite me, but only causes panic.

"Holy shit." I feel her breath whisper against my skin before my shirt even reaches my pecs. "Maybe you would be more comfortable if you kept the shirt on."

What she really means is that *she* would be more comfortable if I kept the shirt on. I'm lucky my pretty face was spared from any lasting damage or I may have never gotten laid again. T or P something doesn't bother to ask what happened or feign sympathy as she kneels back down on her knees and takes me deep into her mouth again.

"*Shit,*" I curse under my breath, as her tongue glides up and swirls around the tip of my cock.

It's almost time for another hit of blow. This chick does have talent, definitely not an amateur when it comes to sucking dick. The feint afterthought that I should have wrapped it up before letting her mouth touch my cock flashes through my inebriated brain. But where was the fun in that? Truth be told I deserve some kind of STD, something that could permanently fuck up my future, but it won't happen. I'm goddamn invincible and no matter how much I test my luck it will never fail me, despite how often I pray it will; begging for punishment like a drowning man searching for air.

My hand lazily finds its way to her head as she takes me deeper and deeper into oblivion. I'm so loaded at this point that I barely remember my own name, so P or T something shouldn't feel bad.

I don't bother to warn her that I'm about to come. I know she will take whatever I have to offer, just like all the ones before her. With a grunt I jet semen down her throat, pulling her hair slightly, causing her to moan in appreciation and sending a nice little vibration around my dick.

Now the welcoming silence descends, my memories wiped clean. Nothing but nothingness.

"Damn, honey, that was something."

I sit up on the bed and tuck myself back into my pants, still managing to hold on to my whiskey like a goddamn pro.

"Mmm-hmmm," she hums. "Now it's my turn. By the way, my name is Samantha," she informs, wiping her mouth seductively with her fingers. *Samantha.* I was way off.

"Whatever, honey." And I also don't give a shit.

She straddles me in one movement and kisses me sloppily while rocking her hips into my lap before I even have time to zip up my pants. Amazing. I treat her like shit and she is still down to screw my brains out. Blondie tastes like tequila and tobacco and shame, but I'm an emotional masochist and all that is wrong with her and this situation only makes my cock hard and ready for round two.

"Give me a second."

Taking a final pull of Jameson I throw the now empty bottle onto the floor where it clanks against the many others playing the songs of my failure and ever progressing self-destruction. I reach into my pocket and pull my wallet free snatching a condom out of one of the folds. As daring as I was with the blow job there is no fucking way I'm sticking my dick in this girl without protection. Shit the last thing I need is a mini-me running around.

Grabbing her hips, I flip her easily around onto my bed, making sure to press her head into the mattress. No need to see her face.

She giggles like a little school girl and I try not to feel repulsed. Whoever told women that sounding like a little girl was sexy should have his fucking head examined. I need to get this over with already.

Pulling my pants down for the second time tonight, I rip the condom wrapper with my teeth and sheath myself.

"You ready for me?" I rasp into her ear, dragging a hand toward the back of her inner thigh and up under her skirt to her center.

I slide a finger into her and she moans. Damn she is dripping wet, more than ready. Her ass begins to grind upward into my hand and her moans become more frantic. She does have a fucking amazing ass I will give her that.

The tip of my dick is hovering right at her entrance when without warning flashes of *that* night play through my mind like a horror movie. *Her* angelic face ghosts through my closed eyes. Torturing me. Tempting me. Killing me.

I shake my head as if that will somehow erase the memory, like my brain is a goddamn Etch-A-Sketch.

Forget. Push past it. Push into her. You will feel release. Become numb.

Before I slam into her, I hear the muffled ringing of my phone from the pocket of my jeans on the floor.

"*Fuck.*" I was so fucking close. Snatching my pants off the floor, I clumsily try to pull my phone out of my pocket.

"Ignore it, baby. It's like two in the morning. Just fuck me already. I'm ready."

"*Don't* call me baby," I snarl.

I know how harsh I sound, but where the hell does this chick get off thinking she can call me baby? Only one girl had that right, and she's dead now.

The caller ID on my phone reads Shayla and I slide a finger across the screen as fast as I can manage. "Shayla? What's up? You okay?"

Trying to hide the panic in my voice is nearly impossible because my sixteen-year-old sister calling at two in the morning can mean nothing good. I discard the condom, because I don't want to talk to my sister with a fucking condom wrapped around my dick, and pull my pants back up over my hips.

"Liam." A faint sniffle shudders through the phone and burns into my ear. She's obviously been crying, and the hairs on the back of my neck stand at attention.

"Who the hell is Shayla?" She flips dramatically around and shoots an icy glare my way as if she has some claim to me.

I thought my not bothering to remember her name would have been the first hint I don't give a shit about her, but apparently that wasn't clear enough. And I do *not* fucking like the way she spits out my sister's name as if it was poison. I cover the speaker of the phone with my hand and walk the short distance from my bed to my bathroom.

"My baby sister. Now shut the fuck up."

Slamming the bathroom door shut I have to lean against the counter to steady my drunk ass, the iridescent lights quickly creating a migraine in my intoxicated brain. *Focus, asshole.*

"You okay? What's wrong?"

The relentless thumping in my chest is warning me that I need to calm the hell down before my heart explodes. I press the Harley keys from my pocket hard into my hand in an attempt to focus my rabid energy. That and because I want to be ready to haul my ass home in order to beat the shit out of anyone that is messing with my sister. I may be too fucked up to drive but the blind rage I've quickly been accustomed to since *that* night is scorching through my veins. Sobering. Me. Right the fuck up.

"I'm fine, Liam. It's dad. He-he can't do it anymore." She sniffs into the phone again. That sound breaks me. My sister is the only one that I allow to evoke some semblance of a real emotion in me anymore; if it were anyone else I would push those emotions someplace deep where they can't affect me.

"What? What do you mean, Shay?"

"It's the cancer. I know he told you he was doing fine and was in remission and he didn't need any help with the bar, but he was lying. The chemo treatments are wearing on him. He's lost so much weight and he is tired all the time. I'm trying to help, but with school I just don't have the time to be there as much. And Dory quit so he doesn't have a manager to help him anymore. He's at the bar all the time. He's killing himself. I don't know what to do. I know he doesn't want you to know, but I'm not sure why. I'm scared, Liam. I just don't...I don't..." She trails off through a faded sob.

How could my dad keep this from me? If he hadn't assured me his cancer was in remission I would have been home months ago to fucking help. Maybe he doesn't believe I can help. Fuck, he'd be right. I'm in no position to help anyone and he can probably sense it. I have an aura about me that screams failure to anyone within a universally wide radius. Damn, maybe he doesn't even want me around. I would be a constant fucking reminder of the night he lost his first-born son while me, his other son, did nothing to help.

But I know that's not the case. No one person; not my mother, my father, my sister, fucking *no one* blames me for what happened. And that makes it so much worse. I would rather their anger and blame than their fucking pity. I don't deserve to be pitied, or forgiven.

"Shhh, Shay, it's okay. You're sixteen, you shouldn't know what to do," I tell her running my hand over my face as I sink onto the bathroom floor. "I'm coming back. I'll hop on the first ferry home to-morrow. Don't worry."

"Promise?" The question came out in a whimper causing me to slam my fist on the linoleum floor. I can't fail her too.

Not her. No fucking way.

How could I be snorting, fucking, and drinking while my baby sister isn't sleeping because she's too busy taking care of her family? Our family. Fuck, I'm such a worthless piece of shit.

She sounds so tired, so worn out. How could I have missed this? Just another thing I refuse to acknowledge because I'm so wrapped up in my own bullshit. Self-loathing can keep a person busy.

"I promise, Shay. Try and get some sleep. You hear me?"

"Okay, big brother. I'm really sorry."

"What?" *Jesus.* "Don't be sorry Shayla. This isn't your fault. Listen go get some sleep. I'll be back on the island first thing tomorrow."

"Okay."

"I'm serious, Shayla. Sleep, you got me?" I command because I want to be very fucking sure she listens.

"Yeah, I got you."

"Good girl. Goodnight, Shay."

"Night. Love you, Liam."

"Me too."

I slide my finger across the screen to end the call while I try my best not to fucking crush the phone in my hand. I don't even realize I am banging my head on the bathroom wall until I hit it a little too hard. But the pain helps. It centers me, it focuses me and with each hit I can feel the anger start to fade away.

"Liam what's going on in there? Are you coming back out here or what? I cut a few lines in case you need a little pick me up, baby."

Shit. I fucking forgot about what's her name. And did she just call me baby again? "I told you not to call me baby. Do you have a hard time understanding fucking English? You need to get your shit and leave. Something's come up."

I don't bother leaving the bathroom; I don't need to deal with her drama. I just want her out of my fucking apartment. I'm sure the gen-tlemanly thing to do is offer to call her a cab and give her money for the ride home, but I'm not a gentleman, she is definitely *not* a fucking lady and I am confident she is a pro at the Walk of Shame so she knows how this works.

"Are you fucking serious?!" She shrieks as she bangs on the bathroom door. Guess that little girl voice has disappeared.

I don't bother to respond, I would just be flaming the fire of her inner drama queen and I have neither the time nor the patience for that bullshit. I hear her mumbling something about me being a one pump chump, blah blah blah, can't get it up and some other nonsense I couldn't give two shits about. Then the front door finally closes with a bang and I work myself up off the bathroom floor. I turn around and do the one thing I haven't done in fucking months.

I look at my reflection in the bathroom mirror.

The person staring back at me is a pathetic excuse for a brother, for a son, for a human being. My pupils are the size of pin needles, probably because of the massive amounts of coke I've inhaled tonight. I haven't shaved in weeks and my skin is gray. Not pale. Fucking Gray.

I guess that's what happens when your main food group consists of whiskey and ramen. Not mixed together. That's fucking disgusting.

I wonder if this is what Shay looks like right now. I haven't seen her beautiful face in months so I wouldn't know. But I know if she looks as bad as me it's because she has worn herself down by doing something admirable, something to be proud of. Like taking care of her family when they need it most. Something I should be doing. I *need* to do.

I have a fucking chance here. A chance to redeem myself. I'm in a hell of my own making and this is my opportunity to get out. I don't know if redemption can be found in hell, but I know it's time to find out. I take one final look at myself in the mirror before I pull my arm up, make a fist, and smash it to fucking pieces.

It's time to go home.

CHAPTER 1

Skylar

"Skylar Joy Barrett and her movie crew are set to wrap their last day of filming today after turning our quiet little island upside down during the most exciting two-month summer we have seen in a while."

Leaning on the wall near the bathroom entry in my small room, I watch as a middle-aged female reporter with pancake makeup stands on a sidewalk which, if I'm not mistaken, appears to be right in front of The Lighthouse Inn, the inn where I'm staying. Fantastic. My shoulders begin to tense and my breathing becomes shallow because I have some semblance of what is coming. They never talk about me as if I'm a person just like them, but more like an object.

"*There have been many sightings of the very troubled twenty-two-year-old starlet, and the general consensus seems to be one of approval. Let's talk to Jessica who says she met Skylar last week at O'Connor's, Orcas Island's favorite bar. Jessica, what was Skylar like when you met her? Did you get to talk to her?*"

And here we go. Not only have I never been to O'Connor's, I've never even heard of it. So I can't wait to see what *Jessica* has to say about this obviously clandestine meeting. Right on cue, the camera pans over to a young brunette woman, probably in her early twenties, surprisingly quite beautiful, and who I can only assume is Jessica.

"*I met her and talked to her! Skylar was over drinking and playing pool, and me and my friends just like walked up and said hello and like asked her if she was having fun on the island filming and everything. She said she loved it here and wished she could stay here.*"

I roll my eyes and give a slight shake of my head, a one-two move I have mastered in my years of watching these same types of news interviews about people that have "met me." It's always the same formula these people use, too. Just like Jessica, the ones before her always see me in a very public place and *always* have "friends" with them as a way to convince the people watching that this indeed happened, because how could someone be lying if their friends were there too?

"*And what did Skylar look like, Jessica? Is she just as beautiful in person?*"

"*Oh yeah, totally. I mean she seemed shorter in real life and maybe skinnier than I thought she was, but they say the camera adds ten pounds. And she wasn't wearing any makeup or anything, so she looked a bit different than she does in the movies. Plainer, I guess. She was still pretty, just, I guess, not as pretty as you would imagine. But she was super cool. She was just like me. I mean, we got along so well...*"

I do love a good old fashioned backhanded compliment. Females are trained to give them from birth as if they are a second language. But at least Jessica got one thing right; I have played pool before.

Well, I've officially had enough. I turn the television to a channel playing some *Law and Order* reruns and decide it's time for that shower I was so looking forward to. As I turn to walk into the bathroom, my phone rings with that damn annoying nostalgic ringtone that makes me want to throw it onto the beach. I really need to change it.

I run over to the bed and lift up my pillow where I know the phone is hiding. Damn it all to hell. The caller ID spells out the last name I'd ever want to see, but probably the first I should expect. Carl.

"Hello, Carl," I say. The eye roll that went with that greeting is one for the record books.

"What's up?" I lie back on the bed, hoping...no...praying to whatever god or spirit or entity or designer I decide to believe in today that this call will be quick and painless. But I already know that this is a futile measure, because nothing with my father is quick, and very rarely is it ever painless. Emotionally or physically, he always finds a way to hurt me.

"I need to know what time you'll be back today so I can set up a meeting with Steve Goodwin," my father demands. My father always demands, and as long as I've known him I've never heard the inflection of his voice rise to the tune of a question.

"Good morning to you too, Carl." I refer to him by his first name whenever he decides to behave more like my manager than my father, which is ninety-eight percent of the time. My only advice to any young actor coming up in this business would be: *don't* hire your parent as your manager. My father jumped on that gravy train when I was too young to have a say, and now I don't have the heart—heart's not the right word—nerve? No, balls. Balls works better. I don't have the balls to fire him.

"Good Morning, Skylar," he says sarcastically. "Now what time will you be back today?"

"I've told you ten times already that I'm not coming home today. The wrap party for the film is tonight, and it won't look good if I bail. I don't need the cast and crew thinking I think I'm too good, or too big of a star to show up."

I've gone over this with him before, and yet the reason he still refuses to acknowledge me is because he believes *I am* too big of a star to show up.

"Skylar, you are too big of a name to even be in this movie."

I knew it.

"And I know I've told you ten times that you need to meet with Steve immediately. He is your attorney, Skylar, and he seems to think this issue with Jeff Roberts is a bigger deal than you do. It's an issue that is not going to go away. Stop being a stubborn selfish little bitch about the whole thing. This will affect us both."

Emotional pain, check.

"You know what, Carl, why don't you just let me have today before I deal with the reality of this? Set up the meeting with Steve for later in the week when it fits into *my* schedule."

I lay that tone on as thick and serious as I can manage and push off the bed. I start pacing back and forth in front of the television. Unfortunately, it's not unusual for my father to talk to me this way, and as much as it wounds me, I continue to allow him to degrade me. I am deserving of his wrath, after all. I took his wife from him. But slowly I'm becoming more and more immune to his attempts at control.

"And when you call Steve, make sure to ask him if those fucking confidentiality agreements he is so fond of having people sign are worth a goddamn thing."

There's a long silence on the other end of the phone, and I assume Carl is throwing a silent temper tantrum, one that will end with a hole in a wall that slightly resembles his fist.

"Carl, are you going to handle this or do I have to?"

"Skylar." Cue the condescending tone. "I really don't think you should put this off any longer. Jeff will start leaking stories about you to the press, and as he was your former bodyguard, he will carry some clout."

I can tell Carl is attempting to say this as slowly as possible, trying to mask the anger that is beginning to fester inside him. As an actress, I've been taught to become adept at listening and reading people in order to emulate the proper reaction in a scene, and I know it's killing him that he's not near enough to physically scare me.

"Set up the meeting for later in the week. Don't call me about this again unless you are giving me the new meeting time."

With a sigh of relief, I hang up the phone before Carl can get another word in. It's easy for me to act brave when talking to him right now because he's three states away.

I drop down onto the bed, and I swear the pillow-top mattress is a magnet pulling my receptive body down. The after effects of an Ambien induced sleep take a little while to wear off, so if I'm not careful I might just get lulled into sleep once again. I don't take it often; in fact I typically try and stay away from it just for this reason. It helps me sleep, but it can make me feel hungover as hell the next morning. It probably doesn't help that I took my Ambien with a Xanax kicker and a shot of tequila. I'm not an addict or anything, and I almost never mix and match my coping mechanisms. I just need a little assistance every now and then when I can't seem to get my brain to shut off, and the doctors in L.A. are all too ready to provide it to "patients" like me. An autographed picture or DVD for the doctor's kid can get me a lifetime prescription pad from Hollywood's most elite physicians.

I run my hands through my hair and release a deep sigh. My anxiety level is at an eight, making its way to a hard ten. Thinking about that pathological liar Jeff makes me sick to my stomach, as in I wish I could literally vomit the fragments of his name and the memory it brings until no remnants are left behind. Hired by Carl as a bodyguard to protect me from aggressive paparazzi, stalkers, and the general creepy super fan, it is simply ironic that he ended up being a man I need protection from.

It just goes to show, you can't trust anyone when you're a celebrity. Right now though, I don't want to think about any of this. I want to enjoy the last day I have on this island—an island that holds an aura of peace and happiness, a type of contentment I've never experienced and know I will lose when I get back home. I walk to the Keurig machine and insert a pod. I need some damn coffee. As I wait, I take a minute to appreciate my small room, giving it one last look.

Maybe small is not the right word; quaint is probably a more apt description. I'm used to larger, more glamorous hotel rooms when shooting on location. Normally I'd be staying in a 5,000-square foot mansion equipped with an indoor/outdoor pool, sauna, media viewing room, and a coke dealer on speed dial, just for good measure, not that I ever touch the stuff. Coke is too cliché for me. My brain already runs at hypersonic speed with a thousand different thoughts bouncing around at the same time, and that's without a chemical boost.

My newest film doesn't have the budget as the ones I've done previously. This is a smaller independent film, and the budget has been mostly used for production costs with nothing left over for the luxuries I usually command, or for that matter the paycheck. I'm certain I'm actually paying to work on this film, and that's okay with me. The script is brilliant and it's not some shitty remake of a once great film, or another sequel to a generically done first film. Career killer, maybe, but at this point I don't care. It's something different. And I *need* something to change. Besides, I made enough money playing Mandy Mayhem as a child that I never have to earn another dollar again. Who knew playing a kid detective that ran around an elementary school solving all kinds of mysteries in a number of serial movies could set someone up for life? It was like Mary Kate and Ashley Olsen meets Nancy Drew, minus an Olsen. And as ridiculous as those movies are, I can't complain. Mandy Mayhem bought me my first house at seventeen and continues to add more than seven figures to my bank account with royalties and merchandising. Mandy Mayhem made me a multi-millionaire more than a few times over.

The sound of the ocean tide grows louder as I approach the French doors. I love that sound; there is something so soothingly forceful about it. More than that, I love the way it smells—the beach and the sand. When I open the doors, coffee in hand, and step out onto the small balcony, the early morning breeze brings in the sea air and it washes over me.

My gaze immediately scans the horizon and stops on a small weathered, seemingly abandoned, but apparently occupied house because there is an equally dilapidated Jeep parked next to it, right on the beach. Whenever I see a house that catches my attention I always imagine what the family that lives there is like.

The sound of my phone beeping interrupts my daydreaming, and I know that time suck of a device is interrupting what will probably be the last moment of introspective silence I'll have today.

Noah's name flashes on the screen, my hair and makeup guru, and also one of only two friends that I have. I never go anywhere or film anything without him. I even have a clause in my contract that states he is to be involved in every movie I am in. Noah is the only one I trust to make me look like the star I am supposed to be, and the only person I just flat out trust, as much as I can anyway.

Noah: Hey there, Morningstar. Just a little FYI, the wrap party is tonight at eight. I know it's early but I guess this island has a 1am curfew. Weird I know. I'll come over and we can get beautiful together. We need to get us some island boys tonight and end this trip with a bang...pun intended. ;)

Despite the less than stellar morning I've had, I can't help but smile looking at his text. Especially when he called me Morningstar.

The origin of that obscure little nickname comes from when he tried texting me Good Morning once and for some ungodly reason his phone auto corrected it to Morningstar. He sent the text before he noticed and we were both unreasonably hysterical about it for hours. I have been Morningstar ever since. Noah always makes me laugh, and he seems to have a sixth sense for when I need a good one.

Me: I'm all for getting ready together, my love, but the island boys are all yours. Where are we meeting?

Noah: Booooo, you whore! You're no fun. Anywho, we'll be meeting at a place called O'Connor's. Don't you just love little bars with Irish names? So deliciously cliché.

O'Connor's. Of course. An incredulous laugh escapes my lips. Maybe I was wrong about Jessica. Maybe she's actually some type of clairvoyant who can see into my serendipitous future.

Me: Okay, sounds fun. Come over at seven and we'll get ready. Love ya!

CHAPTER 2

LIAM

Run. I fucking run. It's how I spend my mornings now, and one of the only things I look forward to anymore, a way to clear my head before the day begins. My feet connecting with the ground in a loud succinct rhythm and my hard breathing tends to drown out the dark thoughts and nightmares left over from my sleepless nights. Since cutting out the drugs entirely and minimizing my weekly booze consumption, I've had to replace the source of my adrenaline intake and mind numbing tactics with other more acceptable options. And the second I hit that runners' high I feel a similar release as when I snort a line or bury my dick deep into pussy. Not that I've given that up. I'm not a fucking saint. Although I have fucked some of those in the last few years.

Turning saints into sinners with a righteous fuck. Gets. Me. Off.

With every deep breath I take I let the smell of the island captivate me. Its salty ocean scent mixed with the evergreen trees and some un-named spice assaults my senses. This makes me sound like a fucking douche, I know, but I read once that the sense of smell is one of the most powerful memory triggers. It can bring on a damn flood of memories because once you smell something new, that scent is forever linked to the person or moment associated with it. I could quote some other scientific shit about the olfactory bulb and its access to the amygdala, which processes emotion, but I won't because I'm not a pretentious asshole. Just because I can recall every fucking word doesn't mean I *understand* every fucking word. The point is, the smell of this island brings me only the good memories. The ones where Trevor was still alive and Shay was just a toddler and we would carry her out to a tiny island when the tide went out, or every year when my parents hosted a huge neighborhood Fourth of July barbecue. Or the day I hung a hammock for Ali in my parents' backyard because she always dreamed of having a hammock to read her books in, but her parents had no place to hang one. Just like a drug though, these runs are only a temporary fix, because once my run is over, these good memories only prove to be more fucking torturous than the bad because I know I can never experience those feelings again.

Six years ago, I would have been running in the late afternoon, when the island was alive with tourists and friends alike. I was friendly with everyone; no one feared me like they do now. Six years ago I had a much different reputation in Eastsound, the town golden boy destined to make a name for myself in the boxing game. But now things are much different. My reputation has been tarnished by my quick temper, and when I fucking snap, everything goes dark. I lose control.

And in a close-knit town like Eastsound, the gossips in it live to remember your failures over your triumphs and never forgive your past. Not that I want or need their forgiveness. I deserve their condemnatory punishment.

As I turn a corner onto Main Street, named that because it's literally the only street in the small town of Eastsound, I feel my shoe loosen around my foot. The goddamn thing is untied.

"Fuck!" I fucking hate when my concentration is broken because all the good memories associated with those smells dissipate from my mind as the momentary lapse in concentration allows a chance for the darkness to descend.

Reluctantly I bend down to tie my shoe and hear a door creak open a short distance away. I glance up instinctively and see her. She walks out onto the balcony from a room on the second floor of The

Lighthouse Inn like a living fantasy. I take a few steps forward toward the edge of the sidewalk to get a better look. Because I know. I *fucking* know this is a sight I would be happy to have seared into my memory from now until the day I die. My breath, which just moments ago had been hard and fast from running, halts in my chest as if time and existence has frozen around me because even the universe can sense how fucking spectacular her presence is. She's quite simply beautiful, breathtaking, and somewhat familiar.

Shit. I know that face. I don't even need a photographic memory to remember who she is. I just need to not live in a fucking cave. Everyone knows her. It's Skylar Barrett. I know she's been filming something around here, the whole island has been talking about it for months, but never thought I'd see her. My sister used to watch that stupid Mandy Mayhem every Saturday morning. It was fucking torture.

And here she is to torture me again, only this time in a *very* different way, because she's all grown up. Her auburn hair drapes messily over one shoulder as she stares out at the ocean. She must have just woken up as she appears to be wearing something she slept in and there is a tranquil vibe about her, a type of calmness that comes before the day fucks you up. A pink tank top fits tightly to her petite body and a pair of white shorts hang off her hipbones.

Fuck me, she has the most perfect body I've seen on any woman. Ever. Trust me when I say I have seen a fucking lot. Unfortunately I'm too far away to see her facial features, more importantly her eyes. Beautiful eyes are my Achilles' heel. That's what drew me to *her*. I shut my eyes to get the image of her out of my head as quickly as fucking possible.

Once upon a time I would have made some grand gesture, like scaling the balcony and asking this girl out on a date, and she would have said yes. Most chicks do, and in less than three hours after meeting one I can have my name replacing God's while they scream it in my bed.

Or theirs.

Or a bar bathroom.

Or the back seat of a car.

Or the front seat of a car.

Or the hood of a car. I'm not picky.

But this chick, this woman, she is one you wife the fuck up. As quickly as possible. And yes, I can tell this just from looking at her. I'm one hundred percent certain I'm not Skylar Barrett material either. I'm not relationship material in general. I can't go down that road again. It will hurt too much in the end, and it *will* end.

Her head turns to her room abruptly; something must have caught her attention, and just like that I am pulled from my self-induced hypnosis. Damn. For a brief second I felt something I have not felt in a long fucking time: alive. Like Doctor Frankenstein just flipped the fucking switch and the monster in me had a fucking beating heart again. I push that shit back down deep because it only stands to remind me of what I've lost. Remind me of how human life is so fucking fleeting and disposable, and the people you care about are no exception. So fuck Skylar Barrett. She is just a poster on a wall you jerk off to anyway. With that last reassuring thought I step back on the sidewalk to continue my run. I want to make it home before the island starts waking up and I'm no longer the last man on earth.

⚜

As I sprint up to the doorway of my house, ending my five-mile run with a strong finish because I always fucking finish strong, I scare the feral black rabbits that run wild on this island out of mom's vegetable garden. I manage a smile as the rabbits scamper away because I know when my mom sees the damage they've done to her garden she'll be livid. It's not that I enjoy seeing my mom mad; in fact she rarely gets angry, I just enjoy knowing the end result is always the same. Dad will suggest setting traps or fencing the garden; once he even suggested poisoning the rabbits, but mom just brushes off every solution with a dramatic sigh saying, "I guess it's good *someone* is enjoying those vegetables."

Truth is, I know she loves those damn rabbits. They make her feel necessary, and her heart is too pure to deny the little fuckers their meal. Not that they would starve without her vegetables.

I open the heavy oak door that allows me entry into my childhood home and I'm hit with the smell of brewing coffee, which can only mean two things: one, I made it home right at eight thirty so I made great fucking time, and two, mom is up.

"Liam, sweetie, is that you?" I hear her ask from the kitchen.

"Yeah, Ma," I say through a ragged breath. "Is the coffee done or did you just put it on?"

I take my shoes off and place them uniformly on the shoe rack under the gilded mirror hanging in the entryway before I walk down the hallway. Everything in this house is done a certain way out of respect for my mom. And I respect the shit out of her, so whatever the hell she wants I'll do. The hallway walls leading me to the kitchen are lined with family photos of camping trips and backyard barbeques, trips to Seattle, and school pictures of me and Trev and Shayla. Anyone can tell within seconds of stepping through the doorway that this is not just a house, it's a home.

When I enter the kitchen, I see my mom at the sink washing her hands, and I engulf her in a bear hug, bending down to kiss her on the cheek. I'm not a mama's boy, I just fucking love and respect the woman who brought me into this world.

Also, I know this hug will gross her the hell out.

"Liam!" she squeals, while squirming out of my embrace. "Come on now, you are all sweaty. And yes, the coffee is done. I poured you a cup," she says, pointing to the dining room table where a large breakfast spread, complete with bagels, fresh fruit, cream cheese, homemade jam, bacon, and an array of muffins has been laid out. This is a typical Saturday morning ritual, a large breakfast to get the weekend started off right. The strawberries are the best. If that makes me sound like a pussy, so be it, but I love a fresh strawberry. And they come fresh from her garden as long as the rabbits don't get to them first.

Fuckers.

"Hey, is dad up yet?" I ask, grabbing a blueberry muffin and taking the seat at the table near my coffee.

"I heard someone rustling around up there. It was either your father or your sister."

"Shay doesn't even know what eight thirty in the morning looks like."

"Hey, I heard that!" Shayla announces, right on cue.

I turn and see Shayla stomping down the creaky wooden steps and into the kitchen. I love my sister as an older brother should. Even when we were younger, I adored her. An eight-year difference separates us, and while most siblings with an age difference that significant may find it hard to get along or have anything in common, we make sibling life look easy. Since losing Trevor, my protectiveness over her has only grown.

I pick up a chocolate chip muffin, Shay's' favorite, and toss it to her as she plops lazily down into the chair next to me.

"I know what eight thirty looks like, skeez." Shay tears a small piece of her muffin off and playfully throws it at my face. Only she can get away with this move. "Not everyone feels the need to get up at the ass crack of dawn and go for a three-hundred-mile run."

"Five miles, drama queen, and maybe you should go running with me. You're eighteen now, and I read somewhere that the female metabolism starts slowing down at that age." I have no idea if this is true or not. It doesn't matter though. Fucking with Shayla is one of my only sources of happiness anymore. She loves it too. It makes her happy, makes her miss Trevor less. I know it.

"Well, I read somewhere that twenty-six-year-old males who live with their parents have serial killer tendencies," she says with a cute-ass attempt at my trademark cocky smirk.

This comment never fazes me, no matter how many times she jokes about me being twenty-six and living at home. We both know the only reason I came back was to help take care of dad after he got sicker. When I got the call from Shay that dad's lung cancer was not yet in remission, I left my apartment in Seattle to go home to my family and help keep our bar running while dad recovered. I was doing nothing fucking productive anyway—although I was doing some productive fucking. Bartending and going through every drug and pussy Seattle had to offer was not anything to be proud of. Not even if the chick attached to that pussy came more than once while wrapped around my dick.

Now dad's cancer is legitimately in remission, and he is back to manning the bar and I am free to go anywhere I want. A place where I can have a fresh start. But I don't know that I deserve one.

"Children, don't make me put you in your time out corners. Don't think you are too old for them. Your mom would agree with me. Ain't that right, Mrs. Lillian O'Connor?"

Shay and I both turn our heads at the same time to see dad coming down the stairs. Sean O'Connor had once been a tall, hefty, barrel-chested man whose large presence could command a room, but since the cancer and the chemotherapy treatments, his frame had shrunk significantly. His demeanor, however, has not changed one bit, and he proves that, despite his now thin frame, he can still command a room. My dad's booming baritone and slightly Irish accented voice, while imposing, is always filled with love and kindness. He's a real life gentle giant who loves his kids and wife more than anything.

I idolize my dad, his skills as a boxer, the way he built a business from scratch, the way he held a family together despite the tragedies, even the way he still worshipped his wife after over thirty years of marriage. True, his wife is our mother, but she will *always* be his wife and true love first. You ask me, that is what makes a marriage defy the fucking odds. One of the reasons I decided to come home is to prove I can be half the man my dad is, but whether I've proven it I can't be sure. No matter how much time I have dedicated to helping the bar stay afloat, I feel like a fucking disappointment because I failed when it truly counted.

Dad saunters into the kitchen and bends his head down to kiss his wife before he makes a cup of coffee. He whispers something in her ear that no one can hear but puts a coy smile on her face.

"Seriously? Again? You guys were just practically mauling each other in the hallway a half-hour ago," Shayla says, rolling her eyes. "You two kiss way too much."

"Don't be jealous just because you have no one to kiss you in the morning," Dad shoots back, not missing a beat.

"Shows what you know, dad."

"Yeah right, Shay. Over my dead body," I warn with a wink as Shayla sticks her tongue out.

I'm only half joking. Shayla happens to be gorgeous—both of us are goddamn winners in the gene pool, and I know how guys look at her. Petite like our mother, and standing at a tiny 5'5", she's thin in the right places and curvy in the *wrong* fucking places with ice blonde hair, bright green eyes, and a smile that could light up a fucking galaxy. Not to mention, Shay has a way of making people feel like they're the only person in a room of hundreds, which can be a dangerous attribute for a girl like her. I know this because I'm a guy and because I'm not as naïve as her, and as her older brother I know it's my job to make sure no one takes advantage of her.

"Liam, I know you have the day off today, but I need you to come into the bar tonight if you can. I got a call late last night that we have a party of twenty people coming in. Maybe more, I can't be sure. I want to put you behind the bar and have Shayla serve. I have Bobby T coming in to help bartend and serve too." He gives me a brief rundown as if only to assure me he really does need me.

"Yeah, I can come in, but a party that large, what happened? Did one of the ferry boats to the mainland crap out?"

"You know that movie they've been shooting here? Well, I guess they're done filming and want to have something called a wrap party. They should be getting to the bar around eight, but I don't know how these actor types are. They may be late or early, who fucking knows," he shrugs.

"SHUT THE FRONT DOOR!" Shayla screams as she jumps off the chair, scaring the ever-loving shit out of me.

Jesus. Fucking. Christ.

"Skylar Barrett is coming into our bar? I can't believe it. I have to start getting ready, like right now!"

"Shay, you've roughly eleven goddamn hours before you need be there. I think you have time," I remind her.

"Liam, language! And don't take the Lord's name in vain."

"Sorry, Ma." My mom scolds us O'Connor men on our language at least ten times a day. But we are like the rabbits: uncontrollable, unresponsive, and loved too much for any real punishment to occur.

"Yes, but I have outfits to look through and makeup to buy. Many, many important things to do. You never know, I could find myself an actor that will whisk me away to L.A. with him. Plus, there's Skylar Barrett to think about. She's Hollywood royalty, and I must impress." And with that last word she runs up the stairs.

"Boy, oh boy, apparently I'll be missing out tonight," my mom says, seemingly still amused by Shay's flair for the dramatic even after all these years.

Shay gets excited about everything. And I do mean fucking everything. I could tell her the sun came out this morning after days of rain and she would flip the hell out, acting like she just won the lottery. But that's what I love most about her. She's a rainbow brightening this bleak fucking world with her color.

I finish my coffee as I reflect back to seeing Skylar Barrett no less than fifteen minutes ago. I feel this jump in my heart for a split second at the mere thought of seeing her again, up close, and in my fucking bar. As I get up to leave the kitchen table and head to the bathroom for a quick shower, I feel a sensation begin to creep up on me. One I have not felt in years: a type of hopeful anticipation. It doesn't make sense. Seeing her would not lead anywhere or mean anything, but fuck me I am going to ride this high as long as I can.

CHAPTER 3

Skylar

I take a final look in the full-length mirror attached to the inside of the closet door in my hotel room. Noah just finished my hair and makeup, and of course he did a superb job. My hair hangs over my shoulders in effortless curls, and the light smoky eyeshadow I'm wearing brings out the blue in my eyes. Instead of lipstick, which would be too obvious for someone as brilliant as Noah, he swiped a clear lip gloss across my full lips and brushed a shell pink eyeshadow over the gloss. The lip color looks pronounced against my sun-kissed skin, making me appear more angelic than I actually am. Noah knows how to make me look appropriate for the occasion, and this occasion calls for simplicity, somewhere between Hollywood and backwoods. I decide to wear my favorite pair of pastel colored Navajo printed shorts and a loose-fitting gray tank top, the buttons coming down just enough to show a hint of cleavage. The mirror in front of me reflects the image everyone else sees. A *Marie Claire* interviewer once described it as chameleon-like beauty. That one minute I can be the girl next door, but with a tweak to my hair, some well-applied makeup, and a slight wardrobe change I can morph into the vixen sex kitten stealing the boy from the girl next door.

I'm not an idiot—I know my looks helped make my career, not that I don't have the talent to back it up. But when I look in the mirror, I see what no one else sees—something on the inside, something dark and tortured. That old proverb is so true. Eyes really are the windows to the soul. And when my eyes stare at my reflection in the mirror, sometimes all I see is a lonely, weak, disturbed girl.

"Girl, I'm ready to have an *amazing* night, and I have a few little green friends to ensure us a good time. Allow me," Noah says, pulling an orange prescription bottle out of his black leather "murse," as he calls it.

Noah is of course dressed to the nines. He tips his head in my direction, flashing that pearly white grin and I marvel at just how handsome he is. His black skinny jeans showcase his long, toned legs, paired with a white dress shirt and gray button-up vest. His shoulder-length hair is slicked back and he's wearing just a hint of his best cologne.

If only he preferred vagina we could have been perfect together.

He slips his arm around my waist and I tense immediately from the contact. I'm not comfortable with being touched. Most of the time I hate it, even if it's someone like Noah that I have known for years. Noah knows this, but occasionally he will touch me in some small way as if to get me used to the idea. When I have to be touched in a scene I never have this problem, but that's work and I'm really good at compartmentalizing. Noah ignores my awkward body language, as he always does, and drops two little green pills into my palm, then turns away for a moment to grab two full champagne flutes from the bedside table.

"What am I taking, my love?" I ask, not really caring what the answer is since I'm going to take it anyway. I know Noah would only give me something to relax me, to help my brain slow down a minute. Filming is over, which means I'll have nothing to occupy my mind until my next project, which is never good for me.

"That, my Morningstar, is Klonopin. It's an anti-anxiety medication my *gorgeous* doctor prescribed to me. All I know is when you take it with a little champagne, you feel like you are flying free as a dove."

"Well, cheers!" I say.

I toss the pills back and take a small sip of champagne, ready to end this trip in style. The last two months filming this movie, a project I've been so passionate about, has been the happiest I have been in a long time. But it's also incredibly bittersweet because I knew each day brought me closer to the last. Orcas Island seems to have brought out the best in me, the bright parts of me, two months with no incidents.

As soon as the pills hit the bottom of my stomach I know I can hold on to the light, even if it is synthetic, for just a few more hours.

≈⊙⌒⊙│⌒⊙⌒≈

We decide to walk to O'Connor's as it's only two blocks away and we can use the exercise. Chances are we may end up a bit too drunk to drive after this party is over. Though it's possible we may be too drunk to walk too now that I think about it. I hope they have cabs around here.

The first thing I notice as we ascend the steps is the sign above the front door. The sign is weathered as if it has seen some unforgiving winters over the years, and forest green lettering spells the name of the bar: O'CONNOR'S, FAMILY OWNED FOR FORTY YEARS.

An odd sense of nostalgia overwhelms me...or maybe déjà vu. This seems odd because I have no reason to feel nostalgic for a place I've never been, but I decide to revel in the feeling because it is one I am unaccustomed to. As an actress it's good to lock on to these types of emotional states, to remember them so you can bust them out in a scene when necessary. This sort of makes me sound like a sociopath, I know, like I'm trying to "learn feelings" or something, but it really does help me hone my craft.

Then, as if my little pharmaceutical miracle has perfect timing, I feel the Klonopin kick in. A light and blissful cloud descends and I'm suddenly very excited to see where the night will take me. When I step through the doors, I instantly fall in love with the ambiance. Warm and inviting, old pictures of the town and pictures that appear as if they were taken in Ireland blanket the walls. Perhaps the owner is actually Irish.

One photograph specifically catches my eye. It hangs on a wall inside one of the booths: a black and white side profile of an older man wearing a newsboy cap with a small grass hill serving as a backdrop.

The man wears a mysterious smile on his face and his eyes look as if they contain a secret, a type of wisdom that comes with age and a life well-lived. They definitely do not have bars like this in L.A.

Bars and clubs in Los Angeles are more like bordellos most of the time; not so much the devils' playground as the devils' circus, overflowing with half-dressed waitresses, copious amounts of drugs, and usually some sort of "inventive" theme, like a bank vault bar, that will make it the new bar of the moment, for at least a few months anyway. Even the "dive bars" are laughable, touting themselves as the "best dive bar" in L.A., which sort of defeats the idea of a dive bar in the first place.

But for all my grievances, I still go to these places I detest so much. Everything and everyone is phony in L.A. I promise I am no exception.

"Where do we sit, my little Morningstar? Seeing as no one is here yet and it's eight-fourteen, it seems as if we get to pick the spot." Noah looks at his watch, obviously a little irritated that none of the cast and crew have arrived.

"How about that booth right there?" I point to the table with my now favorite picture, which also happens to be right next to a few big tables that could fit large groups of people.

"Perfect. Whoa, Skylar, look at the bartender." Noah stops, nudging me in the ribs with his elbow, and points, rather obviously I might add, to the bar in front of us. "Holy walking penis. If he's not the hottest man you've ever seen I'll scrape my eyes out right now."

"Holy walking penis? Really, Noah, thank you so much. Now all I can picture is a walking penis with legs and little feet."

I glance over at the bar, if only to shut Noah up. I'm not expecting much. Noah's barometer for "hot man" is not set high and always varies. It's like playing a game of hottie roulette with him. When I look over this time, however, I find myself staring directly into the gorgeous eyes of the bartender. Am I moving? I think I should try to be moving if I'm not, otherwise I'll just look like a creeper.

Noah was right. The bartender is stunning. Am I allowed to say stunning when describing a man? Is that weird? Anyway, the point is I can't look away.

But I'm trying, I swear.

I know there are other things I should be concentrating on in this bar right now so I don't appear so obvious, but I am frozen, drinking him in as he stares back at me unapologetically. I look behind me briefly to make sure it's really me he's staring at. No one is behind me, so I guess it *is* me.

He's impeccable; tall and muscular, with deep charcoal eyes and a full head of dark brown hair with two-day scruff on his face to match. Not many men can pull off a plain white t-shirt and blue jeans, and he is doing it with ease. But it's not just how he looks; I've seen many good looking men in my line of work. It's how I feel when he looks at me.

Cherished. Wanted.

"Told ya so," Noah says, sending a lightning bolt right through the verve between me and the bartender.

"Yeah, yeah. Let's sit down, Noah. People should be arriving any second now and we're right in the doorway gawking at the bartender. Not a good look."

I try to play it cool, not giving too much of myself away to Noah because he would devotedly run with it, and if I'm not careful I'll find myself in love by the end of the night.

"Okay, Morningstar. Let's sit, you little buzzkill. What kind of shoes do you think it would wear anyway?" Noah asks nonchalantly as he leads me to the booth.

"What? What are you talking about?"

"The walking penis with legs and little feet. What kind of shoes would it wear?"

"Are we talking about your penis right now, or his?"

"Mine. Always."

"Then probably pumps."

Noah erupts in a loud laugh. I love you so much right now. Why are you not a man?"

"Why are you not straight?"

"Because the thought of vagina makes me feel all skeevy inside."

Well, okay then.

By eight forty-five the cast and crew have all arrived along with quite a few locals, and the bar is almost full to capacity. I happen to be enjoying the evening, high not only on the pills and beer but on the conversations going on around me. People reminisce over the two months we all spent together filming a movie we were so passionate about. Darin, the genius behind the script and also the director of the movie, is talking to me about all the film festivals he wants to enter and how he thinks it's the best work I've done, and that with my name attached there is no way the movie can't go the distance. Noah is prattling on about how the sunsets in Washington have inspired a new color palette for a makeup line he has recently decided to start. No doubt the Klonopin talking, I suspect, since this is the first I'm hearing of a makeup line. But I'll support him all the way if it's something he really wants to do.

Thirty people are talking around me, some to me, and I try to remain engaged in conversation, but I can't keep from watching the bartender's every move. I watch as he serves drinks and talks to patrons, and every time he moves his arms I catch the hint of his forearm muscles contracting. Occasionally he reaches up for a bottle of liquor, his shirt raising, and I catch a glimpse of his six pack, muscular oblique's, and the V-shape that leads down to where his pants hang on his hips. Noah always refers to them as sex marks. I want to run my tongue—I mean my hands—down them. I'm about to avert my gaze before he catches me staring when he suddenly looks in my direction, a knowing smirk on his face; almost like he was aware I was staring the whole time.

He just seems so damn cocky, and I love it. Most men are intimidated by me, and the ones that aren't just love to take advantage of me. He clearly doesn't fall under the former, obviously I've no clue as to the latter. But alas, I watch him display the occasional smile as he hands drinks to the striking blonde waitress who he watches attentively, and I realize he's probably not single, and now I feel...jealous, maybe? Another emotion I'm less than familiar with, and I don't think I like it. Shit, I'm spinning now, and I know I have to rein it in. I need to slow down before I become manic. I cannot lose control of my emotions, not tonight.

"Penny for your thoughts my little Skylark? You've been gawking at that hot bartender all night, you little minx," Noah says, trying to get a rise out of me. He does not miss a thing. Especially if a hot boy is involved.

"Ugh, so wrong." I roll my eyes slightly, causing Noah to grin at me knowingly.

What a bitch.

"Okay...maybe I *am* guilty of a bit of stalker-like behavior," I relent.

"So...go talk to him. You are Skylar Joy Barrett, after all. If you can't land that man then he must be gay. In which case, tag me in. You aren't the only one stealing glances, he's been looking at you all night. Every time I look over to stare shamelessly at his beauty, he seems to be eye fucking the shit out of you. Watching over you like any second he's going to go all alpha male, ripping your clothes off and fucking you right on the table."

"Jesus, Noah! Tag you in? What about Erik, your boyfriend, re-member?" I lift my beer up to my mouth in a lame attempt to hide my blush. I do not blush. "Whatever, he's probably just trying to figure out what my tits look like. Besides, I think that blonde waitress might be his girlfriend."

"Always the cynic, Morningstar, but you'll never know unless you grow some balls and go talk to him. And I will have you know that if Erik could see what I'm looking at he would be disappointed if I didn't hit on him. But I guess if you're too scared you could always go talk to that lovely group of rowdy young men across the bar over there. They've *also* been staring your way all night," Noah spits out sarcastically.

Without even looking I know who Noah is referring to. My douche radar has been going off in their direction. A group of four men, scratch that, four guys acting like boys whose balls just dropped, have been loud and obnoxious all night. No, not just loud and obnoxious; I'm used to that. I live in Los Angeles, after all, birthplace of the super douche. But there is something about them that I don't like, something unnerving. Every other word out of their mouths is "bitch this or bitch that," and the "cunt got what she deserved." One in particular, the one wearing a black beanie with a goatee who was playing with an unlit cigarette, seems to enjoy harassing the blonde waitress anytime he gets the chance. He's doing it quietly and under the radar with a small pat on the ass here, a quick caress while she takes their drink order there.

And I can tell she is obviously irritated by the attention from the way she tenses or pulls away. I recognize the game he's playing with the waitress as I have been victim to it too many times to count.

I really hate them.

Just as I'm about to look away I see goatee guy grab the waitress' arm as she walks by him, and he starts to yell at her.

"Dammit, Shayla, stop behaving like a fucking spoiled-ass bitch. I'm trying to talk to you about important shit and you're fucking ignoring me. Do you think you're too good to talk to me now, is that it?" he slurs at her. Obviously there is history there.

"Mason, I don't have time to deal with your crap right now. I'm working! I know that's a foreign concept to you, but take some notes, you might be able to use them in the future," she shoots back as she tries to pull her arm from his tight hold.

Damn, girl has spunk. As jealous as I may or may not be over Shayla's possible relationship with *my* bartender, I have to give the girl credit.

"You are such a cunt," Mason the douche says as he shoots up off the chair drunkenly still holding on to Shayla's arm.

I wince and think maybe I should say something. Someone should. But before I have a chance, movement erupts from behind the bar as the bartender charges forward until he's at Shayla's side, pulling her behind him, shielding her from the asshole. The whole bar goes silent except for the music blaring from the jukebox, and I swear it's Jay Z's 99 Problems. The irony is not lost on me.

"You touch my sister again, Mason, and I *will* end your fucking life." The bartender's dark warning sends a chill through the entire bar so intense it's like you can see it. Yep, there's definitely history there.

"Fuck you, Liam, you can't do shit to me and I will come at your sister anytime I feel like it," Mason shoots back.

Liam. I have a name now. I also have an answer as to who she is to him; his sister.

Although that seems like the last thing I should be focusing on at this second. I watch the scene unfold with everyone else, but unlike the rest of the audience I am not excited or titillated by the idea of watching people beat each other up. Noah is grabbing my arm in anticipation as he stares on, just as Shayla takes hold of Liam's arm in what looks to be an attempt to hold him back. It's clearly lost on Liam, however, because he grabs Mason's shirt and cocks his fist back. I can't breathe. I can't watch but I can't look away.

"LIAM, BACK OFF AND CALM DOWN!"

Everyone, including me, turns and looks toward a booming voice that radiates through the entire building. I turn towards the sound and see a man standing about ten feet behind Liam, a man that looks a lot like him. So much so in fact that I come to the conclusion that this has to be his father or his uncle at the very least. It's in the eyes, those piercingly distinctive gray eyes paired with the darkest eyebrows I have ever seen. I look back at the scene unfolding and my heart is beating out of my chest.

"Liam," the man says, his voice softer and slower than before. "Let go of him and step back. Listen to my voice."

I look at Liam. His chest is heaving so quickly that I think he might burst. The way the man speaks to him is odd. He seems to be trying to calm him down, but is being very cautious, right down to the words he is using. Over the years I've learned to pick up on small idiosyncrasies people use in everyday life, things that may be typically overlooked, because I'm an observer. In order to be the best actress I can be, I have to learn to observe others, become tactical about it.

"Come on, Liam," Shayla whispers, pulling her brother's arm back toward her tenderly. "Everything is fine. I'm okay, big brother."

Well, damn, if that isn't sweet as hell, and it must register with Liam because he lets go of douchebag Mason's shirt, takes a few steps back, and looks around the bar, almost as if he is trying to remember where he is. And for a brief second I swear his eyes fall on mine as if searching for something in them. Embarrassment? Reassurance? He turns around and leads Shayla back behind the bar and into what I assume is the kitchen. The man who is possibly Liam's father, better known now as the man who has clearly prevented a brawl, walks over to the table of douchebags and leans over to say something I can't hear while pointing at the door.

Three of them get up and start walking out of the bar. Mason is the last to move, obviously trying to prove he's in charge while he stares the man down. The man crosses his arms in and stands stoically, not breaking eye contact with Mason for a second. Mason reaches down, grabs his full beer, and chugs the whole thing within a few seconds then slams the bottle back onto the table so hard that remnants of beer and spit fly out of the top. Then he turns and saunters out of the bar, his lackeys following close behind. And as if nothing out of the ordinary has just happened, the whole bar erupts with conversations that were temporarily put on hold as I stare on in disbelief.

"You okay, Skylar?" Noah yells in my ear.

"Yeah, of course, why wouldn't I be?" I say, trying to derail this line of questioning before it goes where I don't want it to.

"You know why. That was pretty intense, and it looks like your skin just got five shades lighter."

Why is he going there? I need to get out of here.

"I'm good. I think I just need a little air. The beer and the pills—"

"And all this testosterone," Noah interrupts, giving me a wink and a smile.

I sigh with relief at this reprieve. Noah knows I don't like to talk about the past, especially with so many strangers around. Anybody could be listening, and the next thing you know my words will be on TMZ or Perez or whatever new celeb bashing site happens to be all the rage. I should have remembered that he always knows when to stop talking. His thoughtfulness is what I love most about him.

"Exactly," I say. "I'm going to go outside and get some air. Watch my drink for me?" I get up from the table. I'm really not interested in a roofie colada tonight.

"Sure thing. Need some company?"

"No, I'm good. Be back in a few minutes." I give Noah a quick wave as I head to the back door I spotted when I got up. I definitely do not want to risk running into Douchebag Team Four who I assume are lurking outside in front of O'Connor's.

I open the back door. A cool breeze touches my face and helps sober me up. Two street lights produce a faint yellow tint in the alley-way, just enough that I can make out my surroundings. A large trash bin sits in front of a chain link fence to my left, and to my right I see a small metal bench. That's kind of odd, but I walk closer and see a round ashtray off to the side. Must be where the smokers go to get a breath of fresh air.

I walk over to the bench and sit down. The cold metal sends goosebumps up my bare legs and arms. I don't feel cold, though, just awake. I run my fingers through my hair and lean back on the chain link fence behind me, and immediately all the tension from my body melts away.

"Didn't anybody tell you that you shouldn't hang out in dark alleys by yourself?" a deep voice scolds.

What the ever-loving hell? I sit up straight, my heart hammering in my chest, and see a figure leaning on the brick wall in front of me. How did I miss that?

Dammit, Skylar, way to not check your surroundings for rapists or murderers or zombies. Stupid. This is scary movie 101, the pretty girl alone always dies first.

The figure steps out of the shadows and immediately I recognize the face. Liam. All my senses light up like a match hitting dry leaves and a slight smile appears on my face. I bite my cheeks to try and hold back a full-blown goofy grin.

"I have heard that before, yes."

"So you've no concern for your personal safety?" Liam asks with a hard yet curious stare as he walks closer to the bench.

My heart starts thumping quicker with each step he takes to close the distance between us. Crap, he is even more gorgeous up close and personal. He has the most perfect full lips I've ever seen and a stare that would make any woman swoon. But I don't want to swoon. I have a zero tolerance rule for anyone or anything remotely swoon-worthy. This includes puppies and kittens and any other cute furry little animal. It's why I don't have a pet.

Liam now stands directly in front of me, and I notice a scar on the left side of his neck. It's impossible not to notice as it's at least six inches long from his ear to his clavicle. I wonder how he acquired it.

My eyes wander the length of him, and damn if he isn't taller than I originally thought he was. Crap. I love tall men, and they're so rare in my line of work. The leading men in Hollywood tend to be on the shorter side. You know how they say the camera adds ten pounds? Well, it also tends to add about five inches in the height department.

Appearances can be very deceiving. Except in Liam's case, clearly, because he has to be easily over six feet tall. Being only 5'5" myself, anyone over six feet seems gigantic.

"If you don't attack me, I promise I won't attack you. Besides, I hear personal safety is overrated," I reply with a smile in a nervous attempt to flirt while I gulp those stupid words down my dry throat.

"Is that so? Well, I make no promises." The wind picks up slightly bringing his scent with it: something woodsy with a hint of sweet that makes it more alluring.

"Well, I figured it was safer out here right now than in there."

His face goes dark for a second and I think maybe I said the wrong thing. It was just a joke, a lame attempt at humor, but maybe this complete stranger who knows *nothing* about me doesn't recognize my sense of humor. Shocking. But the darkness lifts and I see a boyish smile work its way across his perfect face, even reaching to his eyes, dimples peeking out from his cheeks.

"Yeah, sorry about that. Hope I didn't ruin your party."

"You don't need to apologize. They were the ones being scum bums."

I did *not* just say scum bums. But judging by the loud laughter coming from Liam, I'm thinking I must have.

"I'm sorry, but did you just say the word scum bum? What the fuck is a scum bum?" he asks through his laughter.

Okay, rub it in, why don't you?

But my embarrassment quickly morphs into lust because the way he laughs, the deepness of it, how the muscles in his back contract as he does, makes Liam even sexier.

"I really did." I say, giggling. I do not giggle. "I should explain. One of my co-workers has a six-year-old girl who I've been hanging around with for the past few months, and she just loves calling people scum bums. I guess it kind of caught on because apparently you can't swear around a six-year-old, and after two months on the wagon I ended up adapting a more appropriate vocabulary. Plus, I've been told a lady never curses in front of a man."

Jesus what is wrong with me? Who says shit like that other than the cast of *Downton Abbey?*

I need to stop talking. My head falls down into my hands as I die a little inside.

"I see. Damn. Adorable," he says quietly, shaking his head slightly in what seems to be disappointment while looking at the ground as if he's speaking to it instead of me.

What does that even mean? Is my co-worker's daughter adorable? Is he talking about me being adorable? That can't be right since I'm not adorable.

"Do you mind?" he asks, pointing to the bench, interrupting my inner monologue. "My name is Liam by the way." He places his hand in front of me in a proper introduction.

"No, please sit." I scoot down the bench a few inches to make room for him while grabbing his hand to shake it. It's rough against my skin and a bit calloused, and I hold on a little too long to savor his touch for a few more guilty seconds as he sits. "I'm Skylar." I'm careful not to scoot down far because the little hussy in me wants to be close to him. "Was um…was that your dad talking you down in there?" I ask, wanting to keep the conversation going. Maybe if I'm lucky I can see that smile again.

"Yes. His name is Sean. How'd you know?"

"You two look alike. Have the same eyes. He must be the owner of the bar, I take it?"

God, he smells good.

I intimately become aware of how close he is actually sitting now. The heat radiating from his body is actually warming my chilled skin. I can even feel vibrations in my chest when he speaks with that deep growl; almost like a lion purring.

"That he is," he says simply with a sideways contemplative look in my direction, as if he is studying me.

"So that makes your full name Liam O'Connor." Fucking duh, Skylar.

He flashes that smile and I melt.

"It does. Anyone ever tell you how perceptive you are?" Liam winks at me, I assume jokingly, and I'm immediately caught off-guard because for some reason he doesn't catch me as the joking type. More the broody sexy loner type. But I like it, and if me constantly embarrassing myself by babbling like a love-struck teenager who just took a major hit off the crush pipe gets me *that* Liam, then I'll think of a hundred new ways to do it. Although I'm sure I won't have to think very hard; it seems to come easily in his presence. "I know your full name, so I guess it's only fair you know mine," he says.

This is the first time he alludes to knowing who I am. This brief conversation has been going so easily that *I* almost forgot who I am. That I'm someone anyone who hasn't been living under a rock would know. But even though he knows my name, I still feel like a normal girl sitting here next to him. And despite the fact he knows of me, he isn't pretending to actually *know* me like most people do.

"So you, your dad, and your sister all work together?"

"We do." He rests his arms on his legs, his hands clasped together.

"That must be nice. What about your mom?" I ask, leaning back on the chain-link fence.

"Housewife. She stays at home, takes care of us."

"Wow. So perfect family then." A pang of sadness clamps around my heart. No, not sadness because I'm truly happy he has that, maybe just envy.

"I guess it seems that way, but there's no such thing as a perfect family, Sky." He leans back on the fence so that he's now mirroring my pose.

"You just called me Sky."

"Sorry. Do you hate that or something?" he asks, his voice surprisingly laced with an apologetic tone, his eyes gazing at me with concern. "Honestly, I didn't even realize I did it. It seems like such a natural transition from Skylar. Hasn't anybody ever called you Sky before?"

"No. I mean, no I don't hate it at all. My mom used to call me Sky, but oddly enough, no one has called me that since her."

Shut up, Skylar. I need to stop talking.

I don't even know this guy, so I need to stop running my mouth, which is only happening because I'm so damn distracted by my inability to stop lusting after him. If I was smart I'd shut this entire conversation down now and walk away. I have secrets to protect. Skeletons in my walk-in closet that if released, could devastate me so much I would break down and evaporate in their wake. But right now, I don't want to be smart, because smart will end this time with Liam, and I'm not ready for that. So instead I'll do what I do best; evade, distract, change the damn subject. Now.

"Interesting tattoos." My fingers find their way to his left forearm, lightly tracing the outline of a tattoo and over a scar that it covers before I quickly pull my hand away, but not before I notice a slight shiver run through his arm. I'm invading his personal space, and I know if a stranger did this to me I would freak, but my fingers have a mind of their own and they want to touch his skin. If I could reach far enough to the black and white boxing gloves tattooed on his right forearm I would have probably inappropriately touched those too. "What does this one mean?"

The silence is palpable, and a blank look crosses his face. I think maybe I've just made a huge mistake asking this question.

"Um…it's the O'Connor coat of arms."

The tattoo is as gorgeous and intricate and as dark as the man who wears it. Colors of gray and black and green make up the coat of arms. The badge of the coat has a beautiful green tree that grows from strong roots and blossoms into an almost shamrock-like leafy top. A knight's helmet sits atop the badge and the knight's arm holds a sword wrapped with an emerald green snake. Green and gray ribbons explode from behind the badge. The whole tattoo is phenomenal. But the one thing that catches my eye are the three names listed in their own individual ribbon: Ali, Isabelle, and Trevor.

"It's really amazing, Liam." I look up at him, trying to find his eyes, but they remain on the tattoo. "Who are they?" I ask, grazing my index finger above the names protected in ribbon.

As soon as the question is out of my mouth, he freezes and a look passes over his eyes that are now focused on me, a look I am all too familiar with. One that's rife with guilt and sadness. I can't explain it, but I want to protect him from the hurt that will come with his answer. So I decide to evade his demons for him.

"I like boxing!" I blurt out.

Smooth. Way to go, Skylar. You know shit about boxing. Apparently mortification is still on the menu for tonight.

"Excuse me?" He laughs again, and it's worth every bit of

awkwardness.

"Boxing. I like it. You know, because you have boxing gloves on your arm, and I just thought, well, I just thought maybe you liked it too. I watch matches on pay-per-view or in person when I'm in Vegas sometimes." My skin heats with nervous energy as I continue to ramble on.

"Yeah, I like boxing too," he grins, lightly nudging his shoulder against mine. "I used to box professionally, actually. You're cute when you blush, anyone ever tell you that?"

Men have commented on many things about me over the years; my body, my face, my breasts. But never have I been complimented on something as simple and pure as a blush. He reaches up and pulls my finger from my lips and encases my hand in his, sending a quiver of hormones skyrocketing through me. I should hate this. I hate being touched, but I'm sitting here confident, and I would be perfectly content staying in this alley being touched by Liam O'Connor forever.

My newfound life path is short-lived, however, as he lifts himself off the bench and stands in front of me looking ready to leave.

"We should probably get you inside. It's cold out here and you have no coat on. Seriously, were you raised by wolves? Wandering around alone in the dark with no coat at night. Talking to strange men. I think you might need a chaperone, Sky. Let's go, I'll buy you a drink." He winks as he takes my hand, lifting me off the bench and almost right into his arms.

Cocky bastard.

"Yeah, yeah. Anyone ever tell you you're cute when you're being judgmental?" I'm now inches away from him, looking into his eyes, and I feel a surge of carnal energy pulse through the air between us.

After a brief pause he shakes his head at me, mumbling something under his breath, and turns to walk me to the back door, his hand still holding mine. There's something sensual about his touch on my skin, his hand grabbing mine so possessively, each one of his fingers threading through the spaces. I feel safe, and this is definitely not a feeling I am acquainted with.

But the new sensation comes crashing down unexpectedly as I hear male voices drifting toward us. The voices are all too familiar.

They're the same assholes from before, and they're walking straight toward us.

"*Shit*," Liam curses as he pushes his free hand through his hair and turns his now fierce gaze toward me. "Whatever you do, stay behind me, okay? Don't move. You got me?" I nod and stare past Liam toward the approaching threat. "*Speak*, Skylar. You got me?" Liam's eyes burn through mine, his grip on my hand tightening as he waits for me to answer.

"Y-Yeah. I got you," I stutter, because now I'm just a little freaked the hell out.

There are only three of them now and I wonder if maybe asshole Mason and his douchebag friends Pac-Manned the fourth member to recharge their douche points. A half empty bottle of Jack Daniels dangles loosely in Mason's grasp and I know this can mean nothing good. I suddenly wish I was back in the bar. Maybe if we move for the door now we can make it inside before…well…before anything bad happens.

Liam must be thinking the same thing because he quickly starts to make his way to the door, pulling me behind him. But before we make it, one of the guys, the shortest of the three, jumps in front of us and leans his body against the door, effectively blocking the way.

"Well, well, well, what do we have here, Bryce?" As soon as the words leave Mason's mouth, I can smell the alcohol on his breath. I assume Bryce must be the guy leaning on the door. "Is O'Connor getting some strange pussy in the alley? And here I thought you might be batting for the other team."

The other two douchebags chuckle. Liam steps defensively in front of me as Mason stalks toward us and I can feel him tense as his hand clamps even tighter around mine, almost to the point of pain. Heat radiates from his body, causing my heart to start thumping in my chest as Mason and his friend move closer.

"Mase, that ain't strange pussy, that's Skylar Barrett," Bryce says, still leaning on the door.

"That it is! You should get her picture. It'll probably be worth something to those tabloids," the stocky asshole behind Mason so kindly points out, finally opening his mouth. Until this moment I just assumed he was incapable of speech.

"Is that right?" Mason takes his cell phone out of his pocket and attempts to aim it at me.

No, no, no. This cannot be happening. Instinctively, I hide myself even further behind Liam; selfishly using his body to shield me from having my picture taken. He reaches behind and pulls me closer into his back.

"You know what I think, Derek? I think I could get more money with a picture of her sucking my dick. What do you think, Liam?" A smarmy sneer creeps over Mason's face and my mouth goes completely dry.

This is not good. Three against two. Well, technically one because the only thing I can do is run and I'm not very fast, so the outcome of this situation is looking pretty damn miserable at the moment.

Liam takes a small step forward and my free hand reaches up to gently grab the back of his shirt. "I think you should put the fucking phone back in your pocket before I shove it so far up your goddamn ass I break your *fucking* neck. Now back the fuck up and apologize to her before I knock you out, motherfucker."

That was an awful lot of fucks. My spine tingles with a tremor that makes its way up to my chattering teeth. Liam isn't yelling, but there's something frightening in the way he speaks, something primal that both scares me and turns me on simultaneously, and I'm left contemplating if he could actually break someone's neck that way. Nothing about his threat seems idle, and I don't want to see anyone get into trouble because of me, especially Liam. I most definitely do *not* want to see anything shoved up anyone's ass either.

I pull his arm slightly toward my body like his sister had done before. "Hey. It's okay, Liam," I reassure him as his head turns slightly at the sound of my voice. "Besides, I have been asked to do a lot worse by much better men than him. Come on, let's just go through the front entrance. Anyway, he'd have to have a dick for me to suck."

Shit. Why the hell did I just say that?

"What'd you just say, bitch? Trust me, I have a dick. I'll show it to you, slut, and you can autograph it for me." Mason grabs at his crotch and stumbles closer to us as Liam releases my hand to shove Mason back. The whiskey bottle falls from his fingers and shatters, pieces of glass flying everywhere.

Adrenaline courses through my veins so rapidly I instantly feel sick to my stomach. A dam of violence is ready to burst and I have to stop it if only to protect Liam from getting jumped by three guys because I can't keep my damn mouth shut. I step forward, completely ignoring Liam's previous instructions, and place myself between him and Mason. Standing on my tiptoes I grab his face and pull it to mine. What I see almost has me taking a step back in fear however because Liam's once gray eyes, are now black; his pupils completely dilated.

"Look at me, Liam," I command softly. His eyes finally focus on mine but still look dangerously savage. "He's just taunting you. He wants you to react, so don't give him the satisfaction. Don't let him win. Let's just leave and go through the front, okay?"

I can see him regaining focus right before me as his breath slows and his body stops shaking. I didn't even realize his body was shaking until it went still. Probably because I'm shaking too. But there is a distinct difference because I know mine is from fear and he seems to be shaking with anger. Liam shoots the most menacing glance at Mason, like not kicking his ass is the hardest decision he's ever had to make, grabs my hand, and turns to walk toward the street entrance. I breathe a sigh of relief until I feel a sweaty hand seize my wrist and rip me violently from Liam's grasp, sending me careening toward the ground. My left hand instinctively shoots out to break my fall and I feel something sharp pierce painfully through the skin of my palm.

Don't look, Skylar. Don't look.

I look.

A large piece of glass protrudes from my hand, blood spilling from the wound.

An angered roar grabs my attention and I look up just in time to see Liam lunge directly at Mason, grabbing him by the throat with his right hand and landing a solid left hook to his face. Then another. And another. Liam now stands above Mason, pounding him into the ground, as Mason tries to block the decimating blows with his arms. Bryce starts to run at Liam, but Liam must have seen him in his peripheral because he slams his elbow up and into the assailant's face.

Holy shit.

Bryce stumbles backward as blood pours from his nose, hitting the cement with a loud thud as something white flies out of his mouth.

Is that a tooth? Gross.

Derek, the third asshole, takes off running like a coward. Mason pushes himself off the ground and drives his head into Liam's stomach. But Liam fires back, landing solid shots to his kidney and ribs with very concise precision. The hits are so hard I swear I hear a rib crack. To think I was worried about Liam being attacked and outnumbered. Now I'm just worried he'll be arrested for assault…or murder. This has to stop before someone is seriously hurt.

I propel myself off the ground, ripping the glass shard from my hand in one painfully fluid motion, before running toward the back door, stepping over the now unconscious body of Bryce. I swing the door open and scream for help as loud as I can.

A crash comes from the kitchen before three men, including Liam's father, almost knock me out of the way getting through the door.

"Goddamn it, Liam!" his father yells as if it's his fault, while he and two other men move to break up the fight.

I watch in horror as it takes all three of them to pull Liam off of Mason. A hand clamps down on my shoulder and I whip around to see Noah standing behind me, his face looking as panicked as I feel.

"Skylar, what the fuck is going on? What happened? *Jesus,* are you okay? We need to get you out of here!" Noah grabs my wrist as he tries to pull me from the scene.

"Wait. Liam. I need to make sure…" I turn around, trying to get words out, but everything is moving so fast and I'm so confused. All I know is I don't want to leave Liam.

Noah places his hands on my cheeks. "We need to go now before people decide to start taking your picture and you're plastered all over the internet tomorrow. Okay, honey? Let's go."

Before I have a chance to argue, Noah grabs my uninjured hand and starts running through the bar. The last thing I see as I turn to look for Liam is his father, pinning him against the brick wall, saying something I can't make out.

CHAPTER 4

LIAM

"LIAM. Look at me, Son." I hear a familiar voice speaking, the sound muffled like it's coming from underwater, swimming around in my subconscious. "Focus. Listen to me, Liam." I'm trying but everything around me is fucking hazy and murky and I can't see shit.

Fuck. I can't breathe. The pressure on my chest is too much. I keep trying to concentrate on the familiar voice.

"Liam, can you hear me?"

I know that voice. Dad. My vision clears and I see him in front of me, forcing me up against a wall. Fucking trying anyway.

My body is fighting against his hold reflexively and I'm trying to suppress the fury dominating my actions. I don't want to hurt him. And I could. Way too fucking easily. What the hell did I do?

I take in the wreckage left from the storm of rage I released. Bobby R. and Bobby T. are helping a bloody, dazed, and broken Mason off the ground as Bryce wipes blood from his nose and mouth with his shirt sleeve. Then Bryce bends down to pick something up off the ground.

It's his tooth. Hope that hurt you fucking piece of shit.

My breathing starts to even out as I take in the whole scene around me. Blood stains my clothes and the ground around me, my battered knuckles aching with the punishment I clearly inflicted as flashes of the fight start to flood my mind.

Skylar.

A small crowd has gathered in the alleyway and they aren't even trying to hide the enraptured looks on their pathetic fucking faces. Apparently they get off on all the blood. I look through the sea of faces trying to find hers as my dad relaxes his stance.

Big fucking mistake. Because I don't see her anywhere and I'm about to lose it again as snapshots of her on the ground with a piece of fucking glass in her hand and a terrified look in her beautiful eyes starts replaying in my head.

"Where is she, dad?" I try to push him off of me, while my heart attempts to beat right out of my chest.

"What, Son? Where is who? Are you okay? You need to tell me what happened here so I can start to fix this." He releases me from the wall, no longer able to hold me back.

I'm too fucking strong right now.

Too rabid.

I pace helplessly through the alley as I ignore his questions while looking for Skylar like a panicked mental patient.

She has to be here. She has to be okay. This is not like what happened to Ali. *FUCK!*

"Dad, she was *right* fucking here. She was on the ground bleeding. Where is she?" I shove my hands through my hair; a worthless attempt to keep the fear and anger rising within me to a more manageable level. Every second I can't find her is another second that grants permission for my rage to take over. My eyes catch Mason's, who's still trying to stand with the help of Bobby R., images of him ripping Skylar from my hand flooding my thoughts, and that thin thread keeping me sane;

Fucking

Snaps.

I head right for him.

"Who are you talking about?" My dad grabs my shoulder, stopping me before I make it over to Mason. Good fucking thing, too, because I'm gearing up for round two.

"Skylar, dad! Damn! She was right fucking here. Is she okay?"

The small crowd is still standing around staring on in shock as they whisper to each other. This is bound to be all over the island tomorrow, spreading like wildfire. Liam O'Connor loses his shit...*again*.

"Hey, man." I snap my head to the voice coming from my right and see Bobby R. cautiously walking toward me. "I saw her leave. Skylar Barrett, right?" I don't know why but the fact that Bobby just used her full name fucking pisses me off.

Shit. I need to cool it.

"Her friend grabbed her and took her away. She's fine, *hermano*."

My whole body relaxes slightly at this news. She's safe.

"Bobby, help Liam get home while I clean up here," my dad says through a sigh. I'm exhausting him. I know it. I just can't seem to get control of myself anymore.

"I think I can manage to get home, dad."

"Let Bobby take you home. That was *not* a suggestion." He's using his *fuck with me I dare you* tone. I know that tone, I've perfected that tone. It's probably time I leave.

"Come on, Liam. Let's go. It means I get to leave work early so you're doing me a favor," Bobby R. says with a wicked smile.

Bobby is placating me. I'm not a fucking idiot. But looking around at the crowd and Mason specifically, I realize my dad and Bobby are both right. I need to leave.

The night had started out so promising. The thrill of seeing her and feeling like a fucking human being again just talking to her because anytime I smiled or laughed it wasn't forced or for anyone else's benefit or comfort. I know if I continue to stand here, thinking about Sky, about what Mason did to her, or the fact that she is probably somewhere shaking in fear and bleeding, I'm going to lose my shit. Right now Mason is starting to look like the best fucking target. So I let Bobby take me home and write this entire fucking night off as a loss.

⊰⊱⊰⊱⊰⊱

Fuck. My head is killing me. I push my palms into my eyes hoping the pressure relieves some of my pain. Pressure closes off the nerve gates and hits the brain quicker than the sense of pain, or so I read once.

It's too early to be recalling this shit. And too cold. Why the hell am I freezing? The ice-cold wood from my bedroom floor burns into my heated skin.

I'm on my floor again.

I must have had another nightmare if I'm waking up on my floor, crumpled in the corner like a frightened little bitch. Every fucking time I black out this happens. I crawl over to my nightstand, because I lack the fucking strength to stand up at the moment. I snatch the water bottle, knocking my clock off the nightstand, wipe the sweat off my face with my hand, and guzzle the full twenty-four ounces. My dry throat and mouth relax significantly at the immediate relief. Grabbing the clock off my floor, I catch a glimpse of the red lights flashing the time.

9:27 a.m. I'm already late.

Fuck. Fuck. Fuck.

I'm supposed to be at the bar taking inventory of the liquor stock before it opens at eleven. Christ. I feel like I have a massive hangover, despite the fact I didn't touch a drop of liquor last night. Unfortunately, this is a common side effect of my...condition.

Impulsive behavior. PTSD. Explosive anger. Intermittent explosive disorder. Or my personal fucking favorite, rage epilepsy.

Whatever the psychiatrist of the moment wants to call it, I don't really give a shit, I just wish it would stop. But unfortunately I have no clear answer or solution, other than I may have sustained some sort of brain injury the night of the attack that led me here, to the person I am now. Rough. Unpredictable. Violent. Merciless. While the sane have a fight or flight response, I have a fight or kill response. It's fucking ingrained in me now, as much a part of my DNA as my eye color. Without my dad by my side, taming me like a wild animal when I snap, I release an unrelenting hurt. God help the victim of my fury if they are fucking with someone I care about, someone I love, because I will make their punishment painful and lasting. I will *never* let someone I love get hurt again.

But my dad wasn't there in the alley last night. Sky was. I was ready to walk away. For her. Because she asked me to. And that shit is fucking with my head right now.

A firm knock at my door alarms me, bringing me back into the present. I know that knock.

"Yeah. Come in, dad."

He opens the door and walks cautiously into the room looking like he's ready for one of those long discussions he feels he needs to have after an "incident."

"How'd ya' know it was me?"

"You have a very distinctive knock."

"Ah. I thought I'd check on you, Son. Make sure you're up. You're usually awake before any of us." He smiles at me but I can tell he's worried. He pulls out the chair from under my desk and sits down.

I take a seat on my bed across from him, ready to repeat the same discussion we've had many times before.

"I'm fine, just overslept. Guess I needed it." There's an awkward silence, and I'm sure there's something I can say to break it, but there's really no reason. He'll get right to the point.

"What happened last night, Liam?"

Right to the fucking point.

He rests his elbows on his knees and stares at me with a concerned look in his eyes. He thinks he's lost me forever, and he's probably right.

"When you went outside I thought we had everything under control. Next thing I know some girl is screaming for help and you're in the alley beating Mason nearly to death."

"I did have everything under control. I was in the alley talking with Skylar and then Mason came out of nowhere. He and his dumbass friends were harassing her and they just wouldn't stop. She convinced me to leave, and the next thing I know Mason was grabbing her with his disgusting fucking hands and she was on the ground bleeding, and I just...I just *fucking* lost it."

"You were walking away?" he asks, clearly as surprised as I am at the concept of doing it without his help.

But I have no explanation for him other than when I was looking into Skylar's eyes, her hands on my face, pleading with me to leave, I wanted to get her out of there, to keep her safe, to do anything she asked of me. And I'm sure as shit not going to tell him that. It makes me sound like a fucking pussy.

"Yeah. I mean, Skylar asked me to," I say as if this explanation is somehow the Holy Grail. Honestly, it fucking feels like it is.

"Are you and this Skylar girl seeing each other or something? I never heard you mention her before. She must be someone special to get you to walk away from a fight like that."

Christ. He doesn't even know who she is.

"No, I'm not seeing her. I barely know her."

Why do those words burn as they choke out of my mouth? I *don't* know her. I thought she would be some spoiled Hollywood rich bitch, and I was actually counting on that fucking assumption when I saw her sit down on that bench because I wanted nothing more than to seduce, fuck, and forget her in that alley. But she surprised me. She was adorable and sinful and innocent and tragically tortured all at the same time. I saw it in her eyes when she looked at me; it was like staring in a mirror. I *heard* it in her voice when she spoke, well rambled anyway, which I'm assuming she did because she was nervous. And that really hit deep. Skylar Barrett is the epitome of a dichotomy. She's the saint and sinner, the devil and the angel, the savior and the one in need of saving.

My dad looks at me quizzically, as if he sees straight through my bullshit response.

"Where are Mason and Bryce now?" I don't really give two fucks, but I need to know how serious this is, I'm also grasping for a change of subject.

"They should be released from the hospital sometime today."

"They went to the hospital?" I try to mask the excitement and sick pride from my voice, but something tells me the smirk on my face has given me away. All I have are some scraped up knuckles from where my fists connected to their faces. And ribs. And kidneys. And stomach.

"Liam, you broke Mason's eye socket and two ribs, sprained his wrist, and he almost bit the tip of his tongue off."

Shit. Never caused that particular injury before. I bite my own tongue in an attempt to stop my smile.

"And his friend, you broke his nose and he lost two teeth. You caused quite a bit of damage. I'm somewhere between being incredibly pissed at you and exceptionally proud. Mason is a dick and he was an ass to your sister when they dated, so that's the only thing saving you from me," he says with a slightly menacing smile.

Yeah, dad is the shit. But there was a time he could lay me out without even breaking a sweat. He never beat me, but he was my trainer for years so I am very fucking aware of his strength. For all I know, he's still capable of laying me the fuck out with one hit; he'll always be a brawler.

"I'm going to hop in the shower and get ready for work, but do I need to be worried about this thing with Mason? Are the cops going to come knocking?" A valid question because it would not be the first time the cops have come knocking at the O'Connor's door, looking for me.

"They won't come knocking. It's been taken care of."

Well, thank god for that. Getting arrested was not on my fucking to-do list today.

"Thanks, dad. Not sure how you pulled that shit off but I am beyond fucking grateful." I pat his shoulder as I get off my bed and head towards my closet to grab some clothes before I hit the shower.

"As much as I appreciate your well-versed accolades, Son, I didn't do anything this time," he says.

"Then how the hell has this been taken care of?"

That dick Mason has been gunning for me for a while now, especially after Shay dumped his sorry ass, so I know he wouldn't just drop this. The way my dad is looking at me right now has me thinking I'm not going to like the answer.

"How was this taken care of?" I ask again, crossing my arms over my chest as I lean against my closet door. If I appear relaxed, maybe he will be more willing to answer the damn question a little fucking faster.

"I called Mason's stepdad last night to see if we could work this out without involving the police, and he informed me that some little hellcat showed up to the hospital and paid Mason and Bryce's hospital bills. Apparently, she marched right into their rooms and paid them off to keep their mouths shut about the incident, then threatened Mason with assault charges if he filed charges against you. She was not polite about it, either, told both the boys she would unleash her team of lawyers on them so quickly—let me make sure I get this right—'their future unfortunate spawn would still be paying off their backwoods' daddy's legal fees.'"

My dad is smiling like the Cheshire Cat but I am not sharing the same sentiment. I'm pretty fucking livid, actually.

"What the fuck!? What the hell is wrong with that girl?" I launch myself from the closet door and start pulling clothes from my closet with more force than necessary. "What the hell possessed her to walk into the hospital room of her attacker and confront him like that? It's as fucking reckless as sitting in a damn alley at night alone, not to mention Skylar has no fucking business cleaning up my messes."

I need to fucking hit something. Or spank someone. A very specific, obviously feisty, gorgeous someone who needs to mind her business.

Then I hear deep laughter coming from behind me. I snap my head around, my fists clenched as I see my dad getting up while shaking his head.

"What are *you* laughing at, old man?" I ask, because nothing about this fucking situation seems amusing to me.

"It's just good to see you all tied up in a girl again, Son."

I expect guilt to hit me at his accusation, like I'm somehow betraying Ali, but it doesn't. What *does* hit me is fear; fear that he might be right, that I'm a little too mixed up in Skylar *fucking* Barrett. I don't need anything slightly resembling hope or caring, or whatever the fuck feelings come with her bouncing around in my black fucking heart and messing with my head.

"I am *not* tied up in a girl," I huff, well aware I sound like an immature child. Stomping toward my adjoining bathroom probably doesn't help my image either.

He fucking laughs again. "Let me tell you something about the O'Connors, Son. We love with the same emotional intensity we use to hate, which means we have no ability to hide our feelings, they are as transparent as a damn window. Your sister is the same way, although I'm not sure she has it in her to hate a thing, which is why she's always bouncing around all over the place. That girl loves life. Pure of heart, that one." He shakes his head, chuckling softly, with a prideful look in his eyes. It's almost like he can't believe a girl as soft and kind as Shayla came from a man as hard as he is. "Now shower and get ready for work. Those bottles aren't going to count themselves, and I've reached my limit of talking about feelings. My dick is shrinking a little more with each estrogen-filled second, and I can't have that. Another thing about the O'Connors—we're not pussies."

With that last abrupt and slightly convoluted comment, he stalks out my door, leaving me with an image I really did *not* fucking need. I walk into my bathroom and turn the shower on. Flashes of Sky flood my mind, her blue eyes with those tiny flecks of gold, that goddamn bright-ass sincere smile...shit I can even smell her: strawberries. And her skin, I only had a few stolen chances to touch, but it was pure silk.

My cock is getting hard just reminiscing. I turn the nozzle to cold and step into the shower. The freezing water douses my skin but does nothing to lessen my hard-on. Since the cold water is doing nothing to kill my Sky-centric erection, I flip the water to warm, grab my cock, and start pumping. Hard. The memory of her will never leave me, I know this, so I can at least make the best of this fucked-up situation and beat off to her face and body and scent until I come. At least then I will get those few seconds of peace that I crave.

CHAPTER 5

LIAM

"Damn, *hermano*," Bobby R. curses, entering through the double doors that block the kitchen from the bar. "Your sister is driving me insane. I'm telling you, it's unnatural to be that fucking peppy this early in the morning. If she wasn't so adorably hot I would have throttled her by now."

Bobby grabs a set of glasses from a top shelf above where I am crouched on the floor counting vodka bottles and resisting the urge to punch him directly in the kidney. If it wasn't for the fact I've known him for most of my life, he would probably be sprawled out on the fucking floor right now.

I exhale a breath in an effort to calm the hell down. "I fucking know I did not just hear you call my sister hot while threatening to throttle her at the same time," I warn, as I shove the crate of vodka I just finished counting back onto the shelf with a little more force than necessary.

It's not just Bobby's comment that makes me do this—it's the fact that taking inventory is so fucking boring. A far cry from going multiple violent rounds in an arena full of screaming fans.

"Sorry, but *damn*, you know how Shayla can be. She's like a fucking

Care Bear on sunshine crack or some shit. Hard to take first thing in the morning. But I won't apologize for saying she's hot. You should see what she's wearing today, man. Cute little skirt with some kind of thigh-high socks. *Chica* can throw an outfit together, that's for damn sure."

Bobby looks pretty comfortable leaning up against the liquor shelf for a guy that's about to get his ass kicked, friend or not.

"If it makes you feel better, I think you are equally as hot, *hermano*," he says, throwing his hands up in retreat.

That does not make me fucking feel better.

Before I have a chance to say another word, the double doors burst open so hard they swing back and retaliate against the person barreling through them. If it isn't the girl of the moment. I should have guessed by that entrance.

"Crap," Shayla says under her breath as the door almost slams into her face and she practically trips over her own feet.

"Christ, Shay. Be careful," I scold. *Fuck*, Bobby wasn't kidding about her outfit. I make a mental note to have a serious discussion with Shayla about the appropriate length of a skirt, or maybe just go and shred any skirts in her closet so she's forced to wear only pants.

"Sunshine crack, I'm telling ya." Bobby shakes his head, trying to hide his smile as his eyes linger a little too long on her legs.

"Fuck off, B." I smack him over the head, and the son of a bitch actually laughs at me before walking past Shayla and out of the kitchen.

"Liam!" Shay yells, running up to me and grabbing my arms in a pretty impressive grip for a girl her size. Her weird excitement takes me off-guard, and as always seems to be fucking contagious because I find myself smiling while she jumps up and down in front of me, a big ass smile plastered on her face.

"You will never guess who's sitting at the bar right now asking for you!"

"If it's the cops I'm leaving out the back."

"No, fuckwit. If it was the cops you really think I would be this excited? I would be helping you out the back door!"

Fuckwit?

"It's Skylar *freakin'* Barrett."

No fucking way I heard that right. Why would Skylar even come back to this bar after last night? I figured she'd want to stay as far away from O'Connor's as possible, especially if she knows what's good for her. But no. She's here asking for me. Hell, I can't believe she even remembers my name.

"HELLO! Earth to Liam. Did you hear me? Skylar Barrett is asking to talk to you."

I take a few steps back, needing a little distance. "Yeah—yes I heard you. I-I'm coming out, okay? Just give me a second."

Shit. I'm fucking stuttering now.

"Okay. I can keep her company," she says, clapping her hands together excitedly. "Hey, why is she asking for you anyway? Did you hit that and not tell me?" she asks, lightly punching me on the shoulder.

"Give me a break, Shay. Let me put this last crate up and I'll be right out. Try not to embarrass yourself." She flips me off as she turns and strolls back into the bar.

My baby sister. Classy as ever.

After shoving a crate of whiskey back up on the shelf, I brush off the debris and dust that had fallen from the shelves onto my shirt and pants as if it would somehow make me more presentable and worthy to be in Skylar's presence.

I feel like a teenage chick primping for a first date. I need to get my shit under control. I have to go out there, find out what she wants, and then call up one of my regulars and fuck her until the memory of Skylar Barrett is a distant one. I'll probably call Christy, she's always free for me and will let me stick my dick anywhere I want. Hell, she'll probably even let me call her Skylar when I come.

The second I walk through those doors I'm hit with that sexy as hell laugh Sky unknowingly assaulted me with last night, and I see her sitting at the bar engaged in conversation with Shayla. Every second I watch her carry on with Shay so animatedly, smiling and laughing, those dimples coming out in full force, I can feel the scars on my chest and abdomen scorch into me.

As if reminding me. Fucking *warning* me.

I am not allowed to have her. Like the sting you get if you stick your hand on a hot stove; that painful burn that reminds you instinctually to never repeat the same mistake again.

Skylar's gaze lifts to meet mine as I walk up to the bar and stand by Shayla. I don't miss the fact that her smile grows wider across her full lips as her crystal blue eyes light up, and I wonder if it's all meant for me.

"Hi," she says so simply, and the mere fact she greets me first causes me to relax enough to toss a slight smile back at her.

"Hello, Sky," I respond, throwing my hand on Shay's shoulder, hoping she will take the hint and get lost.

She does. Smart girl. "I'm going to go over there...and um...clean something. We open soon so I have to get this place spotless. Okay. Bye, Skylar, it was so awesome to meet you!"

She walks around the bar, and to my shock throws her arms around Sky, embracing her in a hug. Even more shocking is when Sky fucking hugs her back.

What the ever-loving hell was that?

Shay saunters over to a booth at the far side of the bar and starts wiping the table as if she didn't just accost one of the most recognizable faces in the country with a fucking hug. Of course I shouldn't be that surprised, Shay's never been one to adhere to boundaries. She has a tendency to just bulldoze her way into people's lives and personal space without a second thought, and people usually let her get away with it because she just has that welcoming innocent way about her. Bobby was right. Fucking sunshine crack.

When I turn my attention back to Skylar I notice she looks a little shocked as well, maybe even slightly uncomfortable, but still manages to maintain that knock-out smile. I grab the back of my neck in an attempt to release this nervous tension that has suddenly come over me. The urge to have a drink hits me, but I push it back down. I promised myself when I came home I would keep the drinking to a minimum, and never drink in the morning. Whiskey for breakfast is now a thing of the past.

I clear my throat in an attempt to get my mouth to actually form words. Skylar Barrett has me stupid and tied up in all kinds of knots. And I *don't* fucking like it. I need to get this over with and get her off my island already.

"Uh…sorry about Shayla. She can be a little much sometimes. Do you want to go sit at a table? Something more comfortable than a bar-stool?" I offer, pointing to the booth behind her all the while trying to avoid those alluringly sinful eyes.

"Sure. And your sister is quite cute, actually. I don't get to meet girls like her in L.A. Kind of a breath of fresh air," she says as she hops off the barstool and heads to the booth.

I take in the sight of her. She's wearing some kind of short white summer dress that hugs every curve of her perfect body, her auburn hair pulled up in a ponytail, loose tendrils barely touching the curve of her neck. I follow close behind and find my hand twitching with a need to find the small of her back, my teeth grinding at the thought of kissing and biting and licking her bare neck. My dick goes hard as I take in the scent of strawberries left behind in her wake. I watch closely as she slides gracefully into the booth, completely unaware of what she is doing to me. Every sense I have is flooded with a need, and I can feel it quickly coursing through me at an uncontrollable pace.

A need to touch.

To inhale.

To taste.

To fuck.

A need to claim. Fuck. I need to get it together.

I sit down in the booth across from Sky, resisting the immediate urge to take the empty spot right next to her. She places her hands on the table, folding them in front of her, and my hard-on quickly disappears at the sight of her bandaged hand. My lust is replaced with anger as flashes of last night and her on the ground bleeding come crashing back to me. Now the only need I have is a need to fucking hurt someone.

"I'm okay, Liam."

The soft sound of her voice brings me back to the present, but I have no fucking clue what she just said. "Sorry, what'd you say?"

Sky lets out a timid laugh as she glances down at my clenched fists on the table. "I said I'm okay. My hand, I mean. You were staring. It looks worse than it really is. My friend kind of sucks at the whole Florence Nightingale routine so he may have over compensated with the bandages," she explains, picking at a frayed edge of the bandage.

Glass. Blood. Skylar on the ground in shock.

I shut my eyes, trying to block out the flashbacks. My head is starting to pound. It's moments like these that I would give anything to not remember everything.

"Does it hurt?" I ask, running a hand over my face. I don't know why I decide to ask this. Just the idea that she may be hurting because I couldn't help her has me close to falling over the edge.

"No, not really." She's lying to me and it's fucking obvious by the way she avoids making eye contact as she nervously slides her hand under the table.

"Forgive me if I find that hard to fucking believe. I saw that piece of glass in your hand, Sky."

"I swear it doesn't hurt that bad! I've survived much worse, trust me. This one time I accidently gave myself a wicked paper cut on my tongue and couldn't eat or drink anything for days without my tongue stinging like a bitch, and before you ask how I could get a paper cut on my tongue just know that it was for a noble cause, and at the time it didn't occur to me that I could use a glue stick to seal all those envelopes or that there is actually a product out there specifically designed for sealing envelopes."

Just like that my anger dissipates and I try to hide my smile at the realization that I make Skylar Barrett nervous. If her rambling wasn't enough to convince me, the fact that she's now gnawing on that plump lower lip so hard I'm afraid she may puncture it.

I don't know if it's the hottest thing I've ever seen or the most annoying. The small part of me that maintains some type of humanity wants to stop her, to put her at ease. But the other part of me, the primal animalistic side I can't seem to escape, wants to know that I fucking affect her. That I unnerve her to a point where she's unaware of her own physical reactions. I want her to be marked by me.

I haven't *wanted* since Ali. With Ali it was so different though—innocent and pure and loving. We were high school sweethearts. The person I am now would ruin someone like Ali. Sweet. Angelic. *Ali.* Looking across at this anxious blushing girl in front of me, I'm almost tricked into believing she's sweet and angelic too, but I'm not fooled.

She's no Ali. Skylar Barrett may have a sweet and caring side, but I see the dark that hides behind those eyes. I can sense it. Like how animals can sense fear in other animals just from their scent. Call it intuition or fucking instinct, I don't give a shit. I just *know* it's there.

"Anyway, I had to come and see how you are," she says. "Last night got so crazy. Noah heard me yelling, I guess, and wanted to make sure I got out of there before people started to take pictures and stories ended up in the tabloids. In this business, a picture is worth a thousand words and unfortunately none of them have to be true. I-I'm just...I wanted to say I'm sorry for everything and for running away, and to thank you for what you did." She lets out a breath and smiles while fidgeting with her hands on the table.

"You have no reason to apologize, Sky. It was good someone got you out of there. I should've done it before you got hurt." My hand finds its way on top of hers before I even realize it.

Her skin is soft against my rough calloused palms, and I swear a surge of energy travels from her body to mine. Sky reminds me of every time I took a hit of coke or shot of whiskey; intoxicating and dangerously lethal.

"You tried," she says. "Those asshats just refused to let up."

I chuckle, quickly removing my hand from hers. "Noah, huh? Is that your boyfriend?"

Not sure why I ask this question, but I certainly seem to be on a roll today when it comes to asking stupid shit, so why stop now?

"Noah?!" She bursts out laughing, and while it's all kinds of sexy, I'm pretty confused as to what is so fucking funny because I sure as hell am not laughing. "No, definitely not my boyfriend," Skylar says. "Noah is my stylist. He works for me. He also happens to be one of my best friends, and let's just say you're more his type than me. Besides, I'm completely single and without a boyfriend at the moment...uh... not that you asked me if I'm single," she blushes, looking completely flustered. I'm about to speak when she continues on. "Also, I'm pretty sure that announcing I'm completely single also implies that I'm without a boyfriend already, so I guess saying I'm without a boyfriend is kind of redundant." I bite the inside of my cheek so I don't laugh at her, rambling Skylar is pretty fucking cute.

"Got ya. Well I'm relieved to see you're okay." I'm also relieved to hear she's not dating some dick that lets her sit behind a bar alley alone. "I would have called to check on you but had no way to reach you. So, how much longer will you be on Orcas Island?"

"Not long. I was supposed to be leaving today but I have something to do first. Actually, that's why I'm here. What I say next may sound a little crazy." She bites her lip appearing apprehensive, her eyes looking sheepishly up at me, but there's a hint of mischief in them that intrigues the hell out of me. If she's here to ask me to fuck her then I'll truly believe that there is a God.

"I have a job offer for you."

Well, shit. Something tells me this job does not include her pussy and my dick having daily in-depth meetings.

"Say that again?"

"See, told ya. Crazy. It's just that I recently had to fire my last body-guard and unfortunately that's not a position I can leave vacant for very long. Normally I don't handle the hiring of my bodyguards, my manager does, but he hired the last three and...none of them worked out. Do you know what the definition of insanity is, Liam?"

I shake my head as she enthusiastically continues, knowing she won't stop long enough for me to answer anyway.

"It's when you do the same thing over and over again expecting different results. I want to change the results, so I thought maybe if I did the hiring, hire you, I mean, then I could change them."

Bodyguard? What in the ever-loving fuck?

"Look, I'm flattered really, but I don't know a fucking thing about being a bodyguard. I'm not even trained for that kind of job."

"You're just as trained as anyone else I would hire for the position." For a fraction of a second, a pleading look passes over her face as if begging me to say yes, or maybe fearful I would say no, and fuck if that doesn't make my chest ache.

"Most bodyguards hired from private companies are retired cops or ex-military, or former fighters just like you. The way you handled yourself last night was impressive, and to be honest, that might be the most action you see if you work for me. It would be mostly helping me get past hostile paparazzi or fans that get a little too close for comfort.

The hardest part is keeping your cool, especially with the paparazzi. Some of them enjoy pushing until you are forced to push back. Then when you do, they sue, looking for some kind of payday. Damn parasites, most of them."

She's batshit crazy. How could she think the way I handled myself was impressive? I lost control and she ended up hurt. "Listen, Skylar—"

"Wait. Just...wait before you say anything. Let me tell you my offer. I've a three month break before I start filming my next movie. You could just try it out. See if it's a good fit. I have a guesthouse at my home in the Hollywood Hills. You could stay there. If you decide you want to take the job permanently, then I can help you find a place. And the pay is good, I mean, really, *really* good. You would probably make more in three months working for me than you would three years working at a place like this." A look of shame and a slight blush comes over her as Sky's hands move quickly to cover her face out of embarrassment. "Shit, I didn't mean for that to sound insulting. Sometimes I forget how to behave like a human being. I'm so stupid."

Despite the muffled sound of her voice, I hear every word said and it pisses me right off. I reach over and pull her hands away, holding them in my own on top of the table. Those blue eyes lock on to mine and a gasp escapes from her mouth.

"Don't worry about it. I wasn't insulted. But Sky, never hide your face from me and don't *ever* call yourself stupid. You got me."

"I...yeah. Sorry," she says, sliding back slightly in the booth. Realizing I'm still touching her, I jerk my hands away and put them under the table.

"Honestly, Liam, I'm going with my gut on this. I've had some bad experiences with previous bodyguards, ones I knew very little about other than my instincts told me I couldn't trust them. And it turns out I really should have listened because they caused me some serious damage. My instincts, my gut, are telling me I can trust you and this time I plan on listening."

Scrubbing my hand down my face I try and think of the best way to handle this situation. A way to let her down that won't put that sad fucking look back on her face that makes me feel like I just kicked her puppy. "It's not about the money, or a fucking place to stay. You don't *know* me to trust me with a task this…important."

Looking unfazed, Skylar raises an eyebrow as if preparing to put me in my place. I don't like how she seems ready to top me right now. It makes me fucking uncomfortable.

"You're right Liam, I don't know you. But trust isn't necessarily based on knowledge, Liam."

"Then what the hell is it based on?"

"Philosophically, some would say hope. Hope given to someone believed to be trustworthy."

Skylar glances at the ceiling for a brief second, taking a contemplative breath in what I hope is an attempt to think of a way to better explain herself because I have no fucking clue what she means. Then she looks right fucking at me.

"Last night, when we were together, I observed a few things about you. For example, most people would have taken advantage of your situation. Try to cleverly get information out of me so they could sell it to the media. Maybe even come on to me assuming I'm easy because of some tabloid bullshit they've read and they can't wait to brag about the time they banged a movie star." Her sudden rigid posture coupled with her clipped tone leads me to believe she has dealt with these situations often before.

"But not you. You were cautious around me, careful not to touch me. And you never pushed or prodded to get any salacious details about my life. In fact, it seemed like you couldn't have cared less about who I was. On top of that, you can clearly hold your own in a fight. The fact that you didn't initiate it, held out until it became necessary to fight back also speaks to your character. I can't have a bodyguard that throws the first punch. It'll cause me a lot of legal problems. The way you handled the whole situation gave me hope and that hope leads me to believe I can put my trust in you."

I can't fucking hear this shit anymore. Her turning me into some hero, looking at me like I'm capable of protecting her, like I can keep her safe. What a fucking joke. Three people I loved were brutally murdered while I watched. I did nothing to save them. I was weak then. I swore to never be weak again. Skylar is starting to make me weak, and this bullshit needs to end now. I need her to fucking leave.

"Well, *honey*, let me tell you something. You may be observant but you are severely lacking in the common-sense department, and I'm not sure that is something I can handle."

"*Excuse* me?"

"You need me to spell it out for you?"

"Please," she says, folding her arms in front of her chest and sitting up straight as if that would shield her from my onslaught. All it does is cause me to lean predatorily over the table so she pays attention to every damn word I have to say.

"One, you went into an alley behind a bar in the middle of the night. Alone. Which is about as reckless as you can get. What if I hadn't been out there and Mason and his asshole friends found you by yourself? What do you think they would've done to you? Two, you decided to haul that cute little ass of yours down to the hospital and confront the assholes that attacked you all by yourself in an attempt to clean up *my* fucking mess. And last but not least, you are too trusting. You think I was being cautious and careful around you?" I roll my eyes and laugh before delivering the final blow. "How do you know that I wasn't just trying to seduce you? To weaken your defenses to get you under me, to get you in my bed so I could scream to anyone that would listen that I fucked *the* Skylar Barrett."

Her eyes grow wide with shock and I relax knowing I've hit my mark. I showed her the true asshole that I am. But then, within seconds, her lips turn up into a smile, and she fucking laughs at me.

How is it that moments ago I was a predator, and now I feel as if I've become the prey?

"You are something else, slugger." Skylar continues to laugh, shaking her head.

"Excuse me?" I say.

"Would you like *me* to spell it out for you?" She doesn't wait for my response. Thank fuck because I haven't the first clue how to respond. "One"—she lifts her index finger up as if I don't understand the meaning of the number without the visual—"I will give you the lonely girl in the alley thing. That was stupid and I wasn't thinking clearly. Sometimes I forget I'm not untouchable. Two"—and here comes the middle finger. Cute. "Don't assume my trip to the hospital had anything to do with you. I went down there to pay those douchebags off so that they wouldn't run to TMZ or Perez with this story, because next thing I know I'm screwing three guys in an alley or I'm involved in a drug deal gone wrong. Yes, I convinced them to not press charges, but that was because I felt guilty. You wouldn't have been in that situation if it wasn't for me, so I wanted to make sure you were off the hook. But the thing that has me laughing, has me a bit confused, is your last statement."

"And why is that?"

"We both know you are not a man that has either the patience or the need to seduce a woman into bed. A flash of that wicked grin, a wink, and a snap of your fingers will probably have most women on their backs, legs spread and ready. So now I'm wondering, who you are trying to protect with that lie—me or yourself?"

Well, fuck me standing. Where the hell did the flustered, charming girl from two fucking minutes ago, go? Skylar should be running, or at least looking at me like the disrespectful piece of shit that I am. Instead, she's sitting here looking at me satisfied, like she just delivered a successful counterpunch without even blinking. *Damn*, I knew I liked this girl.

I hear a girly little snicker I recognize all too well and turn my gaze just in time to see Shay's smile disappear and her eyes go wide when she realizes I've caught her eavesdropping from behind the bar. She quickly ducks behind the counter and I watch as the door to the kitchen swings open and closed. Sneaky little brat.

"Look, you don't have to answer me now. I was supposed to leave today and head back to Los Angeles, but I delayed it until tomorrow. Do you know where Orcas Island airport is?" Skylar asks casually, as if she didn't just hand me my fucking ass.

"Yeah—yes, I'm aware of it."

"Wow…of course you are. Duh, Skylar. It's a small island," she says, smacking her hand to her forehead.

"It's okay." I can't help but smile, shattering my scowl into pieces. There's the Skylar that first walked in here.

"Well, I have a private plane that's going to take me home tomorrow. It leaves at six in the morning. If you want the job, just meet me at the Orcas Island airport before the plane takes off. Here, I have something for you."

Skylar takes a white envelope out of her purse, a purse that probably costs more than my Harley, then pulls my hand from across the table so she can place the envelope in it.

"The salary details are in there as well as a brief description of the job. My attorney will want you to sign a NDA if you decide to take the job, but I'm not that worried about it this second."

"A NDA?"

"A non-disclosure agreement. It basically means you can't discuss anything that goes on in my life, or anything you witness with anybody. To tabloids, reporters, friends, stuff like that."

"Okay." Makes no difference to me, I wouldn't run my mouth off about her anyway; it's no one's fucking business.

"I know this is last minute, and I'm not giving you much time to think about it, but I know if I go back to Los Angeles without you, my manager will have found me someone else, and I'll be stuck with another asshole bodyguard and I won't have the nerve to ask you again." Skylar lets out a sigh as if she just ran out of words.

She's endearing when she's flustered, but there's something about the way she rambles on nervously but then flips the script so easily that concerns me. I just can't put my finger on it, but it intrigues me because it feels dangerous. *She* feels dangerous.

When my dad was a boxer he went by the name Sean the Swan O'Connor. A lot of fighters would mock the name, laugh at it because they saw it as a pussy name for a boxer. That laughter stopped the minute he pummeled them into the ground within the first few rounds. The thing about swans is while they are beautiful and graceful creatures, they can be mean mother fuckers. Aggressive, territorial, and plain fucking nasty. Swans can tear skin from a body with their beaks, even break a human arm using only their wings. Hidden behind all that elegance lies a crafty animal ready to snap into attack mode at all times.

Skylar is a swan, and damn if she is not tempting me with her perilous splendor. She provides me that risk and adrenaline I'm addicted to. The one boxing once provided, and after that ended, the drugs, the booze, the women, and the rage.

I would be lying to myself if I said I didn't want to take this offer, and not for the fucking money but to be near Skylar, to watch over her, to protect her. The thought of her going back to L.A. and hiring some other dick that could potentially fuck her over has me pissed off. I don't know how her previous ones fucked her over, but given her reaction I can tell it wasn't good, and it has me wanting to shove my fist through someone's face. Which is where my problem lies. I can't control myself when I feel threatened, or when someone I care about is threatened. Rage has now become my closest friend, and it will engulf me, ravage me, and I *will* lose control.

Mason is lucky he isn't breathing through a tube right now after touching my sister and hurting Skylar. My dad saved his life. If I go with Skylar, he won't be there to pull me back from the darkness. I could ruin her reputation just as I have ruined mine. Or worse, destroy her life altogether.

I can't have a bodyguard that throws the first punch. It will cause me a lot of legal problems.

"I'm sure I've monopolized enough of your time, and I want to give you a chance to think about this without me breathing down your neck, because I know if I stay here much longer you might just take the job to shut me up and then I'll feel bad." I can't help but laugh because that fake little pout she just gave me, and those puppy dog eyes, lead me to think she really wouldn't feel bad at all.

"Nah, I like listening to you talk. The speed with which you do it sometimes is very impressive. I promise I'll think about your offer." I place my hand on top of hers because this may be it for us, and I want to make sure I touch her one last time.

Skylar slides out of the booth, grabbing her purse off the table as I sit here like an idiot too scared that if I get up I will follow her all the way to Los Angeles, and I need to make the right decision for her, not me.

"You know, it would be quite fitting if you decided to take the job, don't ya think?" Skylar flashes me a coy grin.

"How's that?"

"Your name."

"What about it?"

"In Irish, one of the meanings of the name Liam is 'determined protector.'"

Well, I'll be damned. She has rendered me speechless. How does she know that and I don't?

"Come on, Liam, don't tell me I just out-Irished you in your own Irish bar. Tsk, tsk. Look alive, slugger." She gives me a sassy wink, covers those seductive eyes with sunglasses, then walks that sexy ass right out O'Connor's.

I am so fucked.

CHAPTER 6

Skylar

oly hell, he's here. He is *actually* here. Wait…why is he here? Liam should be tucked safely in his bed naked or lifting weights shirtless, or whatever it is he does at this ungodly hour, because there's no way he can think I'm sane after our talk yesterday. What person in their right mind offers a complete stranger a job as their personal bodyguard and then invites said stranger to stay in their guesthouse? This is not the behavior of a rational person. Liam was right; I'm severely lacking in common sense.

The truth is, I haven't been able to get Liam out of my head since I met him. When Noah brought me back to my hotel room and helped patch up my hand, I was wishing it was Liam instead. Then, when I was finally able to fall asleep, I didn't have the same abusive nightmares about my mother or father or Jeff Roberts, my previous creepy bodyguard. I didn't wake up gasping for air or screaming for help, sweating and crying until I was able to breathe again. I dreamed of Liam. It was as if my unconscious mind knew to conjure up a vision of him to protect me from my nightmares. He somehow slipped his way into my subconscious thoughts, consuming them in the loveliest and most possessive way possible, and when I woke up *I knew* I needed him with me. And though it was not rational or logical, I had an overwhelming sense that he needed me too.

And maybe he really does because here he is casually leaning up against the brick wall of the small airport building looking like dirty sex incarnate in a pair of navy pants that hang off his hips and a worn black t-shirt stretched across his chest. His hands are shoved into his pockets, causing the veins in his cut forearms to pop out slightly, and now all I can think of is Liam O'Connor picking me up with those arms, slamming me against that wall and screwing my—

"Ms. Barrett, would you like to get out here?"

Right. I'm still in the cab, and I'm sure the driver has better things to do than sit on the tarmac while I silently lust.

"Here is great. Thank you," I say, handing the driver a fifty. Probably more than the actual fare, but the quicker I get out of this cab, the faster I can get to Liam.

As I move to get out of the car, I glance up to see if I can spot him, but the glare from the early morning sun on the windshield blinds me from seeing anything in front of me. The side door opens and my heart picks up for a split second thinking it's him, but when I see a plump hand grab for my suitcase I know those are not the hands I was hoping for. Sliding out of the backseat, ignoring the hand of the cab driver trying to help me out, I grab the suitcase from him.

"Thanks."

"You're welcome Ms. Barrett. It was a pleasure driving you. I've seen all your movies. You're great."

"Oh, wow. Thanks." *Don't ask. Please don't ask. It's way too early.*

"Do you think I could get a picture and an autograph? I got a little girl who loves watching reruns of your show. I would be her hero," the driver all but begs, his hand grasping my wrist lightly to stop me from walking away, and I flinch immediately, pulling it from his grip. He backs off a little which puts me at ease and at the mention of his daughter I cave to his request.

"Uh…yeah, sure. A picture works. You have a camera on your phone?" I am such a sucker when it comes to kids.

I set my suitcase down and wait as he excitedly pulls a cell phone from his pocket.

"What the fuck is going on over here?" A deep baritone voice rumbles so close behind me I can feel the vibrations through my chest.

I turn around but not before I take a deep breath, because I know the minute I see him the possibility of going all spastic Skylar is strong. Keeping my shit together around Liam for some reason is proving to be difficult.

"Morning, Liam. So happy you came," I say, sounding a little too excited. *So happy you came? Jesus, Skylar, just drop your panties now, why don't you?*

"Sky." He lifts his chin slightly, his eyes trained on mine. "Let's go," he orders, grabbing my suitcase then threading the fingers of his free hand into mine causing a slight shiver to dance across my skin. No one has ever held my hand before, not even Cass when we would hang out. Liam has done it twice already, and both times my stomach has done a little flip.

"Oh...uh...sure."

"Hey, what about the picture before you leave, Ms. Barrett?"

Oh yeah. The cab driver. How did I forget he's still standing there? This is clearly the Liam effect.

"Right, sorry. Hold on, Liam, I promised this gentleman a picture for his little girl." I try to pull away from Liam's hold but his hand only grabs tighter onto mine.

"Little girl? Really, Larry? Last I checked, your *little girl* was well over the age of eighteen, and trust me, I checked very fucking thoroughly."

Okay, so clearly Liam knows the cab driver, and the cab driver's daughter. *Really* well. And now I'm trying hard not to picture Liam with some woman. A woman I try to convince myself is probably hideous looking. She probably looks exactly like her father, I'm sure. Short, stocky, and half-balding. Like the love child of Joe Pesci and Danny DeVito.

Stop, Skylar. Jealousy is not a good color on you.

"Larry, how could you lie to me like that? I thought we were friends," I say with a slight smile, trying to defuse the situation because Liam's tense body and Larry's death stare brought on by the realization of his daughter's sexual activities has me on edge.

Larry looks at the ground briefly, at least having the decency to appear slightly ashamed at being caught in his minor fib. "I'm sorry, Ms. Barrett. Just wanted an autograph is all."

"It's fine, Larry. I'm sure you wouldn't be the first to fib to me."

"Let's go, Skylar." Liam pulls me away from Larry and the cab. Tripping over my feet as he all but drags me, I look back and offer a small apologetic wave to Larry. He may have lied but I'm sure the lie was an innocent one.

"You could have been a little nicer to cab driver Larry, Liam. All he wanted was an autograph. That happens sometimes, you know. You can't just snap at people like that, especially my fans."

Liam continues to walk us to the Gulfstream G150 plane that will take us to Los Angeles without saying a word, and I know I was speaking loud and clear, so it seems he's ignoring me on purpose. I refuse to be ignored. I get enough of that from dear old Dad.

"*Hey*, I'm talking to you." I plant my feet so he can't move us any further. He stops, drops my suitcase, and turns to me with a look that should scare me but quite frankly turns me on. Who knows why, maybe it's because I'm not right in the head or maybe it's because he's just so damn close at the moment that I can feel the heat and pheromones and anger pouring off of him. Liam wants me to cower. I refuse.

"Sky, what'd you hire me for? Is this all a fucking joke to you? Are you just some spoiled, bored Hollywood rich bitch looking for a guy to fucking follow you around like a lost puppy, worshipping the ground you walk on? Is this some elaborate way to get me to fuck you?" he asks, releasing my hand as he pulls my body into his and lowers his lips to my ear. "Because, *honey*, all you had to do was ask."

I'm not sure what the hell is happening here but I am *so* not comfortable with his accusation.

Part of what drew me to Liam initially was my attraction to him. He's all maleness and sex, and it causes a sensory overload in my brain, overwhelming me like an undercurrent, trying to pull me under and drown me in all that is Liam O'Connor. I'm also aware I can be impulsive and reckless and make decisions that are not well thought out, especially lately. But this is one choice I made on my own, one that makes sense, and the fact that he seems to think so little of me when I think so highly of him, well it hurts more than I care to admit.

"No, this isn't a joke to me," I say, pulling harshly out of his grasp and blinking back the tears that are starting to form. I will not cry in front of him. I will not let him make me weak. I square my shoulders and look him directly in the eye, like you should do when training a dog. Show no fear. Direct eye contact. Do not be the first to break. Not that I think Liam is a dog, but on occasion the guy seems to show similar characteristics to that of a wild animal. Like now with his pupils dilated, nostrils flaring, and chest heaving, so I'm working with what limited knowledge I have.

"I meant what I said at the bar when I offered you the job, Liam." I shove my palm into his chest—his really well-defined chest—in order to create some safe distance between us. "I need a new bodyguard. Someone I can trust to be in my life, someone I can trust *with* my life. If that isn't you, if you think this is some kind of joke, that I'm just some *spoiled bitch* hard up for a lay, then you can screw off. I can find someone else and you can go back to making vodka crans and pouring beers for the twenty-one and over crowd of Orcas Island."

Grabbing my suitcase, I head toward the plane. He can choose to follow or stay behind, I don't really care. Okay, I do care, but hell if I let him know that. Liam reaches out, grabbing my upper arm, and pulls me to his chest, my back to his front, and suddenly I'm soaking in each singular, erratic breath he releases.

"I'm sorry, Sky," he whispers into my ear, his hand on my arm moving downward to rest on my stomach. I tense slightly at this unexpected touch. "I just saw Larry grab you and fucking lost it for a minute. I know you think what happened with him was innocent, and maybe it was, but I won't take that chance. If you want me to do this job for you I fully fucking intend to take it seriously. One second of me underestimating someone's intentions could make a world of fucking difference. *Trust* me. Can you forgive me?"

The desperation in his voice saddens me, and I give in, relaxing into him instinctively and embracing his warmth and scent and safety as if it's second nature. When I was a child and my mother would get that look in her eyes, the one that told me she was lost to her sickness, I would run and hide in the closet of her bedroom under a pile of her clothes in the back corner. Ironically the scent of her surrounding me relaxed me even if the sight of her frightened me, and I would fall asleep as easily as if I was being held in her arms, a synthetic hug that lured me to a peaceful place. That is what it feels like to be held by Liam. Like he is my new safe place.

"Yes, I forgive you."

I start to walk toward the plane again when he pulls me back into him. "Do you trust me, Sky?" My breath hitches and my skin trembles when the touch of warm air escaping his mouth caresses my ear. I don't even need to think about my answer.

"Yes. I trust you."

"You don't. But you will. We'll get there. I fucking promise."

I suppress my initial reaction, which is to argue with him. Why did he even ask me the question if he wasn't going to believe the answer? But then I realize he *needs* me to allow him to work for my trust. So I say the next best thing I can think of.

"So, you and cab driver Larry's daughter, huh?" Okay, maybe not the next best thing but it's the first thing anyway. "Tell me, how does one thoroughly check the age of a female? I'm assuming you weren't referring to scoping out her driver's license."

"Very cute, Sky." Liam nudges me forward, suppressing a smile as he pulls the suitcase from my grasp and once again grabs my hand. "One suitcase is pretty impressive by the way, especially for such a long stay on the island."

"Well, hold your applause. I sent the rest of my twenty or so bags home with Noah yesterday."

"I see. I got here a little early so my bags are already on the plane," he explains as he walks us up the stairs and into the small plane.

When we reach the middle of the plane I sink into the plush cream colored seat and start picking at a frayed string from my shorts in an effort to not stare at the skin peeking through between Liam's jeans and shirt as he lifts my suitcase into the overhead compartment. I hear the slamming of the compartment above my head and I continue to stare intently at the rogue string as I sense him crouch down in front me. I try and control my breathing so that I'm not panting like I just ran a marathon. I can do this. I can be stealth. He will not be able to tell how much he affects me. I am an actress after all.

All of my acting skills go out the window the second I feel the graze of his hand on my stomach as he reaches for my seatbelt.

"I never really understood the need for seatbelts on planes," I say as he looks up at me silently, clicking the belt into place. I hate nervous silences because I always feel an obligation to fill them. "I mean, if this plane takes a nosedive, I'm sure this strap of nylon will do little to save me from a fiery and no doubt messy death. Have you seen the aftermath of some of those plane crashes? A seatbelt saved no one. It's like kaboom! Then just bloody body parts scattered everywhere."

He chuckles, sliding his hands from the belt, looking up at me with those devious gunmetal eyes. "Maybe. But I wouldn't want to take any chances with your safety, now would I? You're paying me to look after you, so that's what I intend to do."

Before I have a chance to respond, the pilot's voice comes over the intercom, "Welcome aboard, Ms. Barrett. We will be taking off in five minutes. If you and your guest could please buckle up. Mr. Naheer has made sure the refreshments are fully stocked if you or your guest wish for a drink or snack once we even out. We should be landing at LAX around nine a.m. Enjoy your flight."

"Who is Mr. Naheer?" He asks, sinking down into the seat across from mine.

"A friend. He loans me his plane from time to time when I'm in a pinch."

"He loans you his plane?" he asks slowly. "That's a pretty generous *friend*," he scoffs, narrowing his eyes at me disbelievingly.

Seriously?

I swear, if Liam keeps this accusatory attitude up, I will throat punch him right out of this plane the second we hit cruising altitude.

"Paul *is* a pretty generous friend, well, more like a surly great uncle than a friend. Same with his wife of thirty years who I happen to be very close to. Seeing as I missed my flight yesterday due to acquiring an extremely arrogant and seemingly judgmental ass of a bodyguard, Paul was nice enough to make his plane available to me," I snap.

I don't know what type of reaction I expected from him after what I said, but it definitely isn't the cocky grin he is currently sporting. His eyes aren't even on my face anymore. They've dropped to my chest where I've unintentionally put my breasts on display by crossing my arms underneath them. I drop my arms quickly and start rubbing my hands to my thighs which only causes his gaze to lower to my legs. When his tongue slowly swipes across his lower lip my hands quickly find their way back to the safe and completely unsexual armrests.

"So, three hours until we land in L.A., huh," he says, moving his eyes back to mine and placing his hands behind his head. I know he knows he unnerves me. He has to, and that just pisses me off. "That gives us plenty of time, then, doesn't it, Sky?" He knocks his foot playfully against mine.

"Time for what?" I ask.

"I know your mind is probably imagining all the dirty things you want me to do to you on this plane, sweetheart, but I meant time to get to know each other." I can't tell if he's joking or not, but the smirk that followed that comment annoys me. So does the fact that I'm now actually imagining all the dirty things I want him to do to me on this plane. "Look," he sits up straighter, scrubbing a hand down his face. "You told me yesterday it was important for you to trust the person who was looking after you, and I want you to trust me. What better way to build trust than getting to know one another? Three hours stuck in the sky seems like an opportune time to do it."

First he jokes about having sex with me on the plane and now he wants to get to know me? Give me a break. I know this act. I've seen it before. Liam is about to milk me for my stories and my secrets. He's about to use me. How could I have been this stupid? I was clearly blinded by my attraction to him, by the kindred hurt I thought I saw in his eyes, and now I'm about to pay. The unease at his request coupled with the roar of the plane engine firing up and sending a vibration under me has my hands gripping the arm rests tightly. Liam is the picture of relaxation as he sits back, staring me down, waiting for my response which pisses me off. Every part of me is set to defensive mode, and the only way I can shut him down is by punishing him verbally.

"Courtesy of the tabloids, my life is an open book as I'm sure you know. So why don't you just go with what you've read or heard about me? Or better yet, Google me for the most up-to-date information.

That is, if you haven't already," I accuse, rolling my eyes. I should have known better. Carl always beat it into me that the only people you can trust are blood.

He sits up, resting his arms on his legs, and scowls. The sudden change in his demeanor has me shrinking a fraction of an inch back into my chair. "Despite what you may think, Skylar Barrett, not everyone gives a shit what happens in the lives of celebrities. Some of us have our own fucking lives to be concerned with. You think I sit at home on my computer reading gossip sites or spend my hard-earned money on fucking magazines that spew a bunch of speculative vapid bullshit gossip?"

Well, when you put it that way…

"Shit. I'm sorry, Liam. I can't believe I went off like that. And after I made such a production of you calling me a spoiled Hollywood bitch. I guess I am kind of a bitch. It's just that with what I do—"

"Stop, Sky." He reaches over and places a hand on my leg. "Don't call yourself a bitch. I should never have fucking said that to you, and I don't want you saying it about yourself. I know I can be an asshole sometimes, say shit I don't mean, and I'll work on that. Look, I get it. You have issues with trust and I understand why. Being in the public eye has you thinking everyone is out to exploit you, and it's probably good for you to be wary. But I would *never* fucking do that. I could never be that cold or callous. You said outside that you trusted me. Why?"

"I-I don't know."

"You didn't even have to think about the answer, did you?"

"No."

"What was your first thought when I asked you?" he asks, his thumb cautiously moving back and forth across my knee with a tenderness that seems almost as new for him to give as it is for me to receive. "What did you feel when I was holding you to me, Sky? Don't think. Just give me the first word that pops into that pretty little head of yours."

"Safe." Undamaged, untainted, protected, adored, beautifully cherished. But he said the first word, so the rest will remain my own little secret.

He sits back in his chair and clears his throat, appearing uncomfortable with my choice of word. "Good. I need you trust me with every part of you. Your stories, your secrets. Your life. If you want me with you, I *need* this from you. You got me?"

"Yes. I'm sorry for snapping like that." Now I'm the one that's a little uncomfortable. His intensity is definitely something I need to get used to. "Well, at least we already know one thing about each other."

"What's that?"

"We're both pretty awesome when it comes to apologizing."

Liam laughs and relaxes back into his chair, his eyes never leaving mine.

"So, slugger, what do you want to know about me?" I ask.

"Good girl," he praises. "How about you tell me how you got into this business. What made you choose acting?"

A softball question first. I can get behind that. "I didn't really decide it. My father and I moved to L.A. from Portland, Oregon when I was ten. He worked at this computer company and they transferred him to their L.A. office. One day when we were grocery shopping a woman walked up and told my father how beautiful I was and that she was an agent that represented child actors and she thought I would be great for this shampoo commercial. She gave him some line about my sparkling eyes and big smile. Anyway, my father took the bait and I landed the job, along with a hefty paycheck. The potential of the money I could make was incentive enough for my father to keep bringing me to auditions. Eventually he took over as my manager, figured it would be easier, I guess, or he just knew he could make an extra fifteen percent off me. I had a lot of steady work after that and then got cast as Mandy Mayhem when I turned twelve. Once I turned fifteen the movie offers started coming, and then never really stopped."

"Your dad is your manager?"

"Yes. You really don't know anything about me, do you? Do me a favor, never Google me."

Liam lets out that sexy laugh. I really need to brush up on some knock-knock jokes or something so I can hear that laugh daily.

"Why is that?"

"Because I like that you don't know anything about me. You have no judgments or pre-conceived ideas, or reservations. I'm still a mystery to you. I don't get to feel that way very often. If you Google me you may learn some things that will make you think differently about me. I'd like to pretend that a lot of what you would read is a lie, and some of it is, but unfortunately a lot of it's true." I start playing with that pesky string on my shorts again, embarrassed by my admission.

"I promise," he says with a single nod.

"How about you? How did you find your way into boxing?"

"Boxing found its way to me."

Silence.

He provides no further explanation, and I'm beginning to realize that Liam O' Connor is a man of few words. I feel like if I asked a Magic Eight Ball about Liam's life I would learn more than actually asking the man himself. Screw that. If he wants me to let him in, he needs to do the same.

"That is a riveting story. Feel free to expand on that epic personal opus of yours at any time."

"You are such a smartass, you know that?" He kicks my foot again before he continues, "I was a terror as a child."

"Shocking."

"You want to hear my opus or not, Sky?"

"Sorry. You may proceed."

"Anyway, I was a feral fucker, getting into trouble and fights because I couldn't stand to be bored. I had a short fuse and too much time on my hands. I couldn't sit still to save my life. My dad, who used to be a boxer in Ireland, hauled my ass into our garage one day after a particularly brutal fight in which I busted a twelve-year-old-kid's nose. He had hung a heavy bag from the ceiling, and he said to me, 'Boy, you can't fight against your nature but you can fight for it. You can control it instead of letting it control you. Now hit this fucking bag until your knuckles bleed, and then I'll teach you how to become a master to your beast and not a slave to it.' Every day after that he trained me, worked me, taught me how to master my beast. I fought in matches starting at fifteen and fought my way up the ranks quickly. Made a name for myself in no time at all."

"And did you?"

"Did I what?"

"Master your beast?"

"I thought I did. Until the night that beast turned into a monster. And you can't master a fucking monster. You can't control it. It controls you." A detached look consumes him as he absently rubs at the scar on his neck, his eyes glazing over, and I realize I'm watching a person physically draw into themselves, into their darkness, into a past, a moment that changed everything. I know this because I've been there, and I hate that for him. I hate it. I can't watch it anymore.

Do something. Say something. Pull him back. "So what was your superhero boxing name?" Maybe I should have thought that one through a minute.

The hand on his neck drops and he bursts out in laughter. "My what? What the fuck did you just ask me?"

I hope my face is not as red as the heat burning my skin suggests. How can I give speeches at big-ass award shows and charity events in front of thousands of people with no problem and yet be completely unnerved in front of one man?

"You know how boxers have those pet names for each other like Floyd Dollars Mayweather or that um...that Pacman guy?"

Why is he still laughing at me? I mean, *really* laughing at me. He is actually doubled over, head between his legs, sucking in air with one hand up as if to signal to me it's going to be a minute.

"You are something else, Sky. Fuck, I haven't laughed that hard in a long time." He shakes his head and scrubs a hand across his face, gaining back his composure. "First off, boxers do not have superhero names. And we really fucking do *not* have pet names for each other. They're just nicknames. Like Floyd *Money* Mayweather or Manny Pacman Pacquiao."

Oops. I guess it's safe to say he officially knows I know shit about boxing now.

"Second, I'm not telling you until you answer my next question. I do believe it's my turn, after all."

Feeling brave and almost a little high off pulling him back to me, I acquiesce to another question. "Hit me with your best shot."

"Tell me about your mom. What does she do?"

Wrong shot.

Unease creeps through me at the mere prospect of even saying her name, let alone telling him anything about her.

"Sky, look at me."

I do.

"Trust me, remember? I know your mom is a trigger for you. I saw it the other night when you started to talk about her. You held back. Why?"

"Hold on just a second," I say, unbuckling my seatbelt and standing to make my way to the back of the plane where I know Paul keeps his liquor stash.

After pulling some Patrón out of the cabinet, I walk back to my chair and take a seat. I pop the cork out of the bottle and take a giant pull, feeling his judgmental stare on me the whole time. Or maybe his stare is not judgment but worry. I really don't care. If he wants to know about my mother, then he needs to back up and let me have this.

"You want some?" I hand the bottle to him, knowing he will probably decline but no need to forget my manners.

"Thanks, but no. It's a bit early for me, Skylar. You okay?"

"I'm good. Just need a little liquid courage for this one." I go to take one more pull but before the bottle hits my lips, Liam snatches it and the cork from my hands. Placing the cork back in the bottle, he tosses it forcefully onto the empty seat next to him.

"Hey, careful! That's good tequila."

"You don't need that bottle. If you can't tell me without getting loaded, then wait until you *can* tell me."

"Fine. I get it, but you don't have to be so grabby," I joke, hoping to get a smile from him. He doesn't smile back. He just stares at me, waiting for me to speak.

So I sigh, close my eyes for a brief moment, and begin to tell him something only two other people in this world know.

"My mom, Raina, was stunning. She looked like a mix between Brigitte Bardot and Rita Hayworth. She could turn every head in a room."

"Not unlike her daughter, I imagine," he says with a genuine smile. *Don't blush. Don't blush. Don't blush. Dammit, I know I'm blushing.*

"Right, well, for as beautiful as she was on the outside, she was seriously tortured on the inside. She was so sick. Some days were good, some bad. The sun literally rose and set with her. One minute she was carefree and happy, and the next you could see darkness just wash over her. She would change into a whole other person. She would hurt people, hurt herself, create drama where it was unnecessary. I don't remember a lot of it, sometimes only what my father tells me. He told me once when they had a housewarming party to introduce themselves to their new neighbors, she went into the kitchen to grab a bottle of wine, walked right into the dining room, and threw the bottle at one of the women who was wearing a dress that looked similar to hers. Then she walked back into the kitchen, curled up into a ball on the floor, and cried for seven hours straight. That was the first time my father had her committed. She got better. The doctors were able to regulate her meds and she evened out. But then she got pregnant with me. The doctors told her she shouldn't go off her meds. That it was dangerous, but she didn't want to hurt the baby. Hurt *me*. Things never went back to normal after that. They got worse. Something about her hormones changing after giving birth to me sent her spiraling deeper into depression, and at some point, she developed schizophrenia. She would start to hear voices and think demons were following her. My understanding of it from the stories my father told me is that she was convinced when she gave birth to me that she had given birth to the child of Satan, and that when I was born I brought all these demons with me to haunt her. To punish her, I guess."

I start laughing uncomfortably, realizing how ridiculous this whole thing must sound to an outsider, someone who never lived through it.

"Shit, Skylar."

The pity his whispered curse is laced with causes me to cringe. Pity is a wasted emotion because it never progresses into anything positive, and it makes me look weak in the eyes of others. I don't want his pity. I don't want anyone's. I don't want to be weak.

"Yeah. Shit. Anyway, eventually her depression reached the point of no return, so she ended her life." I shrug my shoulders.

The haunted look that claims him tells me more about him than any words he's spoken so far; he is no stranger to loss. "I'm so sorry that happened to you. Losing someone, especially someone you love—"

"I didn't say I loved her, Liam. I didn't even know her. Her being my mother did not entitle her to my love. Don't feel sorry for me based on a misconceived notion that I lost someone I loved," I snap, shocking even myself with that response.

"I think that's enough for today," he relents.

Thank god, because if I don't shut up now, I may end up telling him everything and ruin all of this. Whatever *this* is.

"You play poker?" Liam asks, grabbing a deck of cards from his back pocket. Grateful for the change in pace and surprised by his ability to stop me from spinning out of control with my own thoughts, I find myself laughing slightly in relief.

"Do I play poker? I don't just play poker, I dominate poker." I wipe away the single tear that has formed before it drops to my cheek, and I smile.

"Dominate, huh? We'll see about that. I didn't bring any poker chips with me though."

"Left them in your other pants, I suppose."

"Funny, Sky."

"Hold on. I know where we can get something." I get up from the chair and make my way to the back cabinet, pulling out a bag of Hershey's Kisses I know Paul keeps hidden away.

"We can use these," I say, tossing the bag into his lap. "Paul always keeps chocolate on his plane, it's his only addiction. This is from his stash, and if I value my life I'll make sure to replace the bag before he steps a foot back on this plane."

"Understood. Well, I guess it's game fucking on. Five card draw okay with you?"

"Perfect. Let's do this."

For the next two hours we play poker and talk about our lives. Not the hard parts like before but the stories you love to remember and share over and over again with friends. Liam told me about how his mother decorates for every holiday, including but not limited to Valentine's Day, Halloween, Thanksgiving, the 4th of July, even Memorial and Columbus Day. But her specialty is Christmas, and I loved listening to him talk about how crazy his mom gets with that particular holiday. It was like watching the sun peek out of dark clouds on an otherwise stormy day. He told me how they had three Christmas trees and even a hot cocoa station in the kitchen, and about how his dad was forced to put twinkle lights on everything outside. The roof, outside trees and bushes, even the bird houses had mini lights. I've never decorated for Christmas—I barely even celebrate most years, but I don't have a family like his, and I hope that one day I can experience Christmas the way he does. He even told me about his dad getting cancer, and it truly touched me when he explained how he had come home to take care of his family while his father recovered.

In return I told him how I met the only person I'm proud to call family. Meeting Noah was one of the few happy, untainted memories that I have. He came from a broken home, not unlike me. His father left him, his mother, and his eight-year-old sister when Noah was just fifteen. Noah's mom worked as a waitress at a café in L.A. that I would often frequent. The café was open twenty-four seven, which made it convenient for me with my crazy schedule, not to mention the café had the best macarons, and I'm a macaron slut. Noah would often be there while his younger sister did homework at a spare table in the back because his mom, June, could not afford a babysitter. Because I was there as often as Noah and only a year older than him, we naturally gravitated toward one another, and he immediately ingratiated me into his family.

I wasn't as famous then as I am now and not nearly as jaded, so it was easy to build a friendship with him. I told Liam all about how Noah would come to my house and help me put together outfits for red carpet events and his love of makeup and helping me to apply it. I think he thought I was his own personal Barbie doll, but I loved it because the boy did have a gift. By the time I turned seventeen and bought my own home, I moved Noah into it and hired him as my stylist.

We talked, laughed, and played as if we had known each other for years, and then all too soon the pilot announced the plane was set to land at LAX and asked us to buckle our seatbelts.

I'm terrified this private place we've built between our two worlds will be demolished soon after we enter mine.

"Well, Sky, I do believe you just kicked my ass at poker." Liam clears his cards off the tray and places it back in place. He then buckles my seatbelt again before buckling his own.

"Don't worry. I'll make sure you get a chance to win all your kisses back, slugger."

"I'm counting on it, sweetheart," he says with that cocky crooked smile of his.

"I'm so sure. Oh by the way, when we land don't worry about the bags, I have someone coming for them," I say, attempting to ignore the innuendo in regard to the kisses.

"It's only four bags. I'm sure we can manage."

He only has three bags? For a three month stay? How is that even possible?

"We probably could, but walking through this airport is going to be tough enough as it is without the baggage. I should probably warn you that paparazzi camp out at LAX. It's the perfect place to spot and stalk celebrities. And it will be even worse if it was leaked that I was coming back today. Not to mention the fans and autograph hounds."

"What's the difference between a fan and an autograph hound?"

"A fan knows and loves your work. An autograph hound just knows you're famous and your autograph could fetch them some money on eBay. The fans and hounds are pretty harmless as long as they don't get too hands-on. Typically, you don't have to worry about them. The paparazzi, however, can be dangerous, and they come in swarms. They get too close and the lights of the cameras flash in your face all at once while they ask disrespectful questions, and it's hard to ignore them sometimes. Hopefully my driver is already at the front of the airport so we don't have to wait long. Are you ready for this, Liam? This world...it's much different than yours."

"I wouldn't worry about me, Sky. I've gone twelve rounds with some of the best fucking fighters in the country. I'm sure I can manage a few people with cameras."

Poor, sweet boy.

"Yeah, but you get to use your fists on the fighters," I say as the plane touches down. "Here we go. Let's see what you're made of."

CHAPTER 7

LIAM

*F*uck. My heart is hammering against my chest, thumping faster and faster.

Adrenaline is roaring through me.

My body shaking, jaw clenching.

It's starting to spread through me, taking me over.

Running me.

Owning me.

I know because everyone and everything around me has slowed down. But the rage inside is unyielding and causing every part of me, every molecule, to speed right the fuck up.

I was not prepared for this. Sky warned me how bad LAX would be, but I didn't fucking listen. When we got off the plane it was just a few stragglers flashing their cameras at her, asking her how she enjoyed her trip and welcoming her back home. I kept hold of her the entire time, except when she signed a few autographs for little kids, and even then I hated letting her go. But Sky obviously loved signing for kids because her whole face lit up when she did, so I begrudgingly released her hand whenever one came around.

But in less than two minutes, everything went to shit.

The paparazzi count has gone from four to five to ten to what can only be described as a mob. They are tripping over themselves, walking fucking backwards blindly down the stairs next to the escalator we are about to ride down. I have to let go of her hand because I'm too afraid I'll fucking break it in mine with the way I'm starting to lose control of my body. I push her behind me with my arm and try and use my much larger frame to block her from the onslaught of the bright flashes that are currently blinding me to the point I have to slip on my sunglasses just to be able to see in front of me. She grabs my shirt, pressing her head into my back as if trying to hide herself in me, but she knows there is no safe place to hide because they are fucking everywhere.

Behind us. In front of us. Surrounding the space around us like fucking vultures waiting for their prey to die so they can pick apart and devour the body. Sky is the prey, and fuck if that does not have my blood boiling.

It's fucking chaos.

But what really has me about to destroy everyone with a fucking camera in their hand is the obscene questions they are yelling at her.

"Skylar, how does it feel to be back in L.A.?"

"Hey, Skylar, is this the new boyfriend?"

"Skylar, now that Cassiel Logue is back from tour are you two going to hook up again?"

"Another five-day bender through L.A.?"

"What do you have to say about the rumors that someone is shopping topless photos of you around?"

"Skylar, what do you have to say about the interview Cassiel gave recently in Rolling Stone calling you an animal in the sack?"

"Hey, guy, can you confirm that she is good in bed? How long before she puts out?"

Between the vulgar questions hurled her way and the ambush of paparazzi coming at her, I'm shocked I've not blazed a path of fucking destruction to get her the hell out of here. But with each second that passes, I just focus on her touch against my back, her sweet scent surrounding me, her warm breath that slips through the fabric of my shirt. I absorb her calm. Her being. I anchor my sanity to it.

"Shit," Skylar says as we finally make it outside to the pickup area.

I back her up against the glass wall of the terminal near the door we just walked out of and block her between my arms in an attempt to create some kind of barrier between her and the paparazzi. I bend down slightly so my mouth is right next to her ear. "What's wrong, Sky?"

"The car isn't here yet. I just texted my driver and he said he is two minutes away. We-we have to wait, Liam. I'm so sorry," she whispers past her trembling lips.

Shit.

Clearly she is not as calm as I thought. In fact, she looks like she may cry as she trains her gaze to the ground in front of her. Probably in an attempt to hide from the humiliation these assholes are putting her through.

I feel fucking helpless. Worthless. I can't hit them. I can't even *threaten* them. I turn around, keeping in front of her because the only hope I have right now is being able to spot her driver the second he pulls up. This is exactly what my dad warned me about when I told him my decision to go with Skylar. Our whole fucking conversation is now playing through my mind like a fucked-up afterschool special.

"Do you really think this is a wise decision, Son? I'm not even going to point out the obvious fact that you have no fuckin' clue what the job of a bodyguard entails because I would like to pretend my boy is smart enough to come to that realization himself. But what I will point out is the rather large problem you have dealing with—"

"Dad, don't," I say, throwing my clothes in the duffle bag on my bed while trying to ignore his looming presence in my doorway. *"I've thought about it all, okay? And being a bodyguard doesn't require much, other than getting the person you're protecting from point A to point B safely. I was boxing before I knew how to tie my shoes, and we both know what made me great was my ability to anticipate my opponent's moves before they even knew they were going to make them. So I think I got this fucking covered."*

"Boy, you started boxing at twelve. If ya' didn't know how to tie your shoes at that age then your issues run deeper than I originally thought. But we both know that's not the main concern here. Have you given any thought to how you're going to handle the threats? How you're going to

handle yourself when people start swarming her?" he asks, making his way into my room.

"Stop."

He walks right up into my space, attempting to crowd me as I try my best to ignore him, pulling more clothes off the hangers and shoving them into my bag. I know what he's doing. He's trying to push me. To prove I lack control.

"Does she know about your issues, Son? Did you even tell her?"

"Dad. Stop."

"Who is going to keep you from losing it when people start touching her or grabbing her? Have you given any thought to that because we both know I sure as fuck won't be around to rein you in."

"I said stop, goddammit!" I get in his face, eye to eye, but I don't touch him. I don't want to prove him right. "Just fucking stop," I plead, taking a deep, calming breath. "You think I haven't thought about that? Trust me, I have."

"Right. You've thought about it. For a whole four damn hours and my guess is three and a half of those were thinking with your dick."

"It's not like that. I mean, yeah, she's hot as hell. I'm not fucking blind. But it's not like I'm hard up for pussy, dad. And if this was about sex I could've nailed her the other night." Actually, I'm not so sure about that but no need to admit it to him.

"If you're going to be crass, keep your damn voice down. Your mother is in the kitchen for fuck's sake." Taking a seat on my bed, he runs a hand through his hair which for his age is shockingly still as full as ever. "What is this about then, Liam? Tell me why you are so dead set on leaving with this girl. Give me a reason that puts me at ease here."

I can tell by his defeated tone that he knows he won't change my mind. I'm a stubborn fuckhead. Like father like son. But I want to give him a reason, one that helps him not lose any sleep at night while I'm away.

I sit down on the bed beside him and attempt to explain as best as I can. "Because there is something about her that soothes me. Because she needs me. Because she doesn't know about my issue. Because she fucking made me laugh. Do you know how long it's been since I've laughed, dad? Fucking years. Years since I felt I even deserved to laugh. Skylar made me *forget for a few minutes that my life is complete fucking shit by turning me into someone worthy of protecting her. But this isn't just about her. It's about me too. I can't stay on this island much longer and stay sane. Fuck, dad. The memories here are slowly killing me. It's why I left in the first place. I came back here to help you, to help my family, and I don't regret that because it was time I stepped the fuck up, but everywhere I look I'm tortured by their ghosts. Trev, Izzy, fucking Ali. The guilt eats me up inside enough as it is, and being back home is fucking destroying me. If I don't leave, at least for a little while, I will self-destruct, and my biggest fear is I will destroy you all in the process."*

I can't believe I just admitted all of that to him and I'm hesitant to even look over at him because I feel like a fucking pussy. We are O'Connors. We don't talk about feelings or fears. We fight and drink through our problems until they disappear in a haze of booze or a trail of blood. But when I look at my dad, he almost has a look of pride on his face.

"Well shit, Son," he says, slapping his hand on my shoulder a little harder than necessary. "That is a fucking reason."

Now here I am in an airport about to lose my shit just as my dad predicted. I barely lasted four hours. I should have fucking listened to him.

"Hey, Skylar, where'd you meet the new boy toy?"

"Skylar, what about the topless photos? Are there actually topless photos out there of you?"

"Did you talk to Cassiel Logue while he was away on tour? Someone spotted you at his hotel in London. Is that where you took the photos?"

I don't know how much more of this I can handle. Suddenly I feel Skylar stagger forward into my back as if someone pushed her, and I'm fucking *gone*.

"HEY! BACK THE FUCK OFF!" I push the camera attached to the douche nearest to us so hard the force sends him careening backwards into the crowd.

And it feels fucking great.

The adrenaline rushes through me at a breakneck speed, and I'm starting to get the first hit of that rage high. A few more seconds of this and I will be lost to it. I can't fucking stop it.

"*Christ*! Give her a fucking break! Give her some room to breathe before I use those cameras to break your faces!"

"*Hey, you may want to keep a leash on your boyfriend, Skylar! You're not allowed to touch us, man. That's assault.*"

Assault? If he thinks *that* is assault, he ain't seen nothing yet, and I'm all too fucking excited to introduce him to the true meaning of the word. Before I get the chance to make my move, her hand grabs my wrist gently. "Liam, hang back a second, okay?" Before I have a chance to stop her, she steps in front of me and faces the paparazzi.

What the fuck is she thinking?

"I'll answer your questions." She's giving in? Son of a bitch. She's giving in to keep me from snapping. I fucking know it. "This is not my boyfriend," she continues. "This is my security. Soulless blood-sucking assholes meet Liam, Liam meet soulless blood-sucking assholes. There are no topless photos of me floating around anywhere, so cool your shit. I have not spoken to Cassiel Logue in months and have no comment about his interview in *Rolling Stone*. Anything else or can we be done here?"

Who the fuck is Cassiel Logue?

The flashbulbs continue to go off and questions are still being thrown her way, but I don't hear any of it. I'm too fucking pissed. Pissed at them. Pissed at her. Yet somehow, in the pandemonium, I spot a driver waving in Skylar's direction from about fifty feet away.

I pull her back to me, trying not to be too rough. I'm fucking trying.

"Sky is that your driver?" I growl into her ear like a fucking animal. I don't want to scare her, but I've never quite mastered the art of restraint.

"Yeah. Thank god." She sighs, clearly unaffected by my tone which for some reason irritates me even further. I grab her arm and quickly steer her through the mob. I open the back door to the Town Car and deposit her onto the seat. I quickly follow and slam the door behind me, locking us into a private silence.

I can't breathe.

I'm going to snap.

"SON OF A BITCH!" I yell, slamming my fist into the side of the door. "Why the *fuck* did you do that, Skylar? Why didn't you just stay the hell behind me?"

"Please don't yell at me, Liam," she says so quietly that I barely hear her as our car inches forward.

I'm an asshole.

"Sky. Shit. I'm sorry, baby."

Where did that come from? I just called her baby. I hesitate to even look at her because she probably thinks I'm out of my damn mind. But when I dare to glance in her direction I see that the fear has been erased from her eyes, as if the term of endearment I accidently set free brought her a sense of peace. And fuck if I don't revel in that feeling.

"I didn't mean to yell at you. I'm not mad at you, okay? I'm mad at myself. I could have handled that whole disaster better, but those guys were just fucking animals," I explain the best that I can as I shove my hands through my hair trying to calm my nerves.

"I warned you it would be difficult," she says, placing a hand on my thigh and a little too close to my dick because it definitely takes notice. Who am I kidding? Her hand on my foot is close enough to cause my dick to get a little too excited. She's like a damn cock whisperer.

"You can't touch them, Liam. No matter what they say to me or you. If they don't touch us, you can't retaliate. I was helping you out back there. The last thing I want is for you to get arrested in a futile attempt to defend my honor. But hey, you got through our first encounter with them fairly smooth," she says jokingly, punching me lightly on the side of my arm.

Problem is, I don't find any of this fucking funny or worthy of a joke. But despite that, I still grin slightly. I can't help it. Her cute little smile is apparently contagious and it infects me with a disease I'm all too willing to embrace. Not to mention I'm at a crossroads because I find myself turned the fuck on by her abrasive spunk. Like the way she fearlessly took on the paparazzi and shot attitude at Mason that night in the alley, even the way she called me on my shit and put me in my place in my own fucking bar. Ali never had that edge to her. She was sweet and funny and so fucking pure. The light inside her was so blinding you had no choice but to immerse yourself in it. She was everything I wanted then, but represents everything I would destroy now.

Unfortunately, I have to reconcile, somehow, that I hate that I love that about Sky because I know that fearless mouth of hers will get her into trouble one day, and not the good kind of trouble where she is using it to suck me off.

"Defending your honor is hardly a futile effort, baby."

Jesus fuck. What is wrong with me? I don't have to keep saying it.

"Is it always that bad?" I ask, needing more information so I know what I'm dealing with here.

"No, not always. Clearly someone tipped them off—either that or a bigger celebrity was there before and I was just lucky enough to get the blowback."

"Who the hell would tip them off?"

"The list is endless. The pilot, someone from Orcas Island that knew I was leaving, hell maybe cab driver Larry. It doesn't matter. It's just part of the job, you know," she says, shrugging her shoulders as if what happened is no big deal, but her downcast eyes say otherwise.

"Well, that is one fucked up job responsibility."

Her melodic laughter fills the car. "That it is," she says. The new brightness in her eyes relaxes me just a little bit but not entirely because the questions the paparazzi were asking are still shooting around my mind like a damn pinball. One in particular.

"So, who is Cassiel Logue?"

She stiffens slightly, and I probably wouldn't have noticed if she hadn't pushed that lower lip into her mouth again.

I'm not going to like her answer, I already know it.

"Um…have you ever heard of the band Pathogenic Blood?"

Yes. Supposedly they're the second coming of rock. I even have a few of their songs on my iPod.

"Nope, never heard of them." I'm being a dick but I've already decided I want to delete every song of theirs that I own and forget they exist.

Sky looks over at me suspiciously, as if she knows I'm lying. But whatever, I don't give a shit.

"Cassiel Logue is the lead singer of the band," she says.

I know she doesn't have a boyfriend. She told me that much at the bar yesterday. However, if I'm to believe the questions from the paparazzi, they've clearly had some kind of relationship. But I don't want to listen to anything they say. I want to hear it straight from her.

"And what is he to you, Skylar? An ex-boyfriend?" I ask, pulling her finger from her lip and setting her hand back on my thigh. I like it there.

"No, not really. More like…an ex bad habit."

I'm not even angry about that because god knows I can fucking relate, but what pisses me off is that apparently Cassiel Logue has a big fucking mouth, and I would love nothing more than to shut it for him. "Ex bad habit, huh? I've had quite a few of those myself over the years."

"Oh, *really*," Skylar snaps, pushing away from me slightly, her hand leaving my thigh. "Well, I think you can spare me the details, Liam."

Oh, this is fantastic. I can't help but burst into laughter. I can already tell keeping this arrangement professional is not going to last long. My dick has been aiming to get inside her from the jump, and her being jealous just proves she's having similar thoughts. But I know this is not a girl I want to use up and dispose of, and I'm not sure I'm capable of anything else. I want her to be more than just a weapon for me to use against my pain. She told me about her mom for fuck's sake. She trusted me. And until I know I'm ready to give to her without taking, I have to keep it in my pants. However fucking *hard* it may be.

"Are you laughing at me?" Skylar crosses her arms. She's even pouting now. The embodiment of every straight man's wet dream is sitting next to me, jealous of my past hook-ups and fucking pouting about it. This may go down as one of the best days of my whole life and also the day my ego finally shot out of the fucking stratosphere.

"Skylar Barrett, if I didn't know any better I'd say you're jealous. Anyone ever tell you how cute you look when you're jealous?" I tease, running my finger along her jaw.

"Yeah right. Keep dreaming." She pulls her head back, causing my hand to drop from her skin, which is a damn shame because I like touching her, and based on the small shiver that played across her body, she likes it too.

The car continues to crawl forward at the slowest fucking pace imaginable. The freeway is jam packed. I've always heard horror stories about L.A. traffic, but this is just ridiculous, and the now awkward silence haunting the vehicle is not helping matters.

"So, how long will it take to get to your house anyway?" I ask, breaking through the quiet of the vehicle.

"I live about twenty minutes away."

Thank god.

"But if we take into account that it's nine thirty on a Monday morning, and we're on the 405, we're looking at roughly four hours, give or take an hour or two depending."

"Please tell me you're fucking with me right now." If this ride takes four hours, we're about to get to know each other very fucking well. Those chivalrous thoughts I planned to stick to only a few minutes ago, have about a two-hour shelf life when it comes to confined spaces with this girl. Hell, the last half hour of that flight all I could think about is how easy it would be to slide my hand under those tiny shorts of hers; see how many times I could get her to come while I fucked her with my fingers.

"Yeah, slugger, I'm screwing with you. Calm down. But in all seriousness, it'll probably take over an hour. L.A. traffic truly blows," she says mid-yawn. Now that I'm really looking at her, she looks exhausted.

"You tired?"

"Seems that way. I guess the last few months of little to no sleep are finally catching up with me," she says, resting her head back on the seat. That can't be too comfortable.

"Come on then, Sky. You can put your head down on my lap and rest. I've heard I'm very comfortable."

"Oh yeah? From who?" she says as she puts her head down on my lap without hesitation.

Fuck me. I didn't think this through entirely. I'm going to have to pull something out of my anti-erection photographic memory bank in order to keep my dick down. I think this calls for the time I accidentally stumbled onto the Two Girls One Cup video. Nothing kills a hard-on faster than remembering that.

"What? What'd you say?" I ask her. *Sorry I couldn't hear you because I'm too busy trying to keep my cock from getting in your face.*

Turning her head to face me, she says, "I asked who's telling you these tall tales about how comfortably pliable your lap is for the purpose of napping."

Smartass. "Oh, just some ex bad habits—OUCH!" The little hell-cat fucking *pinched* my thigh!

"Oops, I slipped."

Her head is turned, but from the sound of her voice I can tell she's smiling. Shit. I'm already categorizing the tones of her voice like a pussy-whipped asshole. I look down and take in her relaxed form. Her eyes are already shut. My hands have a mind of their own and start to caress her hair which incidentally feels like fucking silk. The act is intimate and frighteningly completely instinctual. But it shouldn't be. I barely fucking know her, and she doesn't know me. She doesn't know what I've done or about the monster that aches inside of me. Yearning. Desperately desiring escape at every turn. She doesn't know that I'm a complete fucking fraud. That she hired me to do for her what I couldn't for those I loved.

She's asleep now. I can tell by how relaxed her body is. Her breath is steady and she has no idea, no fucking clue that she sleeps so peacefully in the lap of a killer.

CHAPTER 8

LIAM

The Town Car pulls up to a closed wrought-iron gate in the Hollywood Hills, and I immediately know it's her house because a few paparazzi are actually lingering outside her fucking gate on the streets with cameras flashing in the direction of the car. Unfuckingbelievable. Those snakes actually stalk her house. How is this even legal? If I sat outside a woman's house with a camera, I'm pretty sure my ass would get locked up.

Skylar is sound asleep in my lap, while my arm rests across her body. I don't want to wake her up, not until the last possible second, because seeing her so at peace gives me some type of purpose. I want to believe the reason for her total relaxation is due to my presence. That I make her feel protected. Safe. I have to believe this.

The driver's side window rolls down and a hand sneaks out, punching a number into the code box, making me feel a little more comfortable knowing that her house is at least protected by a locked, coded gate. Hopefully she has a good security system set up at the actual house. If not, I'll make sure to take care of it. The gate begins to open slowly as the car moves up the driveway. The partition comes down and the driver begins to speak.

"Ms. Barrett, do you need my assis—" The driver stops speaking as he glances in the rearview mirror and spots Skylar sleeping. I put my finger to my lips, signaling him to be quiet, not ready to wake her quite yet.

Not more than ten seconds later the car comes to a stop, and all too fucking soon for my liking we have arrived and it's time to wake her.

"Sky," I whisper, brushing the hair out of her face and tucking it behind her ear. No movement, nothing. She's dead to the world. "Skylar, baby, you need to wake up. I think you're home."

I've already called her baby twice, so why stop now?

Sky moves leisurely, stretching her body across my legs, reaching her hand up to my face, fingers playing against my skin, refusing to open her eyes.

"Ugh...I don't wanna," she mumbles, her fingers playing blindly across my eyes and down to my lips.

Fucking adorable. "You have to. Back to the real world, sweetheart." I nip at one of her delicate fingers, holding it in my mouth for just a second, long enough for my tongue to sneak a taste of her skin. I know I shouldn't, but I can't seem to stop myself.

"Fine," she sighs dramatically as she sits up and straightens her tank top, patting down her hair and checking her reflection in the tinted window. I wish I could tell her how fucking beautiful she is and that a reflective reassurance isn't necessary, but I know that would be too much.

The driver opens her door and extends his hand, helping her out of the car. I'm right behind her as she exits, and I take her uninjured hand from the driver's so I can hold it in mine. I can't stop touching her. This makes me seem like a fucking psycho, I'm sure, but I don't give a shit.

The times I remember most vividly with Ali are not the ones where I cherished her. Where I hugged her, or held hands or made love to her for hours. Not the times we spent curled up in that damn hammock, or how she would grab my index finger whenever she got nervous. Nope. My fucked up masochistic psyche likes to replay all the times where she stood next to me and I didn't touch her or hold her in some way. The nights we fell asleep wrapped in one another but woke up having drifted apart. Following her death I even became obsessed with all the lost time, and because of my photographic fucking torture device of a memory, I've actually been able to replay and count those lost seconds; adding them up over and over again, tormenting myself.

"Ms. Barrett, a pleasure as always." The driver gives her a nod as he moves to open the door.

"Thanks, Barry. I'll call when I need you next. Say hi to your wife for me."

"Will do Ms. Barrett." He gives her a small wave before he gets in the car. I just stand taking in Sky's house because what I see surprises me.

It's not huge or garish like one might expect from a wealthy actress, but understated and ethereal. Like a house straight out of a fairytale. The villa styled home is tucked away from the main road; bushes and ivy grow in front of a brick wall that surrounds the perimeter of the property giving her the privacy she craves. More ivy strategically creeps over the stucco walls of the front of the home. The house seems small from the front, just a double French door entry and a two-car garage. But something tells me I'm underestimating its size.

"This is a pretty incredible house, Sky," I say, giving her hand a light squeeze.

"Thank you. It's kind of my sanctuary. I rarely leave it when I'm not working," she says quietly, looking up at me, a slight blush coming over her face as if she's embarrassed, or uncertain, I'm not really sure. But one thing I've discovered about Skylar is her inability to accept compliments. She seems as uncomfortable with them as she does being touched. And I really can't fucking fathom why that is. I would think a woman like Skylar would be oozing confidence and assurance, but sometimes she seems a little broken. The sick part is, I think that's one of the reasons I'm so drawn to her.

"So you wanna show me the rest of this dump or what, sweetheart?" I ask, trying to lighten the mood. She just rolls her eyes at me, a small smile playing at the corners of her mouth.

"You have such a sweet way with words, Liam." Her laugh trails behind her as she leads me to the front doors, opening them without a key and walking right the fuck in.

I quickly step in front of her and place my hand on her chest to stop her. "What the hell, Sky? Don't you keep your doors locked? Do you have an alarm system? You can't just leave your house unlocked like this." Even in my small-ass town we lock our doors.

Her eyes open wide and she lets out a sarcastic laugh, or scoff, some kind of noise that tells me she thinks I'm acting ridiculous.

"Come on, Liam, how stupid do you think I am? I *never* leave my doors unlocked when no one's here, and I have a state-of-the-art security system, thank you very much. Winter is here, she's been housesitting."

"Who?"

Before she even opens her mouth to answer, a high-pitched screech comes from behind me. I turn around and see neon red hair barreling down the solarium hallway.

"OH MY GOD, YOU'RE BAAACK! I missed you so much, Skylar!" I figure this must be Winter as she practically knocks me out of the way and engulfs Skylar in a giant hug.

"I missed you too, Win!" Skylar says, a huge smile on her face but tensing against the hug. I can't help but laugh while watching the girly scene unfold in front of me, subsequently catching Winter's attention.

"My, my, Skylar. I see you brought me back a tall, dark, and sexy present from Orcas Island. I would have settled for a necklace or something, but this works too," Winter says, looking me up and down shamelessly. I'm used to this kind of reaction from females. Fuck, I usually love it and start contemplating how many words I have to actually speak before I can have them on their knees with my dick in their mouths, but right now, with Skylar standing next to me, I feel awkward as fuck.

"Yeah, yeah, Winter, bring it down a few notches or you're going to scare him off. Winter Davis, this is Liam O' Connor, the new bodyguard I told you about. Liam, this is Winter Davis. Winter is my personal assistant and my other best friend."

"The cuter best friend. Also, the completely straight best friend in case you were curious," Winter says, winking in my direction and sticking her hand out for me to shake it. Clearly Winter is a flirt, and when I sneak a glance at Sky she just shrugs her shoulders and smiles as if this is typical behavior.

I grab her hand and shake it. "Nice to meet you, Winter, Sky's completely straight friend."

Winter's appearance surprises me. Not that I'm opposed to her style: her bright red hair cascading down her back, her arms covered in sleeve tattoos, a bar piercing right through her left eyebrow. I'm just astonished that she's Skylar's friend. Innocent and angelic looking Skylar. Not just her friend, but her employee. Skylar Barrett continues to shock me.

"The pleasure is all mine, I assure you," Winter purrs seductively, still holding on to my hand.

"Jesus, Winter, knock it off," Skylar warns. "You'll have to forgive her. Winter has no filter and openly lusts after anything attractive with a penis and a pulse."

"Really? That's all it takes is a penis and a pulse to get your girl all worked up? Sky, baby, you're killing my ego here," I say, throwing an arm around her shoulders and pulling her to my side. I'm a fucking addict. I can't go five minutes without contact from her.

"It's true, Liam," Winter says, but I don't miss the brief second she eyes us speculatively, or rather me. "I have issues, but unfortunately they don't have support groups for people with my particular problems, which consist of having an overactive mouth that's only rivaled by my equally overactive vagina. So we all just have to endure my outbursts. But you belong to Skylar, so I'll maintain my distance," Winter says, putting her fingers up in salute.

Skylar turns her head into my chest and groans. "Jesus, Winter. See, I told you," Skylar says, looking up at me. "Liam is not mine. He works for me, okay? Just like you do, although maybe not for much longer."

It's cute how she keeps pretending this is just a working relationship. I'll let it slide for now, but eventually that shit will get straightened the fuck out.

"So when do I get to see the rest of this house, ladies?" I clap my hands together in anticipation. So far I've only seen the cobblestone foyer, but if that's any indication as to the rest of the house, I'm actually looking forward to this tour.

"Let's go," Winter commands, grabbing me by the arm and leading the way. I look back at Skylar who is rolling her eyes as she trails
behind.

The whole showing takes about fifteen minutes, and I figure out
pretty quickly why Skylar picked this house, and why she refers to it
as her sanctuary. When traveling through it I almost forget I'm in Los
Angeles. The house is three stories. There are three bedrooms in total—two are master suites located on the top floor. Skylar occupies one
and the other is Noah's. Each master suite has French doors that lead
to a balcony. On the second floor there's a living room, a dining room
that has been converted into a full bar, and a striking kitchen stocked
with all the latest appliances. The bottom floor is an odd combination
of a well-stocked library, and across the hallway, I can already tell what
will be my fucking favorite room: an in-home gym. The gym has everything: a treadmill, free weights, a rowing machine, stair climber,
and even a heavy bag and speed bag hanging from the wall. The boxing equipment looks new and untouched. I can even smell the leather
of the bags, and now I'm curious if she had all of this set up for my
benefit.

It's a beautiful house, no question, but there's something so cold
about it. There are no personal pictures on the walls, nothing that clues
me in to who Skylar is or where she comes from. It's almost like a mu-
seum and that is fucking depressing.

"And this is where you'll be staying," Skylar announces as she leads
the way past the Grecian style pool to what appears to be a large pool
house.

The pool house is actually a loft, which explains the outside cy-
lindrical build. The bottom floor has a circular couch, matching the
architecture of the actual house and a surprisingly large kitchen. Off
to my right is a spiral staircase that leads to a top floor bedroom and
bathroom. The pool house is bigger than my old apartment in Seattle.
Now I'm wondering how much money this house is worth. I never
really thought about what Sky makes, but I can tell this house is not
cheap and I'm actually starting to feel a little out of my league with this
girl. What can I offer someone like her anyway?

"I know it's not home, but I hope you like it." Skylar is staring up at me with an almost nervous look, and I get an unfamiliar feeling in my chest, equal parts warmth and panic. She's pleading for my approval with those blue green eyes of hers, and I know I'm so fucking unworthy of her admiration, but I selfishly soak it up. I want to drown in it, submerge myself in her misdirected adoration because it makes me feel powerful again. Makes me feel necessary. Needed.

"It's perfect," I assure her, brushing my thumb down her cheek.

"Ahem," Winter says, interrupting our moment. Fuck, I forgot she was even there. We both turn to look at Winter. "Well, I got ahold of Lawrence and all your luggage should be here within the hour," Winter tells us.

"Thanks, Win." Skylar shifts uncomfortably next to me.

"No prob, love. By the way, Skylar, I should warn you…" Winter glances my way for a brief moment, obviously debating if she should continue speaking in my presence.

"It's okay, Winter. Liam's cool, I trust him."

Well, fuck me if that spoken realization doesn't just puff my chest right up.

"Okay…well…Carl has been calling me non-stop this morning. He's really pissed that you haven't been responding to his calls or emails or carrier pigeons for all I know. I told him you should be home around ten so he could call you then, but he told me he was coming over instead. He said, and I quote, 'She's gonna see me whether she likes it or not. I'm tired of her immature avoidance bullshit.'"

"Shit," Skylar says as she quickly makes her way around me and heads toward the main house.

"Hey, Sky, wait…who the fuck is Carl?" I practically yell at her, picking up my pace.

"That's her manager slash father, or as I like to call him, The Devil," Winter calls out, following both of us into the house. I barely hear what Winter is saying to me because my concentration is solely on Sky and figuring out why the fuck she seems so on edge all of a sudden. I follow her right through the back door into the kitchen. When I catch up to her I grab her elbow to stop her, turning her toward me.

"Skylar, stop. Do you not want him here?"

"When it comes to Carl I don't really have a choice, Liam. Besides, I probably have been dodging his calls too much these last few days."

"Damn, you guys are too fast for me," Winter pants as she stumbles into the kitchen. "Listen he'll probably be here any minute, Skylar. I should've told you when you first got here, but I was just so excited you were back and then with meeting Liam and showing him the house, I just got a little distracted."

Why does everyone seem to be at DEFCON fucking five right now? Unease awakens in my gut and all my senses start lighting up under the weight of fear that's being released into the room, both by Sky and Winter.

Sky laughs uncomfortably in an unsuccessful attempt to hide it, burying it in forced humor as a distraction. Won't work with me though. Because once someone experiences true fear, that feeling attaches to every fiber of their being and imprints so it is never forgotten. I can smell it, taste it, absorb the sensation emanating from the people around me. So I caught on pretty fucking quick to the fact that she's scared of her own father.

"It's okay, Win. I should have called him back and not put this on your plate."

"What's going on here, Sky?" I ask. "Is there something I need to know about Carl?"

"No…nothing…it's just…" Right on cue, there's a harsh knock on the door and Winter runs to answer it.

I touch her chin and force her gaze to mine, searching for some sort of wordless explanation. Sky has the most expressive eyes, and she can't hide anything in them. I fucking know something is off here.

"Where is she, Winter? Is she back yet? I am so *goddamn* sick of her shit!" A deep voice curses through the house as heavy steps barrel toward the kitchen. Skylar gently pushes me away, putting distance between the two of us as she turns around.

My heart picks up speed.

My body tenses, readying itself for whatever threat is about to make its way to her.

I don't give a fuck if it's her father. I should but I don't. Rage knows no boundaries. It is a stranger to morality and decorum. Basically, I have no problem fucking him up.

I place my hand on the small of her back in an attempt to assure her that I am here for her and because her skin against mine always seems to calm me.

"There you are! What the fuck, Skylar! You need to learn to answer your goddamn phone. You are being a disrespectful little—" Carl stops the minute he spots me glaring at him from behind her. "Who the hell is this?"

My hand turns into a fist behind Skylar as I grab the back of her shirt, pulling her closer to me. I can see the resemblance between them. He has the same brow and lips, even the same hairline, though he's about five inches taller. But the way he speaks to her is disgusting; no father should speak to his daughter this way. In a million years I could never imagine my dad cursing at me or Shayla like this, no matter how much we may have pushed his buttons.

"Carl, this is Liam. Liam, this is Carl. This is Jeff Roberts' replacement, Carl," Skylar says cautiously. Jeff Roberts must have been her previous bodyguard. I don't lift my hand to shake Carl's, nor does he lift his; this is clearly a standoff wherein we are both establishing our dominance in Skylar's life.

"Jesus, Skylar, please tell me you're joking! I know you didn't hire someone without my consent, behind my back!" he spits angrily.

"It wasn't behind your back. And I definitely did *not* need your consent. I let you hire the last three and look how that turned out. I'll be in control of the hiring of my own people from now on." Skylar backs up slightly into my hand, her breath halting in her chest, and this is when I realize without a doubt that she is terrified of him.

Carl shakes his head, laughing manically. "Skylar, I don't know what the hell has gotten into you these last few months, but this childish behavior ends right this second or else you and I are going to have problems. Now get your ass in my car because we have a meeting with your attorney in twenty minutes." Carl's tone is a little too fucking threatening for my liking, and if he doesn't bring it down I'm going to break his jaw to shut him the fuck up.

See, I recognize the look in Carl's eyes as they bore into Skylar's. That's a man that has a lust for rage, someone who revels in their own anger. A man much like me, only a part of me still fears my rage. People like Carl embrace theirs fully, constantly feeding off of it as if it were as necessary as the air that they breathe.

"I don't think she needs to go anywhere with you, *Carl*. I can take her wherever she needs to go," I say, stepping in front of Skylar, placing myself between them.

"Excuse me, *boy*? Who the hell do you think you are talking to? You do realize that not only am I Skylar's manager, but I'm also her father."

"Yeah, and you really do neither one of those jobs decently," Winter says under her breath as she moves to stand next to Skylar.

"What'd you say to me, Winter?" Carl moves toward her, but I shoot my hand out to stop him from going any further. Carl instantly slaps it away.

"Stop it! All of you," Skylar shouts, stepping out from behind me and placing herself between Carl and me. "You're right, Carl. I'm sorry I didn't call. If you want to meet with Steve about Jeff then let's just go and get this over with. Liam, Winter, I'll see you in a while, okay?" she announces then glances over at Winter. "Winter, will you help Liam get settled, please?"

"He's staying here, Skylar?" Carl shouts, throwing his hands up in the air. "Jesus, I had no idea I raised you to be so damn stupid!"

"Don't call her stupid, jackass," I snap as I start to move toward him. Skylar pushes her weight into me in warning, stopping me from going any further.

"Or what, *boy*?" Carl snarls.

She uses her shoulder to push even harder into me as I try to move forward again. I could blaze past her no problem, slam Carl's face into the kitchen counter, and watch as he bleeds through his disgusting fucking mouth, but I won't. I can't. I want Skylar more than I want to hurt him right now, and I have no idea how to process this. It's like I'm fighting against my own nature and I don't know if I'm winning or losing.

"Let's go, Carl," Sky says, walking up to him. She puts her hands on his shoulders and turns him toward the door. "Go to the car. I'll be right behind you."

Carl stomps out of the kitchen and heads toward the door, cursing the entire way. Skylar takes a deep breath and starts to follow, but I reach for her arm and gently pull her back to me. "Skylar, I don't want you going anywhere alone with him. Let me take you, or at the very least come with you."

Skylar puts her hands on my chest, flashing me a smile that I know is meant to put me at ease, but the smile is fucking fake. I know it. I've seen her real smile, the one that reaches her eyes and lights up her face, and while she may fool some with her acting, I fucking know better.

"I'm fine, Liam," she says grabbing my hand. I move it from under hers and wrap it around her wrist. Her pulse is racing. She is far from fine. Whatever the fuck fine means anyway.

"He's my father, my manager, and it's a lot of responsibility for him, and it puts him on edge sometimes. I don't make it easy for him to handle me either. But he won't hurt me."

Her pulse jumps. I feel it in the tips of my fingers. A lie.

"And he's right," she continues. "I have to go to this meeting. I've been putting it off for too long." Skylar pulls her hand from my grasp and starts to back away. She waves goodbye to Winter and walks through the solarium and out the front door.

"This isn't right," I say, starting after her only to feel Winter's hand on my arm, pulling me back. I shake it off instinctively and with force.

"Let this go, Liam. Trust me. Skylar can handle herself when it comes to him."

"I can't believe that was her father. Does he treat her that way all the time?" I ask, my hands clenched tightly, aching, wanting to hit something. The only thing I can do to calm my nerves is pace. Keep moving. Work the adrenaline out.

"How do you think he earned the name The Devil, love? And this is one of his better days."

Fuck. It gets worse than that? "Why would she put up with his bullshit? She doesn't deserve that. Christ, what kind of father calls their daughter a bitch?" I'm so incensed by the whole scene that just went down that the only thing I can do is place my hands on the kitchen island, lean my head down, and fucking try and breathe.

"Sheesh...oh boy," Winter says, putting her chin in her hands and collapsing into a kitchen chair. "What is going on between you two, Liam?"

I jerk back up, standing tall, as Winter sits in the chair calm as can be, staring right the fuck at me. No, not at me. Through me.

"Nothing," I say defensively. "Skylar hired me to take care of her, and that's all I'm doing."

"No, you were hired as a bodyguard, her security. There's a difference. I'm not blind, love. I saw the two of you during the tour of the house. You looked like a high school couple the day after losing their virginity on prom night. Grabbing and teasing each other, you caressing her face. Not to mention the constant hand holding. The Skylar Barrett I know hates being touched. I barely get away with hugging her. And imagine my shock when you call her *baby* and she doesn't immediately knee you in the balls. Jesus, Cassiel never even dared to drop that on her."

I'm really fucking sick of hearing Cassiel's name.

"Nothing is going on between us." I hope that seems more believable to Winter than it does to me.

Winter groans and curses under her breath. "Noah warned me, but I just thought he was being a drama queen as per his M.O." She is speaking quietly like she's talking to herself. About me. It's fucking annoying.

"You realize I'm still in the room, right? And Noah warned you about what?"

She lifts her head up and looks me directly in the eyes. "How long are you planning to stick around, Liam? Are you going to be here long term, is there a time frame here? Did you and Skylar discuss any of this?"

"I'm not sure that's any of your business."

"Skylar is my business, Liam. Noah's too. We don't just work for her. We're family. Look, I'm not trying to give you crap or pry, it's just... Skylar, she's different than us."

"Right," I say, scrubbing my hand over my face as I start to laugh. Not the genuine laughter I give to Sky but the *you can fuck right off* laughter I've perfected over years of telling people...well...that they can fuck right off. "Is this the part where you tell me she's too good for some low-life bartender who barely scrapes by? Because if it is, I gotta caution you, I have a pretty low fucking tolerance for cliché warnings, especially from people that know dick about me."

Winter sits back in her chair a fraction and her eyes go wide with amusement. "Wow. Jump to conclusions much? Also, I really didn't figure you for a hypocrite."

"Excuse me?" I ask, needing clarification on what the hell is fucking going on right now.

"You essentially just accused me of pre-judging you which in and of itself is a pre-judgment against me. You said I know dick about you. Well, newsflash, you know dick about me! I come from Hollywood royalty, O'Connor. My grandpa is one of the biggest movie producers in the business. My dad has directed more Oscar winners than I can remember, and my mom, she's an oil heiress. Believe me, when I tell you that Skylar is not like us, I'm not comparing bank accounts. Hell, my trust fund alone makes her net worth look like a thirteen-year-old's bank account after his bar mitzvah."

"I'm not really even sure what that odd fucking analogy means, but I'm guessing you are trying to tell me you have more money than she does. So if your vague comment wasn't about my social standing, then what are you trying to tell me here?"

"Look, I'm really impressed with how you stood up to Carl just now, not to mention grateful. Skylar doesn't have many people brave enough to stick up for her like that, especially when it comes to him, and that gives you points in my book."

"I couldn't be more fucking pleased," I deadpan. I'm being an ass-hole, but I've already exerted what little patience I have in waiting for her to get to the fucking point. This is Sky's friend, though, so I should probably try and dial it back. "You going to say what you have to say anytime fucking soon?"

Well, I tried. Shockingly, Winter laughs. "I see why she likes you, O'Connor. What I'm saying is even though I'm impressed with you, I don't know you. See, Skylar has a tendency to be erratic and complete-ly impulsive when it comes to making decisions, and that can be dangerous. But sometimes her recklessness pays off. I'm undecided yet as to which category you fall under. And I get that Skylar thinks she trusts you, but I'm not sure I do, which means I can't tell you exactly what I mean when I say she's not like us, and really, it isn't my story to tell."

That's fucking helpful.

"What I can say is that you need to be observant of her. Skylar has a lot of light in her, but she also has a lot of dark. You should be warned so that you can decide if this is something you are willing to deal with."

"Care to expand on that?"

"No, not really. Give me your phone."

"What?"

"Your phone. Give it to me," she demands, leaving her chair to stand next to me.

I reluctantly pull my phone out of my back pocket and hand it to her. She slides her finger over the screen and begins to type.

"What the fuck are you doing?" I ask.

"I'm *fucking* giving you my number. If you need my help with her or notice a change in her behavior that worries you, shoot me a text. Or call me."

This whole cloak and dagger routine annoys the shit out of me, but what's more annoying is I fucking get it. Winter is being loyal to her friend while still trying to make sure she is looked after, and as desperately as I want to know what the hell she's talking about, I won't push. I respect Winter for not telling me Sky's secrets, and I would rather hear them from her anyway. And fuck me if now I'm not finding myself wanting to prove myself to Winter.

"I like her," I admit. Like that will somehow give me permission from Winter to be around Sky. It's really eating me up that I suddenly crave her approval.

"I know."

"I won't bail on her just because she isn't sunshine and roses all the fucking time." When Winter said Skylar wasn't like *us* she didn't realize she was still being judgmental. Winter doesn't know me. Doesn't know that I am only darkness. That I've not seen light in a long time so nothing Skylar does will ever scare me away.

"We'll see."

Yeah. We will.

"Why do you work for her anyway? You have all this fucking

money, you seem fairly intelligent, and you probably have a lot of other things you could be doing with your life. Why spend your days working as her assistant?" I don't know why I ask this other than I am really wondering why, maybe because I'm just curious as to how all the puzzle pieces of Sky's life fit together.

"Fairly intelligent? Geez, O'Connor. If you keep up with the compliments you're gonna make me blush," she says, rolling her eyes. "I work for her probably for the same reason you decided to work for her. Skylar Barrett has a gift for making the few people she lets into her world feel like they have a purpose, that their mere presence is a necessity, and having that feeling is like a high that you never have to come down from. Especially for people like *us*, Liam. People that need that approval."

I let those words sink in for a minute before appreciating how true they are, and then I feel like someone sucker punched me once they settle because I've come to two realizations: One, Skylar may not have any feelings for me, not like I have for her. I could have misread this entire fucking situation. She may just see me as someone that can protect her, someone she needs for a very specific reason. Giving me a purpose in *her* life. I may be floating in the same boat as Winter, both of us latching on to our need to be needed so we don't drown in a sea of self-condemnation. And the second realization, the only one that seems to matter right now, is that I don't fucking care because Winter is right. It's a high I will never come down from, and if this is all Skylar is willing to give me, it's enough.

CHAPTER 9

Skylar

The drive to my attorney's office in Beverly Hills only takes twenty minutes but it may as well be hours. A thunderous silence fills the car as neither one of us speaks, or even looks, at each other. I know my father well enough to understand that his silence is more terrifying than his verbal outbursts. I don't dare move a muscle, I just train my gaze outside the passenger window, watching my timid breath fog the window, then dissipate across the glass.

Breathe in.

Breathe out.

My mind is running a million miles a minute conjuring up all the scenarios that could play out. Granted, Carl has rarely hit me in the last ten years, not since I was cast as Mandy Mayhem and he realized that bruises would show on camera, that the people doing my makeup would notice and start asking questions. But rarely is not never, and when pushed too far he has been known to release all that pent-up anger he holds back in a very painful way. The times he has slapped me or kicked me or grabbed me just a little too hard start to play through my head, lending momentum to my growing anxiety. And guilt. Guilt that I lied to Liam. That I looked him directly in the eyes and swore to him that my father wouldn't hurt me when I know damn well what Carl is capable of.

But I just *couldn't* tell him. Liam was clearly pissed at Carl's words alone, and I've had a front row seat to what Liam is capable of. Hell, it's why I hired him. If he knew the truth, he would never have let me walk out the door, and what scared me the most is that he may have reacted with violence, giving my calculating, manipulative ass of a father just the ammo he needs to make sure Liam stays away from me for good. The thought of Liam leaving terrifies me. It shouldn't; he's barely been in my life, but I like him in it. His rough touch, his deeply melodic voice, the way he seems determined to look after me—I want it. Need it. Crave it. Never having had a sense of security or even a taste of true intimacy has made me greedy for anything Liam O'Connor is willing to provide.

"Steve cleared his schedule for you today, Skylar." Carl's voice interrupts my thoughts and I realize we have finally made it to Steve's office as he pulls into the parking garage of his swanky Beverly Hills office. "Try and show him more respect than you've shown me. And don't think for a fucking second that I'm going to forget what happened today. We will be discussing that later," he warns, throwing the parking brake on. He exits the car without even glancing in my direction, making sure to slam the door behind him.

"Whatever you say, Carl," I say to a now empty vehicle. I take my seatbelt off and get out of the car, making sure to maintain a safe distance between us.

He's waiting for me in the elevator, his gaze menacing, and I sneak a peek at the door leading to the stairway. I want to escape, but I know if I choose that route I'll just make things worse for myself. So I walk slowly into the elevator, willingly accepting my fate. Seconds after the elevator doors close I feel the same dangerously unyielding hand that gently pushed the fifth-floor button seconds ago on the back of neck, grasping me crudely.

"*Skylar,*" he spits my name out in warning, his hold tightening. "I don't know what's gotten into you lately, but if I were you I would watch the way you talk to me. Especially since your new little bodyguard isn't here to protect you. Don't forget who got you where you are today, and rest assured, I can take it all away if you push me."

"I'm sure you could, Carl, but then who would sign your paychecks?"

This is exactly what he is referring to. Something *has* gotten into me lately. Normally I would be cowering in a corner and bending to his every whim or demand. But over the last few months, I've had to make some life changes in order to come to grips with news that changed my life. News only Cassiel and Noah know, and that wasn't really by my choice. News Cass forced me to realize, and while I'll be forever grateful he did, I will also forever hate him a little for making me come to grips with it.

Before Carl has a chance to respond, the ding of our arrival at Goodwin and Associates has him dropping his hand from my neck. He plasters on that used car salesman's smile just in time for Amy, Steve's secretary, to see as she is standing at the elevator doors waiting for our arrival.

"Good afternoon, Miss Barrett. Mr. Barrett, so good to see you again," Amy says. She's worked for Steve for over three years and has constantly remained professional. No matter how many times I've insisted she call me Skylar, she still refuses, so I finally just gave up.

"Thank you, Amy," I say, following her down the hallway, taking in the new office décor.

About every six months the office is redecorated, and I take so much pleasure in seeing the changes. This time there seems to be some kind of Japanese aesthetic, which is a vast improvement from the weird futuristic western theme his office was rocking the last time I was here. Although I do miss the hanging star lamps and cactus shaped chairs. I guess that's the price he pays for marrying an interior decorator, and bless his heart, he loves her too much to say no.

Amy leads us right into Steve's office, opening the door for us, and then takes her leave. Steve walks out from behind his desk, and I take a second to admire his suit as I always do. Tom Ford; no one can go wrong with a Tom Ford suit.

"Skylar dear, so good to see you. Welcome back. I hope filming went well. Carl," Steve shakes his hand and motions for us both to take a seat on the lush leather chairs as he leans against his desk.

"Good to see you, too, Steve, though I wish it could be under better circumstances," I say to be polite. In all honesty, I cannot think of any enjoyable circumstance that would bring me to an attorney's office, but I like Steve, so no need to be rude. "Love what Clara has done with your offices. Very...Japanese."

He laughs, and I'm struck by how his eyes light up when I mention her name. I'm not sure I've ever noticed it before. Maybe I was too jaded. It's sweet.

"Yes, well, Clara gets an idea in her head and there's no stopping her." He smiles, and I can't help but smile with him; his adoration seems to be contagious.

"I hate to be rude," Carl jumps in, making sure to suck all the pleasantries out of the room, "but we need to get down to business. It was difficult enough to get Skylar here, and I would really like it if we could move this along. I have things to do today."

That would be a first.

"Right," Steve says, straightening up a bit, putting his professional lawyer mask on. Carl really has a way with people. "Skylar, I'm sure your father has filled you in on the details concerning Jeff Roberts, yes?"

"Actually, Steve, my daughter has been dodging my phone calls recently so she's only aware of the basics," Carl chastises. He's trying to shame me, but I refuse to take the bait. I have to be stronger than him so I just roll my eyes in silent protest.

"Okay, then. Let's start from the top, shall we?" Steve says. "You are aware that Jeff Roberts is threatening to sue you for wrongful termination?"

"Yeah, but it's bullshit. He was terminated for very real reasons."

"I'm aware of what you told me, but Jeff and his attorney approached me a few weeks ago, and they are spouting a very different story than the one you gave me. I'm not saying I believe Jeff over you—clearly I must take what you say as truth, but you have to be aware he's ready to start talking to the media."

"Talk to the media about what exactly, Steve?" I ask cautiously.

Steve glances quickly to Carl and then back to me, and I know I'm not going to like what he's about to say. "About you, Skylar. He says he'll go to the media with stories about the nonstop partying he witnessed, the constant drug abuse, and he's also claiming that the real reason you fired him was because you came on to him and he refused your advances. Then you fired him in retaliation."

"WHAT THE FUCK, STEVE!" The sudden burst of anger has me shooting out of my chair. "None of that is fucking true! Jeff is out of his damn mind. This is ridiculous!" I can't even believe this is how Jeff is going to play it. I should believe it; this is what my life usually entails, but it still destroys little pieces of me each time I'm betrayed.

"Skylar, sit down, you're acting like a drama queen," Carl says so nonchalantly, as if nothing of importance is happening.

I sit back down, but not because *he* told me to. I sit because I know I'm starting to spiral. The thoughts in my head are running rampant and I can't make heads or tails of what I should do, what I need to say to make this all go away. I can't focus. My breath is coming in short gasps, anxiety taking the fast track to full-blown panic. I close my eyes and take a deep breath.

I wish Liam was here. Normally I prefer to fly solo on the one-way shit plane that is my life; no one should be brought into this mess. Liam being here wouldn't help me. He can't save me. Only I can, and I need to remember this. Relying on Liam, becoming comfortable with his presence, would be a mistake because eventually he'll leave. But my mind doesn't seem to want to come to an agreement with my heart and body's reaction to Liam O'Connor. It's two against one, and though I suck at math, I'm pretty sure the odds are stacked against me.

"Skylar, I believe you," Steve reassures me. "But Jeff claims he has proof. I haven't seen it and he refuses to show his hand until we all sit down for a meeting."

"He's refusing to show his hand because he has no hand. He is handless!" That doesn't sound quite right, but I'm free falling down an indignant spiral right now so I don't really care.

Steve leans back on his desk, adapting a more relaxed pose in a worthless attempt to try and get me to calm down. "To be honest, Skylar, I believe what Jeff is looking for is a settlement offer. I think he's bluffing in the hopes you'll pay him off to avoid the bad publicity, money, and time involved in a trial," Steve says as if this is supposed to make me feel better.

Carl remains eerily silent during this whole exchange, so silent that I dare to glance his way to make sure he is still awake. He is. He's just sitting in his chair, casual as can be, looking like he has not one care in the world. I keep staring at him, waiting, hoping that he will come to my defense or offer me some kind of fatherly advice. I will him to get angry in my defense, to fight for my truth, to tell me I should rain fire down on Jeff until all of his lies are exposed and I am fully vindicated, but he just continues to stare at Steve in silence. Avoiding me, willfully ignoring my silent pleas. I am on my own.

"What about the non-disclosure agreement, Steve? Jeff signed one, doesn't that mean anything?" I ask hopefully.

"You could certainly sue him for breach of contract if he goes to the media, but there are some issues to consider. You have to prove it was him that leaked the information, which could be difficult. And it may cost you more money than it's worth to sue him for breaking his contract because in the end, even if you win, Jeff has very little money and even less in the way of assets."

"Why even have NDAs then? This is such bullshit. Basically what you are telling me is that I'm being blackmailed under the guise of a wrongful termination lawsuit. Is that what you are saying?"

"I can't tell you that is what's happening beyond a reasonable doubt. All I can do is provide you with my insight and advice."

"Which would be what, exactly?"

"Let me go to him with a settlement offer. I can gauge his intentions and whether or not his silence can be bought. I have a feeling it can be."

What silence? He wants me to pay someone to be silent about events that never happened? This whole scenario is just too much for me. I bury my head in my hands, trying to keep it together. My bandage scrapes slightly against my skin and I focus on the night I got it. Not the fight, not the bad, but the good. The night I met Liam. Images of him laughing, those warm gray eyes, and the feel of my hand in his flash through my thoughts quickly, and I latch on to every one of them hoping they will provide me strength. The type of strength he possesses.

"I think you need to take Steve's advice, Skylar. Let him give Jeff an offer. God knows you can't take any more bad publicity." Oh good. Carl finally speaks up, and shocker of all shockers, it's to somehow insult me.

"So you both think I should just roll over and take this? Is that right? I mean, do you really believe I did the things Jeff said I did? That I partied nonstop and apparently am on a first name basis with a drug dealer? That I came on to him?" I look over at Carl and try one last time to get something out of him. Something that shows me he believes in me, at least a little. "Dad." I almost choke on the emotion that word causes me, "Is that what you are saying?"

Please, please, please stand up for me. Believe in me. Love me.

"To be honest, I don't know what you're up to. And I really don't give a shit. The only thing that matters is that we keep what little is left of your reputation intact," he says, looking me dead in the eyes with a cold unflinching stare that proves I am nothing but a paycheck to him.

My heart drops into my stomach. I always worried that my father hated me, assumed he blamed me for Raina's death. The only time he ever seems proud of me is when I ink another deal for a movie, subsequently adding more and more of a percentage to his ever growing bank account. But my worry can take a back seat now, because looking at Carl while he says this to me I'm hit with the realization that what he feels for me is worse than hate—it is complete indifference. I'm just a tool for him to make money, and I need to come to terms with this. But that is easier said than done; I've already lost a mother, and I'm not sure I'm prepared to lose a father too.

"Fine," I relent. "But before you give him a number, I want to see what evidence he has that is so damaging. Set a meeting. Please, Steve."

"Your wish is my command, Skylar. I think you are taking the right steps here. I'll call his attorney today and let you know what I find out."

"Good decision," Carl says, and I try to hide my cringe at his approval. I feel dirty. "While we are here," he continues, "Skylar has taken it upon herself to hire a new bodyguard, Liam something. I'm not sure how long he'll last, seeing as he came from out of nowhere, but nonetheless, we need an NDA for him to sign."

"You got it. Let me have Amy get the proper paperwork put together for you."

"Actually, that won't be necessary." I give them both the most innocent smile I can muster and stand up.

Carl stands up next to me, no doubt trying to intimidate me, but despite the fact he towers over me and is capable of physical vengeance, I refuse to let him. Something primal and protective comes over me at even the mention of Liam's name from Carl's poisonous mouth.

"What do you mean that won't be necessary?" Carl asks, staring me down. Daring me to defy him. Fuck him.

"Skylar, I would really recommend it," Steve chimes in.

Laughter comes bursting out of me. I can't help it. This is just ridiculous, and the fact that they can't see it has me seriously questioning both their employments.

"Because it worked so well with Jeff? I'm not having Liam sign one. He doesn't need to. I trust him."

"Skylar, we'll talk outside. Steve, we'll be expecting to hear from you soon," Carl says as he grabs my elbow and leads me out of Steve's office and toward the elevator. The trek seems long, especially since it seems we are not stopping for any proper goodbyes.

When he walks me into the elevator I step in cautiously. He pushes the P button that will take us down to the parking garage, and as soon as the doors close, blocking the view to any audience, Carl descends on me, backing me into a corner, his ice blue eyes blazing like the tips of a flame.

"I don't know who Liam is or what gutter you pulled him out of, and frankly I don't give a shit, but if you plan on keeping him around he signs a NDA. Although, if I were you, I would just get rid of him now before he fucks you over worse than Jeff." Carl flashes me a sleazy smile as the elevator doors open, and he turns to make his way to his car.

I'm angry and defensive and I want to stand my ground, not just for me but on behalf of Liam, because I know if the situation were reversed he'd do the same for me, and that is more than I can say for Carl. The way Carl spoke his name with such disdain, insinuating I pulled him out of some gutter, has lit me up.

I walk slowly out of the elevator and stop just outside the doors as they close behind me. I watch as Carl reaches his new Mercedes GL450, the one he purchased with the money I work so hard for, and I know in this second that he has *finally* pushed me too far.

"I'm not going with you," I call out.

"What'd you say?" Carl asks as he opens the driver's side door, not even bothering to look my way, a clear sign that he is not taking me seriously. I don't fault him for that because not once have I truly stood up to him. I was full of strong words but empty actions, my fear of him winning out in the end. But not this time.

"I said I'm not going with you," I repeat, keeping my voice low and steady, my shoulders back. "You embarrassed me up there in Steve's office. You couldn't even say you believed me, your own daughter, not to mention your only client and subsequent meal ticket. Say what you want about Liam, degrade him all you want if it makes you feel like more of a man, but in the last two days he has proven to be more loyal to me than you have in the last thirteen years. *You* go before he does. Are we clear?"

I don't even have time to be proud of how I stood up to him because in a matter of seconds, not even taking the time to close his car door, he is in front of me and grabbing my shoulder, pulling me roughly to the passenger side of the vehicle.

"Get in the *fucking* car, Skylar," he commands, his voice remaining low. Carl looks around the garage briefly, and now my fear really begins to set in. He's making sure no one is down here so no one is a witness to what he might do. But I've come this far and I don't want to back down. Not again.

"I said no. The days of you ordering me around like your puppet are over. In case you forgot how old I am, seeing as you have never celebrated one damn birthday with me in sixteen years, I'm twenty-two. That makes me an adult. And I am *your* boss. Try to remember that."

My voice shakes slightly, but I maintain eye contact. To prove to him that I'm in charge and unafraid; that I hold the authority. Hell, it worked with Liam. It can work here too. A smile creeps over Carl's face as he steps into my space, slowly forcing me back until I am against the car. Then his hand shoots to my neck, seizing it in an unforgiving grasp. He pulls my face close to his and then slams me, hard, against the car. Grabbing my bandaged hand, he squeezes so tightly the wound opens again, and I wince from the sudden, unexpected pain. Up until now, in this horror filled moment, I was not sure Carl even noticed my injured hand seeing as he never even bothered to ask what happened. Clearly he did and was just waiting for the right moment to use it to his advantage.

"Let me make something very clear to you, Skylar," Carl growls in my ear, his warm, stale breath creeping across my skin, the stench of cigarettes invading my senses as he crushes my hand tighter. "I am the reason you are who you are and have what you have," he says, the hand around my throat tightening in tandem with the one on my hand. "Without me you would probably be in a mental institution right now, so doped up you don't know which way is up, just like your mother was at your age. And you can pretend that you are grown up and in charge, but at the end of the day we both know *I. Own. You.*"

Tears start to warm my eyes, both from the pain in my hand and the heartless words he practically sings at me with excitement. Carl knew just how to rip my heart out and stomp on any of the bravery I held moments ago, and he is proud of himself. I see it in his cold eyes, hear it in his pleased tone. I'm stunned, disgusted, and torn between wanting to run from him or drop to my knees and beg for his forgiveness, and that alone makes me sick to my stomach. After everything he has done and said to me, I'm still standing here with his hand wrapped around my throat trying to fight the need to apologize. *To him.*

This is wrong. So wrong. Even Liam was willing to stand up for me against him. He was brave enough, he thinks I'm worth more. Now it's my turn. I try and move from his hold and fight against him but he just pushes harder into me, his grip constricting, making it harder for me to breathe. My saving grace comes in the sounds of voices echoing off the garage walls.

"You better back up, Carl. You wouldn't want to cause a scene, now would you? How would it look if the media found out Skylar Barrett's father gets his kicks intimidating and abusing his daughter in dark parking garages?" I all but whisper to him.

That does the trick. He releases me and steps back, making sure to plaster the fakest smile on his grotesque face. Outwardly he is a good-looking man, even I can admit that, but I see the devil inside, seeping through his pores and unmasking him from the doting father he pretends to be. The public sees me as the actress, the talent, but even I can't out-act Carl Barrett.

"Good luck finding a ride home, *daughter*," he says as he walks to the driver's side door, slamming it shut. The engine roars to life and he peels out of the parking garage, leaving me in the wake of his rejection.

As soon as the car disappears from sight, I fall. My knees hit the pavement as the weight of everything I just did and everything that was done to me comes crashing down.

I can't breathe. I have so many thoughts bouncing around in my head it's like someone kicked over a jigsaw puzzle and I'm trying frantically to pick up the pieces and put myself back together.

Breathe in. Breathe out. Breathe in.

I can't even fathom the repercussions of this; I don't even have the clarity to process where I go from here. I concentrate on the throbbing in my hand. I try and center myself on the pain, using it as a focal point, a way to wade through the emotions that threaten to consume me. The voices get louder as the people I can't yet see are clearly getting closer. I can't be seen here. Not like this.

I pull myself off the concrete, then reach into my back pocket for my phone. I scroll through my contacts until I find Barry's name. I need a ride home, a quiet ride home, one where no one will ask me any questions so I can figure out where the hell I go from here.

CHAPTER 10

Skylar

Thanks to the mid-day traffic, it takes Barry over forty-five minutes before he is pulling into my driveway. I've never been more thankful for L.A. traffic in my life. I was able to spend that time pushing the events that happened deep inside so I didn't have to think about them. To pretend it never happened and wipe it from my mind, temporarily anyway. I'm not delusional to the point I think this intentional memory loss can last forever or that the consequences down the road won't come to bite me in the ass. And probably epically. But I've decided I really don't care about what may or may not happen in the future. I don't care about any repercussions that have yet to come. I just want to go home and be ordinary, and be the version of myself I have always dreamed of. The one whose pictures only ever graced yearbooks or family photo albums, whose first kiss wasn't on screen for thousands to see, the one who had a mom and dad that grounded her for missing curfew. The one that could have a normal relationship with someone without dumping a lifetime of problems on their doorstep. I just want to be Skylar.

"Thanks for picking me up, Barry," I say as I exit the car.

"Anytime, darlin.'" He tips his head toward me, before I turn and walk towards my house.

Opening the unlocked front door, I can't help but smile remembering Liam's reaction when he thought I'd just casually left my house open for anyone to walk in. He blocked my way in, ready to protect me from a nonexistent danger, even going so far as to reprimand me. It was cute, although something tells me he would not like that description applied to his scolding technique. I see Winter walking up to me as I close the door behind me and shove my bloodied hand into my pocket so as not to alarm her or cause her to start hurling unwanted questions at me.

"You going home, Win?"

"Yeah, love," she says, finishing whatever she's doing on her phone then dropping it into her purse. "Got everything taken care of here. The baggage was dropped off so I unpacked everything for you. Liam's all settled as well. Also, your agency FedExed some scripts over for you to read. I put them on your bed."

"Have I ever told you how amazing you are, my little Winter Wonderland? You're a superhero. We should get you a cape and a wand. Definitely a wand."

"I think you're getting your mythologies mixed up there, Skylar. Pretty sure superheroes don't use wands. I think those are reserved for fairies and witches."

"Really? I thought Wonder Woman did. Didn't she?" I ask, trying to think back on her wardrobe. I could have sworn she had a wand.

"Those were cuffs."

"Oops. Wrong accessory."

She shrugs her shoulders. "I'll take the compliment though, but instead of a wand maybe just get me The Rabbit. It's like a wand, only for grownups," she announces with a little too much excitement, as if the possibility of me getting her a vibrator is a real one.

"Rest assured you'll *never* be getting a vibrator from me as a gift. It would completely weird me out thinking you would be using a gift I bought you to get off."

"Skylar, my young, naïve little sex angel," she sighs, shaking her head. "What do you think I've been doing with that thirty-setting luxury showerhead you got me last Christmas? There's a reason they call it a showerhead."

I shove her shoulder. "*Jesus*, is that why you asked me for that? I thought you told me you needed a new one because your other one broke." It's not like I'm prude; far from it, I just don't need to hear about what my friends are doing with their bathroom appliances. Bathroom appliances *I* bought.

"It did. I wore it out," she says with a sly smile. As if I should somehow be impressed she wore a showerhead out with multiple orgasms. Now I have *that* image in my head.

"There is something seriously wrong with you. I can't even look at you right now. Go home, you little nympho."

"Don't hate, love. Not all of us have sex incarnate waiting with bated breath to knock, knock, knock, on heaven's door."

"I think your euphemisms need work." I shake my head at her and try to contain the pink I can already feel warming my cheeks.

"Careful, Skylar. Your crush blush is showing," she says. I've known Winter for so long it's hard to hide anything from her. "Well, as much as I would love to stay here and swap sex toy success stories with you—"

"We weren't swapping stories. You were bombarding me with your shower antics against my will."

"If you say so. Anywho, I gotta get going. Have to go home and feed Kitty." Three years and she still hasn't picked out a real name for her cat. "I'm really hoping Amber has ushered her flavor of the day out of the house before I get there."

Amber. Just the mention of her name makes me feel all skeevy. I dislike her so much I've sworn off even wearing the color. Amber is a socialite succubus, and if she wasn't Winter's cousin, she and I would have zero contact with each other. I don't care who she is related to or how much money she has. And it's not that she's just an epic bitch who constantly has strange men traipsing in and out of Winter's house that annoys me. It's the fact that she's a user and a wannabe, and has been handed everything in life only to take it all for granted.

"Good luck with that."

"Thanks. Oh, before I leave, how did your meeting go?"

"As well as can be expected when you are meeting with an attorney to discuss a frivolous lawsuit from a former employee."

"I never liked Jeff. He was so sleazy."

She doesn't even know the half of it. No one does.

"Tell me about it. I'll figure it all out. I usually do," I say, shrugging my shoulders.

"Well, your Jeff replacement happens to be down in the gym anni-hilating the heavy bag at the moment in case you were curious, which I already know you are so don't even bother trying to deny it." She's waving her hand almost directly in my face to stop me from speaking. I wasn't going to anyway.

"I was half-tempted to go down there and check on him, but I could smell the testosterone and nakedness from here, so I figured it would be safer for him if I stayed upstairs."

"Would you just leave already?" I laugh, turning her around and walking her out the door. "Text me when you get home," I say, giving her a final push.

"You got it, love." She starts to walk to her car but stops midway and turns to me. "You know what you're doing here, right, Skylar? I mean with Liam. It's one thing to hire the guy, but having him live in your house. Are you sure that's a smart move?"

"Technically it's the pool house."

"Skylar, I'm being serious. I just want to make sure I'm not leaving you here with a complete psycho or something. What do you even know about him?"

There is no way I can possibly explain this to her, not in a way she'll understand because truthfully, I don't fully understand, but I can tell her one thing for certain. "I know enough to tell you he is not a psycho. Does that help?"

"How could you possibly know that after a few days?"

I look her directly in the eyes before I tell her the truth. "Because I've known enough psychos in my day to recognize the symptoms."

Winter gives me a sad smile that makes me wish I had not been so forthcoming. I hate to darken the mood. Now I just want her to make another inappropriate comment about what she uses her neck massag-er for or something.

"Fair enough, love. Enjoy your night, and don't do anything I wouldn't do."

"That doesn't exclude much, Winter," I call out after her.

"Oh, I know. See you later." Winter blows me a kiss as I shut the front door.

Immediately I find my way to the stairs that will take me down to the gym, as if my feet have just been aching for the chance to get me closer to Liam. The further down the steps I go, the quicker my heart beats as if it's purposely trying to match the sound of his fists thumping against the bag. I hit the second to last step and freeze. He is turned away from me as he continues to hit the bag, wearing nothing but a pair of athletic shorts, his perfectly defined muscles constricting as he punches with a focused precision. I'm stunned by the tattoo that adorns his back. It's some sort of demon in black with the wings of an angel.

The demon covers his entire back, and the wings spread out to his shoulders, appearing to wrap around his front, the demon's face darkened so you can barely make out the features. That itself would be eye-catching enough, but the true artistry and frightening realism lies in the blazing hellfire erupting behind it. Colors of red and orange and black illuminate the dark angel with such vibrancy it's hard not to be in awe of this piece of art. It's dark and remarkable and frighteningly beautiful. It truly encompasses all that is Liam O'Connor.

"Wow."

Liam stops hitting the bag and whips his head around. Crap. I must have said that out loud.

For a moment I think I see a look of relief flash in his eyes as his gaze slowly works its way over my body, not in a sexual way but in a concerned way. It hadn't even occurred to me that he may have been worried about me. I'm so accustomed to Carl's behavior at this point, and Noah and Winter are used to seeing his temper tantrums that I just assumed Liam would have let it go the minute I left. But the look of relief on his face says he did anything but, and his obvious concern causes my heart to jump.

As his eyes make their way back to mine, a gorgeous smile replaces his previous frown as he takes me in. Again. Okay, now it's sexual.

"You're back," he says, holding the bag against his stomach to steady it, his breathing harsh from his workout.

"Yeah." I practically croak my response. "Just got here. Sorry for spying. I mean, I-I wasn't spying, I just didn't want to interrupt your workout. I was really into it."

His eyebrows shoot up as he bites that full lower lip, trying to contain his laughter.

"I mean, *you* looked really into it!"

I said that way too fast to sound convincing. He's actually laughing at me now and I cover my eyes with my uninjured hand, well aware of the injured one still hiding in the pocket of my shorts. If that hand wasn't bloody, I know I would be using it to cover the *total* embarrassment that I'm sure is clearly written all over my face.

"Just shut up. It's been a long day," I mumble through my hand as I back up a step and lean back against the wall, hoping that maybe if I lean back far enough the wall will just suck me in and I can disappear.

Is Narnia wardrobe specific or can I find that entrance anywhere?

Even though I can't see him I know he's near because I sense the heat of his body closing in on me, smell the scent of his sweat and leftover cologne. Warm fingers wrap around my wrist, the tape on his palms scratching lightly against my skin as he pulls my hand away from my face. I have to bend my neck back slightly just to look into those wickedly piercing steely eyes, the ones that are currently staring directly into mine. He leans close, trapping me in between him and this stupid wall as he brings his lips to my ear.

"Feel free to spy on me anytime you want, sweetheart. It just makes me want to pound it that much harder." His warm breath on my ear causes a shiver to invade my body, and I gulp. I gulp so loud there's probably one of those animated bubbles above my head right now like in the comic books where gulp is actually spelled out. One of his hands is resting on my hip, his breath caressing the shell of my ear. I feel like I might combust. Death by sexual tension.

"Um…well it's top of the line so I think it can take it," I practically whisper because I can't seem to suck enough air into my lungs to say words at a normal volume.

"Who said I was talking about the heavy bag?" I can feel him smiling into the crook of my neck, almost as a private joke to himself because he can probably tell by my tensely trembling body that he's affecting me. His smugness pisses me off. I refuse to be the only one practically panting for some kind of release here.

"Who said *I* was talking about the heavy bag?" I say, mirroring his arrogance and daring to place my hand on his chest. Not hard to drive him away, but lightly to see if he will push into my touch. To find out if he's aching for skin-on-skin contact as much as I am because I truly don't know if he's attracted to me or if this is just Liam's way; a perpetual flirt that enjoys feeding his ego by playing a risky game of sexual chicken.

My answer comes the second he groans while moving into my hand. I absorb the heat as I slowly move my hand down, his breath against my neck picking up speed when my hand travels across the first ridge of his abs. His hold on my hips tightens as he presses into me, willing me to move further. So I do, wanting to touch him entirely, but not too fast. I want to tempt him, torture him, make him beg for me, because if there is one thing I am certain of, it's that Liam O'Connor has never begged a woman in his life. I would really love to be the first. I graze my fingers over the second ridge of muscles and they constrict under my fingers, and I feel...I feel...

"Liam," I whisper shakily under my breath. His entire body stills.

"*Fuck.*" He pushes away from me and turns quickly, stalking to the weight bench where his discarded shirt lays, mumbling something under his breath as he picks it up. I call his name again but he refuses to turn and look at me, the dark angel on his back now taunting me with its owner's silence.

I rush over before he has a chance to pull his shirt on, snatching it from his hands. I don't even know what propels me to do that except I know what I felt and I have to see it with my own eyes. It kills me to think he may be too embarrassed or ashamed to show this to me.

"Skylar," he growls, grabbing my wrists, his shirt still clutched tightly in my hands, as he looks at me pleadingly, silently begging me not to make him show me.

"*Please.* It's okay. I just want to see," I assure him with a small smile.

Taking a deep breath, his hands drop in defeat. I take one step back so I can see his body clearly.

"Oh god," I choke out.

My mouth hangs slack. In shock, in awe, in horror, unwilling to close because I want to be able to say something, the right thing. But as I take in the sight before me I realize there will never be a right thing to say. Circular burn marks are peppered over his chest and stomach, marks similar to those on his arms that are covered by his tattoos. There are two long scars across his lower stomach; they're raised so I know the cut had to have been deep, much like the one on his neck. That alone would cause anyone to drown in empathy, but that isn't even the worst thing. Starting from his lower left abdominal muscle and reaching to the top of his stomach is the number 187 cut—no not cut—*carved* into him. The top edge of the seven is what my hand had touched.

I remain completely silent. There is nothing to say right now. I just reach up tentatively and begin to trace my fingers over each burn mark, every scar, even daring to ghost my fingers fully over the individual numbers.

It's as if I'm reading him like braille. Liam doesn't move, doesn't make a sound as I continue to discover the scars that mar an otherwise perfect canvas. When I've finally finished exploring, I take a small step back, still holding on to his shirt like it's my lifeline. This here, this is real pain, pain I could never imagine or even begin to quantify.

"Wh-what happened to you, Liam?" I ask, trying to hide the slight tremble in my voice because I know he won't want me to pity him, and I don't, but I can't help the fact that my heart broke a little at seeing something so vicious done to someone so strong and so good.

"I was attacked one night after a match in Atlanta," he says robotically as if he has told this story a hundred times before and now is just numb to it all.

"Attacked? By who? Why?"

"Some gang members. As far as all the gory fucking details, I—*shit*," he curses, running a hand roughly through his hair. "I just *can't* fucking talk about it. Not right now. Not with you."

Not with me?

I quickly shake off the insecurities that suddenly plague me with his comment because this is about him, not me. "I'm sorry, I didn't mean to pry," I say, stepping back a little. Reaching out, he gently brushes his thumb across my cheek, catching a tear and wiping it away.

"You didn't. I'm fine, Sky, really. No more fucking tears, okay?" he says, pushing some loose strands of hair behind my ears. "Would it help put a smile back on that gorgeous face if I went back to beating the shit out of that bag so you could enjoy watching some more?"

"Oh my god, you are so unbelievably arrogant," I say, shoving him with my hands. "*Ouch!* Dammit!" I forgot about my hand, and the pain of my skin tearing open just a little more is making me remember all too well.

"What's wrong, Sky?" Liam grabs my wrist, pulling his shirt out of my hand, and immediately sees the damage I tried so hard to hide. "*Shit.* What the fuck happened to your hand?"

Liam actually appears worried as he studies my bloodied bandage, but I refuse to read too much into his behavior.

"Sky?"

"What?"

"Your hand. What the fuck happened?"

"Oh right. It was stupid. I accidentally smacked it against the car, and I think the wound may have opened." Not a total lie and not even close to the complete truth, but it's the only thing I can manage to say especially after seeing his scars. My pain, my darkness is nowhere even in the vicinity of his, and I refuse to cheapen his hurt with my petty family drama.

Liam is silent for a second as he looks at my hand and then at me, his brow furrowing, and I try and paste an *I'm so clumsy* apologetic smile on my face so he can't see through my fib. A great liar breeds an even better actress, and I can act and lie with the best of them.

After what seems like an eternity of silent convincing on my part, he looks at me and sighs. "Where's your first-aid kit?"

"First-aid kit? Um, I think I remember Winter telling me where she put it when she helped me move in here." I nervously tap my fingers against my lower lip, thinking.

"Sky, baby, you're fucking killing me," Liam groans, and his grasp on my wrist tightens slightly with his impatience. "We need to get this patched up before you bleed out in front of me." He releases my wrist and starts to pull the tape off his hands, loosening the edge with his teeth, then unwrapping the rest with his free hand. The whole process is strangely erotic. "Earth to Skylar," he says.

"What? Right, the first-aid kit. I remember she wanted to put it in a place I was most likely to get hurt. Oh! The kitchen! Under the sink!"

"Why would Winter assume that the kitchen is the place you would most likely get hu—you know what? Never mind. We'll cover that later. Hop up here," he says, turning his back to me and lowering into a squat.

What the hell is he doing? Does he want me to leap frog over him or something? "You want me to do what now?"

"Get your cute ass up here and wrap your legs around me. I'm taking you to the kitchen," he announces, jerking his head toward the stairs.

"Liam, my hand is hurt, not my leg. I can walk to the kitchen."

"Nope. Apparently I can't trust that you won't fucking flail your hands everywhere and get hurt again."

"I do not flail!"

"Woman, stop arguing and mount me. I need to get you cleaned up," he demands with a wink.

Trying to contain my giddy smile, I close the distance between us, cautiously wrapping my arms around his neck. As he moves to stand, his arms go under my knees and I instinctively wrap my legs tightly around his waist. Between his sweat slowly seeping through my tank top and the friction he's unintentionally causing when his back rubs against the seam of my shorts, I'm getting a little too turned on for comfort. Thankfully Liam makes it to the kitchen and sets me down on top of the counter by the sink just in time, because I was probably one more step away from moaning accidentally, making a total fool out of myself and furthering the growth of his already monstrous ego.

Liam takes his t-shirt and drapes it around my neck then bends down to grab the first-aid kit from under the sink, giving me the perfect chance to stare at his toned ass. He opens the kit and starts taking out items, placing them uniformly beside me on the counter. He seems to be concentrating so intently that I'm able to steal even more glances at his body. Earlier I was so distracted with the tattoo and the scars that I never really had a chance to silently drool all over his perfectly sculpted form. Abs I could wash my clothes on, check. Obliques, check. Biceps, triceps, whatever the hell that sexy V is that leads me right to what I'm hoping is a large—

"If you're finished checking me out, I would love to look at that hand of yours." He gives me a crooked grin before moving his body in-between my thighs and placing his hands on them to halt my legs from banging anxiously against the cabinets.

"I'm not finished, but feel free to look away. Something tells me I'll have plenty of opportunities in the future."

Laughing, he picks up my left wrist and turns my hand so that my palm is facing upward, then he starts to cut the soiled bandage off. "You're something else, Sky."

I guess maybe he expects me to argue with him or deny my blatant admiration, but why bother? He's insanely attractive, he knows it, I know it, hell, a blind nun would probably figure out within seconds of being around him.

"*Shit*, Sky. This doesn't look good," he says once he gets the bandage all the way off. And he's right. It looks awful. The cut seems deeper and even longer than it was originally, but the dried blood and dirt from when I hit the pavement garage earlier obstructs any view of the real damage.

"I'm going to clean this up and it's probably going to hurt, okay?" A hint of worry laces his warning.

"I can handle it. Do your worst."

He grabs a brown bottle off the counter and pours some of the liquid onto a cotton swab. When he begins to move the cotton toward my cut, I flinch.

"Ouch!" I jerk my hand away.

"Knock it off! I didn't even touch you yet." He rolls his eyes and now I have a full-blown smile on my face as he starts to wipe my hand with the cleanser. It stings a little, but I'm too focused on his close proximity to even care.

"So how did your meeting go? Everything good?" Liam asks as he continues to work his healing magic on me.

"It went. I don't really want to talk about it, though. No more business drama for me today." He glances up from my hand curiously, as if he knows I'm hiding something. Or maybe that's just my paranoia. Either way, I want to change the subject before he presses me for more details, and anyway, there's something I've been curious about since the plane ride.

"Can I ask you something, Liam?"

"Anything, Sky."

"You said on the plane that your dad was a boxer in Ireland. I was just curious how he went from boxing in Ireland to bar owner in Washington. Seems like a big leap."

"That's what you wanted to ask me? You're curious about my dad?"

"Yeah—no, well, sort of. Not about your dad specifically, I'm just curious about you, I guess. You're going to be living in my pool house for the next three months, and it occurred to me that I should probably know more about you. Your origins and all that."

Your origins? Where do I come up with this weirdness?

"Fair enough," he says as he grabs another cotton swab and runs it under the faucet, then starts to clean up more of the blood. I watch his movements curiously because his attentiveness is so foreign to me and I want to revel in the rare moment. "My dad moved to Washington when he was twenty-one. For a girl, actually. My mom. She went to Ireland when she was nineteen, for some study abroad nursing program with her school. She walked into my grandpa Niall's bar one night with her school friends when my dad was hanging out with a few of his friends. He was 'enchanted by her.' His words, by the way, not mine. I would never say something that fucking lame."

"I would never dream you would," I say, shaking my head dramatically.

"Anyway, some douchebag that had come with her—"

"Wait, how do you know he was a douchebag?"

"Because my dad said so, and because the guy wasn't my dad. So he was a fucking douchebag."

"Gotcha. Continue." I try and contain my laughter at his ridiculously adorable matter-of-fact statement.

"So this douchebag ordered a round of some fruity bitch drink for all the girls and Guinness for all the guys at the table." I can't hold it in

anymore and I start to laugh as he begins to swipe some kind of oint-
ment over my cut, but the second he starts to blow on it I forget why I
was laughing in the first place.

Oh yeah, I remember now. "The horror! Ordering drinks for everyone like that. You're so right, what a douche!"

Liam shakes his head and I know he wants to laugh but he's refusing to give me the satisfaction. "He is because he didn't even ask what
anyone wanted. So, everyone at the table happily drinks except for my
mom who ignored hers and watched as the guys drank their beers.
Because my dad was staring at her like a creep all night, he noticed
this. He walked a Guinness right up to the table, handed it to her, and
said 'Mavourneen,' which means my darling" Liam winks at me and I
grin like an idiot. "Mavourneen, you'll never get everything ya' want
out of life if you don't open that pretty little mouth of yours and ask
for it.'"

"He really said that?"

"He really did."

"And what did your mom say?" My eyes widen as big as my smile
in anticipation. Yes, I am a sucker for happy endings; it's my dirty little
secret.

"That's the best part. She smiled at him, swallowed the beer in a
few gulps like the fucking champ she is, and said 'I wanted a shot of
whiskey, darling, and when you bring one back, pull up a chair so I can
tell you more about what I want.' He spent the next two months showing her around Ireland, then he left everything, his boxing career, his
family, his life there to move back to Washington with her."

"Wow. That is incredibly romantic. The kind of thing that only
happens in movies. In fact, I think I might have been in that movie."
Despite the fact his head is still bowed, I catch the smile playing at the
corners of his lips.

"Cute, Sky. So, what are your plans tonight anyway? Are you going
anywhere? We haven't really talked about your schedule or what I need
to do for you."

"I don't really have anything planned for the next few weeks. I
decided to take some time off after this movie to try and relax, read
some scripts, stay indoors where I can be stress free. I may do some

shopping for a few events I am obligated to, or hit up a club with Win and Noah, and I'll need you there. I'll let you know as soon as I know."

Liam's eyes shoot up, his face so close to mine that I can feel the warmth of his breath on my lips. "Let's just plan on anytime you leave this house I am on you like a shadow. Don't fucking go anywhere without me. You go out to get your mail or pet a stray fucking kitten in your driveway, I'm right there with you. After everything I've witnessed this morning, I don't want you going anywhere alone. You got me?"

His demanding tone sends chills through me, and I'm so turned on by his show of dominance that I almost plaster my lips to his. Until something he says actually registers in my lust addled mind.

"Did you just say 'pet a stray kitten in my driveway?'"

"Fuck yeah, I did. You seem like the type that would. And those fucking paparazzi sit outside your house ready for anything, and god knows who else sits out there waiting to catch a glimpse of you, so I would like to play it safe and just make sure I'm around you whenever you exit this house."

"Wait, so is there actually a stray kitten wandering around my property? Where did you see it? Should we set some food out or something?" I don't have any cat food, seeing as I have no cat, but I know I have quite a bit of tuna.

That could work right?

"No, Sky, there is no stray kitten. I'm just making a fucking point."
Never mind then.

"And that point would be? Other than making me feel like a gullible idiot, I mean."

"That you don't think before you leap and you won't take your safety into account first. So, now you get me?"

"Yes, I got you. But just so you know, I would never let a lonely homeless kitten roam around my property with no food or way to survive. But I would have you help me escort the kitten to safety. Do you feel better now?"

"Infinitely. Smartass." He rolls his eyes at me and grabs the gauze to start wrapping it around the bandage he's already placed on my wound. "So what are your plans for tonight, then?" He is definitely doing a better job than Noah's whole slap a Band-Aid over a bunch of gauze and call it good method.

"Well, I sort of have this tradition after I wrap up a movie."

"Oh yeah, and what is that?" Liam asks, putting a final piece of tape on the gauze. Before I have a chance to answer him, he lifts my palm up to his lips and places a chaste kiss on the dressed wound.

This sweet act takes me by complete surprise and now I'm feeling a little shy, which is so unlike me. There is just something about Liam that takes me out of my element, and I love it: his adoration, his attention, the way he never seems to be intimidated by me because of who I am.

"I-I grab a bottle of wine, order a pizza, and have um...a Bill Murray movie marathon night. But you feel free to take a night off. Get yourself settled in and unpacked."

"Bill Murray movie marathon it is, then. I assume you start with *Ghostbusters*," he says, and I realize he's still standing between my legs, leaning into me. Hell, I'm breathing in his air right now.

"No way. *Groundhog Day*," I respond incredulously.

"So, what time does this marathon start?" he asks, his hands resting on my hips as if it is the most normal thing in the world and in no way is making my heart beat right out of my chest.

"You really want to join me?"

"If that's okay? My boss gave me the night off so I have nothing but free time," Liam says in that cocky tone that I find myself physically responding to more and more, almost like he's training me to react to it against my will.

"She must be pretty awesome. Well, its four now so in about an hour I'll be ready. That work for you? I assume you want to shower and get cleaned up. You kind of stink." I place my hand on his chest, daringly teasing him. The air between us is throbbing with desire, and I'm about two seconds and one more flirty comment away from jumping him right here and now. But then I hear a key jiggling in my front door and I know that Noah has come home. He seriously has the worst timing. Ever.

"Hey, Morningstar, you home?" Noah's chipper voice carries down the solarium as he makes his way into the kitchen and subsequently kills my libido. Liam snatches his shirt from around my neck and quickly pulls it over his head, probably to avoid Noah seeing his scars and the questions that are sure to come with it. Liam turns around, but doesn't move away from me like I expected him to. He stays comfortably leaning between my thighs.

"Whoa, what did I just walk in on?" Noah's eyes widen as a smile slowly crosses his lips.

"Nothing," I say a little too quickly. I mean it so why I feel the need to suddenly blurt the word out like I'm yelling *fire* is beyond me. "He was just bandaging me up."

"Oh, is that what the kids are calling it these days? How kinky," Noah teases, waggling his eyebrows at me.

"God, Noah, I meant my hand." I lift it in an attempt to prove nothing torrid has just occurred. Unfortunately. "Is your mind just perpetually in the gutter, or do you come up for air occasionally?" Seriously, what is with my friends? I may need some new ones.

"Skylar, I just walked in on a hot bartender half-naked and sweaty between your legs. It wasn't much of a leap to make it into gutter territory. Nice ink by the way. Totally gruesome. Love it." He nods his head toward Liam.

"Thanks, man." His politeness is rife with sadness. Clearly Liam's tattoo is not one he wishes to be admired.

"Liam, this is Noah Douglas. I'm not sure if you remember him from the other night. Noah is aware of your name and your role here, but for some reason he is insistent on calling you hot bartender. I apologize on his behalf."

"Nice to meet you, Noah. I've heard a lot about you." He moves to shake Noah's hand then once again places himself comfortably between my legs.

"Of course you have. I'm pretty much the most important person in her life, aren't I, my little Morningstar?" he announces, shaking Liam's hand in return. "She probably can't go five minutes without bringing me up," Noah says, winking at me.

"Oh, of course not." I roll my eyes, but really he is the most important person to me; I have no idea what would become of me without him. "Noah, will you be joining us tonight for the Bill Murray movie marathon?" I ask the question just to be polite, but hopefully he caught my *don't even think about saying yes* tone. He may be the most important person to me, but I would love to have some alone time with Liam, not to mention that if Noah hangs out here with us, there will be some guaranteed mortification bestowed upon me. If there is one thing I know about Noah, it's that he never misses an opportunity to embarrass the hell out of me.

"*Us?*" Noah looks up at me with a mischievous twinkle in his eye while I silently warn him with my glare so he knows not to say one word. "Fortunately for you, Morningstar, I'm just here to pack a bag. Headed to the boyfriend's house to spend some much needed one-on-one time together if you know what I mean."

"You want to play some basketball with him?" I ask, feigning innocence.

"Ha. Ha. Very funny."

"Having Erik withdrawals, are you?"

"Skylar, I know you don't know this, seeing as you have never been in a relationship, but spending two months apart from one's significant other is usually not advantageous to the growth of said relationship."

Liam turns to look at me after Noah's admission, and I can sense my cheeks getting flushed. I really haven't had any kind of serious relationships, but I'm also not a blushing virgin or anything. This is a no win for a girl. I could either lie and pretend I've had relationships that have lasted longer than the milk in my refrigerator, try and explain my friends with benefits relationship with Cassiel, or remain silent and come off as a complete slut who sleeps around with no commitment. Which may make some guys think they have hit the mother lode, but I'm seriously doubting that Liam is the kind of guy that would appreciate that kind of revelation.

"I've had relationships, Noah." I go with a half-truth, half-lie which seems to be an ongoing theme when it comes to Liam. I'm just not sure how to be honest with him about anything yet; his intensity is so new to me and makes him unpredictable.

I love that about him.

I hate that about him.

And one day I may come to worship him for it, which makes me fear it above all else.

"You have not had relationships. You, my dear, have had sex-capades. No shame in them, but there is a big difference." And here comes the promised mortification.

"Noah—"

"Is sexcapades not the right term? Sexual time warps? Oh wait, what did Cassiel say recently?"

"Noah, *shut up.*"

Liam's body stiffens against the inside of my thighs, and I officially want to murder Noah. I want to rip out his tongue and bitch slap him with it.

Slapping his hands against my legs, he pushes away from me firm-ly. "Well, Skylar, as much as I would love to fucking hear where this conversation is headed, I'm going to go. Gotta get cleaned up and call my parents. Meet you back here in an hour. Noah, be seeing you."

I watch helplessly as Liam essentially stomps out to the guest house.

"I take it that was hot bartender sarcasm?"

"Nice, Noah. Way to make me look like a slut." I jump off the kitch-en counter, making sure to take care with my freshly bandaged hand.

"What?! Skylar, I was just playing around. Besides, it's not like he hasn't seen all the tabloids and blogs. They may be lies, but it doesn't mean he hasn't come to some assumptive conclusion about your sex life. I just want to make sure he isn't hanging around you because of those assumptions. Based on that borderline caveman exit, I'm going to say he is not hanging around for some easy famous pussy."

"Nice. And you're wrong, Noah. He barely knows anything about me. He doesn't even look at the tabloids."

"How is that possible? Everyone has seen you. On TMZ at the very least."

"Not everyone is into celebrity gossip. He spent most of his life training to box and then the last two years trying to run his father's bar and take care of his family while his dad recovered from lung cancer. Catching up on celebrity gossip seems to be the last thing on his to-do list."

"Shit. That's so tragic," Noah says, putting a hand to his chest. "No time to catch up on celebrity gossip? How does one survive without it?"

I laugh, despite my urge to remain angry at him. This is another reason why I love Noah. He never allows me to stay mad at him, and in a life where I seem to be angry at everyone, at least I have that.

"Come on, my little Morningstar. Help me pack a bag and we can talk all about the feelings you have caught for the hot bartender," Noah says amusingly. It is pointless to argue, so I follow Noah upstairs to his room.

CHAPTER 11

LIAM

I remember this three-way I had with two ring girls, about a month before I was officially kicked out of the professional sport of boxing. They were hot as hell, young with tight little bodies. I was fucking one from behind while she ate out her friend like it was her last meal and she was taking her time savoring the taste; honestly, I was taking notes from this chick on how to properly eat pussy. I've often gone back to that memory when I'm jerking off because the thought of it gets me hard as hell. But the image I'm looking at now easily puts that one to shame. Skylar is standing in her kitchen in barely-there black shorts and a tight as hell blue tank top that is making her tits look fucking fantastic, her hair pulled back into a messy ponytail that bares her neck, and fuck if it won't be hard for me to stop myself from sucking and licking at her skin. I'm so mesmerized by her that I have yet to walk into her house, so I'm just standing at her back door staring at her like a fucking creeper.

Of course the other reason I'm not walking in there yet is because I kind of feel like an asshole for how I left earlier. I was still revved up after watching how Carl treated her, and seeing her hand all cut up again put me in the wrong head space, so maybe my words and actions were too aggressive. But I *won't* fucking apologize because I wasn't wrong in walking out. Why the hell would I want to stay and listen to her and Noah talk about the men she's fucked? So I need to take a deep breath, find my balls, and make sure that the second I walk into the house I do not let the sight of her bring me to my knees like a damn chump.

Skylar turns to open a drawer. The cheeks of her phenomenally tight ass tease me from the bottom hem of her shorts while she pulls a wine opener out and attempts to open the bottle. But apparently she's left-handed.

"Hey. Sky, *wait*," I command as I slide the glass door open and make my way into the kitchen.

She looks at me and smiles cautiously. "Did you want white wine instead of red or something? I didn't know what you preferred. Also, I wasn't sure if you still planned on coming so I just went with red because I knew I would drink it."

Rounding the corner of the kitchen island, I move right behind her, caging her between me and the counter, my front to her back, or rather my fucking hard-on digging into her back. I hear a sharp intake of breath and she drops her hands to the countertop, the wine opener clinking loudly under her hand.

She's into this. Into me. I mean, I'm not a complete fucking idiot, I felt her body's reaction to me earlier in the gym; she was probably ready for me to fuck her against that wall. But I have to admit, after she got a first look at those scars and with my being a total dick to her when I left, I figured her reaction to me would have cooled. But given that she is white knuckling the counter right now and her ass seems to be trying to line up with my cock, I'm going with the assumption that no part of earlier today had a negative effect on her still wanting me. Thank Christ that it doesn't even seem she's waiting for an apology because no fucking way is that happening.

I can sense her breathing pick up as I begin to run my fingers slowly down her left arm, trailing them down to her hand where I grab the wine opener out from under her fingers. Her body shivers under my touch, goosebumps now covering her skin, and fuck if I'm not enjoying every response her body is surrendering to me.

"The wine is not the problem, sweetheart," I tell her. The scent of peaches surrounds me and I'm curious if she tastes as good as she smells. I move my lips right up to her ear, close enough that with a small flick of my tongue I could satisfy my curiosity. "I just wanted to help you get the bottle open. I don't want you to open that wound up again."

Once my breath hits her skin she gasps, and I know I need to fucking move before I bend her over this counter and fuck her until she forgets any man that has ever been inside her. Hell, even the thought of someone else having her has my blood raging and that's not a good thing. It's why I need to pull back from Skylar, just for a while, until I know she can handle me. Until I know I can handle her. Fucking with feelings isn't new to me, but it has been absent for years. I don't know that I'm ready to even take that on.

Move asshole.

Picking up the wine opener in one hand and the bottle in the other, I move to the other side of the island, making sure to keep a safe distance from the evil temptress. I am opening the bottle of wine when she clears her throat and seems to regain her ability to speak, which I already know means I'm in for a nervous earful.

"Well, thank you. Truth be told, I've always had a bit of trouble opening a wine bottle. I know it seems so basic but I always end up getting pieces of the cork in the bottle somehow. I...uh...also ordered some pepperoni pizza. Everybody likes pepperoni, right? Anyway, the guy said he would be here in thirty minutes, which was about twenty-five minutes ago so I guess technically he will be here in about five minutes," she's speaking so quickly her words start to blend together. I don't even think she's remembering to breathe.

"Jesus, Skylar, try and relax." My pleading voice matches the exact moment the cork pops out of the bottle. "Red wine is fine. Pepperoni pizza is perfect. Calm the hell down before you pass out from lack of oxygen." I start to pour the wine into the empty glasses. She stares at me defiantly with her hands on her hips not saying a word. It's actually pretty fucking cute that she seems so pissed.

"I am calm. Well, I *was* calm, then you came in here and started grinding up on me so I apologize if that threw me off kilter a little. I'm only human."

This is why I'm always laughing and comfortable around her. Her honesty is so fucking refreshing but sometimes borders on frightening. Most girls giggle or play hard to get around me, but not her. She just flat out says what she is thinking. Most of the time. That's why it's so hard to discern her truths from her lies. I know she has already lied to me more than once, I just can't be sure about what exactly. Or why. And to be fucking honest, I'm not sure I could handle her truths yet so I've let them slide.

For now.

That saying, "Ignorance is bliss," was meant for uncontrollable fuck-ups like me. People that find out the truths and then destroy them.

So for now, the truths, the lies, the sexual desire will all remain locked in some metaphorical vault deep inside until I think I can manage it all without abolishing everything in my path. Including her.

Especially her.

"Let's just go start this marathon of yours, Sky," I say as I finish pouring the wine into glasses. She stares me down until I grab our glasses and the bottle and head over to her living room, setting everything down on the ottoman. I take a seat on her L-shaped couch and wait for her to finally join me.

"You certainly are a take charge kind of guy aren't you, Liam?" She shakes her head and makes her way to the couch, taking a seat close but not too close. She reaches for her wine and takes a large sip, relaxing back into the couch.

"What can I say, baby, it's my way. Nice pajamas. Not much to them, is there?" I eye her from head to toe, unsure if I am silently chastising or praising her for the choice in clothing, or lack thereof.

She glances down at her chest, shrugs her shoulders, and takes another sip of wine before turning that vixen grin on me. "What can I say, *baby*, it's my way." Reaching for the remote, she starts to hit play on the movie when a loud buzzing vibrates from the house.

"What the hell was that?"

"That was someone at the gate. Pizza guy must be here. I'll go let him in and grab it." She shoots up off the couch and I quickly grab her around the waist, pulling her gently back down.

"Liam, what the hell?!" Sky shrieks, those seductive eyes now wide with shock as she scrambles to her knees to steady herself. Now that is a sight I won't mind remembering. Her on her knees in front of me.

I hear the buzzer again. "I'll take care of it, Skylar. You can't parade yourself in front of the pizza guy dressed like that. You'll give him a heart attack or he'll take a little too much advantage of the view and then I'll have to kick his ass." I turn to walk toward the front door before she starts to think this is up for debate.

"Fine then," she huffs. "You have to punch pound two-one-two-two into the code box by the front door, and that will open the gate. Wait!" I stop by the door and turn to look at her. "Let me give you some money," she says as she starts to get up off the couch.

"Hush, Skylar. Sit," I command, pointing at the couch.

I hope she doesn't think I can't afford a damn pizza. That thought causes me to pound the code into the box a little harder than necessary and slam the door with a little more force. I take the ten seconds it takes the pizza guy to drive up the driveway to pull my shit together. I'm sure Skylar didn't mean anything by that comment, and I have to remember that I'm her employee and not her damn boyfriend, so what does it matter who pays for the fucking pizza?

Some beat up Honda pulls up to me, and a boy probably no older than eighteen gets out of it, pizza in hand.

"Fifteen dollars," is all he says to me as he slowly looks around me toward the house. "Hey, is it true that Skylar Barrett lives here? Do you think she would come out and sign something for me?"

Unfuckingbelievable.

I snatch a twenty out of my wallet and shove it into the guy's chest so hard he stumbles back a little and lets the box fall into my grasp. "Get lost," I warn, my teeth clenching so hard I swear one may have cracked. The kid has enough sense to back up, but he mutters something along the lines of asshole under his breath as he gets into his car. He's lucky he's a kid and I have something better waiting for me inside, otherwise I would take some pleasure in introducing him to an ass kicking into adulthood.

I walk back into the house and make sure to turn every single damn lock on the door and set the alarm the way Winter had shown me earlier. I take a few deep breaths to calm myself so I don't look like an angry psycho when I get back to her. But when I start to head into the living room, any trace of frustration I had disappears and I'm trying to hide a smile, because there on the couch is Skylar, hugging her legs to her chest and doing her best to scowl at me.

"Are you pouting, sweetheart?" I try my best to hide my amusement as I set the pizza down on the ottoman and sit right next to her. Her anger is so different than my own. Mine makes me seem like some sort of rabid fucking Rottweiler while she is more like an adorable puppy whose favorite toy is being held hostage by its owner. But as soon as you give her the toy back, she wags her tail and jumps around excitedly, any trace of irritation forgotten.

"I'm not pouting. I'm pissed. You didn't have to pay for it, and I could have handled a pizza delivery guy. It isn't like this is the first time I've ever ordered one for myself," she says, letting her feet fall to the floor as she straightens her spine and glares at me.

I'm getting the distinct feeling that she hates not being in control. Unfortunately for her, so do I because when I'm not in control, I lose control.

"Do you trust me, Sky?"

"You know I do."

"Then you have to trust that sometimes I may know better than you. Got me?" I'm not really asking for her approval, just an acknowledgment that she hears what I'm telling her. I take a casual sip of my wine, trying my best to ignore her stubborn stare burning a hole into me.

"No," she mumbles so quietly I almost don't hear her. Almost.

"What was that? You're going to need to speak up, sweetheart."

Turning toward me so she is looking me directly in the eyes, she lifts her chin and says, "No. I'm not going to admit you know better than me." Then she does something I was not expecting. She fucking smirks at me. My little hellcat is goading me.

After carefully placing my wine glass down, I throw myself on top of Skylar so she is pinned between me and the couch. She quickly puts her hands to my chest trying to push me off, but I easily snatch up her wrists and begin tickling her ribs with my free hand.

"Admit I know better than you," I command over her laughter.

"STOP, LIAM! Get off!" Sky laughs uncontrollably, writhing beneath me as I continue my assault, and the more she wiggles her hips against my dick the more I struggle to not pull her shorts down and just fuck her here. This punishment has suddenly and unexpectedly become a self-imposed one.

"I'll stop if you admit it." I'll probably stop the next time she shifts her tits up into my chest, but no need for her to think I'm submitting. I don't want her thinking she has the upper hand here.

"Okay!" she screams through her laughter and both those sounds mixed together make me smile. And make my cock hard. So I should probably move the fuck off her now, but she hasn't quite given in to me the way I want.

"Okay, what? Say it, Sky," I say as my hand moves to the other side of her stomach, making sure to hit every rib I can as I graze and tickle my way from her hipbone to right underneath her breast. I accidentally thrust my erection against her at the same time, because apparently once I start touching a female my cock doesn't know how to be polite.

"You know better than me." She doesn't scream the declaration through her laughter like I expected, but moans it in a breathy release, her lips so close to my mouth that I feel the shiver in her lust-filled voice. Now we both are just staring at each other, as if waiting to see who will be the first to make a move. A real move, one that includes ripping each other's clothes off and fucking until we have both satiated our primal needs. But I want to be more than just a primal need to Skylar, and I want her to feel like she is more than that for me, and I'm not sure we're there yet. I launch myself backward to get off of her as quickly as possible without seeming like I'm avoiding her like she's some kind of virus.

"Now that wasn't so hard for you to admit, was it?"

Sky snatches up her glass of wine and says, "You're kind of an asshole. And *that* wasn't too hard to admit."

"I know, baby. It's my way," I reach for my glass of wine and throw my arm casually over the back of the couch while she hits play on the movie.

A bottle of wine and three and a half Bill Murray movies later, I find myself in the corner of the couch, Sky tucked into my chest, my arm draped over her body. We—rather, I haven't talked during the movies, only laughed at the appropriate moments. Skylar, on the other hand, has had something to say during every scene of each of the movies. She spent the first twenty minutes of *Caddyshack* telling me all about how Bill Murray had no script and made everything up as he went along. The rest of the movies were met with same introspective information almost every half hour. I want to be annoyed by the constant interruptions, but I find myself anticipating the moments when I hear her take a breath before she so animatedly brings up all this behind the scenes information she knows. Her passion is contagious, and instead of feeling aggravated, I find myself jonesing for the next bit of useless knowledge from her. Basically, I'm fucked. The last half hour, though, Sky has been silent, and every few minutes my curiosity gets the best of me and I look down to make sure she hasn't fallen asleep.

Finally, she breaks the silence. "Can I ask you something, Liam?"

"Of course."

I do mean that. She can ask me anything, and I wish I was capable of answering anything she is brave enough to ask because I know, especially following this afternoon, she probably has a thousand questions bouncing around in that pretty little head of hers. But I also know me, and the wrong fucking questions will shut me down; it will bring forth hellish memories it took me years of drug abuse, fucking, and drinking whiskey to bury. I don't touch drugs anymore, and I only drink whiskey on occasion, and I haven't fucked a girl in almost a week, so the only default mechanism I have now is to be an asshole. Or to fuck her, distracting myself with either her pussy or my rage so I don't remember.

"The names tattooed on your arm, are they friends of yours?" She begins to caress her fingertips across the tree inked on my arm, paying special attention to the names etched into my skin.

Trevor.

Isabel.

Ali.

Trevor gasping for air, his lungs gurgling. Isabel dead next to him. A man's hands wrapped around Ali's throat as she tries to scream.

My heart rate jacks up with every stroke of her fingers across the names, across my scars, and my body stills as I try to mentally block the memories from fucking flooding my brain.

"They *were* family." I glance toward the movie, trying to distract myself, but I only have a vague awareness of what's happening around me because now all I hear is Ali screaming for help over and over, crying out my name, and as Skylar ghosts her fingers across the names I become strangely aroused and so fucking disgusted with myself at the same time. I know it's wrong to feel so much pleasure attached to something so painful.

"Were?" Realization takes her over; she shifts her body more toward mine and looks up at me with the most innocent, sympathetic brown eyes. No...*fuck.* Sky's eyes are blue, not brown.

"Stop! Please. God, it hurts."

"God, Liam. I'm so sorry. I had no idea. What happened? Were they with you when you were attacked?" She grabs my hand in her soft one and brings it up to her lips, placing a soft kiss on the inside of my rough palm. I can't take it anymore.

"Christ, Skylar! Just fucking *stop* with the twenty questions. What the hell did I tell you earlier?!" I yank my arm away from her and she quickly moves to the other end of the couch as if I've burned her. "I told you I didn't want to fucking talk about this shit!"

The shocked look on her face is enough to wreck me, snapping me back into *this* moment. I scrub my hand down my face, and I feel the dampness from her tender kiss sear my tortured skin.

"I-I'm sorry. I didn't mean to pry." The softness in her voice rips at my chest because I realize I did this to her. I made her scared. I took away her voice, I put those unshed tears in her eyes.

"Fuck, Sky. Don't apologize. I'm the one who's the asshole here." Without thinking, I reach over and wrap my arms around her slender waist, tucking her into my body, bringing her head to my chest. She stiffens immediately and I hate it. I hate myself. I want so badly to tell her, I want to explain why I am the way I am. That I don't just have a temper, I have a fucking incurable sickness, but I can't seem to do it.

I take out her ponytail holder and start to run my fingers through her hair soothingly, both for my benefit and hers. She begins to relax a little more and I try to match my rapid heartbeat to her breathing. "I just don't have it in me to talk to you about this yet. Not tonight."

Skylar puts her hand to my chest and lifts her head just enough so she's looking at me. "When you...I mean, if you ever...never mind." She immediately rests her head on my chest and stares at the movie like she's actually paying attention to the damned thing.

Fuck. "Sky." I place my finger under her chin and tip her gaze upward. "Baby, I meant what I said earlier. You can ask me anything. That blow-up I had, that's on me, not you. That's my own bullshit I'm still dealing with and I shouldn't have taken it out on you the way I did, but I fucking promise I would never hurt you. It would destroy me to think you were too afraid to ask me anything. You got me?"

"Okay," she answers simply but she still seems hesitant to finish her thought. "You never did answer my question on the plane, by the way."

"Oh yeah? And what question would that be?"

"Your pet name when you were boxing. You told me you would tell me on the plane and you never did."

"Jesus. I told you it's not called a pet name, it's a nickname. A ring name."

"Whatever you want to call it, you had one, right?"

"Yes."

"And what was it?"

I think about drawing out her torture after that little pet name comment she made, but I owe her one after the way I'd just treated her, and I'm enjoying the fact that she seems to be warming back up to me, even going so far as to creep one of her hands up under my shirt where it now rests on my stomach.

"It was Lethal Liam O'Connor."

"How did you come by that name? Is it because of your lethally charming personality?" She looks up at me with that mocking little smirk that makes me want to spank the sarcasm right out of her.

"No, smartass, it was because I was lethal in the ring. I could take my opponents out quickly, typically with just one good hit. Never even saw a 12th round."

"How many matches did you fight in?"

"Thirty-two before I went pro. Then four after that."

"And you knocked all of them out before the last round?"

"Every match."

"How'd you manage that?" she asks, her brow furrowing in the cutest way possible.

Dropping my head to the back of the couch, I moan dramatically as if her words hurt, which they kind of do. How could she question my skills? "Sky, you wound me with your lack of confidence in my abilities."

"I'm sure your ego can take the hit. I don't really know anything about boxing, but it just seems statistically with that many fights you should have at least seen the second round at some point. I mean, were you really that good?"

"My dad trained me to be a fucking champ because *he* was a fucking champ, so yes, I am that good, but if I'm being honest I also had something none of the fighters had and I learned how to use it to my advantage."

"Oh, so you had a secret weapon," she says excitedly, flipping over so she's lying completely on top of me. I scoot my back down a little further on the couch so I can lay with her more comfortably.

"Something like that. I have an eidetic memory."

"Like a photographic memory?"

"Yeah. Although I'm surprised you know what that means." Damn. I was kind of hoping she wouldn't know the term so I could screw with her a little more.

She shrugs her shoulders. "I was in a movie once that dealt a little with the subject. You know some doctors claim that it doesn't even exist. That it's a myth and some people just have a more detailed recall than others."

"Well, some doctors are clearly fucking idiots." I tuck Sky's hair behind her ears and wait for her to hit me with more questions.

"I don't understand though. How does having a photographic memory help you box, *Lethal* Liam?"

"Well, *Sexy* Skylar, I would watch tapes of my opponents boxing. I was able to commit their strategies to memory pretty quickly, their weaknesses, their tactics. I was able to predict their moves in the ring just by their body language. A slight jerk of a shoulder or shift in their stance, and I knew exactly what they would do. I would wait for the opening then swing, and I knew just where to hit to take them down quickly. For example, you hit a guy hard enough in the kidney and you can drop him quick. Lethal hands, baby." I wink at her as she rolls her eyes then turns her attention back to the movie.

"Liam?"

"Yeah, Sky?"

"If you ever want to talk about it, I'm here for you. You can tell me anything, I promise."

I blow out a breath and reach behind me to grab the blanket draped over the back of the couch, then throw it over us both.

"I know."

The simplicity of my reassurance means more to me than I'm sure she even realizes. I reach for the remote, turning the volume up on the movie, determined to drown out the awkward silence that now fills the room. It's probably not awkward to her, but I'm not used to this kind of sharing. I would rather just go back to moments ago where she was spouting off inane details about the movie, but I know I probably killed the mood for her tonight, and this was supposed to be a night for her. A fucking tradition, she said. I wish I could be unselfish and walk away, or at least beg some more for her forgiveness for fucking up the night, but I don't have it in me, and honestly, I'm glad Sky saw that side of me. Some sick facet of my personality is drawn to the fact that she didn't run from my outburst or cower or pout and demand an apology for how I treated her, because this is who I am. I can't change, I will never be fixed. I can only ever be accepted.

CHAPTER 12

LIAM

Sunlight shines into the house through the panoramic windows, bathing the whole living room in a bright yellow light and blinding me through my eyelids, waking me from a deep sleep.

Jesus. Why the hell is it so fucking bright in here? Where the fuck am I?

My eyes shoot open as I take in my surroundings. I'm still on the couch in Sky's living room, the DVD menu frozen on the screen, my hand buried in soft strands of her hair. The faint scent of peaches engulfs me and the weight of Skylar's body on mine wakes me right up. Apparently my dick was already aware of this situation because it is wide awake and hard as fuck. Shit. I really did not mean to fall asleep with her, and I'm sure she did not mean to pass out on me. Everything after the halfway mark of *Lost In Translation* is hazy, although I'm not shocked I fell asleep. I was wiped out and I don't care how many people say that movie is fantastic, it's boring as hell.

Something vibrates from inside my pants, and unless my dick got magical powers overnight I'm guessing someone is calling me. Sky shifts slightly on top of me, releasing a quiet a moan while she wraps her arms tight around my waist, burrowing her head deeper into my stomach. I would let my phone keep ringing and be perfectly content just laying with her in my arms, but I never ignore phone calls because the only people that call me are family.

"Sky, sweetheart, I need to grab my phone." I brush the hair away from her face with one hand and attempt to shift myself out from under her.

"There is no Skylar, only Zuul." Her voice is raspy as she rolls off of me and pulls the blanket over her head, refusing to move from the couch.

Quoting *Ghostbusters*, fucking adorable. And she is obviously not a morning person.

I pull the phone out of my pocket and walk to the kitchen. *Fuck*, the tile on her floor is cold. My caller ID identifies that it's Shayla calling, and I answer right before my voicemail picks up.

"Morning, Shay. How is my favorite sister today?"

"Don't try and kiss my ass, Liam. How could you not tell me?" She's feisty this morning, and it's way too early for me to have fucked up already.

"What are you talking about? What didn't I tell you?" I know she knows I'm here since we had a whole discussion about me leaving and she actually seemed way too excited to get rid of me. That probably had to do with the fact she was so star struck over the prospect of me staying with Skylar.

"You told me you were just working for Skylar Barrett, not that you were dating her. When did this happen? You just met her a few days ago, right? And how could you leave me, your only sister and most favorite of people, in the dark? This whole thing is tragic."

"Shayla, what the fuck are you talking about? I *am* only working for her." That isn't entirely true, but there is no reason to get into the details with my baby sister, especially when I'm not quite sure what the hell is going on myself, although I'm confident that there probably is no place in the job description that states falling asleep together.

I hear her typing on her laptop and she sighs before saying, "You and Skylar Barrett are all over the gossip sites this morning. There are pictures and videos of you raging out on paparazzi with the headline, 'Skylar Joy Barrett's new boyfriend has anger issues.'"

"What? That's fucking bullshit!" I push myself off the kitchen counter I was leaning on just minutes before, the anger in my voice causing me to be louder than I intended. Looking over at the couch, I see Skylar gazing at me through half closed eyes, clearly confused, as she lazily swipes the hair out of her eyes.

"So you guys aren't together? Well, what the shit happened at the airport? You look pissed, big brother. Dad is worried you're going to lose it if you stay in that environment with her."

I blow out a breath and try to think of the right words that will help her stop worrying about me. "No, Shay, we aren't together. It was just a crazy scene at the airport that I wasn't prepared for. Shit got out of hand." I turn away from Sky's stare and rest my arms on the counter. For some reason I don't want her to hear this discussion. It makes me feel weak. "You know how I get sometimes. Tell dad I'm good, okay. I have it under control."

"Promise?" Whenever her voice goes quiet like that I feel the weight of her unnecessary concern crushing my conscience. I hate her worrying about me; it should be the other way around.

"I promise, Shayla."

"Bro, you are freakin' famous now!" Worried Shayla has apparently left the building. "So what's it like there? What's her house like? You meet any famous people yet?"

It's way too fucking early for this. "Look, Shayla, you know I love you, but I just woke up. Can we save the interrogation for another time?" Preferably never.

"Okay, okay, I can see the fame has already gone to your head. No time for the little people anymore."

"Yeah, yeah. Stay out of trouble, Shay."

"Same goes for you, big brother. Oh, wait! Can you do me a favor? Pretty please with rainbow flavored whiskey on top."

"What the hell is rainbow flavored whiskey? You know what, never mind. What's the favor?"

"Can you take a picture of her closet for me?" *Why the fuck would she want a picture of her closet?*

"No, I'm not doing that."

"Oh, come on. She wouldn't care. We're pretty much best friends now and she stole my brother, so she owes me."

"She didn't steal me. She hired me, and I'm not doing that so just forget it." I turn around and catch a glimpse of Sky who is now fixing her sleep disheveled hair by pulling it up into a ponytail. Even just waking up, her face free of makeup and with messy hair, she is still the most beautiful person I've ever seen. "Seriously, stay out of trouble. If Mason gives you any more shit, you tell me or Dad, you got me?"

"Just one picture of her closet, one that shows the most shoes. Come on, just ask her, Liam. She will understand. It's totally a girl thing."

She just dodged me. I don't like that. Not one fucking bit. "Shayla, did you hear me? Is Mason giving you trouble? You would tell me, right?"

"Yes, I heard you, Liam. And no, he isn't giving me trouble. You just worry about yourself, okay?" *Easier said than done.* "Love you, big brother."

"Me too."

"Don't forget to send me the picture."

"No. Bye, Shayla."

"You suck today."

"I know."

I put the phone in my pocket and lean back on the kitchen island, watching as Sky stretches and shakes her head, clearly trying to wake herself up, seemingly unconcerned that we ended up falling asleep together.

"What was that about?" she asks through a yawn.

Fuck, I don't even want to tell her. I'm too afraid the story that is now being spun will piss her off and she'll send me packing to avoid the problems I'm currently creating in her life, but I guess she will find out soon enough.

"That was my sister. Apparently we are all over the gossip sites."

She raises her brow at me and a small naughty smile creeps across her face. "Really? What are the stalkerazzi saying now?"

Not exactly the response I was expecting. "They're saying that your new boyfriend, meaning me apparently, has anger issues. I guess because of the airport incident." Sky jumps over the back of the couch and makes her way over to the kitchen, hopping her cute ass right up onto the counter so she is sitting right next to where I'm standing.

"Hmmm." She shrugs her shoulders nonchalantly.

"Hmmm? What does hmmm mean? Aren't you pissed?" I ask, moving myself so I'm directly in front of her, my arms bracing the counter on either side of her. She still seems so much smaller than me. Tiny, delicate, easy to break. I know Sky's not as fragile as she seems, but that still does nothing to ease that protective instinct that continues to rise the more I am around her.

"Why would I be pissed?"

"They're calling me your boyfriend and they have video of me shoving a guy. I don't want to ruin your reputation here, Sky."

Sweet, unexpected laughter fills the room. Definitely not the reaction I was expecting. "Liam, I trashed my reputation a while ago, and as far as fake boyfriends go, I think I kind of lucked out with you. It could have been much worse. Although I did always sort of picture Colin Farrell filling that role, but I suppose you'll do."

"Colin Farrell? Really?" *Fuck Colin Farrell.*

"What can I say, I have a thing for Irish boys." She winks at me and starts banging the heels of her feet against the counter while sporting a mischievous grin. I want to fucking kiss her. Grab her face and kiss that flirty teasing look right off it.

"I'm hungry," she announces. "I can't believe it's ten in the morning. I never sleep in this late. You want to get some breakfast?"

Ten in the morning? I don't think I've slept in this long in fucking ever.

"Sure, I could eat. We should probably change first, get cleaned up." I give her barely there shorts and tank top a once-over. Her cold kitchen floor must have chilled her too because right now her nipples are poking the fabric of her shirt, just begging me to put my mouth on them.

"I think I'm good to go now. It is L.A. in July. It'll be hot and muggy outside, so the less clothes the better as I always say. Keep my glowing reputation intact," she jokes. I know she's fucking with me and it's endearing, really, but I'm hungry as hell and I don't want to play this game with her so I wrap my arms around her waist, picking her up off the counter and throwing her over my shoulder.

"Liam! Put me down, dammit!" She's shrieking and laughing while she tries to wiggle her body out of my grasp.

I hold on tight, making my way up the stairs, and to the bedroom. "I'm taking you to your room to change because we both know you won't step out of this house in what you're wearing. Then we'll get some breakfast." Kicking her bedroom door open with my foot, I step over to her bed and throw her on top of it. Sky looks sinful on top of the white covers—sinfully pissed off. I wrap my hand around the back of her neck and place a rough kiss on top of her head. I'm not sure why, I just fucking wanted to.

"Change and meet me downstairs. Maybe wear something that brings out the blue in your eyes."

"You know, a please would go a long way. Manhandling is not necessary," she pouts, crossing her arms over her chest.

"Probably true." But it's not as much fun.

"You are also kind of an ass."

"Definitely true, baby," I tell her as I walk out and close the bedroom door behind me. But like a sucker, I just stand outside it, my arms braced against the door jamb. As soon as I hear the shower turn on though, I back away because the thought of her naked and wet is just a little too much to handle.

∿⊶⊰⊙⊱⊷∿

"Skylar, you done up there yet? I'm starving, woman!" I've been sitting on the bottom step in her solarium for the last ten minutes, waiting for her to finish getting ready. It took me ten fucking minutes, and I get that women take longer, but she's naturally beautiful so really Sky should be able to shower, throw some fucking clothes on, and be done with it.

"I'm coming, slugger. Calm down."

I stand up and turn around, watching as Sky skips down the stairs, taking two at a time, and I could not be more fucking thrilled that she's decided to wear a short green summery dress that makes the blue in her eyes stand out against her sun-kissed skin and auburn hair. Not to mention, prop her tits up in the most perfect way possible. I almost smile at the fact she listened to me. *Almost.*

"You look beautiful," I compliment, placing my hand under the fall of her hair and around her neck, giving her a quick kiss on the cheek.

"Thanks. Thank you. I mean, it's just breakfast, I know, but I'm kind of a dress girl. Not that I don't like pants or anything, I definitely like the pants you're wearing," she nervously states, tucking her hair behind her ears.

Okay, now I'm smiling. "Did you call your driver to come pick us up already?" I release my hold on her neck. It seems to make her a little anxious, and as much as I love when Sky gets flustered around me, I would really love to move this along so I can have breakfast.

"No. Why would I call my driver? I have you, don't I? You can drive us."

"I didn't realize you have your own car. I figured you just had people."

"I do have people, but I also have cars. Two in fact. It is L.A. Everyone drives at some point." A grin grows on her face, one that is telling me she has a secret she can't wait to tell me all about. "Come on. Let's go to the garage and I'll let you pick which one we take."

Grabbing my hand, she pulls me through the foyer and to a door that I'm assuming leads to the garage. How we managed to avoid the garage during the tour I have no idea. I didn't even think to ask where this door led. The second she flicks the light on, I realize why she was acting so excited.

"Holy fuck, Sky. These aren't cars, they're works of art." I want to live in her garage. I will move all my shit from the pool house right into this space and sleep on the cold concrete of the garage floor just to be closer to these cars. The one nearest to me is a sleek black Lotus Exige Roadster, a car I've never actually seen in person and now I'm so close that I can see my reflection in the pristinely clean doors. And as if the Lotus wasn't impressive enough, parked right next to it is a mint condition midnight blue '68 Mustang Fastback. This girl has a fucking Fastback.

"You approve?"

Sky's leaning back on the Lotus as if she is just aching to be my prey, waiting for me to push her onto the hood and bury myself balls deep inside of her, marking this flawless vehicle with the imprint of her even more perfect ass. I scrub my hand over my face just to try and get that image out of my head. "I most definitely approve," I assure her. "I can't believe you have a Fastback, and in perfect condition like this. Shit, my dad is going to fucking love you."

She pushes off the Lotus and saunters over to the hook on the wall holding the keys and snatches them. "Mustang it is, then. It's my favorite too. I saw Steve McQueen in *Bullitt* when I was fifteen and I thought he was just so damn sexy. The way he handled that car gave me chills." She must really mean that because a slight shiver runs through her body. "So when I turned sixteen, I bought one. I bought the Exige last year. I was feeling a bit dangerous and daring when I bought her. Here." Sky tosses the keys to me and I catch them with ease as she makes her way over to the Mustang. Daring and dangerous for me usually ends in blood and pain. Apparently for her it ends in buying cars worth more than a hundred grand. I like her way better.

"I'm a *Bullitt* fan too, only not for the same weird reasons that you are." I walk over and open the passenger side door to let her in.

Grabbing the top of the open door, she narrows her eyes at me. "Oh yeah, and why were you into the movie?"

"For the fucking car, baby."

"And how is that less weird than why I was into the movie?"

"You were underage and clearly had an unhealthy obsession with an older man, who's dead by the way. It's fucking weird."

"First off, I was not obsessed, and every girl has lusted over an older man at some point in her life. Second off—"

"Second of all, you mean."

"Yes, ass. Second of all, it's a lot less *weird* to obsess over a person than an inanimate object. Like, say, a car." Sky taps the top of my nose with her index finger before sliding herself gracefully into the seat.

I shake my head as I shut the door then walk around the front of the car to the driver's side. There's a difference between obsession and appreciation; I am *not* obsessed.

Sky pushes a button and the garage door starts to lift up just as I open my door and get in. I ache so bad to get this car started that the key is in the ignition before my ass even hits the seat. The first thing I hear is the treble of the exhaust roaring to life. I don't shut my door yet; I just sit back in my seat and tap at the gas pedal so I can listen to the engine wake up.

"You know the '67-'68 Mustangs were the first Mustangs to incorporate the V-8 into their mechanical design," I tell her, gripping the steering wheel as I take it all in: the smell of the leather, the sound of the engine, and the way it vibrates the entire interior of the car just from its power.

I could die here happily.

The sound of Sky's coughing grabs my attention. She's staring at me, hands covering her mouth, obviously stifling laughter.

"What?" I ask her. Shit, she's making me feel self-conscious all of a sudden. I think that's what this feeling is anyway. Her hands move away from her face and she is sporting a full-blown smile. "What's up, Sky? Why are you looking at me like that?" I almost check my face in the rearview mirror to see if something's on it.

"Nothing. It's just, you've had a smile attached to your face for," she pauses, making a point to look at her left wrist as if she is checking the time; she isn't even wearing a damn watch, "over twenty seconds now. You look like a little boy who just got his favorite Autobot for Christmas."

Shit. She's right. My face almost hurts from it.

"Sky, you know how it turns me on when you talk Transformers to me."

"Liam O' Connor, was that a joke you just made? Would you like me to give you and the car some alone time before we head out for breakfast?"

That idea actually doesn't sound too bad, but when I see her dress hike up slightly on her thigh as she fakes an attempt to get out of her car, I pull my shit together.

"Maybe later. Right now I just need to get some food, so tell me where I should go."

Sky recites the directions to some restaurant called The Regal—which apparently is her go-to place because they serve fresh made macarons daily, and I shut my car door and shift into drive.

"Should only take us ten minutes to get there," she tells me as I'm pulling out of her driveway. There seems to be no photographers outside her gate which fucking elates me. Maybe today won't be as chaotically distressing as yesterday.

"Sounds good. So, you bought this car when you were sixteen? Must have made you quite the popular girl in school." Fuck, my brother had a used '69 Z28 Camaro with a bent bumper and chipped paint when we were in high school and he was constantly getting laid because of it. And now I'm hoping the same doesn't go for girls in school because I really don't want to picture the line of guys ready to fuck Skylar, even without this car.

"Well, it might have if I had gone to high school."

"You didn't go to high school?"

"Nope." She pops the P and shrugs her shoulders, looking a little uncomfortable, picking at the bandage on her hand, reminding me that I should probably check her wound again when we get back. "Carl thought it would be better if I just used tutors. That way I would be available to work more. So I basically was homeschooled, well, more like trailer-schooled. The tutors would come to my trailer on and off during whatever free time or breaks I had. So when I wasn't working, I was in school all by myself. I begged him a few times to let me take some classes in a private school, to cut back on work so I had time, but he would just get angry and accuse me of being lazy."

The hatred that I have for Carl is beginning to fester; it's a poison that's starting to contaminate and pollute my insides, and eventually I won't be able to stop it from spreading. I know what it's like to miss out on some of the fun my friends were having due to my training schedule, but I still got to go to school. My dad made sure I was able to maintain some sort of social life so that I had a semblance of normality. My happiest memories were from school; I had no problem making friends back then, and I had Ali and my brother who was only two years older than me.

For all the hard work I put in, my dad made sure I was paid back with love and affection, and he cut me a motherfucking break. And he *never* degraded me. The thought that Carl has done worse to her has been fucking eating at me since yesterday; she didn't want to talk about it then but now seems like the perfect time to bring it up.

"Does Carl do that a lot?" I refuse to call him her dad because from what I've seen and heard of him so far, he doesn't deserve the title.

"Do what?"

"Get angry and fucking belittle you. I know you know this shit isn't right, Skylar. You know that, don't you? The way he was yesterday…" My hands are choking the steering wheel at this point, aching to wrap around his throat as I remember the whole scene. "Has he done anything worse than what I've already seen?"

"Why are we talking about this right now?"

"Because it needs to be fucking talked about and you didn't want to talk about it yesterday, so I didn't pressure you, but you're crazy if you think I'm going to let that shit go."

"*Don't* call me crazy." Her face snaps toward mine, the blue eyes I had admired before now burning a hole through me.

"Don't take it so literally." In retrospect, the crazy comment may have been a dick move given what she told me about her mom, but I don't really do retrospect. "Listen, Carl looked like he would have hit you if I hadn't been fucking standing there. Actually, he looked like he didn't give a shit if I was standing there or not, which I have to tell you, Sky, is really fucking disconcerting."

"He wouldn't," she mumbles so quietly that I am less than convinced.

"What's that? Speak up, Skylar."

"Liam, I appreciate your concern but this is family business, not your business."

Luckily we've stopped at a red light because I want to look at her when I say what I'm about to. "Fucking. Bullshit." My brusque tone causes her to look right at me in shock. She's probably not used to people that work for her talking to her this way, but I don't really fucking care because she needs to listen. "I thought we cleared this up yesterday, but since you seem to have forgotten, let me remind you. You hired me to protect you, so until you fire me I don't give a flying fuck if it's your father, a fan, or your goddamn priest. If they are a threat to you, I need to know."

She silently assesses me for a few seconds, her eyes softening the way they do whenever it seems like she's receiving a compliment for the first time. "Well, Carl, won't be much of anything to me anymore."

"What does that mean?"

"It means I plan on firing him. I've actually been planning on it for a few months. I was just waiting until I got back to do it. I also wasn't a hundred percent on the idea, but after yesterday...well he sealed his fate."

I know men like Carl, and there is no way his anger just died out the moment they left her house. He took it out on her in some way. I fucking know it. "Did anything else happen yesterday that I should know about?"

"No. Unless you count that really naughty dream I had about you last night."

"Nice try, sweetheart, but I'm not that easily distracted." But my dick is, so I really hope she doesn't start going into details. Or maybe I do. *Fuck.* I wonder just how naughty we are talking here.

She pulls her bottom lip into her mouth and makes it a point to slowly check me out from head to toe, her gaze becoming more heated the second I shift gears. I know that look. That is the same look I give a chick when I'm wondering what she looks like completely naked and coming on my dick. Now she really has me wondering where the hell I can pull this car over in the middle of a busy L.A. street so I can fuck her. That is, until she starts to break out into laughter.

"You're fucking with me, aren't you?"

"It was just so easy."

"Oh, you are so going to pay for that." I want to be more pissed, but hearing her laughter is a next-level endorphin shooting through my veins, like I've got an IV line open just for her and every smile is one big push.

"Maybe later, slugger, but right now just make a left into that parking lot," she says, pointing over to a small pink stucco building, almost tucked away, two much larger more industrial buildings on either side of it dwarfing it in size. The Regal's lit up vintage sign reminds me of those old diners I've seen in fifties movies, the ones where James Dean would be leaning over a pool table.

By the look of the parking lot, the place isn't that full, which is kind of surprising. Old diners like this tend to have a packed house in Seattle. But my guess is this is why Sky chooses this spot to eat. It's somewhat secluded and absent of any large crowds, and more importantly, there doesn't seem to be any paparazzi in sight.

I'm out of the car and already to the passenger side door before she barely has her seatbelt off, probably because she spent an extra twenty seconds checking her reflection in the visor mirror primping and fixing her hair. I don't know why girls feel the need to do that shit, it's not like we drove through a tornado. Sky looks just as beautiful as she did ten fucking minutes ago.

I whip open her door and grab her hand to pull her out, then back her up against the door, using her body to shut it. She gasps my name, her breaths frantic as I push my hips further into hers, my arms braced tightly on the roof of the car. I bend my head so my lips are a whisper away from her ear. "You shouldn't tease me like that unless you're willing to deal with the consequences. And, baby"—I know the second she feels my hard cock press into her stomach because her eyes widen just a little more—"don't think that little stunt has me forgetting about Carl, either. You don't want to go into details right now, fine. But when you're ready to fire him, you better make sure you do it on the fucking phone or bring me with you. You got me?"

Her hands grab at my waist hesitantly and I don't know if it's because she wants to push me away or pull me closer, but I do know she hasn't answered the damn question. She won't even meet my eyes, and I really don't like being ignored.

"Sky." My impatience has me growling her name, and everything about being this close to her has me in some kind of fucking sensory overload—her scent and her warmth and the small whimper she lets loose as my lip grazes the skin of her neck. The next thing I know I'm biting the soft lobe of her ear and sucking it into my mouth, and I'm not even being fucking gentle about it.

Because I want her to answer me. Obey me. Fucking submit to me. Too many times over the last few days she has tried to tempt me. Tease and torture me. Fucking top me. I know what she's doing because I've been doing the same damn thing. Only with her it's like she thinks it's a game. For me, I fucking *need* the control.

"Do You. Get. Me?"

"Ye-yes."

She's stuttering. Perfect. Stuttering I can work with.

CHAPTER 13

LIAM

"I can't believe you're eating cookies for breakfast, Sky," I chastise while she grabs another brightly colored pastel cookie off the plate that sits directly in front of her.

"These are not just cookies, they are macarons. There's a difference. And why not? People eat donuts for breakfast and that's just cake with a different costume. Plus I probably wouldn't be eating as many cookies if someone didn't eat half of my breakfast."

I shrug my shoulders and smile at her. "I was still hungry."

Pointing at me almost accusatorily she says, "You should have ordered something other than the Jogger's Breakfast then."

"Well, I was too fucking hungry to pay attention to the menu. I'm a runner. The title of the breakfast implied it would be something a runner would eat. Like eggs, bacon, steak, some fucking carbs. Not egg whites and fruity yogurt. If I ate that and tried running five miles I would pass the fuck out before I hit mile three."

This is how the last three hours have been. Small talk and joking around with one another. I hadn't even realized how long we had been here until a half hour ago when I noticed they changed out the breakfast menus for the lunch ones, and the crowd on the outside patio where we are sitting started to grow. I can't remember the last time I ever lost track of time. The previous three years have been nothing but suffering the minutes, the hours, the days as they were constantly plagued with the debris of everything I'd lost. There has never been any reprieve, not even during sleep when the nightmares plague me.

"Honestly, I never order that much food for breakfast. I knew you were going to regret what you ordered, so I got the special so you would actually have something to eat," she says, winking at me.

"Why didn't you just tell me to order something else if you knew?"

"Because I figured it would be more fun to see the look on your face after they set it down in front of you." She smiles before running her tongue around the edge of the cookie, trying to catch the crumbs in her mouth.

Jesus. I can tell she's completely unaware of what she's doing because her attention seems to be solely on that cookie. It only takes her two bites to finish it and she makes sure to suck her fingers clean before she grabs for another. I reach my hand under the table and adjust my pants slightly to give my dick a little room. She actually has me squirming in my seat.

"So, do you have any other plans for the day, sweetheart? Aside from tongue fucking those cookies right in front of me, I mean?"

Her eyes widen slightly right before she rolls them at me. "That was hardly me tongue fucking. Trust me. I like to use a lot more tongue than that."

I shake my head at her, having no idea what to say to that. I really don't want to give her a reaction; she's trying to punish me for earlier at the car, I know it.

She finishes her last macaron and brushes her hands together. "I actually need to do some shopping today. I have a few dresses I need to get for some events I'm supposed to go to next month."

"Sounds like torture." I fucking hate shopping.

"Well, you are being paid well for the torture, so suck it up, slugger," she says before taking a sip of her iced tea through the straw she has all but massacred with her teeth, chewing on it throughout breakfast. I can't believe she can even suck anything through it at this point.

And now she has me cringing at the reminder I'm even being paid to do this. The idea of it has yet to sit right with me. Before I even have a chance to shoot some kind of smartass response her way, I see her whole body tense as she looks toward the restaurant door leading to the patio, scoots down in her chair, and says, "Oh shit."

"What?" I quickly turn my head to see what the fuck suddenly has her on edge. I clock his ass immediately. I know who the fuck this is. Cassiel Logue. And I find it a little more than convenient that his ass happens to show up at this place at exactly the same time Sky happens to be here. He doesn't have that stereotypical rock star look to him. His lack of ink, blond hair, and his unique singing voice has earned him the title 'Angel of Rock'.

His behavior is far from angelic though. I know this because I Googled the motherfucker the second I got done unpacking last night. I may have promised Sky I wouldn't Google her, but I never said anything about Cassiel, and hearing his name fifty fucking times yesterday made me think I should probably brush up on the asshole. For work purposes. The guy is into everything: drugs, booze, women, and he has an arrest record spanning from public intoxication to petty theft to assault. He puts the version of me two years ago to shame. And for some reason, Sky was with this dick. Photographed with him stumbling out of clubs and bars, but their relationship status never seemed to be clear in any of the shit I read, and he was pictured with many other women during that same period.

And this dick has the balls to stride right over to our table, throw an arm around Skylar, and kiss her on the cheek.

"Hey there, Speedy, you're a sight for sore eyes," he says, pulling out an empty chair from our table as if someone invited him to sit here and join us.

"You know I hate when you call me that, Cass." She moves her body away from him, scooting as far into her chair as she can manage. It is clear as fucking day she doesn't want him touching her, but she still smiles genuinely like she is happy to see him. I can't get a read on this situation and it's starting to piss me off.

"Can I help you?" I know he saw me the second he stepped up to the table. I'm hard to fucking miss. He wants to play some game with me, but I don't need to stake my claim or play 'who has the bigger dick.' I already know. Sky moves into my touch, never away from it; she craves it. And I honestly don't give two fucks about his dick size.

"Liam, this is Cassiel. Cass, this is Liam, my new bodyguard." The introduction could not seem more forced and unwanted, as if she could have gone her whole life without the two of us ever meeting.

"Yeah. Saw you two all over the gossip sites this morning. Hey, bro." He gives me a chin lift then turns his attention back to Sky.

"I'm not your fucking bro." My knee is bouncing anxiously, spiked with the adrenaline that is spearing through me as he just sits there calm as ever. This ass has been running his mouth all about their sex life, and he has the balls to walk up to her and talk and touch her like he did nothing fucking wrong and she isn't even calling him out on it.

"Ok then," he says, essentially brushing me off with a roll of his eyes. "So, Speedy, I tried calling you but your number changed again. Can't believe you didn't give me your new one. Breakin' my heart, dar-lin'. Luckily I happened to see the 'Stang sitting in the parking lot, so I decided I would just come see you."

'Stang? What a douchebag. "Oh yeah? And where did you happen to see her 'Stang from? I didn't see any stalker bushes out front."

He just smirks at me. "From my condo, *bodyguard*."

I'm going to hit him.

"He lives across the street, Liam. It's how I found out about this place. Sorry I didn't give you my new number, Cass, it just slipped my mind." She places her hand on his arm and rubs him slightly as if to assure him. It fucking irritates me that she doesn't seem to mind him being here. "Anyway, what's up? Did you need something?"

"I just wanted to tell you the boys and I have a show coming up next Friday at the Viper Room, and then we're throwing a welcome home party at Club 7 now that the tour is over. I figured since you're back we could make it a kind of joint party. Celebrate our homecoming with a bang like we used too. Wouldn't be the same without you, Speedy," he says as he reaches out and grabs a lock of her hair, tugging at it and causing her to back away again.

Motherfucking asshole. "Are you fucking deaf, Logue?"

Both their gazes shoot over to me in surprise. Where just seconds ago I was on edge, now I've adapted a more casual stance. My laid-back demeanor at the moment is the complete opposite of the storm raging inside me. But I want to observe before I attack. It was a skill I used to be very familiar with, patience and attention to detail before I went on the offensive. Like, for example, the way he sits straighter in his chair now, his hands clenched at his sides, the right more than the left, his jaw tight and breath short, his eyes narrowed right fucking at me. He gets rattled quick, which means if he comes at me, he will come hard and erratic. He would go for my face first because he is cocky enough to think he can take me out with one punch. The second he goes to hit me, he'll leave the right side of his body open which is where I could land one hit. Hard. Directly into his kidney. I could have Cassiel Logue pissing blood for a week and barely break a sweat.

"Excuse me?" He keeps his tone low and angry, almost like he is trying to growl at me as if that would scare me. I'm shaking in my boots.

"I said. Are. You. Fucking. Deaf? Sky just told you she hates when you call her Speedy. I know this because I can hear." Cassiel looks over at Sky, who is looking at me. Shock registers on her face, but there is something else. Something almost appreciative. As if it's rare that any-one would stand up for her.

"*Sky*, is it?" he sneers, still looking at her.

"Look at me, don't look at her. I'm the one talking to you."

His eyes meet mine, and I can tell he is close to snapping.

"What the hell is your problem, dude?"

"My *problem* is I'm not your bro, I'm not your dude, and the lady asked you not to call her that name, so show some *fucking* respect."

The small smile I see from Sky just now is worth any trouble that is about to come my way. But as much as my instinct is telling me to end him here and now, I actually have the forethought to look around and see the people surrounding us. The audience. Any outburst from me will affect Sky, and I don't want that. But then he makes the mistake of opening his mouth with a smarmy fucking grin plastered to his face.

"Lady, huh? I take it you haven't know Skylar Barrett that long. Liam, is it? I think she lost that lady status a while ago. Right, Speedy?"

Before I even have time to register and react to what he just spewed from his mouth, Sky is out of her seat looking pissed as fuck.

"Cass, you need to leave. You are not allowed to disrespect me or Liam that way."

Cassiel slides his chair back and stands up. I follow suit because I'm fucking ready now. My patience is gone.

"Sorry, Skylar. That was rude of me. I've got to get going anyway. Please come Friday. It won't be the same without you. I need you there." His manipulative apology almost seems sincere. But I know better.

"I'll think about it, okay?" This is just fucking perfect. What is between these two? She can think about it all she wants. She isn't going anywhere with him.

"Thanks, Spee—Skylar. Don't forget to send me your new number." He gives her a quick peck on the cheek then looks over at me and smirks. "Stand down, bodyguard."

Cassiel Logue is a self-righteous, arrogant fucking bitch, and I can think of no greater pleasure than wiping that smirk off his fucking bitch face, but as I make a move toward him, Sky shakes her head. My teeth clench at having to stand down as he walks out the front door, but as I glare at Skylar I notice her breathing becoming labored. *Shit.* She's hyperventilating. Unshed tears begin to form as she tries to shakily find her way back down to her chair.

"Sky, what's wrong? Jesus, are you okay?" I run over to steady her in my arms before she collapses.

"I-I'm fine," she stutters through shortened breaths. "I'm just...I'm just humiliated. I'm so sorry, Liam."

"Why are you sorry? You have no reason to apologize for that asshole." I pull her into me, feeling her tears wet my shirt. Why the hell is she apologizing to me? Cradling her head as she cries into my chest, I look around and notice people are beginning to stare. I need to get her the hell out of here. "Come on. Let's go to the car, okay?"

Taking more than enough money out of my wallet, I throw it onto the table and lead her toward the parking lot, tucking her into the crook of my arm so few people can see her cry as possible. As soon as we reach the car, I open the passenger door and set her gently down on the seat. Tears still fall from her eyes, and I want nothing more than to stop them. They cause an ache in my chest and I don't fucking like it.

"Sky, *look* at me," I say, cupping my hands around her face. She complies, her red teary eyes locking with mine. "You have to stop crying sweetheart. If you don't I'm going to get fucking angry and ruin Logue's face. Then what will the tabloids say about your fake boyfriend?" I say, working for that gorgeous smile. She does one better and laughs through her tears.

"God, I am being so ridiculous, aren't I? I just..." Skylar buries her face in her hands.

"You just what, Sky?" I say, pulling her hands from her face.

"I just don't want you to see me that way. The way Cass sees me, the way my own father portrays me, the way the tabloids paint me, even Noah. I mean, I know Noah was joking with the whole sexcapades comment, but I don't want you to think I'm some kind of... ignorant slut."

"*Stop* talking, Skylar." I take a deep breath and try calming myself before I end up snapping at her again. "I would *never* think that about you. I don't give a shit what anybody says about you, especially assholes like Logue and your father who, no offense, happens to be the biggest fucking prick I've ever met. You are intelligent and beautiful and incredibly strong. That is how I see you," I say, wiping the tears from her cheeks with my thumbs.

Time seems to stand still as I wait for her to say something. *Anything.* But there she goes, yet again, staring at me curiously like it's the first compliment she's ever received. Her face moves closer to mine, and I can now feel her hot frantic breath on my lips. My hands slide from her cheeks to her neck where I can feel her pulse thumping wildly through my fingers. My skin, my blood, every fucking fiber of my being burns with a raw primal desire for her.

Without warning, Skylar closes the small space between us and presses her soft lips to mine so passionately that it almost knocks me back from the door of the car and onto the pavement.

Fucking hell. I pull back in shock because I was not fucking expecting that, and everything about this seems wrong—the wrong time and definitely the wrong place. The car is in a busy parking lot on the side of The Regal, in full view of the public; anyone can see us. Definitely not how I pictured our first kiss.

First kiss? What the fuck. I'm a man not a pre-teen girl. After a kiss like that though, one thing is clear.

I need more.

I launch myself into the car, my lips crashing into hers as I reach back to pull the passenger door closed. She accommodates my brash movement by working her way backwards into the driver's seat. Her legs fall open, allowing me to press my body into hers, and cause her dress to hike just enough that I can see the small strap from her lacy pink thong.

Fuck me.

Not being able to get enough of her mouth as quickly as I fucking need it, I devour and stroke her with my tongue then bite her lower lip and suck it into my mouth. *Hard.* Maybe too hard because I get a faint taste of blood on my tongue. I'm too unrestrained. Like a fucking untamed animal starved for his next meal, and god she tastes as good as she smells—sweet like those damn macarons she was eating. Skylar pulls her mouth from mine, panting and pulling air into her lungs but I don't stop. I can't stop.

I lick and bite and suck my way down her throat as my hand runs up her soft bare thigh, pushing her dress even higher. I hook my fingers into the side of her thong, preparing to shred it from her body. I need to slow down. She can't possibly want this, want me. Not like this.

"God Liam, *please.*"

I guess I'm wrong because she is fucking begging me now. *Shit* I don't think I've ever been this hard in my life. My dick is pushing so painfully against my zipper I wouldn't be surprised if it bust my pants open.

My cock is a genius. When I grind my hips into her looking for some kind of friction, she moans as one hand pulls at my hair and the other reaches back and slams against the now foggy window.

Her hips push up into mine, matching my frenzied pace. I can feel the heat coming off her pussy and it fucking brands me. My lips find their way back to hers, and we're kissing and grinding as the world around us disappears. Skylar pulls me closer with her hands around my neck, practically whimpering into my mouth each time I thrust my hips into her.

"Sky, you are so fucking perfect."

I don't even realize the words I'm saying to her because I'm so drunk off her soft skin and full lips, her scent. Everything about her is overriding the logical part of my brain, the part that is telling me to stop.

To pull back.

Not here.

But when Skylar's fingers move under my t-shirt and she clumsily tries to take it off, my dick goes back to doing the thinking. I break free from her mouth helping to pull the shirt over my head, then I toss it onto the floor, hastily returning to her lips. Her soft hands caress my chest and abs, gently stroking each scar she comes across, until her fingers find their way to the waistband of my jeans. I'm going to come way too fucking soon if we don't slow the hell down.

My lips move back up her neck, kissing the curve of her throat as she moves her hands up through my hair, willing me to keep going. Voices outside catch my attention, a few errant catcalls and whistles—people know what is going on in the vehicle. Luckily the windows are so fogged up that no one can see us. The last thing Skylar needs is to be caught making out with me in a parking lot, and if I don't stop this now it won't be long until it passes the making out stage right into the me shoving my dick into her pussy stage.

Moving up to her ear, I lick the outside rim. "Skylar, we need to stop," I whisper, my hips still thrusting, my fingers pulling at the lace edge of her panties. *Don't* pull. *Don't* rip. Remove your hand from her panties, asshole.

With a strength I didn't know I possessed, I remove my hands from the lace and bring it shakily up to brush the hair away from her face. I know I'm less than convincing in my attempt to derail this situation we seem to have worked our way into.

"I know," she says, her eyes hooded as I bring my face back up to hers while she kisses and playfully nips at my lower lip.

"Christ you are so damn intoxicating," I swear under my breath as my head falls into her chest.

She runs her fingers through my hair while we both try to catch our breath and regain some composure.

How can she be this gentle with me after I practically mauled her in her car?

"I don't think I did a very good job convincing you I'm not a slut."

"What the fuck, Skylar!" I sit up angrily and grab my shirt off the car floor, pulling it over my head. "I don't like it when you talk about yourself that way, even if you are joking." I grab her chin and place a deep kiss on her lips so that she really fucking gets what I'm telling her.

"Crap! I can't believe I did that. I just couldn't hold back anymore," she says, hiding her face in her damn hands. I fucking hate that she hides from me.

"What did I tell you about hiding your face from me, Skylar?" I refuse to pull her hands away this time. I want her to do it.

"Sorry." She removes her hands from her face.

"What do you mean you couldn't hold back anymore?" I ask, but she won't look at me, her hands grasping the steering wheel so tight her knuckles are turning white. "Sky. What did you mean by that?"

After a few seconds of torturous silence, she finally speaks. "There's something here, right? Between us? I'm not-I'm not imaging this, am I? When I first saw you I felt it, and every time you touch me, it's like something...I don't know. Maybe I'm wrong, I know I mix stuff up in my head sometimes and don't always see things how they are. Crap I'm not explaining myself right..." She trails off, trying to describe something so simple.

I stroke her hand and pull her fingers off the steering wheel one by one, then I bring it to my chest, placing it over my erratic heart, which is quite telling of my feelings for her at the moment because what I really want to do is place it on my cock. "You're saying you're attracted to me. I get it, Sky, and yeah I'm fucking attracted to you too. And before you start overthinking things in that pretty little head of yours, no I don't just mean physically attracted." *My dick does, but I don't.* "But Sky, I work for you. I practically live with you right now."

"Right, I know." She quickly pulls her hand from my chest. "I'm so stupid. I should never have kissed you. It's like sexual harassment or assault or something. I'm so sorry. Can we just forget this happened? We can go back to—"

I slap my palm over her mouth to shut her up for a second because no way in hell am I going to let her ramble on and talk herself out of this, and I really fucking *hate* when she calls herself stupid. "Sky, calm down. Stop talking and listen. You're misunderstanding me. Especially if you think I could just forget this happened. Now, if I take my hand off your mouth, do you think you can stay quiet long enough to let me finish talking?"

CHAPTER 14

Skylar

I went from being humiliated to hyperventilating to essentially attacking Liam in the front seat of my car. In a public parking lot no less. All in under ten minutes. That has to be an emotional rollercoaster record for me. Quite frankly, I'm a little worried he can see how crazy I am, and I would be more concerned about it except for the fact that he has his hand over my mouth right now, physically shushing me, which is actually rather obnoxious and *really* annoying.

"Nod your head if you understand me, sweetheart."

I wrap my hand around his wrist and pull his hand away from my face. "I understand that if you ever put your hand over my mouth to quiet me again I will bite off one of your fingers." I smile sweetly.

"There's my little hellcat," he says right before he winks at me, causing me to forget why I'm even irritated in the first place. I'm kind of starting to loathe that he has this kind of pull over me. "Now, let's talk about what just happened."

I'm literally biting my tongue, making sure I don't spew word vomit all over him again because I'm pretty sure saying, 'you mean that whole totally mind blowing dry hump session where I almost came before you even got your pants off' is not what he wants to talk about.

"Okay." See, that was much more concise.

"What do you want from me in this, Sky?"

"What do you mean?"

"What I mean is, am I just some quick itch you want to scratch? You want to fuck me whenever you're in need of a fix, or are you looking for something more than that?"

If I hadn't been looking in those totally hypnotic gray eyes of his when he asked that completely crass question, I would have thought he was just trying to insult me. But I can tell he honestly wants to know. It seems unfair that he is asking me that question while rubbing his fingers against my bare thigh, though. Is he trying to confuse me?

"Well, what do you want from me?" I ask.

His palm stills on my leg and he applies a slight amount of pressure. "Don't do that. I asked you what *you* wanted."

I absentmindedly start tracing his knuckles lightly with my fingers thinking only one thing. "What if I answer wrong? Then you won't want to be around me anymore." I can tell by the pitying look on his face that I just said that out loud. *Shit, shit, shit.*

"Christ, Skylar. I'm not looking for a way out here. I just want to set some ground rules. I've had *one* relationship in my life and it didn't end well. In fact, the ending was so fucking devastating that for years now I've just been sticking my dick in disposable pussy over and over, hoping it would just help me forget. I don't even know if I'm capable of anything deeper than sex anymore. It sounds messed up, I know, but I'm trying to be honest because if you tell me here and now that you are looking for more than a meaningless fuck, I'll try. For *you*, I will try. But any attempt I make will come with a whole lot of issues you would have to deal with, and I don't think you want or need that burden."

He's been in a relationship. That seems to be the only thing he said that is sticking with me. It's not that it's surprising; the surprising thing is that he has only had one and that one scarred him. And that one is one I would have to compete with. I want so badly to know more about what I'm up against, but I know if I ask he'll pull away or snap at me like last night. I know he won't hurt me, and knowing that makes me unafraid to ask the question, but one thing I've learned about Liam is that he comes with a *Proceed with Caution* stamp directly on his perfectly gorgeous face. So I have to pick the right time to start to wade into the already murky waters of relationships past, and this is not it.

But I have to say something.

"So, my options are a relationship that comes with some baggage, or to be disposable pussy. Aww." My hands fly to my cheeks. "It's like you're my real-life Prince Charming," I say, biting my lip.

"This isn't a joke, Sky." His tone is sullen as he grabs my wrist, wrapping his fingers around it. I'm sure he can feel my pulse start to quicken. "And I wouldn't call it baggage. You can get rid of baggage, remove it, unpack it, clean it up and make it disappear. I'm filth. I'll stain you. I'm rude, selfish, territorial, possessive. Fucking controlling. I have a quick trigger temper that is practically impossible to control. I'm a fuck-up on my best day. On my worst, I'm completely destructive."

"You can't stain something that's already dirty." The words come out in a whisper and I'm not sure if he even heard, but I wish that I hadn't said them in the first place.

"What?" he asks.

I roll down the window a bit, needing some fresh air and to clear the condensation off the windows. This is it. The perfect opening. The most appropriate time to tell him the parts of my life that I left out on the plane ride here. About my mother, about me. I could lay it all out for him so he can see that I'm not as pure and perfect as he seems to think I am. But his words from before keep repeating in my head. *"You are intelligent and beautiful and incredibly strong. That is how I see you..."*

I just want to be seen like that for a little while longer.

I take his hand and thread my fingers through his. "I guess what I'm trying to say is that I don't believe you are those things, and that even if you are, the good in you outweighs the bad, and well, I like you. A lot actually." Enough to let him destroy me just a little bit more.

"Sky, you don't know what you're—"

A flashing light from outside the car window grabs our attention, interrupting Liam and practically blinding me. I look out the now clear windows and see two people taking pictures with a camera aimed right at me. Looks like our time is up.

"*Motherfuckers.* Sky, when I get out, scoot over into the passenger seat."

"What? Why? I can drive us out of here. You don't have to go out there, Liam."

He throws the door open and exits the car before leaning his head back in. He's holding on to the door frame so tightly I'm afraid he might bend it. "Don't argue with me, just move over." His tone is low and demanding and sends shivers up my spine. There is obviously no use in arguing.

He slams the door and slowly walks around the front of the car while I scurry over into the passenger seat, careful not to give the paparazzi and growing crowd a free show of my ass. I see they are trying to fire off questions at me, but between being in the car and the sound of my heart thumping hard in my chest, I can't hear any of it.

With every step Liam takes closer to the people with cameras and the casual onlookers, his jaw clenches tighter and tighter. The muscles in his arm constrict the harder his fingers curl into his palm.

"Come on, Liam. Just get in the car," I quietly murmur. I'm trying to duck my head in my hands so they don't get a clear shot of me, but I can't take my eyes off of Liam. If he flips out I need to bring him back. I let out a breath when he reaches the driver's door and pulls it open.

"*Hey, Skylar, what were you two doing in the car? You into screwing in public now?*"

Okay, that question I definitely heard. Liam's eyes go dark and he bows his head so I can't see them anymore. His chest is heaving and his nostrils are flaring. I swear I'm seeing true anger manifest before me.

"*Skylar, we heard Cassiel Logue was here earlier. Are you with both guys?*"

"Liam. *Look* at me."

He does, but says nothing. The look on his face breaks me more than it scares me. The anguish, the hurt, the rage, I see it all pass through his features, almost as if it physically pains him to not go after the pricks asking the questions.

"Get in the car. I want to go home." I'm shocked I'm able to keep my voice steady, hiding any hurt or embarrassment I may be feeling because I know it will make him lose it. "Don't forget you work for me.

I'm telling you I want to leave. Take me home. *Now*."

I hate myself the moment I have to throw this job in his face, but it's the only thing I can think of to stop him from going after those assholes. Thank god it works. He all but launches himself into the car, slamming the door so hard that I'm surprised it didn't break my window. The engine roars to life, and before I can even blink he backs the car up and peels out of the parking lot, leaving the crowd behind.

"Liam." I place my hand gently on his arm, surprised by the heat coming off his skin. He quickly jerks away from my touch as if I've burned him instead of the other way around.

"*Don't*."

That's it. That's all he says. One word, a single command, and the weight of it is crushing me with its finality. The whole drive home I remain silent, somehow managing not to cry in front of him, but with each passing second I actually find myself wanting to fight with him. Fight for us. He will fight for me. We were getting somewhere before we had a damn audience, and then that moment was taken from us. I'm so fucking sick of having my life dictated and controlled and ruined by everyone. The paparazzi, the media, directors, my agent, my father.

By the time he pulls into my garage, shuts the car off, and all but stomps into the house, I've finally reached majorly pissed-off status. And it's about time. I'm not weak, I have a voice, and it's time I finally start speaking up.

With my resolve final to confront this head-on, I get out of the car and head into my house. I hear the loud thumping the minute I walk in and know exactly where he is. Taking the steps down to my gym two at a time, I stop the second I hit the last one and watch as he pounds the heavy bag mercilessly. No shirt. No gloves. No control.

"Liam," I call out to him as I walk further into the gym. He doesn't even spare me a glance, but I know he hears me because when I call out his name again I see the muscle in his jaw twitch. One thing I hate more than being shushed is being outright ignored. I'm starting to learn I deserve more, and how ironic that the one person who is starting to make me believe that is the one currently ignoring me.

I walk right up to the bag as it swings from his hits and grab hold of it, hugging the thing in an attempt to get it to still, so that he finally has to stop and listen to me. In retrospect, seeing as I'm now on my ass, that idea was probably not the smartest one I've ever had.

"What the fuck, Sky? Are you okay?" Liam rushes over to me, grabbing my elbows and lifting me off the floor.

"Aside from being a little embarrassed, yeah, I'm fine," I assure him, brushing my hands down my dress.

"Embarrassed?! *Jesus Christ.*" he barks out, his hold on my elbow tightening. "What the hell were you thinking? Don't *ever* get in front of a bag when someone is hitting it. You could have been seriously fucking hurt."

"Well, I know that now obviously."

"*Fuck.* Are you sure you're okay? Let me look at you." The concern in his voice softens my anger at him.

"Liam, I landed on my butt, you really want to take a look?" The slight twitch of his lips has me realizing how stupid that question was. "Never mind, don't answer that. I wouldn't have to go to such drastic measures to get your attention if you would have stopped to talk to me when I called your name."

Just like that, any trace of concern seems to disappear and he is back to being pissed off, and now so am I.

"I don't want to fucking talk to you right now," he says.

"Well, too bad. I want to finish what we were discussing in the car. About us."

"Skylar, there is no us. What happened in the car was a mistake. You were right. We need to forget it ever happened."

"That's bullshit."

"Excuse me?"

"You heard me. Less than half an hour ago you told me you would try. For *me*, you would try. Then we have a little run-in with the cock-block-arazzi and now you want to throw in the towel. I thought you had more balls than that, O'Connor. I also didn't figure you for a liar."

"Stop pushing me *baby*. I'm not in the fucking mood," he warns.

"No," I say, jabbing my finger into his hard chest. "Not until you tell me what the hell changed."

"You really don't want to know the answer to that. Now march your ass back up those stairs and get out of my face."

"*Don't* tell me what I want. I'm asking, aren't I? And I'm not leaving until you answer the question. I'm not scared of you, Liam, so stop trying to intimidate me."

"YOU SHOULD BE FUCKING SCARED!" he yells, and the sudden change in the volume of his voice causes me to jump, but not out of fear. Liam starts to crowd me, backing me up until I hit the wall behind me. He braces his hands on either side of my body and gets right in my face. I wait for the fear to settle in, like it does when I'm with Carl, but I feel nothing. In the deepest part of my soul, I know Liam would never hurt me, and that thought keeps me from breaking eye contact with him. Because I know the second I do he will think he's right, that I'm scared. "*You* should be fucking terrified," he says again. "Do you know what I wanted to do to those fuckers that were shoving a camera at your car? What I wanted to do to Logue? I wanted to *hurt* them. I *needed* to hurt them worse than they were hurting you. With every disgusting question they hurled your way I pictured breaking another bone. Legs. Arms. Hands. Nose. I wanted to see them bleed. Do you think those are the thoughts of a fucking sane man, Skylar?"

"But you didn't." I cup his face in my hands, but he jerks his head away, leaving my hands to fall back down. "You got in the car. Having those thoughts and actually acting on them are two very different things, Liam."

"I got in the car because you asked me to, and you know what? I fucking *hate* that I got in." His fist wraps around my hair, tugging slightly so that I'm even closer to his face than before. I'm panting now, my adrenaline spiking. With irritation, with lust. I can't decide if I want to slap him or kiss him. "You want to know something else, Sky? Part of me even hates you for asking me to."

"I don't believe you," I tell him with every ounce of conviction I possess.

A deep growl comes from his throat. That's the only warning I get before he crashes his lips to mine. His grip on my hair strengthens as he basically fucks my mouth. His tongue exploring my mouth like he has to taste every part of me, his teeth nipping at my lips; the sting a welcome addition to my pleasure. I grab his hips and pull him closer to me, close enough that I can feel his erection digging into my stomach. He moans into my mouth at the contact, puts his hands under my thighs, and lifts me so that my legs wrap around him, then slams me back against the wall.

"*Fuck,*" he groans, ripping his mouth away from mine as he starts kissing and sucking down my throat until he reaches the tendon at the base of my neck. The second he bites down I feel him shred my panties from my body.

"Liam, *shit.* Don't stop." I'm so desperate for release at this point that I'm begging.

Seconds later, I feel his hot breath trail down my skin until it reaches my ear. "Tell me, baby, how wet are you? Wet enough to take my cock?"

I can't even form a coherent sentence right now and he is asking me questions.

"Skylar, fucking answer me." He rocks into me, the friction of his zipper against my clit almost causing me to come.

"Y-Yes. Just fuck me. *Please, Liam.*"

His lips are back on mine and I hear the faint sound of a buckle and a zipper before I feel the tip of his dick teasing my entrance. Holy hell. This is really about to happen.

Tearing his lips away from mine he says, "You better be fucking sure about this, Sky. There's no going back."

"Huhhhm," is all I manage to get out because the only thing I can concentrate on is the sensation of his dick so close to being inside me. I try and move my hips down so he sinks deeper, but his grip around my waist tightens and stills me.

"Jesus, fuck, you're soaking my cock," he rasps, his body shuddering with the need to lose control. "*Stop* moving. Look at me and answer the question or I won't fuck you." He groans when I wiggle just a fraction more over him. "On second thought, maybe I will, I just won't let you come." I snap my eyes open at the threat. "Tell me you're sure about this, Sky. This will change everything."

I bite his lower lip, sucking it hard into my mouth before I release it. "I'm sure."

Dropping his forehead to mine he says, "You want me? You trust me to take care of you?"

The muscles in my pussy begin to contract, trying to get him inside me, causing Liam to slide in a little more.

"Yes, Liam. I do. I swear."

With that last promise, he slams into me. Hard. The size of him shocks me, and it takes me a second to fully stretch around him. I can already tell I may not fully get used to him this time, but it feels so amazing that I don't even care.

"*Fuck*. Sky, you feel so fucking good."

He thrusts into me again and again. There is no rhythm or gentleness to the onslaught, and all I can do is hold on to the back of his neck as he fucks me relentlessly against the wall with wild abandon. I'm lost to the overwhelming ecstasy, and the only words I manage to get out are *more* and *harder*. At some point his fingers find the strap of my dress and he pulls it down, tearing it from my body and freeing my breasts. Thank god I went without a bra today otherwise not one item of clothing would have made it out unscathed.

Before I have time to even mourn my dress, Liam's wet, warm mouth is wrapped around my nipple, sucking it into his mouth. *Fuck that dress.* He moves to my other breast, licking and sucking and nipping as he continues to pound into me. When he bites down on my nipple I scream out his name, lost to the sensation of pain and pleasure.

"*Sky. Shit, fuck.* Please tell me you're fucking close," he begs before he's back to kissing me again. I don't even have a chance to answer before his calloused fingers press down on my clit.

I come so hard I feel my thighs squeeze around his waist as my pussy tightens around his cock.

"Sky, I need to—pu-shit, I can't stop. *Fuck*," He slams his fist against the wall next to my head then I feel him release inside me.

Liam's knees give way and he sinks to the floor, taking me with him. We're both panting, trying to catch our breath. I hold his head against my chest and relish the feel of his dick still moving inside me. I'm not sure how long we sit this way, and I would almost be worried I killed him or something except I can feel his heart beating hard against my hand.

"Liam, you didn't, like, pass out on me or anything, did you?"

I hear him chuckle before he lifts his head from the crook of my neck. "I'm not sure, sweetheart but it's possible. I think I saw God for a second."

"Oh yeah, what did he look like?"

"An awful lot like your tits."

"You're a pig," I scold him but I can't even attempt to hide my smile. Liam grabs the back of my head and brings me in for a hard kiss as he pulls out of me, leaving me feeling empty. He backs himself up so he's sitting against the wall, and he brings me with him so I'm resting against his chest.

"I didn't use a condom."

"I can kind of tell by your cum dripping down my thighs."

"*Fuck.*" He groans as if in pain. "Don't say shit like that to me right now. It'll just make me want to fuck you again, and I really need to at least get my vision back fully before that happens," he says, scrubbing his hand over his face.

"I'm clean, you know," I assure him. "And I'm on the pill. I have been for a while."

"I'm clean too. Plus, I haven't gone bareback in years. But I shouldn't have been that reckless. I shouldn't have let that happen before we talked about it." He starts to stroke my hair, running his fingers through the strands.

"It's okay. I meant what I said. I trust you to take care of me. So, what does this mean? For us?" I wrap my arm around his middle and relax my head into his hard chest, inhaling his scent: all sweat and sex and pheromones that almost make me want to jump him again.

"I told you, this changes everything. We take it day by day, see where this goes. But you need to know I don't share. No one else can have you while you're with me."

"I don't screw around, Liam. I'm not like that." My tone comes out sharp as I immediately go on the defensive.

"Shhh. I didn't think you were. I just want to make sure we are both on the same page. This is probably the most backwards and un-conventional way I can think of to start any type of relationship, but I want to try. I can't promise it will be easy; in fact I have a feeling we have a hard fucking road ahead of us, but…" He takes a deep breath and moves his hand from my hair down to my bare arm where he begins to lightly stroke his fingers against my skin.

"But what?" I ask, looking up at him.

"But the sex was so fucking mind blowing that I'm willing to take the chance, at least for a little while."

"Oh my god, you are such an ass!" I elbow him lightly in the stomach and move to get up. Liam's laughter is loud enough that it echoes off the wall in the gym. I don't think I've ever heard anything so beautiful before. He wraps his arms around my waist before I have a chance to go very far, pulling me back down.

"You sure this isn't moving too fast for you, Sky? Because I don't go halfway into anything. I will consume you."

"My whole life has been fast. Like warp speed, breaking the sound barrier fast. I've never gone about anything slowly, and definitely not by choice, because I never really had any." The way he looks at me now, with a curious and doubtful stare, has me scrambling for a way to explain it to him.

"Like, you know how girls always imagine what their first kiss will be like?"

"No. Do they do that?" I feel him smiling against my cheek.

"Of course they do. They wonder when it will happen, where, and who with. Will it be a little sloppy with some tongue, or just a sweet kiss stolen when no one is looking?" My fingers start lazily tracing over his skin and his scars.

"Aww. That is so sweet, Sky." His tone is playful with a hint mockery, but his arms tightening around my waist almost make me forget that he's making fun of me.

"Whatever." I roll my eyes, even though I know he can't see it. It's the principle of the thing, really. "My point is, a girl spends a better part of her pre-teen years just imagining all the scenarios of this perfectly innocent first kiss. Even if it's a complete disaster, it would be a special one because it's yours. When I was fifteen, I had my very first kiss with an actor that was twice my age. On camera. In front of a director who was busy giving me directions on how to do it properly and a crew of twenty people. For a movie I didn't even want to do, one Carl pretty much forced me into because he said it would help further my career. To let the audience see past my Mandy Mayhem persona because I would be playing some Lolita-type character that was seducing an older man. The depressing part was that Carl was right. The movie catapulted my career into more adult roles, ones where I was taken more seriously. But you know what, I hated every second of it. I knew after that day that I would never have a normal life, or grow up like most kids my age. I would never have that innocent first kiss or first date, or even get to go to something as stupid as prom. But do you want to know something?"

"What?" He starts to stroke my hair, tucking it behind my ears.

"*Our* first kiss, and this moment right here, is the only choice I've ever made on my own that I don't regret. I think I would have given all the rest of this up if it meant my first kiss could have been with you, in the car, or even in that alley behind your bar. So yes, I'm sure this is not moving too fast for me."

"Sky."

"Yes?"

"At the risk of sounding like a total pussy, I'm going to tell you this anyway. That may have been the most romantic thing anyone has ever said to me."

"Liam?"

"Yeah?"

"Where's your wallet?"

"In my pants. Why?"

I turn toward him and start to sneak my hand into the pocket. "I just thought that maybe it was time your man card was confiscated."

"You think you're so funny, don't you?" he says, pulling my hand away from his pants and flipping me onto my back, pinning me to the floor. "Baby, I've got good news," he growls into my ear before he bites my earlobe.

"Oh yeah? What is it?"

"I think my vision is back. You ready for round two?"

He doesn't even wait for me to answer before he's buried deep inside me and I'm a goner.

CHAPTER 15

Skylar

"I'm dying. This is how I go out. My obituary that TMZ will so kindly pen will read: Actress Skylar Joy Barrett collapses to her untimely death on a morning jog with her bodyguard who coerced her into the run against her will."

I've stopped halfway up the hill, not far from my house, and I refuse to move another muscle, aside from the ones I'm using to collapse onto the sidewalk. I don't even care that I'm lying on the gross cement right now because it's cooling my heated, disgustingly sweaty skin. A tall shadow moves over me, blocking the early morning sun, and I close my eyes, hoping he'll go away and leave me to my misery. He is the cause of it, after all.

"Being a little overdramatic, don't you think, Sky? And I did not coerce you into running," Liam says as I feel him squat down next to me.

"You so did! You slapped my ass while I was still comfortably asleep in bed and told me that I had to come running with you. Then when I refused, you said, and I quote, 'I don't know this area, baby. I could get lost and some lonely Hollywood Hills cougar housewife could snatch me up and use me as her sex slave.'"

The slapping of the ass part I was so not opposed to, but that's because I thought it was going to lead to an entirely different type of physical excursion, especially seeing as that is all we have been doing for the last week. That and coming up for food.

Food. That sounds amazing right now.

"That was a valid fucking concern, not coercion. And we've barely gone two miles. You can't be this exhausted already. With a body like yours I assumed you worked out daily."

"Well, sorry to disappoint, but I don't. Maybe the occasional Pilates session if Carl is telling me my ass and thighs are getting bigger, but that's it."

"Jesus, I really fucking hate your father. I can't wait until you fire his ass," he growls. When I dare to open my eyes again, he's lying on the dirty sidewalk next to me.

"So you've mentioned." Over and over. Ever since I dropped the bomb that I was planning to fire Carl, Liam has been not so casually dropping hints to remind me that I said it, almost as if he's afraid I'm going to back out, and honestly I'm not really sure how I feel about any of it. I did mean it when I said I wanted to fire Carl, but I didn't expect Liam to be so adamant or involved about the whole thing.

When I pause to take in all of Liam, I suddenly become breathless again. This man does for track shorts and wife-beaters what James Bond does for a suit. Daniel Craig/Sean Connery James Bond not Pierce Brosnan James Bond…or Roger Moore or that other guy no one cares about.

"Damn, this is so unfair," I groan. "How do you still look so good after that marathon we just ran and I look like some wet hairball pulled from a shower drain?" I ask, throwing my arm over my eyes. I no longer want to look at his muscled non-sweaty perfection.

"Baby, a marathon is twenty-six miles. We've barely gone two," he so helpfully informs before he rolls over so that his top half is resting on me. "And you do not look like a fucking hairball," he kisses me deep and without warning. "In fact," he moves his lips lower, slightly grazing my cheek until I can feel his warm breath against my ear, causing me to shiver, "I think you look all kinds of fucking sexy like this in just a sports bra and tight yoga pants that I have to say make your ass look fucking phenomenal." He shockingly licks a path from my collarbone up to my ear.

"Liam, stop. I'm all sweaty and nasty and—*oh god*," I moan as his tongue traces the shell of my ear, his nylon shorts doing nothing to block the erection that is clearly pressing into my thigh. I should be worried that we will be seen, that at any moment someone will pop up from behind a bush or something and start snapping pictures. I should be worried about all these things because it's second nature to me. But I'm not. I find myself not even caring because I'm happy and if someone wants to plaster my happy all over the tabloids, so be it.

"Sweaty and nasty is the way I prefer you, sweetheart," he groans into my neck right before he grabs my wrists and lifts himself up off the ground, taking me with him. "Now let's at least try and go one more mile, then we can head back and you can work at trying to make me all sweaty and nasty too."

"Nope. No way," I say, stepping away, dodging his attempt to grab me. "The only way I am running ever again is if—"

"Is this where you get all fucking cliché and tell me you're only running if someone is chasing you?"

"What? Hell no. I'm not even running if someone is chasing me."

"Then how do you expect to get away?" he asks, chuckling at me as if I'm being the ridiculous one.

"Um...duh. That's what I have you for. I expect that if someone is chasing me you can just hit them in the face or something, and I'll find my way to the nearest vehicle so I can drive away. Like a sane person. No, the only way I'm ever running again is if I'm running by proxy."

"What in the fuck does that mean?"

"It means that the only way I'm doing it is if it's you running and I attach myself to your back." I know I'm totally rambling at this point because I look down at my hands and realize I have posed them like claws to emphasize my point. I look back up at Liam and he has the biggest grin on his face, his dimples out in full force.

Stalking closer, practically towering over me, he wraps my ponytail around his hand, tugging at it so I'm looking up into his eyes and not at his chest. "You are so fucking cute, you know that?" He states it in a way where he is asking a question that leaves no room for an actual answer. "Let me take you on a date today, Skylar."

Say what now? "Um, what?"

"Go out with me today. On a date."

"Why?"

He releases my hair and takes a step, putting distance between us. "Why? Seriously? Jesus, Sky, why do you think?" For a split-second I swear I see something akin to hurt and maybe anger flicker through his gray eyes.

"I just mean…you don't have to, you know. I'm not one of those girls that demands you feed and water them after sex."

His hands skate through his hair roughly, sweat flying off, and not that I thought it was possible, but it actually makes him look sexier. "What the fuck, Skylar? You can be so infuriating sometimes. We've been in your house for days, haven't left once. Now I don't know if it's because you're afraid to take me out in public or you're afraid to be out in public, but either way it doesn't fucking sit well with me. Not to mention that now I'm really annoyed you think whatever this is between us is just fucking."

Crap, I didn't mean to offend him. "Hey," I say, grabbing his hands to pull him back to me. "I didn't mean that how it sounded. I just, I've never really done this before. The whole dating thing. Hell, I don't think I've ever really been on a real date before."

He tilts his head to the side and eyes me curiously. "You've never been on a real date before?"

"No. I mean, I don't think so."

"You don't think so? You do know what a date is, right?"

"Stop looking at me like that, and yes I know what a date is. I've gone to movie premieres and events with someone on my arm but it's never been a date type thing. More a publicity thing."

"Well, what about your old boyfriends? What about that douche Logue? None of them ever took you out to dinner or a movie? Hell, even bowling would be something. I mean it's fucking lame but it's something."

"Don't you listen, slugger? I just told you I've never done this whole thing before. None of it. I also told you it wasn't like that between Cass and me. It was just a sex th—" Before I can finish the sentence, he slaps his large palm over my mouth.

"First lesson in having a boyfriend, sweetheart. You don't mention the fact that you fucked other guys, especially with someone like me. I warned you I'm territorial." His already low voice seems to drop an entire octave on that last statement.

I'm turned on, but I'm pissed off because he put his hand over my mouth—again—and now I'm a little giddy because it just hit me that he referred to himself as my boyfriend. So I do the most natural thing I can think of.

"Ow! What the hell? You just bit me!"

"You put your hand over my mouth. Again. And by the way, you brought up Cassiel, not me, so I was just reminding you that Cass and I were just about the se—" His eyes narrow at me in warning as he continues shaking his hand. "I was just reminding you that Cass and I are just...friends."

"I still can't believe you actually bit me. Fucking hellcat," he mutters under his breath.

"You're my boyfriend," I mutter under my own.

"What?"

"You said, 'the first lesson in having a boyfriend' which implies that you are calling yourself my boyfriend." I bite my lip, trying to hide my smile, but I lose the battle and smile anyway. Big. Then he smiles back too. Kind of. Okay, his lips twitch a little, but for Liam it may as well be a smile.

"What's your point? I thought we already covered this days ago, right before my cock claimed your pussy."

"How romantic," I say, rolling my eyes. "Blackmailing me with an orgasm is hardly putting a title on us. I would have agreed to give you anything at that point. Hell, I would have agreed to give you Noah. Don't you think you could have at least asked first?" I ask, placing my hands on my hips. Not that I would have said no, and while I realize I'm in my twenties and this whole label is childish, I still want to be at least asked. Just once. Just to see how it feels.

"No. This isn't fucking high school, baby."

I pout and give him the saddest eyes I can manage before laying on the guilt trip. "Oh, I wouldn't know. I never got to go to one."

I look up through my eyelashes to see him shaking his head at me, a full smile now adorning his gorgeous face. "You're really laying it on fucking thick, aren't you?" He steps closer to me on the sidewalk, and my immediate reaction is to back away from the predator, but I don't. *Liam won't hurt me.* His hand comes up to my face and I almost back away again, my breath picking up as his palm lightly grasps the side of my neck.

"Skylar." My name is released in a tone somewhere between a whisper and a growl. "Will you pretty fucking please do me the honor of being my girlfriend?"

"I don't know. The term boyfriend just seems so juvenile, don't you think? Can't we just say we're exclusive or something?" I ask without missing a beat.

He leans his neck back just enough so that he can look into my eyes. His face remains completely masked, and I can't read his reaction at my flippant remark. Then something unexpected happens. Liam laughs. Not like the small laughs he has let free on occasion, the kind where he pulls back almost as if he doesn't think he deserves to. No, this one takes him over, starting from his chest and growing momentum until it racks his whole body. The sound of it, the intensity, is something to be cherished. To some something as simple as laughter is taken for granted because it flows through them so freely, but I know how rare true laughter can be—unforced and authentic and even vulnerable. And here in front of me, the strongest man I've ever met is breaking down and cracking up.

Liam cups my face in his large hands and pulls my lips to his, kissing me deeply and with purpose, as if I just gifted him with something rare and now he is returning the favor.

"You are a trip, Skylar Barrett," he says after releasing his lips from mine. He descends one more time, placing a much softer kiss to my punished lips. "I don't care what the fuck you want to call us as long as we're together. You and me only, baby. Now hop on," he commands while kneeling down on the sidewalk in front of me. I already know what he means, what he wants. I've been here before. I jump onto his back and wrap my legs around his waist.

"I'm going to let you ride me home, then I'm going to let you ride me dirty, then we'll clean each other up and go on a fucking date, yeah?"

"Sure, but I'm warning you that a date with me may be difficult. Paparazzi, fans. Zero privacy," I warn, wrapping my arms even tighter around his neck.

"Most things with you have proven to be difficult. I would expect nothing less."

"Aww, you say the sweetest things." He turns his head slightly and manages to kiss me on the cheek before he starts running to the house with ease.

～⌘～

"Boom! And Liam O' Connor for the fucking win. Again." He turns from the pinball machine to face me with that oh-so-cocky smirk. I should be pissed because I really hate to lose, I mean really *hate* it, to the point where I actually used to release all the pieces to the Connect Four game if I thought Noah was about to beat me when we were younger. But watching Liam bang away at this pinball machine, his sleeves pushed up, the veins on his muscular forearms popping out with each movement, the view of his perfect ass always present, I could hardly call that a loss.

"Despite my lack of experience in this whole dating thing, I do believe you are supposed to let your date win. I've also heard it's bad form to gloat in front of said date." I hop off my barstool, taking a quick sip of my beer before making my way over to where he leans arrogantly against the pinball machine. I link my fingers through his belt loops, using them to pull myself closer. I don't even bother looking around to see if anyone is staring or taking pictures because not one person here seems to care what is going on around them, all too invested in their games. My guess is Liam planned it that way, and that kind of forethought, that ability to know what I need and be able to provide, well, that makes me fall a little more in like with him.

"Baby, I lose to no one. Not even a date as fuckable as you." He grasps my hips, pulling me closer to him, so close I can actually feel him start to get hard. "Gotta tell you, Sky," Liam buries his nose in my hair, his lips grazing my ear, causing a shiver to roll through me, "as much as I love those little dresses you wear, the way these jeans hug your ass is magical." He pulls the lobe of my ear into his warm, wet mouth, a move I'm learning is his favorite, and one that's becoming my favorite as well.

"How did you even find this place, Liam?" I ask after he releases my ear. I pull away just a little before I let my hormones dictate my next move and maul him like a sex-starved teenager. "I've lived in L.A. pretty much my whole life and I've been to Venice Beach a gazillion times, but I never even knew this existed."

Seriously, it's like some kind of secret vintage arcade hidden in a mythical alleyway right on Venice Boulevard.

"My brother Trevor actually heard about it from some Venice local the last time we came to L.A. for one of my amateur fights. He was always obsessed with videogames, and not the new Grand Theft Halo whatever bullshit. Trev liked the vintage games." Liam isn't even looking at me as he talks about his brother, and his eyes drift off as if they are literally in the memory, recalling and immersing in every detail. I stand as still as possible fearing if I move an inch he'll shut down and deny me this small peek into his life I so crave. "Fucking kicked my ass at *Street Fighter* every time, which is ironic seeing as I could kick his pansy ass in the ring."

"In the ring? He boxed too?"

"Trev? No, not like me. He helped train me with dad though, sparred with me, sat in my corner every fucking fight."

It's right on the tip of my tongue. I want to ask so badly what happened to his brother, to ask him about the other names inked right next to Trevor's, but I know it's not the time. A part of me hurts each time he refers to his brother in the past tense. I know what that's like; even though I may not have been as close to my mother, even though most the memories I have of her are tainted with her sickness, there are times I still miss her. Times when the good memories slip through and make it harder to deal with the reality that she's gone and has now become past tense.

"Was Trevor the older or younger brother?"

"Older." The waitress chooses this moment to bring us the burgers we ordered, setting them down on our table, and I see the second Liam decides to take that interruption as his way out.

"Can I get you two anything else? Another pitcher of beer?"

"That'd be great," Liam says, throwing his arm around my shoulders and leading me over to our small table, where he pulls my high barstool out so I can sit, before he takes the chair next to me.

"By two years."

"What?"

"Trevor. He was older by two years." Liam reaches over for the pitcher and begins refilling my glass and I can't help but smile at the fact I was wrong as he continues to talk about his brother. "Why are you smiling like that?"

"I'm just imagining how pleasant it must have been for Shayla growing up with two older brothers, especially if Trevor was anything like you," I tell him, not wanting to divulge the true reason behind my smile.

"What do you mean?" he asks, popping a fry into his mouth. "Of course it was pleasant. Shay fucking worships us. She adores the hell out of me."

"Oh, come on. Two older brothers, who I can only assume were protective as hell and also happen to box, not to mention an intimidating father. Her dating life probably makes my barely existent one look exciting."

"You think my father is intimidating?"

"Please. You don't? He was frightening as hell when he was talking you down in the bar, then telling those assholes to leave. I was ready to apologize to him and I didn't even do anything. You are very much your father's son in that department," I say before taking a huge bite of my bacon burger. Normally I would be much more ladylike when I'm eating for fear of a less than desirable picture popping up in the tabloids, but Liam really did choose the perfect place for this date. No one seems to care who I am, and the arcade is hidden far enough away from the crowded boulevard.

"Do I intimidate you, Sky?" he asks, eyeing me above his glass before taking another drink of his beer.

"No."

"No? And why not?" A devilish smirk crosses his lips, almost like a silent dare.

"Because I don't find you frightening. I'm not scared of you."

I've always believed that if you want to truly get to know someone, you figure out more about them in their silences. Those small moments when the conversation seems to cease and the person you are talking to reflects a lifetime of emotion in just their facial responses. The silence with Liam is a puzzle of reactions, from his furrowed brow to his hard gaze to a now blank stare; I just want to be able to put the pieces together.

"You know the more you keep telling me that, the less I believe you."

"Well, I could kick your ass in a game of *Street Fighter* if that will help ease your worry," I tease, tapping him with my foot under the table.

"As much as I would love to see you move your whole body around like a monkey having fucking seizures when trying to control your player, we need to finish eating. Need to get to the second part of the date."

A flush creeps across my cheeks and my mouth drops open. He did not just say that. "I so do not look like that."

"Yeah, you do, baby. You do realize that you only have to move your hands when playing pinball, right? The ball doesn't move in the same direction as your entire body."

"Shut up, jerk. It's my first time playing pinball. Cut me some slack," I pout, shoving another french fry in my mouth, resisting the urge to chuck it at his smirking face. "What is the second part of this date, by the way? I'm assuming it has something to do with the fact that you borrowed Noah's Range Rover."

I don't even bother asking him what it is; Liam's made it pretty clear he was telling me nothing this morning, even after I tried to bribe him with sex on the kitchen counter. Which we ended up having anyway, because, well, because I'm clearly a slut for Liam O'Connor.

"That it does, Sexy Skylar," he winks, throwing back the rest of his beer before setting the glass back down on the table. If I wasn't so involved with finishing my amazing burger, I probably would have noticed that Liam's attention was no longer on me and rather trained on the window behind me that faces the street. "That and the fact it's less recognizable than your cars and comes equipped with tinted windows. Figured it would be harder for you to be spotted. Give us more privacy from *those* blood suckers."

The way he says *those* has me jumping to attention. Liam's eyes are narrowed and he's pointing right behind me. When I turn to look, sure enough, there are two paparazzi standing outside the arcade window snapping pictures. Of our date.

Great. I bet they got an epic shot of me shoving this burger in my face.

"Told you it would be difficult going on a date with me." I shrug.

He reaches into his wallet and throws some cash down on the table. "Time to go." He grabs my elbow, lifting me from my chair.

"I really wish you would stop paying for all the meals," I huff, grabbing my purse off the chair next to me.

"It's a date, Skylar, so I'm paying. Now stop being difficult so we can get the fuck out of here before the parasites multiply." When he starts pulling me toward the back door that leads to the alley, I plant my feet because there is something I want to do before we leave. It's crazy and reckless and will probably come with a shit ton of consequences, but I don't care.

"Wait."

"Sky, we need to get out of here."

"I know. But kiss me first."

"What?" he asks, his brows furrowing as he quickly glances around the arcade, probably trying to gauge if we have more of an audience than just outside. But quite frankly, I don't care.

"Just—"I don't even finish the sentence. I stand on the tips of my toes so I can wrap my hands around his neck and crush my lips to his. Liam's trepidation lasts about two seconds before he takes total control, throwing his arms around my hips and pulling me into him until my feet lift slightly off the ground. His tongue plays and caresses mine until we are both practically out of breath. Then before he stops the kiss entirely, he pulls my lower lip in with his teeth, biting it, sucking it, a move that has me squeezing my thighs together in order to calm the ache I now have for his cock. The moan that slips from my mouth when he finally releases me is nothing short of embarrassing.

Setting me back down on the ground, he gently tucks my hair behind my ears while I try and unscramble my brain. "What was that for?" he asks.

I press my fingers to my tingling lips and attempt to hide the giant smile I know is trying to escape. I fail miserably. "Um…I…that was for the parasites. I just wanted everyone to know I'm yours. I guess there will be no disputing that now."

Moving his lips close to my ear he whispers, "If it wouldn't make me want to kick the shit out of every guy in here after, I would bend you over that pinball machine and fuck you until all of Venice Beach heard you worshipping my cock like it's your own personal deity."

A shiver runs through me. All I want to do is say amen and drive the hell home.

"What are the odds the second part of this date is us at home, in my bed? Because right now I'm very tempted to get religious with you."

"Sorry, sweetheart. No such luck. Now let's get the fuck out of here."

CHAPTER 16

LIAM

"I still can't believe you brought me to a drive-in movie!" Sky is jumping up and down in the backseat of the Range Rover like I just took her to the fucking moon or something. Her rambunctious energy forces a smile from me and I throw my arm around her to pull her in closer. "And even got me cotton candy. I haven't had cotton candy in years," she says, peeling off another piece of the pink fluff and licking it off her fingers. I wish I could say that innocent action didn't turn me on, but like Pinocchio's nose my continuously growing cock would prove me a fucking liar. Snatching her around the waist, I pull her even closer to me in the backseat.

"Now I know why you wanted to borrow Noah's Range Rover," she says, snuggling into my side like it's second nature to her. And I easily accept her because doing so seems to be fucking first nature for me. Again I wait for the guilt I'm sure will hit me at any moment, but it still has yet to come. Almost as if it's Ali herself giving me permission to move on.

Knowing Ali, she would have too. When I was fucking my way through bar sluts—well really every kind of slut, no need to get bar specific—I heard Ali in my head all the time. Chastising me, berating me, telling me I was better than what I had become. Now, with Sky, there is just silence. Even when she's tucked into my side as if she is a part of me, a missing limb reattaching itself, I never hear Ali.

I have to believe it's Ali's blessing.

I need it to be.

"And why is that?" I ask, snatching the hand that is holding another piece of cotton candy, bringing it to my lips, and sucking the piece from her fingers. She looks up at me with desire in her eyes as a shiver takes over her body.

"Because you're hoping to get lucky with me in the backseat and you knew it would be easier here than in one of my cars." She trails her finger from the inside of my mouth to my chin. "Although I do have to tell you, even though I've yet to see *The Shining*, I'm fairly confident this movie is not designed to get me in the mood, so your plan seems to have backfired" she says before playfully tapping my nose.

I'm still shocked as shit that she's yet to see *The Shining*. Especially because she's such a fucking film fanatic. The second we drove in to the theater, she freaked out in that really adorable way of hers, yelling that she'd always wanted to see this movie and asking if I got that piece of information from Noah. To which I responded:

"No fucking way. I have a dick. I don't need to ask another guy where I should take my woman on a date."

She just rolled her eyes and giggled like I was joking.

I wasn't.

"Baby, trust me, I would have no issue fucking you in either of your cars. When it comes to me getting my dick inside you, I can make any location work, and you should already know I'll have no problem getting you in the mood. We could be watching *Human Centipede* and I'd still be able to get your pussy wet."

"That is morbid, and also, cocky much?"

"Just confident."

"Oh yeah?"

"Absolutely."

Turning her body so she is facing me, a wicked little smirk adorning her gorgeous face, she speaks two words in a dare, words that make my dick hard: "Prove it."

I have her on her back, her small wrists trapped in my grip above her head, before she even has a chance to blink.

"Hey, I was really enjoying that cotton candy," she pouts, eyeing the pink fluff that is now on the floor of the car.

"Fuck the cotton candy. I warned you that if you teased me you better be ready for the consequences."

"So my punishment is the destruction of my sugary pink heaven? You bastard."

"You wish. No, your punishment is going to be much more fun. Tongue, fingers, or cock?"

"What?" A whimper escapes Sky the second I grind myself into her.

"Choose. Tongue, fingers, or cock." I rock into her again, pulling the lobe of her ear into my mouth.

"Jesus. Cock. Your cock."

"Tongue it is."

From the sound coming out of the speakers in the car, I can tell what part of the movie is playing. That creepy little kid is using his fucking freaky ass Tommy voice for the first time. Yeah, I managed to make it past the credits before I started mauling Skylar. Trust me, I should get an award for holding out through the previews. Even with the demon child's weird voice, I would bet my left nut that as soon as I stick my hand down Sky's panties, I'll find her wet.

Yep. My left nut is safe.

"Oh god, Liam," she murmurs the second my finger strokes her clit. "Please."

"Please what?" I ask, applying more pressure as I stroke her faster.

"Please just fuck me."

I pull my fingers away and jerk her jeans off her body which I should get a fucking award for doing so smoothly seeing as I'm working with limited space here.

"No fucking right now, sweetheart. Only my tongue."

"Why make me choose then?" she whines, a whine that turns into a moan the second I rip her panties away.

"Well, it wouldn't be much of a punishment if I gave you what you wanted, now would it?"

She braces herself on her elbows, and I can tell she is about to open that sassy mouth of hers and give me hell, but before she gets a syllable out, my tongue is on her pussy.

Her hips buck as a curse leaves her mouth. My thumb works her clit at the same time my tongue fucks her pussy. Her worshipping my name and praising me as god, while much appreciated, is starting to get too loud for a drive-in movie where anyone can hear her. I stop, pulling my face away.

"What the hell, Liam?"

I laugh while reaching behind my neck to pull my shirt over my head. "Don't worry. I'm not finished. Here," I throw my shirt at her and she catches it easily.

"You stopped my orgasm to give me your shirt? This is just a whole new level of arrogance, even for you. Congratulations."

"Smartass," I say, shaking my head. "Bite it."

"Excuse me?"

"The shirt. Put it in your mouth and bite down. I'm about to make you scream, baby, and we don't need everyone in this park hearing."

She eyes the shirt speculatively before grinning at me. "Mighty sure of yourself there, aren't you, slugger?"

I don't even bother answering. I just lower my mouth above her clit and watch her stomach as it contracts quickly with just the whisper of my breath brushing across her skin. Right when I think she can't stand it anymore, I lick.

I lick, I suck, I nibble on her clit until she moans into the shirt and pulls my head further into her cunt.

I devour her pussy with my mouth, my tongue, my teeth. Sky pants and grinds herself into my mouth with such abandon that I finally have to wrap my hands around her small waist just to get her to stay still.

Between her taste and the sounds she's making, my blood can't help but pump fiercely through my veins, making a path right toward my dick, causing me to grind myself into the seat so I can feel some type of friction. The fingers wrapped around her left hipbone start to sneak under her ass, more and more, every time she lifts it slightly. Before I know it my thumb is right there seeking entrance, and once

I'm able to catch some of her wetness with it, I push into her ass and she comes.

Hard.

"Liam!"

My shirt has obviously fallen from her mouth seeing as she is screaming my name, and I can't take it anymore. I pull my pants down far enough to free my cock, then I move up and slam into her. She starts to cry out louder so I slap my hand over her mouth while I continue to ride her. I'm about five seconds away from coming and I don't even care that I've barely lasted a minute. Seeing Skylar get so worked up, feeling her come in my mouth while my thumb was in her ass, I can't help myself.

"Oh god—fuck, *fuck*, Sky," I curse, releasing into her, reveling and shaking, the bite of her nails scratching down my back causing me to come even harder. I'm panting into her neck as her similar harsh breath teases my ear.

"Wow," she says shakily.

I lift my head, chuckling, "Yeah, wow is a bit of an understatement, sweetheart." I tuck her loose hair, which is now damp with sweat, behind her ears before kissing her gently. I just fucked her like a horny animal with my thumb in her ass; a soft kiss seems necessary at the moment.

Her half-drugged, post-orgasm smile pleases me and I find myself just staring at her for a few seconds, not saying a thing.

I've never been selfish when it comes to fucking women; I've always made sure they come at least once before I do—I'm a gentleman that way, but it's been a long fucking time since actually seeing a girl get off has been enough to get *me* off.

"You are going to be in soooo much trouble," Sky taunts, breaking me from my trance.

"Why? Is there a fucking cop outside the car or something?"

"No. Worse. You've made a mess in Noah's car. This is his baby, and you just defiled it." She bites her lower lip like she's trying to hold back a laugh. I pull my shirt off the ground and shift it under us at the same time I pull out. She shivers when I start to clean her up as best I can with it before tossing it back on the floor.

"I'm pretty sure the defiling was a team effort, sweetheart." I wink, tucking my cock back into my pants. She just rolls her eyes at me while attempting to sit up and fix herself.

"Nope. No way." She shakes her head. "No way am I taking any of the blame for this. Noah loves this car. It was his first big purchase. As far as I'm concerned, I turned you down and you ended up having your way with yourself in the back seat."

I can't help but laugh as she rights herself, fixing her shirt, her hair, zipping back up her pants. "I can't believe you'd throw me under the bus like that. I thought we had something here." I pull her into my side, the perfect position so that we can now actually see the rest of the movie.

"We do have something," she replies, snuggling into the crook of my arm, wrapping her arm around my bare stomach. "But Noah and I had something first."

She must feel me tense at that comment—it's a fucking reflex at this point—because she immediately launches into rambling Skylar.

"I mean, we don't have the same something that you and I have. We have a different something. Like the non-sexual type of something. We just came first. I mean, we just knew each other first. Obviously seeing as I only met you a few—"

I kiss her. I kiss her because as cute as her running her mouth is, someone needs to save her from herself, and I'm always ready and willing to save Sky from any enemy, even if that enemy is her own mouth.

"Relax, Sky. I'll get the car detailed before I return it. Although I hardly think Noah will notice. It's not like my dick is a firehose spraying cum everywhere. Most of what I released is in your cunt right now, where it belongs."

"Such a romantic."

"I try."

We relax into a comfortable silence as the movie continues to play. Well, not complete silence; Skylar and silence do not go hand in hand when watching a movie. The girl has a wealth of useless fucking knowledge when it comes to films. It's one of the reasons I wanted to take her to one. It's obvious she has a passion for movies that goes beyond just starring in them, and watching her enjoy her passion has almost become an obsession.

I stroke her arm lazily as she stays cuddled up underneath my arm, absentmindedly tracing her fingers over my scars, and I wait patiently for that rise in her chest, that slight hitch in her breathing that tells me she's about to talk again. I am still actually watching the movie. I'm not that much of a fucking creeper. When she starts rubbing her lip against her teeth, I know I'm in for it.

"Can I ask you a question?" she asks.

"I'm certain I can't stop you."

"Probably true, but it is kind of super personal, so I don't know if I should ask."

"Sky, I just had my finger in your ass and my tongue in your cunt. I'm pretty sure we passed super personal ten minutes ago."

"You did not just say that."

I chuckle and start playing with the ends of her hair. If she's about to get personal I don't want to fucking snap at her on accident. Touching her like this helps soothe me. "Just ask already. The suspense is killing me."

She blows out a breath. "Okay, well, I understand the tattoos on your forearms for the most part." I tense, wondering where this is going, willing myself to stay calm. "But the one on your back, the evil looking angel demon thing. What's that one about?"

Okay, that's not so bad. Her description of it is, but I can at least gloss over the answer without getting too deep. I can't blame her for asking, that's for sure; you can't get a fucking tattoo like that and not expect questions.

"That angel-demon thing is Abaddon. In Hebrew he's an angel of destruction and ruin. He's considered the angel of the bottomless pit."

"Damn, that's bleak, Liam. Is that how you see yourself? Don't get me wrong, it's an amazing tattoo. Scary and dark and beautiful, just like you, actually. But you can't believe that about yourself, right?"

"You did not just call me beautiful."

"I did, deal with it." She smirks. "But seriously, why this Abandon guy?"

"It's Abaddon, and I guess"—I can't believe I'm about to admit this to her—"I guess, yeah, it's because that's how I see myself. It reminds me of what I'm capable of, reminds me that I destroy."

"I don't think you destroy."

"No offense, but I don't think you know what you're talking about." I feel like an asshole, what else is new.

"We must be soulmates then because I, too, am like Ababbon, at least if you ask Carl."

"It's Abaddon," I correct, even though I think she's probably just fucking with me, trying to be cute. Which she is. "And what the hell are you talking about?"

She shrugs, eyes trained on the movie screen. "Carl always accuses me of the destruction of our family. Which, to be honest, I've always kind of understood. I think that's why I let him get away with so much."

What the hell? "What do you mean he accuses you of destroying your family? That makes no sense. I thought you said your mom killed herself."

"She did, but only because I was born."

"Again, what the fuck are you talking about?" I sit up slightly, taking her with me.

"I told you this already, on the plane, remember?"

"I remember you said she was sick. Then she got pregnant, stopped taking her meds, and got more sick. What part of any of that is your fault?"

"Listen, I'm not completely delusional. I know it's not all my fault. But let's be real, Liam. If she hadn't gotten pregnant with me, or maybe even if I had been a better child, less rambunctious so she could have handled me easier, she wouldn't have gotten so sick. Maybe she would have stayed on her meds."

"Sky, baby, you were a child. For fuck's sake, she died when you were six."

"Yeah, but she hated me. It had to have been something I was doing wrong in some way. Even Carl said—"

"Stop. Sky, your mom was sick. That had nothing to do with you. She was sick before you, and she would have been sick after you without the proper treatment. And let me tell you something else. I don't give two fucks what Carl said. The guy is nothing but a controlling, manipulative prick."

She looks at me, her eyes clearly questioning what I've said, taking it all in as a few more tears trail down her cheek. But then she smiles, and I swear that smile, as small as it is, hits my fucking heart.

"Carl really is a prick, isn't he?"

"He is legitimately the worst. The only good thing he ever did, as far as I can tell, is dump his sperm into your mom to create you."

"That's so…weird. Sweet but weird."

"Seriously, Sky. How someone as amazing as you came from the DNA of those two is a damn miracle." I kiss the top of her head as she relaxes onto my bare chest, the movie still playing in the background, but since forgotten by us both. The condensation from the windows starts to evaporate, and before it disappears entirely, she quietly says something in a tone so unlike her.

"Never forget that I am made from their DNA, Liam. They are a part of me as much as I am a part of them."

I hold her tightly in my arms, to comfort her, to assure her of what I know to be true. "From what I've seen so far, you're not even close. Now let's stop with all this and enjoy the movie, yeah?"

CHAPTER 17

Skylar

"**S**o you get to watch him do this every day?"

"Yep."

Noah and I are sitting on the steps leading to the gym, sharing a bag of gummy bears and doing what can only be described as gawking at a shirtless, sweaty, muscular Liam pounding away on the heavy bag. In about two minutes he'll switch to the speed bag, and then five minutes after that he'll go to the weight bench. That part is my favorite.

"Man, I need to start coming home more often. Do you think he knows he has an audience?"

"I doubt it." We're sitting high enough on the steps that I don't think he's noticed us, and Eminem, which I've learned is his favorite music to work out to, happens to be blasting through the speakers so I don't think he even heard us come down. Not to mention that when Liam works out, he always seems to zone out.

"He wouldn't say anything even if he did. He's being all pouty right now."

Noah sticks his hand in the bag of gummy bears I'm holding and grabs another handful, popping one into his mouth. "Why, did you not 'squeeze your pussy' around his cock hard enough this morning?"

"Oh my god, Noah!" I slap him on the shoulder, causing him to choke slightly. "Can't you just forget that happened?"

"Skylar, it just happened yesterday. How could I possibly forget that? I got an eye and earful."

"Well, maybe you should have knocked first, ass!"

"How was I supposed to know I needed to knock on the garage door in my own house? What, I should have just anticipated that hot bartender would have you bent over the hood of the Lotus? *You* didn't even tell me you two were banging. Although I wasn't surprised."

We've been together a few weeks now. We've played, talked, fought, been on dates, and most definitely fucked. I even, somehow, let him talk me into running with him in the mornings. I'm still totally confused as to how that happened.

Needless to say, my thighs are still sore as hell and I can barely make it a mile without collapsing to the ground, dramatically of course, because I've come to find out that he can actually run while carrying me on his back. Now that part is fun. For me anyway.

"What has his tighty-whities all in a twist this morning?" Noah asks.

"He doesn't wear tighty-whities."

"Boxers or briefs?"

"Commando."

"Damn that's hot." His eyes roll dramatically as he tosses back another gummy bear.

"Tell me about it. He says it cuts down on laundry. Anyway, he's mad that I told him I think it's best he doesn't come to the meeting with Steve today."

When I sprung on Liam last night that I was meeting with Jeff and our attorneys to discuss a settlement offer over an issue Liam was not even aware of, it pretty much turned into World War III. He accused me of withholding information from him, claimed I was being too secretive about my life, and that meant I didn't trust him. Then, like a ten-year-old shouting "I know you are but what am I," I threw it in his face that he still keeps some pretty big parts of his life from me too. But it all went nuclear when I told him I planned on going to the meeting alone. For the first time since he got here, we slept separately last night and he hasn't said a word to me all morning.

"Shit," he curses under his breath, running his hand through his hair. It hadn't really occurred to me that Noah would be upset by this too. "That's today? Is Jeff going to be there with his attorney too?"

"Yep. We're going to try and get this thing settled. I just want it to be over with so it's not constantly hanging over my head anymore. I want to move on from it, even if it costs me a chunk of money."

Once I have this wrapped up, I only have one more loose end I need to tie up, but something tells me firing Carl is going to be a lot more difficult than that.

"And you're not bringing Liam…why? You two are together, right? Hell, you hired him to be your bodyguard. Maybe you should bring him along for protection."

"I'll be at an attorney's office, Noah. It's not like Jeff will do anything to me there. Let's not be dramatic. Besides, you're supposed to side with me on this. You're *my* friend."

"That's right, I'm *your* friend. I want what's best for you, Skylar, what keeps you safe. Jeff is a creep and a total ass. It doesn't hurt for you to have someone like Liam sitting in your corner, intimidating the hell out of him. Did you ever think that maybe Liam *needs* to be there for you?"

No. "I just don't want to burden him. He isn't used to this life, you know? Every day it seems I have more drama and shit going on than the last. Between the media and Carl and people accosting me the second I walk out the door, it just gets to be too much. Especially for someone that has never dealt with it before. I mean, Jesus, we couldn't even go on a date without being bothered. If Liam goes to this meeting, I'm afraid he'll get fed up and decide that he's had enough."

Of me.

My biggest fear is that Liam will finally recognize my life is too much trouble to deal with. It's why we've barely gone out, not that I was a huge social butterfly before. In fact, *homebody and proud* should be tattooed on my forehead. The few times we actually left the house to shop or grab food, there always seemed to be fans begging for pictures or paparazzi stealing them. And with every encounter, I could see what little patience Liam possessed to begin with starting to wane. Even the unanswered and ignored phone calls Carl bombarded me with throughout this last week seemed to test his sanity.

I really need to find my lady balls and fire Carl already.

See, Liam wasn't lying when he said he had a quick temper, and I know he's capable of violence; the protective streak in him is one to be rivaled. While I love it in so many ways, I fear it, too. Not for my sake. but for his. Because, I too, am protective of him, and if he gets in trouble because of me, I will never forgive myself.

"Baby girl, you hired Liam for a job. You can't forget that just because you two are boning now, otherwise you may make him feel like a paid escort. Not to mention, that if you two are in a relationship, you need to trust that he can handle whatever your life throws at you. That he will help you shoulder that burden because, Skylar, you need to let someone help you."

"Noah—"

"Oh look, he's going to the weight bench. Damn, I could watch this channel all day."

So could I.

"Look, go talk to him. Let him do what you brought him here to do." Noah knows about the scars, has even seen them, obviously, and also knows that Liam has not yet told me about them. But there is one thing Noah doesn't know.

"I told him about my mom."

"Like, that you have one?"

"No, jackass. I *told* him about my mom."

"Wow."

"Yep."

"You actually have let him in then. Skylar, I mean, shit."

Based on the shaking of his head and the running of his hand through his hair, I'm guessing that is not a positive for Noah.

"What?" I ask him.

"Listen, just be careful. I know I said let him in a little, and I meant that, it's just...fuck."

"What? Just spit it out, Noah."

"No one knows the real story about your mom aside from Carl

and me. And you only told me because you were incredibly wasted." The public knows that my mom died when I was young. Public records and all. But what they don't know is that she committed suicide. It was a tidbit Carl was actually able to cover up. He was friends with someone in the police department, and in a small town it isn't hard to fudge the paperwork a little. It was ruled an accidental drowning and left at that. "Winter doesn't even know the truth. When I say let him in a little, I mean just that. A little. Just until you know him better, understand his motives more. The more he proves he's trustworthy, the more you can let him in."

"I'm not stupid, Noah. I know. I trust him, okay?"

"Okay, Morningstar. If you say it, then I trust it. As fun as this show is, I have to go. Gotta go meet with my business manager and then Erik and I are having lunch. Catch ya later, lover." He kisses me on the cheek before he stands to leave. "I'm taking these with me," he says, snatching the bag of gummy bears from my hand.

Jerk. With a deep inhale, I make my way over to the weight bench. He knows I'm standing right in front of him. There's no possible way he can't, seeing as the bench is inclined. I just stand there, watching as he presses the bar up and down, up and down. I can tell that with each breath he expels he is counting the reps in his head.

"Are you just going to continue to pretend I'm not here?" I ask, folding my arms across my chest. I even make it a point to fold them under my breasts so they plump up a little. Yes, I know it's a cheap trick, but I'm trying to get the guy's attention, and I know my boobs are his weakness.

Silence. Lift. Silence.

Fine. He wants to play this game, I can play too.

I walk closer to the weight bench and throw my leg over, straddling him as he continues to lift the weights above his head. The small tortured groan and slight shift of his hips is the only acknowledgment I get from him. That and the feel of his growing erection against my ass. I can't help the smirk that teases my lips, knowing that I'm affecting him this way, but damn if he isn't stubborn, continuing to spare me even a glance.

"Liam," I purr, wiggling slightly over his hips, my hands pressing down on his sweat covered bare chest. "Would you mind putting the weights down so I can speak to you for a second?"

He continues to lift, and I can feel the shift of his abs constricting under me with each movement, working me up, causing friction against my clit. I almost regret wearing a dress. I know this has to be torturing him as much as it is me.

"Your panties are either incredibly thin or I must be getting you pretty fucking wet, because, baby, I can feel you soaking through to my skin," he accuses, continuing to lift.

"Not exactly how I pictured this conversation going, but I will take it over your obstinate silence."

"Don't confuse me pointing out how much I turn you on as an opening for us to converse. In fact, if the next words out of that pretty little mouth of yours aren't, 'Liam please come with me to the attorney's office,' then just keep it shut. Or on second thought, leave it open and get on your knees. I'm sure I can find another use for it."

The music switches to another song, the beat slower and more methodical, the lyrics waxing poetic about a girl who loves her man one day, and the next is so cold. Which seems to hit a little too close to home right now.

"I'm surprised with how we left things earlier that you're not afraid I'm going to bite you."

"Nope, not worried at all. You made it pretty clear that's the only part of me you have any use for."

"Oh come on, Liam. Don't be like that. What I said this morning wasn't meant to insult you. I was just trying to protect you. This—"

"Protect me?" he says in an outrage before sitting up so fast I have no choice but to jump off of him. "Protect me, Skylar? I'm supposed to be the one protecting you!"

"I know that. Look, I know. I know." I cautiously place my hand on his arm, not because I'm afraid of him but because I notice my touch somehow calms him. I notice that he takes a deep breath when my skin touches his, like the tension and unreleased violence has dissipated from his body. "I made a mistake. I know that now. You do a job for me, and we are together, and I need to learn to balance those two things. Noah was helping me understand that."

"So, great, then I'm coming."

"If you want to, absolutely."

"Then what are we even arguing about, baby?" He smirks at me and I just get annoyed.

"We wouldn't have been arguing if you had just let me speak instead of ignoring me or snapping at me."

"Yeah, but then how would I get your wet pussy on me?"

"You're disgusting."

"Yeah, but you kind of love it." He pulls me in for a kiss and I relent because he's right. I kind of do.

CHAPTER 18

LIAM

Steve, Sky's attorney, has his hand on the sleek black door, ready to pull it open, and in a matter of seconds I will be sitting across from Jeff Roberts trying my best not to rip his fucking throat out. I know I told Sky on the car ride over here that I could handle this, and I really will try, but to be honest I was speaking under the influence of the best fucking head I've ever received in my life so I can't guarantee shit. It's the equivalent to getting drunk and assuring your friend you'll help him move out of his house the next day. Probably not going to happen, but you meant it at the time.

Sky filled me in briefly on the story with Jeff. He's suing her for being fired and threatening to go to the media with lies about her. But as it always seems to go with her, I know I'm only getting half the story. Which pisses me off. And I've got a feeling I'm about to learn some things I really don't want to hear. So I hold on to Sky's hand, soaking up her strength. Her perceived calm.

The door opens into a private conference room and I zero in on the two men sitting at a large conference table, both looking our way, and I already know which one is Jeff. Because his eyes open wide as he takes me in, his gaze shooting to Sky's hand in mine and then over to Skylar. I know that look he has in his eyes. That is a look of pure jealousy.

Holy fuck. This is worse than I thought. This son of a bitch might be in love with her.

"Gentlemen," Steve says, loosening the buttons on his suit jacket as he takes a seat. I pull out Sky's chair, and she sits. I take the chair right next to her, my eyes never leaving Jeff's. This table is not nearly wide enough because I know if he makes one wrong move I don't have to reach very far to pull that asshole right over it and pound his face in. He's in his late thirties, probably ex-military because he still wears his hair like he's serving. Doesn't matter. I know I can take him.

I can do this. For her, I can do this.

Wrapping my hand around Sky's wrist under the table, I sense her pulse, trying to absorb the slower rhythm. I look over at her and she gives me the smallest, most unconvincing fucking smile as if trying to relax me.

"Let's get right to it, shall we? I think we can all agree this has gone on long enough, and Ms. Barrett would really like to move on," Steve says. "So, Tim, let's not beat around the bush. What exactly is your client looking for in order to not run his bullshit mouth off to the press? And let's be realistic on the number seeing as how Jeff did sign a non-disclosure agreement, and if we really wanted to, we could drag this case out for so long your client would end up losing every dime he has just trying to pay your exorbitant legal fees. Then, when we win, we'll come back and sue his sorry ass for *her* legal fees. The only reason I am even entertaining this meeting is because Ms. Barrett would like to put this whole thing behind her so she never has to deal with your client again."

I really fucking like Steve.

A small cough comes from Jeff's attorney. "I gave you our number, Steve. Ten million and my client remains silent on the indiscretions and mistreatment shown to Mr. Roberts by Ms. Barrett. Mr. Roberts maintains that Ms. Barrett came on to him, and when he denied her advances, she fired him. And this is just the tip of the iceberg."

Holy fucking shit. Ten million.

Skylar sits up straighter, her pulse picking up speed as Jeff stares right at her. "Mistreatment?! Fucking bullshit, Jeff," she says, pointing right at him.

There's my hellcat.

"Was it mistreatment when you stole my panties and tried to sell them on eBay or whatever the fuck it is you did with them?"

Nope, no way I heard that right.

"Or what about leaking private information to the media or tipping off the paparazzi to where I was going to be?"

"Skylar," Steve interrupts her.

"No, Steve, this is so messed up. What about when I woke up and you were in my room taking pictures of me when I was sleeping?"

What the fuck did she just say? Now I'm truly fucking glaring at Jeff, who is looking at Skylar as if she's his prey. He's breathing heavy as she stares him dead in the eye while she reams his pathetic ass. Jeff hasn't even realized that I'm watching him the same way he is her. Because he is *my* fucking prey. I'm suddenly finding this thin conference table perfect for what I have in mind.

"Listen to me very carefully, Jeff." Sky's voice is deceptively calm as my grip on her wrist tightens, her pulse beating quickly causing mine to catch up to its pace. "I'm not paying you one dime. You go to the media and run whatever bullshit stories you want because I would rather my career ruined than give you one more penny."

Neither one of those things is going to happen. I'll make sure of it. Jeff sits silently and that worries me. No one says a thing for what seems like hours, all of us stunned into silence by Skylar's warning.

"Well then," Jeff's attorney says. "I guess we will see you in court."

"Wait." Jeff finally opens his dumb-ass mouth and I've already thought of ten different ways to make sure he never speaks again using just my right hand. Possibly three ways with my left. Maybe I'll even throw a foot or shoulder in there just for good measure. I love to branch out and get fucking creative. "Skylar." He clears his throat, attempting to get her name out. "Can we have a minute? Alone," he says, looking around the room at the attorneys and then lastly at me. If he thinks I'm leaving Sky alone in here with him he is the dumbest motherfucker on the planet. Skylar tugs her wrist from my hand, and I'm about to pull her out of the room before she decides to make a bad decision, but then she puts her hand over mine and holds it steady.

"Fine. But Liam stays."

"I got you, baby," I say, kissing her temple while never breaking eye contact with Jeff. He is seething. Fucking perfect. Now he knows.

She is mine.

"Skylar, I would really advise—"

"Steve, I've got this, okay? Please give us a minute," she says, dismissing him from the room.

Both attorneys pick up their files, which I'm convinced are just filled with blank papers and bullshit to make their professional dicks look bigger, and walk out of the room.

"Who the hell is this guy, Skylar? And why the fuck is Carl not here?" Jeff snaps the minute the door closes.

"Watch your fucking mouth when you speak to her, asshole." Sky's hand squeezes mine in warning.

"We're alone now, Jeff. What do you want?" she asks, getting straight to the point. If I didn't know any better, I would think she is angrier than I am. But that's fucking impossible. I still can't believe this dick crept into her room. She and I need to have a serious fucking talk when we get home.

"Skylar, I never wanted it to come to this. You don't understand. What happened, what's happening now, it's not what you think. I'm not the bad guy here."

"Oh really? Who is then, Jeff? Because you're the only person trying to blackmail me right now and you're doing it with lies. Are you telling me it wasn't you tipping the tabloids off to every place I went? Or leaking stories only you could know about? Do you think I'm stupid?"

"No, it wasn't me," he scrambles. "I mean, it was, but it's not for the reasons you're thinking and I wasn't tipping off the paparazzi. Not directly. It's not me you should be concerned about, Skylar. I'm the last person you should worry about. I would never do anything to hurt you if I could help it. Skylar, I love—"

I slam my hands on the table, using the force to push myself up so I'm towering over him from across the table. I'm. Fucking. Done.

"Don't say another fucking word to her."

"She needs to hear what I have to tell her," he says, almost looking panicked. The slight quiver in his voice gives him away and leaves me still trying to figure out what his game is. "Skylar, you have to pay me the ten million or it will get worse for you. You think what happened before is bad, that's only—"

That's all the threat he gets out before I reach over, grab him by the neck, and drag him across the table. I knew I had enough space.

Skylar pushes her chair back and stands. "Liam," she says, my name leaving her lips in a plea.

I hate the fear in her voice, but this ends now. Rage is my friend and I'm taking advantage of our agreed upon terms. I will manage the fallout with her later.

"Listen to me *very* fucking carefully, Jeff," I say, squeezing just a little bit harder as he grabs at my arms, trying to pull them away from his neck. He won't be able to. His face has just the perfect amount of red, but no purple yet, so I keep my grip steady. "Sky is not going to give you a damn thing. From here on out, you forget you even know her name." Keeping one hand on his throat while my forearm holds him down against the edge of the table, I reach into his back left pocket and lift his wallet out. His ID is visible through the clear plastic, and I peruse it quickly, taking in his full address and storing it in my memory. "I know where you live now, asshole. Rest assured, if you talk to Skylar, look at her, hell, if you even buy a magazine that has a picture of her on it I will come to your house and beat you within an inch of your miserable fucking life. You get me, *Jeff*?"

His trachea works against my hand trying to suck in air, making pitiful gulping sounds as he tries to swallow. The idea that I could kill him right now titillates my mind and feeds my fury. It would be so easy to break his neck, his would not be the first I've broken, and I could rid this parasite from Sky's life forever. I squeeze just a little harder as he attempts to say something to me.

Then I feel it. Her skin against mine. Her hand reaching under my shirt, making full contact. She instinctively knows what to do to bring me in from the kill. She is trying to power me down.

"Liam, let him go. *Please*," she cautiously begs. The sound of her voice plays at my senses, toying with my want to destroy him here and now to keep her safe, and my need to let him go for ironically the same reason. I release him. I won't do her any good in prison.

"Don't say another fucking word, Jeff. Walk out that door before I change my mind and end you here."

"Skylar, please…" Jeff says, reaching toward her as he makes his way toward the door.

Before I have a chance to go for him again, Sky throws her arms around my waist in an attempt to hold me back. Jeff stops and places his hand on the door. I think he is about to say something to Skylar but he bravely looks in my direction and speaks.

"If you care about her at all, you'll open your fucking eyes and realize I'm not the enemy. She needs to pay the ten million or you might as well dig a grave for her now."

Yep. I'm going to kill him. Fucking kill him. I'm in an office building full of lawyers so this is as good a place as any. But Sky's hold on me tightens and my temper seems to play slave to her embrace. Jeff Roberts walks out the door and heads to the elevator unscathed. He's lucky, but I'm not. I still feel my pulse thrashing wildly, my blood is on fire, and I need a release. I need something. Something to calm me. To bring me back. I walk over to the conference room door and flip the lock. Luckily every window in this room is covered by blinds so it makes what I want that much easier.

I stalk toward Skylar, backing her against the conference table, placing my hands on top of the surface so that I'm surrounding her. She looks at me with a hint of fear in her eyes, but the lust she is experiencing pours out of her so heavily I can almost smell it.

"I want something from you, Skylar, and I *need* you to let me take it. *Now.* Or I will go after him. I will *end* him."

She is breathless, feeding and absorbing my emotional state, and says exactly what I need to hear. "I'll never deny you anything, Liam."

Those words make my cock so hard I immediately flip her around and bend her over the table, my hand wrapping around the back of her neck. This is the only way I can work my aggression out. I have to use her or I will hurt him. I want to pretend she knows this. Fuck, I hope she knows it. At this point, I have two roads to choose from, and the one where I use my cock on her instead of my fists on him seems like the best one to go down.

Shoving my free hand up her dress, I push it past her hips, my fingers finding their way to her panties where I rip the thin fabric away. She moans and backs her ass up into my erection.

"Shhh. You're going to have to be very quiet, Skylar," I growl into her ear, squeezing her neck just a little harder as I free my cock from my jeans. I tease the tip of my dick right over her clit, sweeping it back and forth until I feel her get wetter. "This is going to be quick and fucking hard, baby, so you better hold on," I warn seconds before slamming into her.

"*Liam!*" she yells, and I remove my hand from her neck, placing my palm over her mouth, gripping her hip so hard that I'm sure I'm bruising her delicate skin. Her hands are slipping over the marble conference table, looking for something to hold on to as I drive into her repeatedly. Pushing into her over and over. Using her, degrading her.

I try and focus on her teeth scraping against my skin, the feel of her warm, wet cunt tightening around me, the smell and taste of her skin as I drag my tongue from the base of her neck to her ear and bite down. But no matter how hard I try to overload my senses with Sky, memories begin to creep in. I see Ali dying, then her face morphs into Sky's. Ali's killer becomes Jeff. So I thrust harder into Skylar, trying to rid myself of the poisonous images.

"*Sky,*" her name comes out as if I'm pleading. Praying to her. Fucking *begging* her to make it all go away. That's when she turns her head, my hand falling from her mouth, and pushes herself up off the table. Her arms come around the back of my neck, her blue eyes staring into mine when she pulls my face down and kisses me so softly that I'm almost brought to my knees. Wrapping my arms around her waist, I continue to thrust into her. Once. Twice, and then I come so hard the force of it pushes me down against Sky's back until we both lie flat against the table.

I quickly pull out of her and turn her into my arms, hugging her close to my chest as we both catch our breath.

"I'm sorry, Sky. I'm so sorry. I don't know." I'm stroking her hair as if to calm her down, but I'm the one losing it.

"Shhh, Liam." She leans back from me and gently grabs my face. "I've got you, but let's not talk here. You don't need to apologize, I get it. Let's get out of here, okay? We'll go somewhere and talk about what just happened, but I think if we stay in here any longer Steve is going to send in a search party, and they'll get a full-on view of that phenomenal ass. As much as I love it, I doubt they'll feel the same way."

I fucking hate that she is doing this. I used her, and even worse I thought of Ali when I was inside of her. I'm so ashamed, so aware of how unworthy I am, and here she stands, trying to comfort my worthless ass. Trying to make me fucking laugh. That attribute has been something I've loved about Sky from the moment I met her, but in this second it's become something I loathe; I don't deserve her reprieve.

Now she wants to go someplace and talk. Sky knows me well enough at this point to know that what happened wasn't normal, even for me. She has seen me have similar fits, beginnings of rage blackouts or memories flooding so fast through my brain that they incapacitate me. But I've never bothered to explain them or use her like this in a way that absolves me and damages her. After what happened here, she needs to know. Hell, she deserves to fucking know what they did to me, what they took from me. Even what I've done. My stomach churns at the thought, and I pull her into me, holding tightly so I can burn the feel of her into my skin and memory. I will need this reminder to comfort me in the future lonely nights I'm about to face. Because after I tell her the truth, her need for me will be gone. Sky will leave me. She'll disappear back into the torturous fucking fantasy she emerged from.

CHAPTER 19

Skylar

Silence has never been so glaringly loud or uncomfortable before. I swear I would cut off my pinky finger for a Xanax right now. Where is Noah when I need him?

I can't stop my knee from bouncing or my palms from sweating no matter how many times I wipe them on my dress, and I can't decide what I want more. To be out of this car or for this ride to last forever so that I can delay whatever outcome is going to come from whatever the hell happened at Steve's office.

Of three things I am certain: I have no idea what I'm going to do about Jeff but I'm starting to become increasingly grateful for all those hours I spent watching the *Investigation Discovery* channel because I'm pretty confident I know just enough to get away with his murder.

Two, Liam just used me to fuck his anger away, and while I can tell by his behavior afterward that he felt guilty about it, I liked it. I wanted him to use me, craved it even. During that whole meeting my mind was spinning. I couldn't focus. I felt myself slowly falling deeper and deeper into a dark place. I acted all tough and take-charge, but inside I was completely lost and hopeless. When he bent me over that table and drove into me again and again, every thrust brought me closer to ecstasy and further from the dark. It anchored me. Centered me.

And finally, I have a very bad feeling about what Liam plans to do next. He's protective, and I know if he thinks he's hurting me, he'll leave. Liam will protect me from himself even if I don't want or need it. The thought of him leaving scares me, and the idea of not knowing what's about to happen with him makes me nervous. And being scared and nervous makes me ramble and say really stupid things.

"I was a spy when I was a kid," I blurt out.

"What now?"

See?

"I mean, not a real spy or anything."

"You don't say," he deadpans.

"Shut up," I say, rolling my eyes. "My favorite book was *Harriet the Spy*. I must have read it a hundred times. It was the only book my mom ever gave me, even though I was too young to read it at the time. Anyway, when Carl moved us to California after my mom died, he would go to work and leave me alone all day. I was seven. No babysitter and no grandparents to watch over me, so naturally I got bored. I found a spiral notebook and these binoculars Carl had, and I would spy on all the neighbors. Take notes. Watch their lives unfold. Especially the homes with kids. I would pretend their lives were mine. That I was sitting with my mom and dad at the dining room table, eating a real meal. Or playing in the backyard with a brother or sister, sliding down the slide and climbing back up just to go down again."

Watching the Kensington family had always been my favorite. They ate dinner every night at seven. Every Saturday morning Riley and her brother John played outside in their backyard. Their parents always sat on the porch watching and drinking their morning coffee. They even had an honest-to-god white picket fence.

"Anyway, when I went to audition for Mandy Mayhem, I nailed it. Probably because I had a few years' practice pretending I was a spy, so I really had a head start on that whole child detective thing."

"Baby, as adorable as that story is, what's your point?" he asks, one hand on the steering wheel, the other playing with a lock of my hair. Liam always seems to be doing that, finding ways to touch me. Lately I've even been timing how long he can last without touching me in some small way; grazing his fingers across my thigh when I walk by, his arm around my neck, his rough fingers playing with my hair. His personal best has been twenty-one minutes, and as desperate and pathetic as it may sound, those twenty-one minutes kind of sucked.

"My point is that it's okay to pretend with me. Hell, I've made a career out of it. You don't have to tell me anything if you don't want to. Not about Ali, or your brother, or Isabel. I'll pretend right along with you, because sometimes, if you pretend long enough, that fake life can become your new reality."

I expect to see a relieved look on his face, that maybe he would be happy I was unburdening him, but as we pulled up to my gate he looked over to me with the saddest expression. Almost like I was a child he pitied, and my heart splintered just a little at that realization.

"Sky, that isn't how life works, sweetheart. That is most definitely not how relationships work," he admonishes while punching the code into the gate. He may as well be punching me in the stomach because I swear that's what his words feel like. He just made me out to be some naïve girl who has no idea how life works. Well, fuck him.

"I'm not stupid, Liam."

"What?"

"I said I'm not stupid," I repeat, trying to keep the tears in my eyes from falling.

"Sky, I never said you were stupid. Where is this coming from?" When he looks over at me I see concern and hurt, and for some reason, that pisses me off even more. A part of me realizes that he never said or implied I was stupid, but I can't stop from lashing out because deep, deep down I know. He's touched on my biggest insecurity, the one that has taunted me for years, that had me fearing ever getting truly intimate with someone.

"I know how relationships work." *I don't.* "You don't have to have been in one to know how one works." *Yeah, but you probably would have needed to witness a successful one at least once in your life. Or know how it feels to be truly loved by someone. A mother, a father, a friend you don't pay.*

Tears finally wet my cheeks. Not a lot of them, just a few. Enough for Liam to take notice when I quickly swipe them away. The car has

been stopped at the end of the driveway for far too long and I just want
him to move it so I can run inside and hide under my covers for the
rest of the day.

"Baby, why are you crying? You have to clue me in on what the
fuck is going through your head right now because I have no idea how
we got here." Liam reaches out to wipe a tear away but I quickly move
from his touch. It wasn't even intentional, just an instinctive reaction
to hating the fact that he is witnessing me being this vulnerable.

"What the fuck, Skylar." He grabs my chin gently, turning my face
so I'm forced to look at him. "Don't ever, fucking *ever*, jump away from
my touch. Especially not when you're crying and all I want to do is
help make it go away. Be pissed. Be sad. Cry. Fucking yell at me, hit me,
kiss me like you hate me. Fuck me like you despise me. But *never* turn
away from me. You get me?"

The sun shines brightly outside, rays bouncing off the windshield.
Birds are chirping from the palm trees that line the street; everything
beyond this car is the personification of cheerful and happy. But inside, it may as well be pouring rain and striking lightning directly on
us because this storm is just beginning, and the only thing I can do to
prevent a total disaster is agree. So I nod my head, and in return he
punishes my lips with a harsh kiss before driving us up to the house.
And that's when I realize everything is about to get so much worse, because parked in front of my house is the last person I want to see right
now, but the first person I should have expected.

"Whose car is that?"

I take a deep breath and on the exhale spit out his name. "Carl's."

"You have got to be fucking kidding me." Fury pours off of him
and I seriously almost fear for Carl in this moment. Almost.

Liam throws his door open and stalks over to Carl's Escalade,
looking ready to commit murder. I unclip my seatbelt quickly, jumping out of the Lotus in an attempt to intercept him. It's true I can't find
it in me to care what happens to Carl one way or another, but I do care
what happens to Liam. I know that my father is not here out of the
goodness of his heart, and whatever he says may push an already on
the edge Liam right over. Carl will not hesitate to play dirty. If Liam
touches him in any way, even if provoked, Carl will have him thrown

in jail.

"Whoa, Liam. Hold on," I say, throwing myself in front of him, palms pressed to his chest. Sometimes it's easy to forget just how much bigger he really is than me. Not just in strength, but in height too. I feel like Tinkerbell trying to stop a raging bull.

"He's not even in the car. Where the hell is he?"

I know he's not going to like this answer.

"He's probably in the house."

Taking a slow step back, he puts some distance between us, his menacing stare burning through me. Yep. He's pissed.

"In the house," he states.

I swallow hard before answering. "Yes."

"That motherfucker has had a key and the alarm code to your house this entire time?"

I'm really not appreciating his accusatory tone. "Yes, as a matter of fact he has, and you know what, I don't owe you any type of explanation for that. You haven't been in my life that long, and despite your disdain for Carl, he is still my father and manager. So, yes, he has a key and the alarm code to my house because why the hell wouldn't he?"

Trust me, at this point I regret ever giving him access to my house, but I'd been under his control for so long that I never really thought I had a choice when he demanded it from me. Not to mention, I was technically a minor at the time I purchased the house, so as far as I knew, he had every right to a key. Looking back on it now, I know it was just another control tactic he used to make sure I was never far from his reach, but I've only recently started to truly separate myself from him, and I honestly forgot about the key. But I stand by what I said to Liam. He can be pissed all he wants, but I did nothing wrong.

He snatches my wrist and walks us to the front door. "You're right. You don't owe me an explanation as to why you gave him a key, but you should have told me he had easy access to your house." He stops us right in front of the door and turns to face me, my wrist still in his grasp, his thumb pressing against my pulse. "But right now, none of that matters because we are going in there and I'm going to stand there while you do what you should have done the first day I met him."

Despite the issue that still hangs heavy between us, the one I know we will have to deal with later, I can't help the small smirk that I wear proudly. Liam is right. I finally get to do what I should have done a long time ago, and I have zero excuses to not pull the proverbial trigger now. And I can't wait.

"You have to swear to me, Liam, that you will keep your shit together. Let me handle it. Carl knows the right buttons to push and he'll punish you if you react. And I'm not talking about physical punishment. He's manipulative and dangerous. You understand what I'm telling you?"

Liam's lips, the ones I love to be on any part of my skin, form a scowl. A scowl that tells me he is currently weighing the pros and cons of going in there ready for a fight with Carl, or bracing for the fight with me afterward if he goes after him.

"Fine, but if he gets out of line or approaches you like before, I can't promise shit."

"I expect nothing less. After all, that is what I pay you for."

"It's not about that."

"I know." I reach out to lightly stroke his cheek before kissing him softly on the mouth. "Well, what are you waiting for, slugger? Open the door."

He grins back right before placing a kiss on my forehead. "With fucking pleasure, sweetheart."

The sight of Carl used to cause knots in my stomach, nervous ones like the ones I would sometimes get right before an audition, because that's how I always felt around him. Like I was auditioning for the role of perfect daughter, one that he could love and respect and take care of. Only these knots were also tied with fear because the outcome of losing with him was so much worse than losing a role.

Now looking at Carl as he leans casually against my kitchen counter, resentment and contempt burning through eyes that mirror my own, I feel empowered. It could be argued that my sudden burst of confidence is solely due to the 6'3" trained boxer-turned-bodyguard boyfriend standing next to me, but I know, deep in my heart, that it's all me. This strength is mine to claim.

"What are you doing here, Carl? Because I sure as hell didn't invite you. I also know you never called to say you were coming."

Carl looks from me to Liam then down to my wrist which is still firmly in Liam's grasp while he takes a protective stance by my side. He rolls his eyes and scoffs, as if the sight of us together is one big joke to him.

"Nice to see you too, daughter, and since when do I need to be invited?" He straightens up from the counter where he was leaning. "Also, calling seems to be a pointless fucking effort with you these days seeing as you don't answer your damn phone."

He has a point there. Avoidance has been my best friend as of late.

"Cut the shit, Carl, and tell me what you want. Then make sure to give me my key back on your way out."

I hear Liam whisper a faint *"hellcat"* and I can't stop the slight shiver I get from his warm breath caressing my ear or the small smile that appears on my lips. Liam knows exactly what I need in this moment: for him to stand back, not far enough back to make me feel alone, but just enough to let me close this door myself.

"Cut the shit? Oh, I see. Now that you have your latest fuck toy on a leash you think that makes you safe to mouth off to me?"

"Hey—"

"Liam." I turn my head slightly, shaking it in warning. "Like I said, Carl, cut the bullshit. You are not to disrespect me or Liam, especially not in my own house, so hurry up and get to the point of this little visit, or *leave.*"

"Okay, fine." He starts to roll up the sleeves on his blue button-down shirt slowly, a move I know very well; it's intended to intimidate me because it usually means he's gearing up to slap me around. "Let's talk about the fact that you had a meeting with your previous fuck toy and Steve earlier and didn't bother to inform me about it. I should have been there, Skylar. I'm your goddamn manager."

Okay, now I'm pissed. So pissed that I don't care if the outburst I'm about to have leads to me getting hit.

"I never touched Jeff, and you know it! I can't believe you!" Strong arms wrap around my waist and haul me back.

"Easy there, sweetheart. If anyone gets a go at him, it's me," he says into my ear so that only I can hear him.

"I already told you once that I don't really give a shit what your relationship with Jeff is, Skylar. All I care about is getting another one of your messes cleaned up before the media finds out what a grade-A fuck-up you are."

"Hey, asshole! I already told you once to watch your tone with her, or I'll be the one coming after you," Liam warns, his hold on my waist tightening.

Carl's composure is that of someone completely at ease, as if he's just swatting an annoying fly rather than getting threatened by someone who could kick his ass as easy as he blinks.

"I'd acknowledge your threat but then that would mean I'd have to acknowledge your presence, and quite frankly that seems pointless."

He lets go of my waist and stalks a little closer to Carl. "Seeing as I'm here to protect your daughter, it's in your best fucking interest to acknowledge me."

"As I was saying, *Skylar*," he says, emphasizing my name pointedly as he looks around Liam to me. "You should've had me at that meeting so I could've made sure you paid him off like we decided. Instead, you brought reject Rocky over here who almost destroyed any chance of making this go away," he says, waving his hand toward Liam.

I step forward slowly, making sure to put myself in front of Liam so Carl sees my eyes when I speak to him. "First of all, do *not* call him a reject. And *we* did not decide anything. I told you I wasn't going to pay Jeff off, but you refused to accept my decision. And last but certainly not least, I didn't want you at that meeting. That's why you weren't there. It's over, Carl. This business arrangement we have is done."

Shit, that felt good. Better than good. Fucking amazing. That is, until I hear Carl's laugh. The one that is clearly meant to patronize me and prove to me I'm nothing but a joke he can laugh at, and I know it makes me weak to admit it, but it's starting to work. The confidence and inner strength I so bravely walked in here with is starting to dissipate ever so slightly.

"We both know you aren't going to fire me. You would be nothing without me, Skylar. You'll be even less than that without me now. Don't forget, daughter. You owe me, which means I own you."

"*You* shut the fuck up! You don't own her. She can make her own decisions, and her choice is to let you the fuck go, and I couldn't agree more. I *see* you, Carl. You're a low-life scumbag piece of shit that gets off on scaring and intimidating your daughter in order to maintain control over her because you know if she ever finds out the real truth, you're fucked."

"And what truth is that, boy?"

"*You* would be nothing without *her*."

I can't help but stare at Liam in front of me, inches away from Carl, and I do mean stare. Possibly even full on gaping. A full on total gaping dreamy stare.

Although when I say it like that, it seems less on the romantic side and more on the weird stalker porn-y side.

Carl finally shows an emotion other than indifference. In fact, he looks pissed and maybe even a little scared at the realization that this should be taken seriously. For the first time ever he looks threatened.

Or so I had the pleasure of thinking for all of about fifteen seconds, before he brings everything crashing down around us.

"Since you seem eager to bring up truths, let's bring up some of yours." That's when I see the folder on the kitchen counter, the one his fingers are currently tapping. I look over at Liam only to realize he notices the folder too, and his face pales immediately. I don't know what's about to happen, but I'm certain I don't want it to.

"You want to know who you have on your side, in your corner, Skylar? The guy you hired to watch after you and I'm guessing let fuck you, especially if you're anything like your mother."

"Don't." Liam warns in a tone I've never heard before and I'm not sure if it's more for me or him.

Gauging by the smarmy smile on Carl's face, I guess I have my answer; it's more for his. "Has your little bodyguard told you that he put someone in a coma once?"

No.

"Did he tell you that he was involved with gang members that murdered people close to him?"

Oh god.

"Did he happen to mention to you, I don't know, maybe during some pillow talk, that he's also a murderer?"

Murderer.

Liam murdered someone? That can't possibly be true. It has to be a lie, just another manipulative tactic Carl is using to distract me from firing him and to turn me against Liam instead. But Liam remains silent, saying nothing to deny the allegations, and when I look at his face, it's completely void of any emotion or indication that this is all bullshit. It doesn't make him guilty, though; he was just accused of murder, and while I know something bad happened to Liam in his past, I know he's not a murderer. If he won't speak up for himself, I will.

"I don't believe you, and it changes nothing. Liam could have killed ten people and I would still be firing you." I don't miss Liam's wince, causing a tiny amount of doubt to creep in. "He has nothing to do with my decision. I'm done letting you take my choices from me. You were always a shitty father, but you made for an even shittier manager, which I must say is pretty impressive. You think I would be nowhere without you, Carl? You might be right. But I would rather be a nobody living on the streets than to have to spend one more day under your control, paying you money *I* earn, money that I sacrifice my life and privacy for. You have been nothing but a cancer in my life, and lucky for me, you can be easily eradicated. Get the hell out of my house."

Now this is the reaction I've been waiting for. His face is starting to turn red, his nostrils flaring ever so slightly, his hands fisted by his sides as his cold eyes glare into mine. He steps forward, but Liam makes sure to move in front of me.

"I wouldn't if I were you," Liam warns.

"Don't worry, boy. I'm heading toward the door like Skylar wants. If she wants to ignore my warning about you, that's on her. You know, you two really do make a fitting couple. You're both excellent at hiding secrets. Isn't that right, Skylar? You haven't told him, have you?"

"Get out now!" I yell before he has a chance to say anything else.

Liam can't know. Not like this, not now, and not from Carl who will spin everything in a way that will have Liam hating me. I know Carl will keep his mouth shut if he still thinks he has a chance to weasel his way back into my life, and if this secret gets out it will destroy me and him in the process.

"With pleasure. This isn't over, Skylar. You and I both know that, so enjoy my absence while it lasts." He makes his way toward the front door, making sure to shove into Liam's shoulder on his way out.

When the door finally slams shut I walk over to the kitchen counter, bracing my hands on the edge. With my head down, I draw in deep breaths, trying to slow my racing heart. I'd almost lost everything. Just when I thought Carl couldn't get any crueler, he teases me with the threat of how terrible he can really make things for me. The red color of the folder catches the corner of my eye and I'm hit with another wave of anxiety. I have no idea what information it contains, but I know whatever it is may have the power to ruin us, and I can't handle that right now.

Liam's hand begins to stroke my back softly. "Sky, you need to breathe."

That's easier said than done. Moving out from under his touch, I step away. "Liam, I can't do this right now. I can't handle any of this. Can you go? Please, can you just go to the pool house? I need time."

A mixture of confusion and defeat crosses his otherwise gorgeous face, and I want nothing more than to kiss him and assure him everything will be okay, but I can't find the strength. His head drops, then he nods slightly as he heads to the back door. Before he opens it, he calls my name. When I turn to look, his back is to me, his head turned slightly so all I can see is his profile.

"Yeah?"

"Don't open that folder. For me, okay? Let me be the one to tell you when you're ready."

Without waiting for my reply, he exits out the back and heads to the pool house. I grab the folder off the counter and throw it into the trash before heading up to my room where I can cry for us both.

CHAPTER 20

LIAM

There's a light tapping on my bedroom window and I can't help but laugh and shake my head. Ali loves to sneak in at night even though it's completely unnecessary and ridiculous. Mom and dad have no problem with her coming over at any time; she could easily knock on the door and they would welcome her in, but no. At night she insists on sneaking in through the window, says that makes it more romantic. So I always keep a small crate I brought home from the bar outside to make sure she can reach the window easily and tap away until her heart's content.

Some nights I like to play around with her. Like tonight, where I let her tap on the window for over a minute, trying to hide my laugh as she knocks a little louder and starts to whisper my name. She is so fucking cute sometimes.

"Liam, are you there?"

I finally give in, pulling back the curtains and opening my bedroom window. Her fucking smile when she sees me brightens up the night sky around her.

"What can I do for you, angel?" I've always called her angel because that's what she is. My fucking angel, so good and pure that whenever I *get my hands on her I feel like I'm in danger of corrupting her a little, but I don't fucking care because I love her, and when bathed in her light I feel worthy.*

"I need my secret weapon," she whispers coyly, biting her lower lip.

As much as I wish she was talking about my dick, I know that's not the case. "Tonight? And here I thought you were sneaking in to take advantage of me."

"You wish."

"You have no idea how much."

"Come on, Liam, it's perfect out right now. So clear we'll be able to see all the stars." With her lip all pouty, her blonde hair shining in the light of the moon, and those damn cupcake pajama pants on, how can I turn her down?

"All right, all right, I'm coming,"

I start to close the window but she says, "Wait, what are you doing?"

"What do you think I'm doing? I'm going to come out there just like you asked."

"Just crawl through the window," she says, rolling her eyes at me like I'm being the ridiculous one.

"You are a weird one angel. You know that, right?" I snatch a blanket off my bed and grab the windowsill, pulling myself out easily. The second I'm upright, I waste no time in pulling her to me, lifting her off the ground and kissing the shit out of her. Ali throws her arms around my neck, taking everything I have to give.

"Well, it's nice to see you too," she says. Even in the dark I can see the blush that stains her cheeks. I smile down at her and kiss her forehead before tugging the zipper on her pink hoodie all the way up to her neck and throwing the hood over her head. It may be summer, but the beach here always seems to be chilly at night no matter the season.

"Wouldn't want you getting sick before our trip to Atlanta, baby."

"Me? Never," she says and grabs my hand. "Come on. We're wasting precious time."

It's only ten, not even that late, but I don't bother arguing with her, I just let her drag me the short distance to our hammock. I climb in first, making sure it's steady before Ali drops in next to me.

When I first put the hammock up, there were a few mishaps, and by mishaps I mean crashes to the ground. Believe it or not, hammocks are fucking hard to master with two people. Ali and I spent more time on the ground the first few tries than in the actual hammock, laughing so hard that we could barely get off the ground to try again. But we mastered it and are now lying comfortably together, swaying back and forth with the breeze coming in from the ocean, staring at the stars.

"So." Her sweet melodic voice softly grazes my ear "Which one were we on?"

I point up to the sky, trying as best I can to show her the last star we left off at. "We were at Peacock, baby," I tell her, throwing the blanket over us.

"Ah yes. Peacock. Number nine zero six. Such a bizarre name for a star, don't you think?"

"No more bizarre than the idea we can count every visible star in the sky together," I chuckle, tightening my arm around her to bring her closer.

"Hey, that's not bizarre! You heard what Mr. Bond said." Mr. Bond was our Astronomy teacher in high school. Ali was obsessed with Astronomy and I was obsessed with Ali so I made it my mission to pay close attention and remember everything that was taught to us in that class. I even studied star maps just to be able to impress her with my knowledge. At the time she had no idea I had a photographic memory, so when I took her on our first date I was able to really impress her with my knowledge of the constellations. Once we started getting serious, though, Trevor outed me and Ali found out the truth. I thought she would be pissed, but instead she told me that she loved me. It shocked the shit out of me, but I fucking loved her first so I couldn't have been happier with her admission.

"No one really knows how many visible stars can be seen with the naked eye because no one has tried to count them all. It could be any-where between five and ten thousand. With your gift and my dedication, I'm positive we can figure this out together. And who knows, maybe we can even become famous for it. They could name a star after us as a re-ward." She winks at me before placing a chaste kiss on my cheek, and I swear I can see the stars sparkling right through her brown eyes.

"You know you can just pay to have a star named after you, right? You want that, I'll make it happen."

"It's not the same though," she says. *"Are you nervous for the fight next week?"*

"Nervous? Come on now, angel. You know I'm undefeated. No one can touch me."

"Be serious, Liam. You've been practicing harder than normal these last few months, studying those fight tapes like it's your religion. I know this one is something different for you."

Sometimes I forget how well Ali knows me. It can be unnerving, but there's also something soothing about it. Maybe because I don't have to pretend with her.

"Yeah, there is something different with this one."

"What is it?"

"Darius Tate is a different type of boxer than I've fought before."

"How so?"

"He has more to lose and a shit ton to gain if he beats me. He's trying to make it out of the shitty part of the city he lives in. Working hard so he stays out of the gang life, unlike his brother who's heavily into it. So when Darius fights, he's more wild and unpredictable. He can switch from fighting with his head to demolishing with his heart in seconds. I can't track his movements as easy as the others I've fought."

There are a few moments of silence, where all I can hear are the waves crashing against the beach and Ali's soft breathing.

"If that's all it is, then you got this," she says, sneaking her hand under my shirt so her skin is on mine.

I reach down to adjust my jeans because the simplest touch from her always causes my cock to start paying attention. After I make myself more comfortable, I put my hand on top of hers.

"And what makes you so confident? I mean, other than the fact that you're totally aware of, and have accepted, my overall awesomeness in all things."

She giggles and my dick gets harder. We haven't tried it yet, but I'm pretty sure I can fuck her in this hammock. *"Because he's just like you. That's how you fight. In all aspects of your life. Try not to overthink this one, Liam. Use your natural instincts. Trust them and you'll beat Darius."*

God, I love her so fucking much.

We swing back and forth, counting the stars, and I tell her their names as I remember them from the maps. We make it to 941 before her eyes start to droop and she begins to nod off. I'm not far behind. This memory thing with the star maps wears me out mentally sometimes, but I wouldn't trade these nights for anything. Ali is worth it.

"Come on, babe. Let me take you to bed."

"No. No way. I'm awake, I swear. We have to make it to a thousand."

"Ali, we can do it when we get back in a few weeks. Gives us something to look forward to, yeah?"

She yawns big. "Yeah, okay. But can we sleep out here tonight? It's nice out and I don't want to move," she says, burrowing in closer to my chest.

"Sure," I concede, because honestly I'm quite content here too. "I love you, Ali."

"I love you, too."

"Oh yeah? More than the stars?"

"More than anything." She kisses my chest before closing her eyes. I almost think she's fallen completely asleep when she says, "Hey, Liam?"

"Yeah?"

"How long do you think it will take us to count them all?"

"I don't know. A long fucking time probably," I tell her as my own eyes become heavy with the promise of sleep.

"Then it's probably good we'll have each other for a long fucking time, isn't it?"

I laugh when she curses because it sounds so foreign and cute coming from her innocent lips. I kiss the top of her head. "It's definitely good. Better than good. Fucking amazing. Now go to sleep, angel."

Her breathing starts to even out quickly, and I know she's out.

I just wish I had stayed up like she wanted so we could have at the very fucking least made it to the thousandth star.

◈◈◈◈◈

"What are you doing out here?" Sky's voice draws me out of my bittersweet memory, the one that has haunted me for fucking years.

"Looking at the stars." I take a long pull from my beer, leaning back a little further in the lounge chair. Seeing as she's probably about to leave my ass I may as well get comfortable, and hopefully drunk too.

At least if Skylar is about to dump me she'll look fucking hot doing it; something about her in tiny cotton shorts and a tight tank top always seems to make me instantly hard.

She sits at the foot of my lounge chair, steals the beer right out of my hand, and takes a long pull. "This is L.A. You can't see the stars here. Kind of ironic if you think about it."

Tapping my head, I tell her, "Trust me, sweetheart. I can see them all up here." I contemplate reaching over, grabbing her around the waist, and pulling her to me so I can have just a few seconds of peace before she tears me apart, but I know now is not the time.

"I didn't read the file, Liam."

Now I kind of wished I'd told her to read it so I don't have to re-live this fucking nightmare. "Good for you. Shocked to see that you listened to me for once," I snap on reflex. I'm being an asshole. I don't want to be, but self-preservation seems to be forcing that tactic out of me.

"That's not fair and you know it. Don't do that."

"Do what?"

"Be a dick to me so that I run and you don't have to tell me what happened. I gave you an out in the car before Carl showed up, before he spewed his venom all over us, and you told me that's not how rela-tionships work. You were right."

I turn and grab another beer from the six-pack next to me. She reaches over and grabs my face so that I'm forced to look at her. "Hey. I said you were right. I want this relationship to work, so don't pretend with me. I want to know your reality, Liam."

I've never thought to compare Ali and Skylar. They're both so dif-ferent that it never even occurred to me. But the one thing they seem to have in common is an ability to read me, and that may be the only explanation I need as to why I'm falling for someone so different than the one who came before.

"I'm sorry. Shit, I'm sorry, Sky." This time I reach over and bring her closer to me, burying my face into the crook of her neck, breathing in her sweet scent and hoping it calms me just enough to get through this. "It's not what you think."

"Liam, I know. I know you're not a murderer. I'm well aware of how Carl works. I just needed to take a break from everything, not just you. I'm sorry if I made you think otherwise."

"I was never convicted of murder." She shivers slightly when I speak, goosebumps spreading across her neck.

"I never thought you were. Liam, I know you could never kill someone." She starts running her fingers through my hair in a reassuring gesture that doesn't go unnoticed but is entirely undeserved.

My eyes squeeze shut and I swallow hard. "No, Skylar. I was never convicted of murder, but that doesn't mean I didn't kill someone."

Skylar stills, and the hand stroking my hair halts before disappearing altogether. When I dare to finally look up, confusion is plastered all over her perfect face. "I don't understand. You killed someone?"

If what I'm about to tell her wasn't so fucked up, I would take a few extra moments to appreciate how fucking adorable she looks with her brow slightly furrowed and her nose scrunched up.

"Liam, are you telling me you killed someone?" She starts to scoot back, putting space between us, but I grab the back of her neck to stop her. I can't let her leave before I have a chance to explain.

"Liam, let go of me."

"No." She tries to pull away again, but I'm stronger. Placing my forehead against hers, I look directly into her eyes. "Promise me you'll let me explain first. If I let you go, swear to me you won't fucking run. Please. Just trust me," I plead.

Indecision has never appeared more evident, and as the seconds tick by and the pulse in her neck speeds up against my fingers, I begin to lose confidence that she will stay. I close my eyes, readying myself to release the hold I have on her neck to let her walk away, but then I feel her nod against me.

Fucking thank Christ. I release my hold, allowing her to move further down the lounge chair, away from me. Though I know she needs the space, I don't fucking like it.

"You're going to tell me everything, right?"

"Yes, baby I swear. The reason I—"

"No, wait!" She throws her hands up quickly to stop me.

"What?"

"Can you let me ask questions instead? I ask, you answer."

I would ask her why she wants to do it this way, but I'm a fucking expert at what it is Sky is seeking here. "You want to control how this goes?"

She nods slightly before softly saying please.

"Why?" I ask.

"Because I have a feeling that whatever you're about to tell me could break my heart, and I just need to be able to regulate the shatter."

Fuck if that revelation doesn't cause my own heart to crack a little. I guess I should be thankful to Skylar in this moment because the pain I'm feeling means I still fucking have one.

"Okay. You ask, I'll answer."

"So...you killed someone?"

"We're just jumping right in then." I sigh, scrubbing a hand over my face.

"Seems to sort of be the pink T-Rex in the room."

The fuck? "I think you mean white elephant, Sky."

"No, the white elephant in the room is, 'Oh hey, I actually have a live-in ex-girlfriend I never mentioned,' or, 'I once got arrested for stealing credit cards from my grandma's friends.' You just admitted to killing someone. That is a damn pink T-Rex."

I bark out an inappropriately timed laugh. How she is making me laugh in this moment, I have no idea. "That logic oddly makes fucking sense. And it was two."

"What?"

"It was two someone's. I killed two people."

"Oh. Shit."

"Yeah."

"But, I'm assuming you had a reason, right?"

"Yes."

"Did it happen the night of the attack? The night you got the scars?"

"Yes."

"The two you killed, did they hurt you?"

I only manage to nod, suddenly finding it harder and harder to answer, to confirm what had happened. I hate being reminded that it isn't just some nightmare I can wake from at any moment.

"And they killed them?" she asks, pointing to my arm that has the names inked on it.

"Yes."

She begins to move closer. Once she's sitting right next to me, she reaches over and pulls apart my clasped hands, turning the arm closest to her over.

"Trevor," she points to his name, "is your brother. Who were Isabel and Ali?" This time I let her touch the names. I force myself not to pull away or cringe, even though that's my first instinct.

"Izzy—Isabel—was my brother's wife. She was a firecracker, cussed like a fucking sailor. She was the only person I knew that could put Trevor in his place. Ali was my girlfriend."

I can't go into detail about Ali. Not now. Not fucking ever with Sky. It's not fair to me or to her.

"How did it happen?" she asks, linking her fingers through mine. The gesture is so fucking gentle and reassuring.

"Remember when I told you it was a random gang attack?"

"Yeah, I remember. You said it happened in Atlanta."

"It did. But I wasn't completely honest. It wasn't a random attack."

"I don't understand. Were you part of a gang or something?"

I chuckle dryly, brushing the windblown strands of her hair behind her ears. "No, baby. I wasn't a gang banger. Me, Trev, Isabel, and Ali all went to Atlanta for a fight I had lined up. It was a big one for me. I was actually pretty fucking nervous about it."

"Really? I don't think I could ever picture you being nervous. About anything."

"Well, I was. My opponent, Darius Tate, was pure fighter to the core. It wasn't just about the competition for him. He fought to thrive and survive. The way he competed, shit, I knew not to underestimate him. Darius was unpredictable, fast, and fuck he could hit hard."

"You respected him."

"I did, and knowing that he'd be a real challenge fucking excited me to no end. I was nervous, but I was also pumped. I trained the hardest I'd ever trained, watched his fights on repeat. I was prepared. And Darius, he respected me too. Neither one of us engaged in any public shit talking or bullshit weigh-in dramatics. My dad said it kind of reminded him of the old days, when boxing was more about the sport than the fucking antics. Anyway, the match went eight extremely bloody rounds. We went at it like goddamn street fighters, just pummeling the hell out of each another. Every time I thought I had him, he countered with something unexpected. By the eighth round, we both just started throwing haymakers, blindly going for a knockout, because at that point I think we both knew that was how it was going to end, how it had to end. Whether it was fucking luck or skill I still don't know, but I landed a huge left hit to his temple, and before he could shake it off, I caught him with an uppercut."

"You knocked him out?"

"I didn't just knock him out, Sky. I put him in a fucking coma."

"A coma? You put someone in a coma?" I guess she forgot that part of Carl's debriefing, and the look of shock and disappointment on her face breaks me down just a little more.

"Yes. It happens sometimes in boxing. Not often, but it can happen." What I'm telling her is the truth. It's rare, but not unheard of, and all boxers know the risks before they step into the ring. Broken bones, comas, the possibility of early dementia, and in the rarest of cases, even death. We accept the possibility of these dangerous outcomes because the thought of ignoring our passion, what we were born to do, is far worse.

"Wait. Hold on. I don't understand. What does all of this have to do with the attack? With the gang members?"

"Darius's piece of shit brother Marcus was a member of a collective gang out of Atlanta—The 187s." Her gaze quickly shoots to my shirt-covered chest and I see the recognition hit. The scars begin to burn under the weight of her stare, and heat spreads throughout my entire body. My heart pounds against my chest as the images of that night start to ravage my brain.

I have to release Sky's hand so I don't accidentally fucking break it because I recognize that my rage is taking hold of me, but it won't recognize her. When I stand up, I hear Sky say my name but all I can do is hold a finger, signaling for her to give me a minute. I have to finish telling her everything. I snatch another beer and pop the top with my forearm hoping the bite of pain will do something to distract me from the images, from my anger. It doesn't, so I take a long pull of the beer, killing half of it in one swig.

Fuck, I could use something harder than this beer right now.

"Eleven minutes, Skylar," I blurt out, digging the palms of my hands into my eyes. "I was only gone from them for eleven fucking minutes."

"What?" There is a tremble in her voice that punishes my ears, and she begins to stand up and move towards me, but I can't have her near me right now, not when I'm explaining how I failed to protect the people I loved.

"Don't move! Fuck!" That came out harsher than I meant it to. "I'm sorry. Just stay seated. *Please,* Sky. It will help me get through this." She nods and sits back down, but I don't miss the sheen of tears starting to build in her eyes.

I blow out a relieved breath. "Thank you." I swallow hard before I get up the nerve to continue.

"We were hanging out at this casino two nights after the fight. We decided to stay back in Atlanta a little longer because my guilty ass wanted to make sure I was around when Darius woke up. His doctor told me his recovery was promising. Darius's mind and body were already responding to stimuli. He was going to wake up. Anyway, it was pretty late when we finally decided to call it a night. Right when we were leaving the casino I got stopped by a few fans for some autographs. You have to understand, that was a new thing for me. Being recognized. And I ate that shit up too, like some cocky asshole. I told my brother to take the girls to the car. Kissed Ali and told her I would only be ten minutes behind them. Eleven minutes later I was out that casino door and into the parking lot." I kill the last half of the beer, grasping the neck of the bottle in my hand as I start to hear the sound all over again, piercing through my ears.

Over and over.

Louder and louder.

On torturous repeat.

Gutting me and breaking my heart all over again.

"I heard her screams before I even saw the car in the back of the lot. I took off running. By the time I got close enough to see what was happening, I realized I was too late. Both the rear doors were open. Marcus was on one side holding Ali's arms down while another guy was on top of her. He-he was fucking *raping* her."

"Oh god, Liam." The tears start to flow more freely now and she makes no effort to hide them or brush them away.

"When I finally made it to Ali, I tore the guy off of her and snapped his fucking neck without a thought. I never noticed the eight guys on the other side of the vehicle. By the time the first one reached me, I was so blind with rage that I hit him so hard I actually crushed his nose into his brain. Killed him on impact. But I couldn't take on the six left no matter how hard I fought. The rest is all a blur, just blurry snapshots of that night mixed with blackness. I kept drifting in and out of consciousness when they started torturing me. Burning me with the barrel of their guns, the ones they used to shoot my brother and Isabel with before I even got there. Marcus carved the 187 tag into my chest with a serrated knife. The same one he used to slit Ali's throat with right in front of me."

"H-how—" she stutters on the cusp of a sob, and seeing her cry almost has me following suit. I can even feel the unwanted moisture gathering in my eyes. "How are you alive? Why didn't they kill you too?"

And ain't that the million-dollar question, the one that has haunted me for years. Why didn't Marcus kill me? I was the one that put his brother in a coma. His anger should have been directed at me.

Somewhere between the booze and the drugs and the endless pussy I finally came across the answer, and it was as simple as the question.

"Because Marcus is a psychopath, and he is well aware that there are some punishments worse than death."

CHAPTER 21

Skylar

This is so much worse than anything I imagined. I wish I had read whatever Carl put in that stupid file so he wouldn't have had to relive this nightmare. When he told me he killed two people I was ready to run as far away from him as possible. When he told me why, I wanted nothing more than to run to him, wrap my arms around him, and take his pain away. It was in that moment that I knew I must love Liam, because if I could take on all his pain, even on top of my own, I would have. Even if it meant I could somehow give him Ali back.

But I can't, because life just fucking sucks that way. So I lie here in bed, running my fingers through his hair and down his bare back as his head rests on my stomach. He finally fell asleep an hour ago but I can't even seem to close my eyes for five minutes because I still have yet to process all that he has told me.

We spent two hours by the pool as he divulged everything. Not only did he tell me about the horrific attack, but he told me about the hell that followed after. The drugs and the constant drinking, the end of his professional boxing career, and the beginning of his uncontrollable violent outbursts.

Luckily Liam was never charged, let alone sent to jail for killing the two gang members. It was obvious that his actions had been in self-defense. But Marcus and the six other gang members were not so lucky. They were jacked up on a crystal meth and cocaine cocktail when they committed the crime, which somewhat explained the idiocy behind their rash and ridiculous revenge decision. It also meant that on top of the murder and rape charges, they also got charged with possession and intent to distribute. Every single one of them will die behind their prison walls, and rightfully so. But when Liam told me he ended up in the same hospital as Darius, and that Darius had actually apologized on his brother's behalf, I shed tears for them both. Liam told me that was his final breaking point because he couldn't find it in his heart to forgive Darius. Despite the fact he wasn't even close to his brother, Liam was so full of hate and anger that he couldn't accept an apology from a man that had no obligation to give one.

"*He put his hand over my hand and apologized for everything his brother had done, while I laid there in a hospital bed recovering from my injuries, and what did I do? I fucking hit him, Sky. I totally lost my shit. Didn't even register my own pain, or the fact I ripped out my IV as I attempted to beat a man I'd put into a coma. A man that had nothing to do with what happened, but I didn't give a shit. In that moment, all I saw was red. I didn't care that he was innocent, I just wanted to kill him because his blood took everything from me, and I wanted nothing more than to see that same blood spilled in front of me.*"

Even after Liam cleaned up his act to take care of his family, he still refused to forgive Darius or himself. The hatred and guilt that continues to rot inside him is incredibly destructive, a self-imposed punishment Liam does not deserve, and I will make him realize that even if he hates me for it afterward.

"You stopped." A deep rumble vibrates against my stomach and my heart nearly leaps out of my chest as my back shoots off the mattress.

"Holy shitballs! I thought you were asleep!"

He laughs lightly and moves to lean against the headboard next to me. "I was until you stopped rubbing my head with these sweet little fingers of yours." He grabs my hand and lifts it up to his lips, kissing my fingers one by one. "How long was I out?"

"About an hour." I rest my head on his shoulder.

"Weird. Feels like I slept right into the next day."

"Nope. Still have about two hours until it's officially tomorrow."

He kisses my temple before saying, "You have that photoshoot and interview pretty early in the morning. You should try and get some sleep, Sky."

I almost forgot about that. Time off for me isn't the same as it is for everyone else. I don't have to film, but Carl went ahead and booked me for some additional interviews and campaigns. I was able to re-schedule most of them, but this one I actually wanted to do. It's with *Fame Magazine* and they promised me I could use the interview as a platform to promote the indie I just finished wrapping up. I want to make sure I do everything I can to help this project succeed. I believe in it and *finally* have a passion project.

That doesn't mean I can manage to fall asleep though.

"I'm not tired yet."

"Yeah, me either. Are we good? After everything I told you to-night, I wouldn't blame you if you wanted to kick me to the curb."

"What are you talking about? What you told me changes nothing about me wanting to be with you. How could you even think that?" I ask, shifting slightly so I can see his face.

"Skylar, I killed two people."

"It was in self-defense, Liam. Jesus, you were protecting your family."

"No, I wasn't. If I was protecting them they would be here right now. They would be alive. Instead, I was off stroking my own fucking ego like an arrogant asshole while my family paid for my mistake."

I straddle his lap, wanting to be as close as possible when I tell him this so he really listens to what I'm saying. I ignore the way his whole body tenses, and I grab his chin when he tries to lower his head. "What happened that night was not your fault, Liam."

"Don't—"

"No. You look at me. I'm sure you've heard this a hundred times— from your parents, from Shayla, hell, you've probably heard the same mantra from Ali and Isabel's family." I can tell by the way his fingers tighten around my waist that I'm right in my assumption. "You refuse to believe it because something you did accidentally set that tragic night in motion, and you feel responsible. You revel in that guilt because you think it's deserved. That you earned that penance through their deaths, but that line of thinking is so incredibly misguided."

"No, it fucking isn't! *I* put Darius in a coma. *I* stayed inside that casino to sign autographs for people instead of leaving with them. You weren't there, Skylar, so you don't get to have an opinion on this. So just back the hell off!"

I know I may live to regret what I say next, the words will be purposely harsh, but I can't get through to a guy like Liam with motivational clichés and positive platitudes. So I take a deep breath and just go for it.

"It wasn't your fault, Liam. I mean, if you really think about it, this was all your dad's fault. Those deaths are on him, right?"

The fuse is lit.

I don't move.

I can't breathe.

I watch as the wick burns away, as Liam realizes what I said, and I wait helplessly for the bomb to explode.

"What the fuck did you just say to me?"

He quickly lifts me off of him and I'm shocked, with the anger radiating off him right now, that he doesn't just toss me off the bed. God knows I deserve it. He flips the light on and I really wish he hadn't because the sight of him both scares me and makes me want to get on my knees and beg for his forgiveness. But I can't. I won't. I have to get through this so Liam can finally let his guilt go.

"I asked you a fucking question, Skylar!"

"I realize that."

"Then have the fucking courtesy to answer me!"

"You forcing me to repeat it won't change what I said."

"Oh, that's fucking great! So then you really are just a bitch who blamed my dad for the death of his own son." Okay, ouch. "You listen to me, and you listen well." His jaw clenches so hard I'm surprised his teeth don't shatter, then he speaks slowly like I'm a child he's reprimanding. "Don't ever try to project your twisted daddy issues on to me. My dad had nothing to do with this, and you damn well know it, so shut your mouth and stop fucking with me."

If he had slapped me it would have hurt less, but I don't stop. I *can't* until he hears me. "How can you possibly be mad at me? I'm using your logic here, Liam."

"What the hell are you talking about?"

"If your dad hadn't gotten you into boxing, then you would have never been in Atlanta. Never put Darius in a coma. His psycho whack job brother would have never darkened your world by taking your loved ones from you and putting his marks on you." I point directly at his bare chest.

As the silence ticks on, I think that maybe I've gotten through to him. He roughly drags his hands through his hair. Those eyes I've grown to worship are trained at the ceiling as if they hold the words he's searching for. When he turns his back on me and starts toward the bedroom door, I hang my head down in defeat; I seriously fucked up.

My heart shatters like shards of glass, the pieces splintering my chest and causing pain I've never felt before. I can't find the will to even move, to go after him and stop him from leaving. The loud thud, the one that sounds like a fist meeting drywall, confirms that he is in fact done with me.

Then I look up.

Where I thought I would see only vacant space, I see him. His hands are braced in the doorway, not looking for an exit, but looking in, at me. Before I even register that he hasn't left, he destroys the space between us until he's right in front of me. He buries his hands in my hair and tilts my head up so I'm forced to look into his eyes.

"That is the stupidest fucking thing I've ever heard, Sky." I don't know how to respond or if I'm even supposed to. I'm not sure if I'm witnessing a breakdown or a breakthrough. When his lips descend to mine harshly, I almost burst into tears because I know.

He gets it. Finally, he understands.

"I know," I say the second his lips release mine. "It's so stupid."

"It wasn't his fault."

"No."

"It wasn't my fault."

I smile big as if he's just given me the biggest gift. "No, slugger, it wasn't."

He continues kissing me, raw with passion, as if he's releasing five years of guilt. His hands roam wildly as if he's desperate to touch my skin. I didn't even realize we were moving until I feel the mattress hit the back of my knees. When I fall backwards onto the bed, he finally releases my lips. Standing to his full height, he reaches behind his neck and pulls off his shirt.

God, that is sexy. He really is a sight to behold. There is something beyond just looks, something in the feral way he moves, the way his dangerous eyes appraise me, and those same eyes flash with a moment of vulnerability, an emotion I haven't witnessed in him before. I only have seconds to appreciate the rare sentiment because his warm, rough hands are now under my shirt, caressing my skin with a gentleness I have yet to experience with Liam. In fact, everything he does after is nothing but soft caresses punctuated by his tongue and mouth slowly tasting my skin. When he finally enters me, it's with a gentle thrust, and every movement after is made with care and passion.

This is different.

He is different.

And though I have no experience with it, and the thought of it once seemed liked fiction to me, I would almost describe it as what I imagine making love is like. Like he wants to possess me. Learn and own me. Force me to desire and need him by creating an addiction with his attentive touches and whispered words of how perfect and beautiful he finds me. When he comes, he doesn't curse before groaning my own name at me. Instead, he whispers and praises it. As if he's thanking me and assuring me that I am only meant for him.

When we finally have fucked to the point of exhaustion, he can't even find the strength to grab a towel to clean me, which he has always done before. Instead, I just curl up against his chest and he holds me close. I graze my fingers across his scars, tracing and memorizing each one, even daring to run my fingers across the ink on his arm, over the names of the loved ones he lost. It isn't until he falls asleep that I let the tears fall. Because I know there is no way this can last. I'll never be able to measure up to his first love, or be as perfect as Ali was, and once he finds out my secret, it will be made crystal clear to him. Liam can do better than me, and after what he has already been through, he deserves better because I'll be nothing but a burden.

But until that moment comes, I'll live in my denial and soak up every second I can with the man I'm in love with.

CHAPTER 22

Skylar

"**S**kylar Joy Barrett, stop hanging off your man like a damn octopus and get your ass in the pool right this second before I get out and throw you in!"

"You'd have to get past my bodyguard first, Erik!" I wrap my arms around Liam's firm waist as he flips the burgers on the grill. I slip my hands under his shirt, wanting to touch his skin, wishing he could take his shirt off like Noah and Erik, but he's not ready for the questions or stares. And frankly, I don't blame him. I'm a little sad that I can't openly gawk at his godlike body—scars and all, but I get it.

Since Liam's admission and subsequent breakthrough, I've been incredibly happy and carefree, so I decided on the spur of the moment to have some of my friends over for a small get together. Noah, who's been spending more time at Erik's house than ours, brought him along. I'd forgotten how much fun I always have with Erik around. Winter brought Amber, well not so much brought Amber as Amber decided to bring herself as she tends to do. That girl is like herpes in human form. No one wants it around, but surprise! Here it is to ruin your party. And if she keeps eye-fucking Liam I'll deflate one of her implants with her ridiculous heels.

"That's right, baby." Liam turns slightly, slaying me with that wicked smile of his, before placing a light kiss on the tip of my nose, making those butterflies take flight in my stomach. That is, until Amber speaks and massacres every one of them with her annoying voice.

"Well, if that's all it takes to get manhandled by Liam, I'll gladly toss you in the pool, Skylar."

"Letting that slut flag fly a little early today, aren't we, Amber?" Noah snaps at her from the lounge chair where he is currently tanning himself. He doesn't even bother to open his eyes to spare her a glance either.

"Did you just call me a slut, Noah?" She actually looks offended, though I've no clue why. He never misses a chance to joke about her whorish ways.

"Cut the innocent act, Amber. Everyone knows your vag has accepted more semen donations than a sperm bank."

"Oh shit." Winter chokes on a laugh and a little of the beer she just sipped. I try and hide my smile behind Liam, who's currently shaking with silent laughter.

Amber purses her lips, and if it weren't for her oversized sunglasses, I'm sure we would be able to see the daggers she's shooting at Noah. "Why do you always have to be such an ass to me?"

"Now, children, let's not fight. This is supposed to be a fun day, remember?" Winter chimes in playfully, throwing her arm around Erik's shoulder.

Noah finally sits up, sliding his sunglasses to the top of his head. They're sitting on opposite sides of the pool, but he's glaring at her like she's five feet in front of him. "Amber, you came to Skylar's house uninvited and then proceeded to hit on her man. Maybe start to show her some respect and I'll be less of an ass."

"Oh whatever, it was a joke. You knew it was a joke didn't you, Liam?"

The way she addresses him and not me only goes to prove Noah's point, and has me finally speaking up. "What are the odds she's like a T-Rex? If we stand still and don't speak is she still able to see us?" I direct toward Liam.

"I heard that."

"I would hope so," I say directly to her so there is no confusion.

I've never been a big fan of ganging up on one person; it all seems a little too *Mean Girls* to me, and I of all people can sympathize. But when it comes to Amber, I can't seem to give a shit. The girl is what I like to refer to as TST.

Tabloid Socialite Trash.

She gets off on being in the tabloids in any capacity. The only reason paparazzi care about her in the first place is because she's related to Hollywood royalty. Her uncle, Winter's dad, is a legendary director. She was merely famous by association for years until a sex tape of her banging a married A-list actor was mysteriously "stolen" and sold to a porn company. But she failed where the Kardashians didn't. Turns out Amber didn't even have enough talent to get a reality show off the ground, so instead she just kind of created her own reality show using the paparazzi as her cameramen and her absence of morality as her director.

"Whatever. You were never this touchy when it came to Cass."

Oh yeah, and she slept with Cass.

It's not that I was jealous and it was after I ended our friends-with-benefits arrangement, so thankfully nothing that was ever in her touched me, but it just shows you the kind of girl she is.

"Speaking of Cass, where is our moody little rock star? Isn't he supposed to be here today?" Winter asks as Liam slams his beer down a little harder than necessary but wisely keeps his mouth shut on the matter.

He had plenty to say about it last night when he found out I was inviting Cassiel to this impromptu pool party. I get why he has a problem with Cass; they didn't exactly look like they were eager to become besties the first time they met. Cass came out of the gate with his full on *I don't give a shit* attitude, and if Liam thinks that behavior was reserved only for him, he has so much to learn about Cass.

Cassiel constantly spits that trademark indifference my way, too. Liam thought his behavior that day at breakfast stemmed from some unrequited longing for me; that he was jealous seeing me there with Liam, but that couldn't be further from the truth. Liam doesn't know Cass like I do and trying to explain it to him would do more harm than good.

So, in my infinite wisdom, I decided what better way to fix this than to invite Cass? I can show Liam firsthand why he has nothing to worry about because I need them to at least be civil to one another. I won't abandon Cassiel; he will always be a part of my life. He's earned my loyalty and I know that sooner rather than later I need to explain why to Liam.

"He should be coming. He texted me last night and said he was in, but you know Cass. It's like he's allergic to reliability."

Liam grunts before saying, "With any luck, he's allergic to barbeques, pools, and you."

"Liam," I say in slight warning.

Despite those hot as hell aviator sunglasses he's wearing, I know just by the slight rise of his eyebrows that he's daring me to fight with him on this. Last night he told me he would "allow" Cass to come over, but that he didn't have to like it. Then I proceeded to inform him that he doesn't "allow" me to do anything, which led to an aggressive argument punctuated by sex. Angry, passionate, life-altering sex that had me forgetting my own name and screaming his.

And this arrogant bastard knows just how much it affected me judging by the smirk that was on his face and the way I practically panted his name while I was attempting to scold him with it.

Tugging on his T-shirt, I pull him directly in front of me and stand on my tiptoes so I can whisper, "Stop. We don't want a repeat of last night. Not when I have friends here."

"Speak for yourself, baby. If I had my way, I'd kick them all out, drag you inside, and bend you over the couch."

"What is up, my people!" a loud voice bellows through my backyard, quickly breaking us apart. A quiet *fuck* slips from Liam's lips before he grasps the back of my neck and kisses me. Hard. Because he knows who just walked into my backyard and this is his way of pissing on me so that there is no question of who I belong to. But as suspected, Liam has nothing to worry about because here Cass stands, arm slung around his girlfriend, the beautiful, yet seemingly shy Paige. She is one of the reasons I wanted Cassiel to come. There is rarely a time when he *doesn't* have a girlfriend. Cass typically only does relationships. They last a few months, then for reasons unknown to me they end abruptly and our arrangement would kick in again.

"Speak of the devil," Winter says, pulling herself out of the pool to greet Cass with a hug.

"That's angel, sweet pea, and don't you forget it. You're getting me all wet here, darlin'. That's my job," he flirts, kissing Winter on the cheek.

"Don't be a pig." She shoves his shoulder before giving a hug to Paige, who seems completely unaffected by his comment to Winter. If Liam said anything like that to a girl in my presence, I would have thrown his ass in the pool, after I drained it.

But that's just how Cass is, and his girlfriends always seem blissfully pliant. Noah gives a lazy wave toward them and continues to get his tan on while Erik gets out and gives him a man hug while mentioning it's good to see him again.

Then Cassiel lifts his shades and aims his devious gaze towards me. "Where's my hug, Speedy?"

Shit. There's that nickname again.

I hate everything it represents, and the fact that he knows it and still continues to use it bugs the hell out of me, but I refuse to acknowledge it today. I'm happy, I want to have a good time, and I want Liam and Cass to at least play nice. If Liam believes I'm uncomfortable with something Cassiel has done or said to me, I know he will not hesitate to shut him up.

So I squeeze Liam's hand in reassurance, giving him a quick wink and a smile before I make my way to Cassiel, feeling his eyes burning through my back with each step I take.

"Cass, glad you could make it." He lets go of Paige and walks toward me in that slow, cocky way that only he can. I even take a second to admire how good he looks. Board shorts hanging low, a black vintage Bowie concert tee, the one we found together at a thrift store when we were seventeen, stretching tight across his chest. He looks good. Healthy. Healthier than the last time I saw him which means he's probably clean again. When he hijacked our breakfast weeks ago, I suspected he may be using again—he gets nasty when he uses—but by the look of it, he's now flying straight.

"Damn, I've missed you," he says, picking me up and spinning me around.

"Missed you too." I separate from him quickly. Funny how I can be comfortable having sex with him, but that intimacy factor, something even as simple as a hug, has my muscles tensing like I was just thrown into a tub of ice water.

Except with Liam.

"Hey, Paige, nice to meet you finally."

"Hey, Skylar. Nice to meet you, too. Thanks for inviting me."

"Of course! You guys can head over to the bar. There are beers in the fridge and a pitcher of vodka lemonade on the counter. Liam's grilling up some food now."

"Why don't you go get us a drink babe?" Cass points Paige to the bar before turning his attention back to me. "So, bodyguard got a promotion to cook, then," he says low enough that only I can hear.

"Cassiel."

"Skylar."

"Knock it off. Don't be an ass. I want you two to get along. Please."

He flashes me a grin before conceding, "You got it, Speedy. You know I can never have enough friends." He saunters up to Liam. When he gets to him he shoves his hand out.

"Good to see you again, bodyguard."

Liam stares at Cass's hand as if it's infected with Ebola and he would rather gnaw his own hand off than shake it.

"Well, okay then," Cass says before pulling his hand back.

Cass looks over at me and shrugs before heading to the patio bar.

"You could have been a little nicer to Cass." I poke Liam in the ribs trying to take his attention away from the damn barbeque.

"I could've been," he replies dryly, his attention still on the grill. "Hand me the cheese slices, baby." I pick up the package of deli cheese and shove it hard into his chest. "Jesus. What the fuck, Sky?"

"Stop being an ass and try to be nice. He brought his damn girlfriend for crying out loud. There's no reason to be all dickish with him."

"I am being nice. For me, this *is* nice. If I wasn't being nice, his ass would be at the bottom of the pool after I drained it." Holy shitballs. Can he read my mind or something? "And you're delusional if you think he is even remotely serious about that girl. He gave you a hug like he hadn't seen you in years and he just found you during a zombie apocalypse. Meanwhile, he just made her get her own drink in a house she's never been in, at a party with people it seems she's never met. He still hasn't introduced her to anyone else here except you. Look at him now. He's over there talking to Erik while she's standing back at the bar looking like a lost little puppy."

I take a quick glance over and, sure enough, Paige is staring blankly into her glass at the outdoor bar while Cass chats up Erik near the pool. I've seen Cass go through his share of girlfriends, but his inability to stay committed has nothing to do with some unrequited love for me, that much I know. But I'm sick of trying to defend myself. I just want to have a good time.

I've been craving some excitement for a few days now. It's been itching at me, the need to do something crazy and dangerous. Mix it up a little. That's why I wanted this pool party to begin with. I'm starting to feel antsy and fucking ready to party. I need a release.

"Hey!" I take a sip of my drink while everyone around me stops what they're doing to look my way. Even Amber, who I wish wasn't here, but whatever, in for a penny, in for a pound and all that. "So, I was thinking, now that we're all here, we should go to Vacancy on Saturday. I think we're long overdue for a night out."

Noah chokes slightly on his drink, while Cass and Winter just give me a blank stare. You would think I just told them I plan to birth an alien baby on Saturday.

"Um, are you sure you want to do that, Skylar?" Concern laces Winter's tone.

"What is Vacancy?" Liam asks before closing the lid on the barbeque.

"It's a club," Noah says.

"Not *just* a club," Amber cuts in with a giddy purr that has me rolling my eyes. "It's *the* club in LA. Can't even get in unless you're one of the chosen to have the password."

"Password? To get into a club? Fucking seriously?"

"Yes, Liam, seriously." I don't know why that comment grates on me. Maybe it's because to him it may seem stupid, but this is my life.

The side I want him to see and appreciate. Part of me knows I'm being overly sensitive, but I can't help that it bothers me.

Before I have a chance to give him more details his cell phone rings. I already know it has to be a member of his family as he goes to answer it. They are the only ones that ever call him. When he mouths *mom* to me I nod my head and he disappears into the house.

"So," Cassiel says, sidling up to me. "Vacancy?"

"What about it? Don't tell me you have an issue with that, you practically live there. I'm pretty sure they named a drink after you."

"I have no problem going to Vacancy. You know I'm always up for a good time. I just know it's not good when *you* finally get up for that time."

I throw back some of my drink, letting the cool sweet lemon flavor quench my thirst while barely registering the slight burn of vodka that comes with it.

"And you're drinking again," Cass says, interrupting my enjoyment of the drink. I ignore him because I do not, under any circumstances, want to follow where this conversation is headed right now.

"So what if I'm drinking? It's not like I'm an alcoholic, Cassiel." I start to walk away but he wraps his arm around my arm and pulls me back.

"I know that," he speaks low enough so that only I can hear him. But it does not escape my attention that Noah and Winter are trying their best not to watch this exchange, both failing miserably.

"And you know very well that is not what I'm getting at. Don't treat me like I'm a stranger or some random bodyguard fling that doesn't know any better," he warns in that deep, husky growl that used to turn me on but recently, and by recently, I mean this very second, is pissing me off.

"Liam is not a fling," I hiss.

"Yeah whatever, Speedy. The—"

"And stop calling me Speedy! You know how much I hate when you call me that and you continue to do it! Knock it the hell off!" I warn, shrugging out of his grip.

"No, I won't knock it the hell off. You know why I continue to call you that? Because I know you fucking hate it. I know what the nickname does to you. What it means to you. And if that's the only way I can knock some fucking reality into the land of denial you're living in right now, then I will call you Speedy until your ears bleed."

"You're being an ass on purpose to trigger me? How sweet of you Cass," I roll my eyes. "And I am not living in denial."

"Yes, you fucking are. And yea I'm being a dick because you won't pay attention otherwise. The past confirms that don't ya think Skylar?"

"I just got done filming a movie, Cass. Three months and I did just fine."

"Dammit, Skylar, have you not seen anyone? Done any of the research? You can be fine for fifty-one weeks out of the fucking year. But that last week, that's the one that will get you, and you should know that. I can tell within the first ten minutes of being here how different you are."

"Shut up."

"How edgy and excitable and fidgety you are."

"Knock it off, Cass. I mean it."

"Hell, you rarely drink, and my guess is you've had more than one of these," he sticks his finger in my glass and pulls it out of my hand, throwing the rest back in one large gulp before slamming it onto the table next to him.

"Have you even told him yet?"

"Look at me, Cass. I'm fine, okay? Did you ever think that I'm just happy? Am I not allowed to be happy or go to a club without you second-guessing me? You're not my parent or my keeper, just like I'm not yours. You don't hear me interrogating you over Paige, do you?"

"Nice attempt at a subject change." He rolls his eyes at me. "Just promise me that this is handled otherwise the same rules apply as before. I still have those pictures—"

I quickly slap my palm over his mouth. "Cassiel Logue, *shut up.*" I thought that demand came out quietly but I can feel all eyes on me now. Sure enough, when I glance around, everyone is gawking at us. I dare to take a quick look behind me, making sure Liam is still inside the house before I properly tear into Cass. He's still on the phone, pacing back and forth with a small smile on his face.

Perfect. The coast is clear. "Don't you dare threaten me with those photos again. You played that card once, and I won't let you do it again. You're supposed to be my friend."

"I'm being your friend the only way I know how."

"No, you aren't. A friend would be happy that I'm happy. A friend would relax and enjoy a freaking pool party at my house. And a friend would go to Vacancy with me and tell me all about his new girlfriend even if it is the tenth one this year." I blow out an exasperated breath.

A disarmingly shy smile works its way across Cassiel's face, the dangerous one to women everywhere, the one that suddenly transforms him into a picture of innocence. The one that helped him earn the name The Angel of Rock. He's not anything close to shy and innocent, but damn if that smile doesn't make you forget he's made of nothing but mysterious shadows and dangerous dark.

"She's actually only the sixth, thank you very much." He bites his lower lip while looking over at Paige, waving his pinky finger at her. Paige is seated at the bar, now talking with Erik and Noah, but the second Cass bestows that small bit of attention, her entire face lights up, the blush on her cheeks evident that she's completely soaking it up.

"Well, whatever, she seems sweet," I tell him, my shoulders sagging in relief. I hadn't even realized how tense I was until now.

"She is. That's how I like them. The sweeter they are, the more fun they are to ruin."

"You're a real asshole, you know that?" I shove a hand into his shoulder. He purposefully stumbles backward until he falls into the pool. I didn't even push him that hard. Drama queen.

Laughter erupts from everyone as Cass stands up in the pool, spitting water out of his mouth.

"That was fantastic," Noah says with a shit-eating grin plastered to his face, his phone pointed toward Cass. "I got it all on video and I'm uploading it to Instagram as we speak."

"And I will so be reposting that to Skylar's Instagram." Winter pulls out her phone and starts typing away.

"Why bother? Noah's already posting it, he'll just tag me in it."

"Because, Skylar." Oh great, she's using her mom tone. "Rose says you need to be posting to your Instagram and Twitter at least four times a week."

Ah yes. Rose, my super-agent. Who I actually rather like, and not just because Carl loathes her and was completely against me hiring her in the first place. That was one of the biggest selling points for me.

"Yeah, but you know how much I despise that social media bullshit." Instagram, Snapchat, Facebook, Twitter, I hate them all. Posting anything on them is pretty much like playing Russian roulette with my confidence. People will either hate to love me or love to hate me or just hate to hate me.

"I know, which is why I'm posting it for you." When I roll my eyes at her, she shakes her head. "What? You have a problem making six figures for a stupid Instagram post? Such a hardship."

"You make money from an Instagram post?" A deep voice rumbles behind me and I about jump out of my skin, almost falling into the pool. Luckily Liam's hand wraps around my arm, pulling me back just in time.

"Whoa there, sweetheart. You're always so jumpy." He chuckles, kissing me on top of my head.

"I'm not jumpy! You just make no noise when you approach. It's like you're training to be the next member of Seal Team Six or something."

"Baby, I opened and closed those doors," he says, pointing behind him as if I don't know where my own doors are. "Then I popped the cap off this beer. I'm not the one with the problem. It's your cute jumpy ass that's the problem."

Before I get a chance to defend myself, Cass chooses this moment to finally agree with my boyfriend. "Oh, I know. She's more skittish than a seeing-impaired kitten," he says, lifting himself out of the pool.

"Tell me about it. Anytime I open a door to a room she's in she jumps about ten feet and looks like she's about to have a heart attack. You'd think I was a serial killer, or that she's been attacked by a rogue door at some point in her life," Liam finally engaging with Cass in a conversation would normally make me ecstatic, except it's at my expense and they are both full of shit. The need to defend myself overwhelms my want to see their sudden camaraderie, but before I get a chance to say anything, Noah decides to pipe in.

"You are super jumpy, Morningstar. Remember that time you

shot out of your chair at the Golden Globes after Ronan Connolly set your drink down on the table and accidentally sent your elbow into his balls?" He laughs, everyone else joining in.

"Well, who sneaks up on someone with a drink?!"

"Skylar, he asked you if he could get you a drink while he was up, you said yes, and he came back five minutes later!"

Liam is laughing his ass off and I'm torn between being irritated that they are all ganging up on me and ecstatic that at least everyone is getting along. Even Amber has yet to speak up and annoy me.

"Let me get this straight. You nailed A-list movie star Ronan Connolly in the nuts?" Liam throws his arms around me, still laughing, only softer now, and whispers in my ear, "You are so fucking adorable I can hardly stand it sometimes."

"Yo, bodyguard!" Cass yells out, causing Liam to release me. "Your meat's burning," he says, pointing to the grill. I look over and, sure enough, smoke is spilling out of the grill.

"Oh shit!" Liam runs over and throws open the lid, waving the plumes of smoke out of his face. "I think it's all good. Thanks for the heads-up."

Cass salutes Liam and shoots me a wink before turning to Paige and nuzzling her neck, making her giggle. Right now I couldn't be happier. I haven't heard from Carl or gotten news about Jeff in weeks. With Liam in my bed, I've stopped having nightmares about my mom, and right now everyone that matters to me is getting along. Minus Amber, but at the very least she's fallen asleep on her lounger so I don't have to hear her speak.

I feel on top of the world. Cass is so wrong. There is nothing going on with me. My life is fucking perfect right now, and I can't wait to share it all with Liam.

CHAPTER 23

LIAM

This is the fifth day I've woken up in this bed alone, and I'm really starting to fucking hate it. Not just because I've been waking up hard and ready to get my dick wet, but because I've actually found myself enjoying her body wrapped around mine. It hasn't escaped my attention that Skylar has barely slept in the last five days, waking from nightmares she won't tell me anything about because she claims she can't remember them. She gets up early every morning, sneaking out of bed because she has so much "work" to do. The first three mornings this happened my ego actually took a major fucking hit. How could she not want to wake up next to me like I do her?

Yet every time I go down those stairs to find and confront her about ditching me, she has the brightest fucking smile and the wildest energy I've ever seen her have, bouncing around, and always with a new project she is working on. Yesterday she was writing a script for an idea she had for a movie, which I had no idea she could do, and the day before that she had completely reorganized her closet.

That one woke me up.

But I won't complain because Sky ended up riding me on top of a pile of clothes she had thrown off the hangers. She was wild and free, and it was fucking amazing. Sex with her during these days has been nothing short of phenomenal and constant. Her stamina has almost put mine to shame. On the fourth morning I started peeking through her drawers and purses thinking she had drugs stashed somewhere. Maybe some coke hidden away that she was snorting behind my back. I found nothing and also felt like fucking shit for doing it, but I'm at a total loss as to what to do here.

While I can appreciate all the benefits of this side of Sky, I can't help but feel this unease growing in my gut, and I'm done fucking ignoring it. It's six in the morning for fuck's sake and we didn't even fall asleep until after two. So I toss the covers off and grab my track pants from the floor. I'm not going to bother with my morning run today because Sky and I need to sort this shit out.

Imagine my surprise when I hit the bottom of the stairway and hear *two* voices rattling on. I recognize the second voice as Winter's, and while she works for Sky and has been around these last few weeks, I can't fathom why she is here this early.

"Morning!" Sky runs over and throws herself around me so hard I actually fall back a little.

"Morning, baby." I kiss her on top of her head before moving to her lips, my previous issue with her almost forgotten and buried under her excitement. "Morning, Winter." I nod in her direction, and the slight apologetic look on her face almost escapes my notice. Almost.

Something is up here.

"What's going on?" I direct this to both of them because I'm honestly curious, and I don't know which one of them will be honest and tell me.

"What do you mean?" Sky asks, a mischievous look gracing her face.

"I mean, what the fuck is going on? Why is Winter here at six in the morning? Why are you not in bed with me right now?"

"Winter is here to help me."

"Help you with what?"

"Skylar, do you really want to do this right now?"

Okay, now I'm even more intrigued. Winter looks panicked and Skylar looks like a kid on Christmas, before said kid realized Santa was just a fake-ass creepy mascot.

"Yes. Why wouldn't I?"

"Do what?" I ask.

Winter looks at me as if she's trying to silently convey a message, one I can't decipher because, as it turns out, I still can't fucking read minds. Before I get a chance to say another word, Sky is pulling me out the front door. By the time we hit the driveway, I only have one question:

"What the fuck is that?" I ask, pointing to the sleek black car parked next to Winter's. "You bought yourself a '65 GT40?!" I slide my hand across the hood; my girls got good fucking taste.

"No."

"What? Then what's it doing here?"

"I mean, yes, I bought the car, but not for me." Sky reaches into her back pocket and pulls out a set of keys, then tosses them over to me. I easily catch them by the time she announces, "It's yours."

"Excuse me?" I know I heard that wrong. As soon as that beaming smile starts to dim, I realize that my tone was harsher than I meant it to be. Or maybe it wasn't. I mean, fuck, if she really bought me a car, that, in this condition, probably ran her about two-hundred grand, my tone is probably about to get a lot fucking harsher.

"It's yours! It's your car. I got it for you today! Okay, not today. Yesterday, actually. I called a friend of mine that deals in vintage cars, but Win was able to pick it up from him this morning and bring it to me. I figured it would be perfect for you to drive me to Vacancy in."

My head is spinning. That's the only way to describe it, because honestly I can't latch on to one single emotion right now. I'm pissed, confused, insulted, irritated, and fucking worried about her. But when I look at her face, all I see is enthusiastic, gleeful blue eyes staring back at me. And for some reason, that makes the pissed off feeling beat out all the rest.

I toss the keys right back to her. "This isn't my fucking car. Take it back, return it, drive it yourself, I don't really care. But this car is not mine."

I turn around, walking back into her house, passing a wary look-ing Winter on the way. Even she gets it. How the hell can the girl I've been inside countless times, slept next to and divulged secrets to over the last few months not?

"Liam!" Skylar's confused voice carries from behind me.

"What?" I bark at her, causing her to falter. I hate that I've caused her to suddenly hesitate, but at the same time I also don't give a shit. I know she can handle my temper. Not to mention, Sky can give as good as she can take. If she couldn't, we wouldn't have lasted this long.

"What? Seriously, Liam. How about what the hell is your problem?"

"You bought me a fucking car, that's what!"

She throws her hands in the air. "And?! So what! I bought you a gift Liam, I didn't rip off your balls. Calm down."

Normally her sass coupled with her tiny shorts and tight tank top would have my cock standing at attention. But right now, I'm too fucking pissed to notice.

Until she pushes her chest out a little. I'm still a fucking man, and right now my mind is starting to imagine what it would be like to fuck my anger out on her.

Where the hell were we again?

Oh, right. "Don't be a smartass! Why would you think I would ever need or want you to buy me a car, Skylar? I have a bike at home. At *my* home. If I need some form of transportation I will go and get it. Or I'll buy my own fucking car if I need one here! Believe it or not, I can afford one, even without the money you pay me. I'm not some boy-toy that needs or wants to be kept!"

"Okay," Winter says from behind Skylar. "Maybe let's take it down a notch or two. It's a little early in the morning to start World War Three."

"I wasn't implying you need to be kept! I just wanted to give you a present. Isn't that what couples do? Give each other gifts and show their affection?" Sky snaps, completely ignoring Winter.

"Yeah, that's what couples do. They buy candy or flowers or a fucking shirt. They *don't* buy two-hundred thousand dollar cars after a month of dating. Especially not when one part of the couple is in the other's employment. Though in all seriousness, I have no clue what I'm being paid for anymore because you barely go out enough to need a damn bodyguard. I mean, seriously, what the fuck?!" I snap, instantly feeling like shit, especially when I see confusion and sadness wash over her beautiful face. I didn't mean to demean what we have based on the length of our relationship because I'm pretty fucking close to being in love with her anyway, or to throw my job in her face, but I seriously can't seem to shut the fuck up.

I need to apologize. "Look, Skylar—"

"Don't." She shakes her head, stepping back when I go to reach for her. "Obviously I somehow fucked up when I bought you a car. Forgive me for trying to show my gratitude. But you're right. You need to work more. Earn your paycheck so you stop feeling like a 'boy-toy.' Lucky for you, we are all going to Vacancy tomorrow night. The pool house is still yours, so feel free to sleep there tonight. Be ready by ten tomorrow. And let's make sure we keep it professional, so it's completely clear what the fuck you are actually being paid for."

She throws my words back at me before stomping her cute little ass upstairs, making sure to slam her bedroom door for good measure. I know I fucked up, but I also know there's something not right here, and though my need to go after Skylar is manifesting, I stay put. Whatever this is she's going through, she has to be ready to come to me on her own.

"Well, that's one way to handle it, O'Connor. Way to hit every insecurity of hers in one breath," Winter says from behind me. Shit, I was so caught up that I forgot she was still here.

"Fucking forgive me for lacking sensitivity at six in the damn morning after I just got gifted an expensive as fuck car from my girlfriend, who incidentally has been acting off for the last few days. This doesn't seem at all odd to you?"

"I told you she wasn't like us."

"Yeah, and I still don't know what that cryptic bullshit means. Is she…" I rub the back of my neck, drawing in a deep breath before I speak because honestly, I don't know if I'm ready for the answer to this. "Does she have a drug problem or something?"

Winter laughs like I'm joking, but I find nothing funny about it. "No, she doesn't have a damn drug problem. Are you for real right now?"

"Are you? I'm not an idiot, Winter, and believe me when I tell you

I've been around the block a few fucking times. The erratic behavior, she's barely slept in days but that hasn't slowed her down one fucking bit. Sky seems to be turned up to fucking ten all the time. I can tell you that is *exactly* how I was acting when I was doing coke." She's even been fucking me like she's high on the shit, but I decide to leave that part out.

"Jesus, you did coke?"

"Oh please. You live in LA, don't act like I'm the first person you've ever met who's done it. And I haven't touched the shit in years."

"Look, just give it a few more days and she'll be back to her old self. Skylar gets this way sometimes, and no, maybe it isn't exactly normal behavior, but nothing about her life is normal. How many seventeen-year-olds that you know buy a freaking mansion to live in? How many girls you know whose pictures are all over magazines by age twelve? And don't even get me started on her dick of a father. Skylar handles her life differently, that's all, and if you can't handle that you should move on now before she falls in love with you, if she hasn't already."

"Well, I need to get going. I have a lot to do today, including apparently returning this car to the dealership. Just give Skylar some space and give her a break. See ya tomorrow night, O'Connor," she says, grabbing the keys to the car off the floor where Sky threw them before walking out the door.

Winter's words are hardly comforting, and it's still possible Skylar has a drug problem and is really fucking good at hiding it. Her previous fuckwit of a bodyguard even included that accusation in the lawsuit he's threatening to file against her. It wouldn't matter to me if she had one. I'm the last person who should judge her for that. But it does matter that she isn't being up front with me, that if she does have one she doesn't trust me to help her.

"Oh fuck no."

Nope.

No.

No fucking way is Skylar going out to a club in that sorry excuse for a dress she has plastered to her sexy as fuck body right now.

"Noah, is everyone else ready?" she asks, refusing to look at me, completely ignoring my outburst.

"Yep. Winter, Amber, and Erik are in Barry's limo outside. Cass texted Winter earlier. He changed his plans and decided to meet us there. You look gorgeous, by the way. Knew the Posen dress was the way to go." He kisses her on the cheek then smirks at me as if he knows I'm about to lose my fucking shit.

What she is wearing is no dress. It's just purple lace that's almost completely see-through, thicker appliqués of lace barely covering her tits and pussy. It's a long-sleeved dress, it hits her thighs just right, and it isn't even that low cut, but it's sexy as fuck and has no place being seen in public.

"Great! Let's head out," She turns to grab her purse off the table, and that's when I really lose my shit because all I see is the naked, smooth skin of her back.

"Where the fuck is the rest of your dress?" I growl.

"And that's my cue to go." Noah laughs awkwardly. "I'll tell everyone you're on your way out in five, okay?"

"Don't bother," I tell him, my eyes still locked on a pissed off Skylar. "We're taking her car. We'll follow you." There's no way I'm going to go to a club and not have a way for us to get home on our own whenever we want. We could also use some privacy to talk about what happened yesterday. I'm not spending another night in a bed without her warm body next to me.

"Skylar, you good with that?"

My jaw clenches as I stare her down, silently daring her to say no.

"It's fine. Go ahead, Noah. We'll meet you at the club."

"All right. See you soon then." He winks at her before walking out the door. "You really do look beautiful, by the way," he yells before the door shuts.

Jackass. She turns to look at her reflection in the mirror hanging in the entryway, swiping a finger across her lower lip before pulling her ponytail a little tighter. When she's finally done, she looks at me through the mirror. "You clean up nice," she says in a dry tone that irritates me.

Although I would never admit it to her, I did agonize slightly on what to wear to a club like this. I had no fucking clue and I didn't want to look like a slob standing next to Skylar. I actually called Shay to ask for advice. After having to answer fifty-five fucking questions, she finally told me to wear my Lucky jeans and the black Kenneth Cole dress shirt she bought me for Christmas last year. Thank god I bothered to pack both.

"Let's go then." She turns and walks towards me—no, not towards me, past me—to the garage. Before she's able to make it, I grab her elbow and turn her around to face me. I take her other arm and march her backwards until her back is to the wall, placing my other hand next to her head so I'm caging her in. Her pupils immediately dilate, her breath coming in short gasps, her eyes trained on my mouth. It's been a whole day since I've kissed those full, pouty lips so I don't waste a second before pressing my mouth to hers.

She can be pissed at me, that's fine, but she can prove it with her mouth rather than her fucking attitude.

And damn does she ever.

She sucks my tongue into her mouth, biting my lower lip and running her fingers through my hair while grinding her pussy into my thigh that has found its way between her legs. When my hands grab her ass and I realize she isn't wearing any panties, I swear I almost come on the spot. By the time we finally break apart, getting some much-needed air, I grab her ponytail, pulling it so her eyes meet mine. I make sure she is looking at me when I speak to her.

"Part of me wants to rip this fucking dress off of you and tear it to shreds so no one sees you in it," I rasp into her ear before sucking the earlobe into my mouth, causing her to moan and grind harder. "But there's another part of me that wants to watch you walk around that club knowing that every motherfucker in there will be lusting after what's mine." I kiss her again, hard, for good measure. I'm two seconds away from pulling down my zipper and taking my cock out so I can fuck her against this wall when she suddenly places her hands on my chest and shoves me backward.

"Good thing you don't have to decide then, isn't it Liam, seeing as a bodyguard has no input into what I decide to wear." She shoulders past me and into the garage.

Fuck. "Listen, Sky, we need to talk about what happened yesterday."

"Actually, Liam, we don't. You made your point. Winter took the car back, and now I want to go out and have some fun."

"That was about more than the car and you fucking know it." She can't play dumb with me. Sky may have her friends walking on egg-shells around her, but not me. I care too fucking much.

She sighs. "Liam, look, you want to talk about what happened yesterday, fine. We can do it tomorrow. But tonight I just want to go out, have fun, and pretend I'm like every other normal girl out there. One that knows how inappropriate it is to buy her boyfriend-of-the-month a car, one that gets out of the house more than once or twice in any given week because she's not scared or worried about paparazzi or strangers hounding her. One whose boyfriend also isn't employed by her, making everything apparently more awkward than she realized. Does that work for you, or would you like to continue to dictate to me how you think I should behave?"

She doesn't even sound mad when she says it, just defeated. Fucking fuck me, I fucking suck. I literally want to punch myself in my own face. I could start this night out with an apology, but I'm not actually sorry because I'm not in the wrong. Empty apologies are for assholes. There is something I can do for her though.

Sky wants a fun, carefree night, then the least I can do is help give it to her. Whatever our issues are can wait. My main concern is getting her smile back. Snatching the keys to her Lotus from the hook, I stride over to the passenger's side where she stands and open the door, caus-ing her to back up. "You want fun, sweetheart?" I grab the back of her neck and pull her lips to mine, kissing her roughly. "I can give you fun."

"Fun or *fucking* fun? I have to say, without the fucking from you I don't feel you're truly committed." She slides into the seat and I'm right behind her, starting the car and pressing the garage door opener, all while trying not to smile at her sassy as fuck comment.

"Cute, baby. Now why don't you tell me where I need to go so we can get your fun on? The sooner we do that the sooner we can get the fun out of the way, come back here, and get the fucking going."

She rattles off directions. I like that she's back to teasing me. I also really like the thought of fucking her later. This dress is going to be the death of me, or at the very least the death of my cock by the zipper that is currently cutting into it. When I feel fingers creep up my thigh, I jump, my foot accidentally slipping against the gas pedal. I look at the small delicate hand inching closer to my dick then up to Sky's face. The corner of her lower lip is held captive by her teeth, making her face look mischievous.

"What are you doing, Skylar?" I practically pant her name.

"I missed you last night." Her voice drops to a sultry octave, her hand rubbing my length through my pants. By the time I hit the first red light, she has her seatbelt undone, my zipper down, and my cock in her warm, wet mouth.

"*Fuck*, baby," I groan. I'm so aware we should not be doing this, that it's dangerous on so many levels, but when my dick hits the back of her throat and she gags on it, my hand has a mind of its own and pushes her head down even further. A car horn sounds behind me, and when my eyes open I see the light has turned green.

How the fuck am I supposed to remember where to go when all I can concentrate on right now is her tongue swirling around the head of my dick?

"Fuck, Sky, your mouth is killing me, but you need to stop before I end up killing us." That demand didn't even sound believable to me, which is probably why she doesn't stop, continuing to fuck me with her mouth. I grasp the back of her neck tightly, feeling my balls tighten and that familiar tingle at the base of my spine. When she moans, it sends a vibration over my sensitive skin and I know I'm about to lose it.

"I'm about to come, Skylar, and if you don't want to ruin that pretty dress, you better fucking swallow."

She sucks harder, moves up and down my shaft faster, and when she gags yet again, I lose it. I come so fucking hard that the damn steering wheel almost snaps under my grip.

"Wow." Fucking understatement of the century, I know, but I have no words. I've had road head before, but nothing like this, and never in a million years did I think Skylar would want to suck me off in her car where anyone might be able to see. All it takes is one person with a camera phone on the sidewalk to notice. It's not like we're on the freeway here.

"Did you like that?" she asks, while doing me the favor of tucking my now soft cock back into my pants.

"Like it? Sweetheart, I like pizza. That was fucking phenomenal."

"To be fair, pizza is also phenomenal." She pulls the visor down and fixes her hair, adding some type of lip gloss to her mouth meant to erase any sign that my cock was just in it. I'm about to ask why she did it when we've barely spoken since yesterday, but before I get a chance, she speaks first. "We're here!"

CHAPTER 24

LIAM

This can't be right. This can't be the club Sky was talking about. It looks like a vacant building. No sign, no line, no paparazzi. It looks more like a warehouse than a nightclub.

"Baby, are you sure this is it?"

She laughs. "Of course I am. I've been here once or twice before. Pull in over there."

I turn right and drive down an alley, immediately spotting the underground garage. "There's a code to open this gate?" Why is there a coded gate to get into a parking garage for a club?

"Yeah. Just type in seven, six, seven, one, one, five."

I do, and the gate opens. I drive down the ramp to the parking spaces and...holy fuck.

"Skylar, what is this place?" The parking spaces are filled with the newest Ferraris, Lambos, Porsche Carreras...three of them in fact, and a few Aston Martins for good measure, not to mention a Rolls Royce. Each car is more impressive than the last. I feel like I just entered Willy Wonka's side business. I'm starting to get hard just looking at them.

"It's Vacancy. Well, it's the parking lot anyway. Oh! There's an empty spot over there by that black and yellow car."

"Black and yellow car?" I groan and shake my head at her. "Sky, that's a Bugatti Veyron Supersport."

"Hmm." She shrugs her shoulders.

"Hmmm? That's a four-million-dollar car and there are two parked down here. No wonder this place is fucking coded."

The thought that maybe this is why she bought me that car this morning suddenly worms its way into my mind. Like maybe she would be embarrassed that I don't have a car like this of my own to park down here. I quickly dismiss it, though; that isn't her. She has never once seemed materialistic or judgmental of my finances.

"I think this one is my friend Radar's, actually. He only takes it out on special occasions."

"Radar? As in the rapper?" She nods, smiling sweetly at me. "I think I forget who you are sometimes. This is all kinds of surreal right now." I turn the car off and get ready to exit when she stops me with a hand on my arm. When she pulls me in for a kiss, I'm stunned. When she straddles me, I'm even more shocked, and fucking impressed that she was able to cross the console so easily. That voice inside my head keeps whispering, though. *This isn't her, this isn't her, this isn't her.*

Something isn't right.

But between her sweet berry scent invading my senses, her pussy grinding into my cock, and that addictive tongue of hers working its way inside my mouth, it's hard to fucking concentrate. When she pulls back, trying to catch her breath, I cup the sides of her face and look into her eyes. "What was that about?"

"That was about me making sure our night starts off right. Yesterday sucked." She presses into me even further and I grip her hips to stop her. I'm hanging on by a fucking thread, and as much as I want to fuck her, now is not the time. "Let's make up for it tonight, bodyguard."

"*Don't.* Don't fucking call me that."

"Sorry." She places a soft kiss to my cheek before getting out of the car, making sure to pull her dress down. Not that it matters, the fucking length isn't the problem. With a heavy sigh I follow behind her, making sure not to slam the car door as hard as I fucking want to. Both of us being a brat tonight isn't going to help anyone. This night has started out bad and I have a feeling it's going to end worse.

"Morningstar! Hurry your ass up, love. We need you for the password!" Noah is running toward Sky. He latches on to her arm and pulls her quickly ahead toward the rest of the group who are all congregated near a door I'm assuming is the entrance. She turns while being pulled along and yells to me, "Damn, I'm just so wanted," and throws her free hand into the air. A little cocky but cute as hell. Just like that day she walked into my bar.

That's *my* Skylar.

I jog up to the door and catch them before she gets too far out of sight. I'm the last to go through, right behind Amber and Winter, following them into a plain, small concrete room. Some young guy dressed in all black is standing at a podium and behind him is a half-naked chick dressed in a jeweled bikini, dancing in a cage to a song I don't recognize. It's oddly hypnotic.

What in the hell is this place?

When he comes around the podium, I move to stand closer to Sky. He starts handing clipboards with some type of document to everyone, and when he hands me mine I just stand there staring like a damn idiot.

"Sir, you need to sign this before you go in."

Sir? Seriously. He can't be more than five years younger than me.

"What the fuck is it?"

"It's the NDA, Liam," Sky whispers, handing over her pen. "There are a lot of celebrities in there, a lot of things that go on that they don't want getting out to the public. It's just a precautionary measure to ensure that it doesn't."

Everyone else is signing away without even fucking reading it, so I do the same because what other option do I have? I go where she goes. She must sense my wariness because she says, "Trust me, Liam. It's all just smoke and mirrors to help the overindulgent Hollywood elite feel more comfortable in their natural habitat. It basically just says, 'keep your mouth shut or we'll bankrupt you.'" She grins. "Doesn't really matter in the end though, does it?" The last part is said under her breath, but I still heard it and I know exactly what she's referring to. That piece of shit Jeff.

"Can we go in now or what?" Amber huffs from the far corner of the room. She's dressed in a short red dress that makes her look cheap, one that really puts into perspective what Sky is wearing. As much as I fucking hate the dress, it's not because it makes her look cheap or slutty, quite the opposite actually; she looks fucking stunning, elegant even.

Amber must mistake my lingering look as an invitation. "Looking good, Liam." She winks at me.

Gross.

Sky looks between me and Amber, and I realize I probably have the face of a guy caught doing something he shouldn't be. Yes, I was looking at Amber, but only with disgust because I realize how much time I've wasted on girls like her after Ali's death. I'm about to say something when a throat clears. It's host boy.

"Ms. Barrett, can I get the password?" He flashes her a crooked smile and suddenly my palm twitches with the need to smack him over the head.

Sky leaves my side, sauntering behind the podium, walking as if she fucking owns the place, like she is about to own him. When she reaches his side, she fucking whispers in his ear with her hand grazing his back like they are fucking lovers, and I swear to god my body temperature rises about ten degrees. What the hell does she think she's doing?

This is not my Skylar.

And this little whisper session is going on much longer than speaking a fucking stupid password should.

"Are we finished here?" I snap. "Can we go in or is she reciting the damn dictionary to you?" I hear Erik curse under his breath and Noah makes some indistinguishable sound. Skylar has the fucking nerve to mouth "what the hell" to me as if I'm the one doing something wrong. If her idea of having a fun night is flirting with anything that has a dick, she has a rude awakening coming her way.

Host boy remains stoic, professional, completely ignoring my outburst which further enrages me. The least he could do is have the decency to look scared, seeing as I could break his jaw without even breaking a sweat. He turns to the girl in the cage and nods. She pulls the lever and the cage opens, revealing a spiral staircase.

As pissed as I am, I can still recognize that was pretty fucking cool. Skylar leads the way down the staircase, and I follow close behind as everyone else falls in line. A haunting hip-hop version of Amy Winehouse's "Back to Black" blasts through the club appropriately setting the scene before me. I thought I'd seen just about everything there is to see when it comes to the party scene, both when I had been boxing and then when I lost everything and descended into a darker level of what's out there. But this, this is something else altogether.

The waitresses look like they stepped out of a Victoria Secret catalogue, walking around in nothing but body paint serving drinks to patrons seated on their own private suede and leather couches. More girls dressed like the one in front dance in similar gilded cages, some even hanging from the ceiling. As I walk by one table I see yet another supermodel lying naked on the table with sushi covering her body, people eating it off her. Famous people. People I recognize from award shows and music videos and fucking blockbuster movies. Even goddamn athletes. One eats a roll off her stomach, leaving an empty space. The person sitting next to him decides it's the perfect spot to spread a line of coke and snort it right off her skin. The table past sushi coke girl's table has a bowl filled with all kinds of colorful pills and thousand dollar champagne bottles.

I feel like I'm in the fucking *Twilight Zone*. Not that I'm one to judge; a place like this would have been my playground years ago. But this is hardly a place I can picture Sky in. Everyone seems to be snorting, smoking, or swallowing something, and it's really starting to further strengthen my belief that Skylar has a drug problem. Sober people do not hang in a place like this.

"Skylar fucking Barrett, you sexy little minx." A man no older than thirty comes running towards her, picking her up off the ground in a hug.

"Hey, what the fuck, man!" I quickly pull them apart and push Sky behind me. This night is truly fucking testing my patience.

"Liam, it's cool." Her hand wraps around my bicep as she moves out from behind me. "Liam, this is Monty, the club's manager. Monty, this is Liam, my new bodyguard."

Bodyguard. Not boyfriend. I thought with the blowjob in the car followed by the almost fucking, she had let yesterday go. I, however, am starting to get the distinct feeling she is punishing me.

"Hey man, nice to meet you." He reaches his hand in my direction and I shake it. He seems harmless enough; maybe it's the 90s spiked boy band hair and cheesy club promoter smile that somehow makes me not see him as a threat. A douche, but not a threat.

"I have your area all set up. Cass is already over there waiting. Come on, I'll walk you over." He links his arm with hers as he leads us all down a small set of stairs to a circular couch. I want to be pissed at him for touching her, but I know it's not fair to him. My real anger at this moment is with her. She's barely touched or acknowledged me since we got out of the car. Sky doesn't push him away and take my arm instead. Monty doesn't even know she's taken because she introduced me as her fucking bodyguard. Which I am, but still.

"God, you've been MIA around here for a while now. Vacancy is never the same without you, Speedy."

There's that nickname again. The one that makes her cringe. Apparently it isn't Cassiel-specific. Speaking of Cassiel, he sits on the couch downing a bottle of vodka, his arm thrown around a girl that is very much not Paige.

"My people!" He stands up, opening his arms like he's the fucking welcoming committee. Christ, we're almost dressed the fucking same. I would burn this shirt when I get home if it wasn't a gift from Shay.

Sky immediately goes to hug him, making me want to punch him even more. Winter, Noah, and Erik all go in for a hug, too, before sitting down. When Amber walks up to him, he eyes her up and down like he wants to take her in the back and fuck her brains out. Which he can certainly do as long as it keeps him from touching my girl and keeps Amber away from eye fucking me like she's getting paid.

"Hey there, Amber, I see you brought my favorite accessories out to play tonight" Cass says, grabbing her hip while he stares at her tits unapologetically. She giggles, eating up the attention and by the way they look at one another I'd be willing to bet if they did end up in the back of the club fucking, it wouldn't be their first time.

I take a seat on the couch, Noah and Erik flanking my left leaving the right side open for Skylar. Unfortunately, Skylar is busy saying her goodbye to Monty and Amber takes that as her cue to sit. Right fucking next to me. I'm about to get up and move until Skylar turns around and sees us sitting side by side, her eyes narrowing on Amber's leg, which is entirely too fucking close to mine. But the fact that she's clearly jealous pleases me to no end. She wants to play games tonight and flirt with any guy she runs into, fine. She can have a taste of her own medicine.

She goes to take the empty seat next to Cass, like I figured she would. "So, Cass, where is Paige tonight?" Skylar asks, eyeing the girl sitting next to him.

"Paige is done, Speedy. She told me she loved me, and you know how much I love to hear those three words."

I shake my head. Fucking typical.

"What was that, bodyguard?" he snaps at me. Guess I said that out loud.

"I said typical," I yell over the music to make sure he hears me.

"How so?"

"You're just that typical guy afraid of love and commitment. Anytime someone says the dreaded fucking L-word, you run because it scares you. Pretty cliché, rock star."

Skylar staring daggers at me makes me aware that she's not impressed with my outburst. That combined with the fact that Amber has brazenly placed her hand on my thigh and I've yet to remove it. If Skylar has a problem with it, she can fucking say something. I expect Cass to shoot back with some smartass comment meant to provoke me, but instead he does the opposite. He laughs.

"Oh, bodyguard, you have no idea how wrong you are. I actually love hearing the dreaded L-word. I wait for it. Makes me fucking hard every time a girl says it to me. It's the after that bores me. Much more fun to have fifty fucking girls tell me they love me than one, don't you think?" His pupils are dilated and his jaw wiggles back and forth.

Jesus. He's high as fuck.

"I personally love, love. How 'bout you, Liam?"

Amber's hand creeps higher up my thigh and my dick doesn't even twitch, though Skylar's eye does. When she gets off the couch I'm ready for her to call me out. Hell, I fucking crave it from her at this point. Instead, she pours herself a shot from one of the top shelf booze bottles littering our table.

"I want to make a toast!" She shouts it so loud that the DJ actually turns the music down and some of the people on the surrounding couches stop to pay attention. Apparently she can command a room of full-fledged celebrities and not even blink an eye. They all grab their drinks and hold them up, almost like it's a practiced fucking dance they've performed before. Noah's whispered "here we go" leads me to believe it has been.

"Let's hear it, Speedy!" Cass encourages, throwing his shot back before she even makes a toast, then pouring himself another. Amber tries to shove a shot in my face and I wave her off. I'm not fucking drinking when I'm supposed to be watching her.

"Aww, come on, Liam. One won't hurt." She runs a hand through my hair and I back up, but not before Sky sees it. Shit. This is getting out of hand too fast.

Then she holds her shot in the air and speaks.

"To L.A.'s angels! May we all continue to collaborate down here in hell, where the liquor endlessly flows, the best drugs come free, and the roads are paved with cheap women," Skylar makes sure to direct that last comment right at Amber before turning her icy glare toward me. "And if the night ends in ruin, let those left in our wake be spared from burning in hell with us. Sláinte Mhath!"

Skylar slams the double shot back as everyone around her does the same, the music turns back on, and everyone goes back to having a good fucking time. Except for me. Because now I'm really pissed. That toast was aimed at me. It wasn't just her death stare in my direction that tipped me off, it was her parting words. I've heard my dad say the same thing many times in his bar before. It's a specific Irish toast, and she shot it right at me. I so badly want to get her out of here. My muscles are screaming at me to remove her from this fucking club and force her to tell me what the hell is wrong with her. I don't want to play these games. I don't want to allow Amber to flirt with me just so I can get an equal rise out of Skylar. This whole night is a mistake like I knew it would be.

When I make a move to grab her arm, she breezes right past me. I don't even think she noticed. She grabs for Winter and ushers her out onto the dance floor, and I sit back down feeling fucking defeated.

"Liam, sit down. You're making me nervous," Noah sighs. I run my hands through my hair realizing that I probably look like a caged fucking animal right now. "You good, man? Need a drink or something?" he says, clapping me on the shoulder.

"Not going to drink while I'm supposed to be watching her," I motion to Skylar who is now looking sexy as fuck with her hands in the air swaying to the music next to Winter. I will say one thing about this club; everyone seems to keep their distance when dancing. No guys are even coming near her, probably because they all have their own girls with them.

"Hard to watch, isn't it?" Noah nods his head in Sky's direction on the dancefloor.

"What's that?"

Noah grabs a pack of cigarettes out of his pocket before motioning over to Skylar on the dance floor. He lights one up and offers it to me.

"No thanks. Don't think you're allowed to smoke in here, Noah."

He laughs. "Look around you, man. Smoking is the least of the sins going on in this place." He lights up and takes a long drag. "She's not always like this, you know. I see what she's doing right now, and don't take it personally. She goes through phases."

"Look, you're good for her. I can see that. She needs a strong hand. No one really holds her accountable for anything, me included. She doesn't have family, really. That dick of a father doesn't count, so I cave when it comes to her. Same with Winter." He takes another long drag and I keep my eye on Skylar. It's hard not to; seeing her dancing is making me crazy. "She's had a shit hand in life and I think both Winter and I are so concerned with just making things easier for her that we forget how to actually help her."

I nod because I get it. I'm about to ask more questions when a figure in the back corner across from me catches my eye.

It's Jeff. And his eyes are on my girl.

CHAPTER 25

LIAM

"What the hell are you doing here, you sick fuck!" It wasn't really a question so much as a demand. One that he can't really respond to, seeing as my forearm is against his trachea. Luckily for me, since he decided to creep in the corner of this fucking hear no evil, see no evil club, no one seems to notice or care. When I hear him start to choke on his own spit, I let up a little.

He coughs and chokes, his red face starting to turn pink. I'm fucking angry right now, so he's lucky I don't slip and accidentally break his neck.

"Fuck man! What the hell?"

"I told you, I warned you not to breathe the same fucking air as her, yet here you are." I come for him again, but he backs up.

"I'm not here for her, asshole!"

"Oh right, so this is just some big fucking coincidence then. You got dressed up in some fancy fucking douche suit to come party with a bunch of your Hollywood friends. Fucking spare me."

"Jesus, you're a real prick."

"You have no idea. Now get the fuck out of here before I put you out."

"I'm here on a job! I can't fucking leave."

"What?" I ask in disbelief. When he points over to an actor I recognize, I call him on his bullshit.

"Give me a fucking break. You expect me to believe that?"

"I don't care what you believe, Liam. Go ask him yourself if you don't believe me."

"I saw you watching her!"

"Yeah, because I was shocked to see her here. It's just a fuckin coincidence, and yeah, I was looking because I was surprised and happy to see her doing so well. Having some damn fun."

"Stop talking about her like you know her." I shove him, not being able to contain myself. I'm shocked as shit when he shoves me right back. And still no one steps in or says a damn thing.

"I do know her. Knew her longer than you."

"Don't test me, Jeff. I'm starting to get the distinct feeling that I could kill you in here and no one would even fucking notice."

He straightens his tie and runs a hand across his hair, attempting to fix it, I'm guessing. "Listen, I already told you I'm not the one you need to worry about, and I meant it. Things aren't always what they seem, Liam. If you care about her, if you love her—"

"You mean like you think you do," I sneer in his face.

"I do care about her, yes. Love her too." I'm going to hit him. "But not in the way you think. Jesus, I'm almost twenty years older than her. I have a daughter close to her age."

Twenty years? Never would have guessed that, not that age really matters. He could still be obsessed with her. She caught him in her room for fuck's sake.

"Then why sue her? If you care about her, why fucking sue her?"

He shakes his head, having the decency to look ashamed. "I can't tell you that."

This is fucking pointless. "You're a pathetic lying piece of shit."

"You're probably right. But right now you should stop worrying about me and start wondering why your girl walked into the garage with Cassiel Logue a few minutes ago."

I snap my head around, looking for Sky on the dance floor where she was before. She isn't there.

"Fuck!" I take off through the club, bumping and pushing my way through the people dancing until I make my way to the exit. Or entrance. Whatever the fuck it is. I immediately see Skylar and Logue in the back of the parking lot. I slow my pace down as I approach, trying to keep my anger in check, but it's clear whatever they are talking about is intense because Cassiel is getting a little too fucking animated for my liking, encroaching into her personal space. The closer I get the more I hear.

"Cass, you're high. Go home."

"As if you care anymore, Speedy. You got bodyguard to fuck you whenever you need it now, don't you?" He takes a pull of his beer. I can tell neither one of them hears me approaching, and I'm curious as to where this conversation is going.

"Stop calling me that, Cass, for the last time! And this has nothing to do with Liam. You and I decided to stick to being friends a long time ago. You need to sleep whatever this is off before you do something you regret."

That's when Cass sees me. He points his bottle at me, causing Skylar to look. "You think he's going to stick with you, Skylar? You think he'll stay with you when he finds out how fucked up you really are?"

"Fuck you!" she screams at him.

"No, fuck you, you bitch!" he spits, actually fucking spits at her feet, and I fucking lose it. I run up and hit him so hard in the face that he lands with a sick thud on the ground. I'm about to go at him again when Skylar's hand pulls my arm back.

"Liam, don't!"

I don't hit him again, but I also know I'm about to if we don't leave right fucking now. "Let's go, Skylar. In the car. Now."

"We need to make sure he's okay!"

"Are you fucking kidding me right now? Get in the fucking car or I will go back there and hit him again, I swear to god." She looks back at him, almost like she might choose him over me, but then thinks better of it and gets into the car. We both slam our doors and I start the engine. I'm so fucking pissed that I feel like I can't breathe. I can't believe I actually stopped, though, that I didn't black out and end him.

"You didn't have to hit him, Liam."

Is she serious? "Oh really? So you're okay with him calling you a bitch and spitting on you? You think that's how you deserve to be treated?"

"He was messed up."

"Well, he's definitely messed up now."

She gets out her cellphone and starts furiously texting away. Curiosity gets the better of me. "Who the hell are you texting?"

"Noah. I need to make sure Cass gets home okay."

"Oh for fuck's sake."

She snaps at me. "What is your deal? He's a friend. I care about him and you hit him, not to mention he's high on god knows what."

"You care about him? How could you care about someone that treats you like that, Skylar? You are so fucking infuriating sometimes." I so badly want to lose my shit right now.

"Excuse me?"

"You fucking heard me."

"Care to elaborate on that?" She's talking to me like I'm an idiot and I won't placate her.

"Nope," I snap. And those are the last words we speak to each other until we get home, the tension and silence growing so thick it begins to choke us until it's almost impossible to be in this car. I know it's the same for her because the second the car is parked she is out the fucking door. If she thinks I'm going to just let this go she is so very fucking wrong.

CHAPTER 26

Skylar

"**S**kylar, get the hell back here!"

Despite the rather loud sound of blood rushing through my ears and the fact that Liam is still in the car, I can hear him cursing and slamming his hand against something. But I don't care. And I don't stop walking, making my way through the garage and into the house, stomping my way up to my room. I'm pissed at Liam, pissed at myself; I'm feeling violent and lost all at the same time. I don't feel like me at all and that thought makes me scared. Scared and angry is what has me slamming my bedroom door and locking it because I know Liam is on his way up to have it out with me and right now I want nothing to do with him. Right as I start taking off my heels I hear his heavy footsteps on the staircase and I know he is just as pissed at me. The doorknob rattles as he tries to open it.

Good luck, asshat.

"Unlock the fucking door right the fuck now, Skylar. I mean it."

"Go to hell!" I yell, throwing my shoe into the corner of my room. One resolute pound on my door follows and I just roll my eyes.

"You open this goddamn door or I swear I'll kick it the fuck down. We're not done talking," he says, not loud, but deadly calm.

The obstinate, angry side of me wants to leave him outside my room and dare him to break down my door. But I know he won't hesitate to do it and I like my door on its hinges, intact. I am also strangely aching for this fight to happen. Some sick part of me wants to argue with him. To loathe him and lust after him all at the same time because I know when he gets this way it's all I can focus on, and I need my anchor.

So I flip the lock.

I step back.

And I wait for my torturous salvation.

The door opens slowly, not fast and hard like I imagined it would, and the predatory look in his eyes has me backing up in small steps. He looks down at my chest almost like he can see my heart beating out of it and then glares, no burns, his gaze straight through my eyes and to my soul. He is daring me to talk first, so I do because I'm not in the mood for games. I want him to either fuck me or fight with me and he better make that decision fast.

"You have a problem, Liam?" He cocks his head to the side, studying me silently as if deciding how to handle me. Suddenly he kicks the door closed, never once taking his eyes off of me.

"No. Right now *you* are the one with a fucking problem, or should I say problems?" His voice is deceptively low, almost a growl, as he slowly begins to remove his jacket. When he tosses it on the ground I swear I see my previous confidence fall right to the floor with it.

"You know what? You're right," I sneer. "You seem to be a big problem for me tonight."

"I won't argue with you there, sweetheart. I'm about to be a big fucking problem for you. But let's go through the list, shall we?"

"What's the point? You don't listen to me anyway. In fact, why don't we just cut to how this ends, *sweetheart*?" I turn away, make my way to the bed, and bend over the foot, placing both my hands on the mattress. The back of my dress hikes up, just a small amount, enough that I can feel a cool breeze against the back of my thighs. When I look back and meet his eyes, I can't help but smirk. His pupils dilate as he takes in my posture and his tongue grazes his full bottom lip. I have him. In this moment, I own him. "Isn't this what you want, to fuck me into submission? To use my body's need for you against me until I just agree to whatever you want? Well, go for it, Liam. You don't even have to prep me. I'm already incredibly wet for you."

I have no idea where any of this is coming from. I'm typically not the aggressor. The words and actions feel so foreign, almost wrong, like I'm not myself, which I know makes no sense because I'm the one speaking, provoking, wanting. A part of me likes this side of me, the other part fears and despises it. Just like before in the car.

A deep growl comes from him. He looks pissed. Downright lethal, and I'm not sure why, but this turns me on even more. My adrenaline spikes and it's as if every obscure, foreign feeling and all the darkness that has crept through me over the last few days is halted. It ceases to infect my mind because the only thing I can focus on is Liam and what he plans to do with me, how good he will make my body feel, and how he will punish me to the point of blissful pleasure.

"Stand up," he commands while unbuttoning his shirt. I don't argue or question, I just stand and obey. "Turn around." I turn.

Even the scars on his perfectly sculpted body seem to glow red, as if his anger is reflecting through his skin, and if it weren't for the growing bulge in his pants, the one that has my lips lifting in the smallest of smiles, I would worry that I made a mistake challenging him.

"You find something funny about this, Skylar?" I say nothing. "I must say, I thought I'd have to shove something in your mouth to finally keep you quiet tonight. Why don't you make this easier for the both of us and get on your knees?"

That condescending comment snaps me right to attention. "You want easy, maybe you should have just gone home with Amber." The second that comment leaves my mouth, I regret it.

"Fuck Amber. I don't give two shits about her. And fuck you for even throwing that in my face. I won't play these games with you, Skylar. Now. Kneel," he demands as he whips his belt loose.

Again I say nothing, but I kneel. The wood from the floor is uncomfortable, but I welcome the bite. My chest rises and falls so quickly, heavy with anticipation, and I accept the burn in my lungs from my own harsh breathing. Liam is standing in front of me now, towering above me as if I'm meant to worship him, the belt dangling menacingly from his left hand.

"Of all the things you've done wrong tonight, Sky, you know what the worst one is?" He crouches down on the floor so that he is eye level with me and I can't help but be drawn into the storm brewing in his tortured gray eyes. His arms move above my head and drop, effectively draping the belt around my neck. "It wasn't that fucking car you bought for me, or this sad excuse of a dress, or the fact that you flirted with every guy that looked your way," he loops the end of the belt through the buckle and begins to tighten it slowly, methodically, to the point where I can feel the leather surrounding the delicate skin of my neck. "It wasn't even when you ran off to the garage with Logue."

"I didn't run off—"

"Shut up." The belt tightens along the back of my neck as he uses it to draw me up so that I'm standing. "Your biggest mistake tonight was not trusting me. Not trusting me like you've claimed, like you've promised me you would."

I have no chance to say anything, to ask what he means, because he turns me around and my arms shoot out to brace myself above the bed. The belt around my neck tightens with the brash movement. The warmth of his body surrounds me and I can feel his hard cock pressing into my ass. His lips linger on my ear, his breath against my skin causing me to shiver. His rough fingertips skim down my spine before he reaches the scoop of my dress right above my ass. His calloused skin scrapes slightly against me right before he tears the flimsy lace fabric away, and I can't hide the whimper that escapes my lips. Or my involuntary grinding against his dick. The harsh slap against my ass turns my whimper into a moan.

"Stop, Skylar. Stay the fuck still." The belt closes in around my neck; why I haven't even questioned it, I have no idea. Probably because I'm too excited at the prospect of being choked while he fucks me. "I hate this fucking dress," he growls right before I hear the unmistakable sound of a zipper. Grasping the sheets and practically gasping, I'm ready to burn the ten-thousand-dollar dress and beg forgiveness if it means he will pardon me with his cock. When I feel the head of his dick at my entrance, I'm expecting to be teased, tortured, eased into it. Instead, he slams right into me, and like a wanton slut I come easily.

"Shit. Fuck." Each curse is punctuated with another thrust. "You came already, didn't you, baby?"

When I don't answer, he pulls out and slams back into me, then his free hand slaps my ass. "Answer me or I stop."

"Y-yes, I came." I drop my head to the mattress in defeat, bracing myself for the next orgasm that I know is not far behind. His hand grabs the belt, and I feel his knuckles scrape against the back of my neck. Then he pulls me up until my back is pressed against his chest.

"You're wrong about one thing." He slams into me again and the lack of air makes me light headed, almost euphoric. "I don't want to fuck you into submission—submission is easy. Using your body's need for me against you, even easier." His hand slides down to my clit, fingers pressing hard until I come again.

"Oh god. Fuck! Liam!" I start to fall forward onto the bed again, but he uses the belt around my neck to keep me up.

"See, baby? Too easy. I'm not about easy. This is about admission." *Thrust.* "Confession." *Thrust.* "I'm going to fuck you until you tell me what the hell is going on with you." He bites the lobe of my ear as he continues to pound into me, pinching my nipples, pulling the belt every time he thinks I've started to catch my breath. Right as I'm about to come again, he stops. Warm breath caresses my ear, but the question coming out of his mouth does the opposite.

"Why have you been acting differently these last few days?"

"I-I haven't." Have I? I don't know. I'm different, but still me. He just doesn't know this version of me yet.

"Skylar." Rather than call me out for lying, he growls my name in warning. But I know his body so well by now that I can tell by his tightened muscles and stilted movements, his cock jerking inside me, that it's taking everything in him not to come. And I don't want to tell him. Not like this.

"Are you using?" *What? He thinks I'm using drugs?* When I fail to answer right away, his fingers find my clit again. "Fucking answer me," he demands. I'm so focused on his cock inside of me, his fingers playing with me and the belt that continues to tighten, that I can't. And this is one answer I can give him honestly. Liam's head falls to my shoulder. "*Please, Sky. Answer me.*" He's begging because he's about to come.

"No, Liam. I swear I'm not using drugs," I pant, and it seems to set him free. With one hand on my hip and one on the belt, he pushes into me, over and over, punishing me with his cock but worshipping me with his mouth. His lips press against my neck until he reaches my ear and licks. He releases his hold on the belt, wraps his fingers around my jaw, and tugs my mouth to his own.

The second his full lips hit my own he comes, taking me with him. There is something so tragically poetic about it all. Poetic because in this moment I feel his love for me, a love matching my own. Final because even though I told him one truth, I coupled it with a lie, and the moment I correct that mistake, this will be over.

"Holy shit." Liam pulls out of me and then releases the belt, tossing it to the floor so I can actually collapse onto the bed, then he falls down next to me, both of us sweaty and breathless and completely sedated. His fingers lightly trace up my spine until they hit the base of my neck, then he begins to massage, and I sigh.

"Are you okay? Did I hurt you, with the belt, I mean?"

"No. I kind of liked it actually. Is that weird?"

He chuckles, which seems like such a juxtaposition. "You're asking me if it's weird? I was the one that wrapped it around your neck. Hold on, let me get something to clean you up." When he gets up I manage to crawl my way to the top of the bed. I remove the elastic band from my hair and rest my head on the pillow. I feel his weight on the mattress but I don't open my eyes. I jump when the warm cloth wipes between my legs, but still I keep my eyes closed.

"Is that something you've always been into?" I ask.

"What's that?"

"The bondage belt thing?"

"Bondage belt thing? Is that the technical term?" He laughs, pulling the covers out from under me and then throwing them over the both of us. When he pulls me into his naked chest, I relax instantly.

"Well, I don't know what it's called. Figured you would, seeing as it's your thing."

"I think the term is actually erotic asphyxiation, and it's not my thing. I've actually never done it before tonight, and to be honest I shouldn't have." He starts to run his fingers through my hair and I melt.

I want to tell him so badly that I love him, but the moment seems wrong, even if the sentiment is right.

"Why?"

"Because it's something that takes some knowledge to practice safely, and I don't have that. I just went on instinct. I felt like I was losing control with you, with me, with us. It's been a five day build-up of twenty fucking questions that went unanswered because I couldn't ask them. Between yesterday and tonight...I just fucking panicked. I thought I was losing you, and in my fucked-up mind, this was the only thing I could think of to keep you with me, even if it was just temporary."

I stop breathing. It's like he can read my soul, can sense exactly what I need. But he's right about one thing—it can only work temporarily. But I do want to be clear about one thing.

"I'm not doing drugs, Liam. I swear to you, I don't touch the—"

"Shhh. I believe you," he whispers soothingly, pressing a kiss to my forehead. "But you get that I had to ask, right? I've been worried about you. You've barely been sleeping, and you're way too fucking energetic for as little sleep as you've been getting. Seeing you at that fucking club tonight, around all those people, it just helped foster that idea. Fuck, I even asked Winter about it yesterday."

"You asked Winter if I was using drugs?" I wonder why she didn't tell me.

"Yeah. I was at a loss."

"Well, you could have just asked me."

"I tried. Trust me. I just stopped myself every time because I think instinctively I knew it wasn't the case. There's something else I need to tell you. Jeff was at Vacancy tonight."

I freeze, and my blood turns cold. "What?" It's only when he squeezes me tighter that I realize I'm shaking.

"He was at the club. I saw him, confronted him, and he said he was there on another job. That he wasn't there for you."

"Do you believe him? Should I be worried?"

"I don't know if I believe him," he says, scrubbing his hand over his face. "He spouted off the same shit as before. That he's not the one you need to be watching out for, but I found that hard to believe seeing as he just happened to be at the same place as you when he was saying it. I was going to ask the so-called client he was now working with to see if his story checked out, but when he told me he saw you leave with Logue, I got sidetracked."

"I'm sorry, Liam, I had no idea. And I'm sorry about Cass. I should have handled that differently. it just didn't occur to me that I was handling it wrong in the first place. I—"

"Listen, I get it okay? Kind of. Winter explained some shit to me yesterday. You grew up under different circumstances and that causes you to handle shit in a different way, and I'm going to try and be more empathetic to that." He buries a hand in my hair and takes a deep breath. "But I'm not sure I can deal with Logue again Sky. I know you think he's your friend or whatever, and you have some weird loyalty to him I don't understand, but how he was with you tonight is unacceptable, not to mention he was clearly high as fuck and you shouldn't be around that."

Tears burn my eyes but I hold them back, I don't want Liam to know I'm crying for Cass right now. "Cassiel and I have known each other since we were sixteen, Liam. It's easy to relate to one another, because we've grown up in this business together. Cass has his issues. Just like I have mine, or *you* have yours. He's not in a good place right now, I agree, and I'll be cautious of that. But I-I can't abandon him because of it. If he asks for my help, I won't turn him away."

He stills for second, then starts to stroke his fingers lightly down my back. "Let's just sleep now, okay? We can talk about it later." His response wasn't what I was hoping for, but it was at least enough to help me relax so I could sleep, knowing that he was leaving the discussion open for another day.

CHAPTER 27

Skylar

I wake with a jolt. It wasn't a nightmare that got me this time. Last night I slept rather soundly, and apparently longer than six hours seeing as the clock on my nightstand is telling me it's eight. Liam isn't in bed, which isn't a surprise given the time. He probably went out for his run. Thank god he didn't wake me for that. I think I gave up on the morning runs when I stopped sleeping through the night. When I hear beeping, I realize what it was that must have interrupted my sleep. I grab my phone off the nightstand and unlock it.

"Holy shit." Forty-two missed calls, twenty-seven voicemails, and fourteen unopened text messages. That's a lot for eight a.m., even for me. When I go to check my messages, the phone shuts off. Dead battery. Of course. Where the hell did I even put my charger?

Throwing back the covers, I grab Liam's shirt off the floor and put it on, along with a pair of shorts. I'm so going to need some coffee before I deal with the case of the missing phone charger, and definitely before I check these messages. When I step outside into the hall, I see Noah's door wide open with a very naked Erik sprawled out on top of the covers, no doubt sleeping off a wicked hangover. I can't believe I slept through them coming into the house. I guess rough sex plus a deep conversation equals a sleep coma. Not that I'm complaining, I needed some sleep.

I start down the stairs, then take them two at a time the second I smell coffee. When I hit the landing, I hear Noah talking in the living room, panic in his voice. At first I think he may be talking to Liam, but I quickly realize the conversation is one-sided. He must be on the phone.

"No. I don't know what to do. Just this morning. It's everywhere, Win. She is going to freak. I had no idea. He saw it."

Feeling a little sleazy for eavesdropping, I alert him to my presence as I walk toward the coffee maker. "Morning."

"Win, Skylar just walked downstairs." Noah spares me a tentative glance. "Okay. Yeah, I will. I will. Okay, bye."

Okay, seriously, what the hell? "What's up?" I ask him cautiously as I reach into the cupboard for a coffee cup. I am willing to bet this has something to do with Liam and Cass's fight last night, and there is no way I want to rehash that without coffee first, so I don't even give him a chance to answer. "You know, if Erik is going to sleep ass naked in your bed I would recommend closing the bedroom door so that we all don't get a free show." I smile at him while pouring the coffee into my mug. The smell of it hits my nose before the liquid even touches my lips, and I'm instantly awake. Now I'm ready to talk about this nonsense. But when I look at Noah, he almost looks scared. "Noah...I was just joking. Shit." Silence and a pitying look. "Okay, Noah, what's up? You're starting to freak me out. And where is Liam? Is he out on his run?"

"Skylar, honey, come sit down on the couch next to me for a second." Noah moves to take a seat on the couch. Is he for real right now?

"No thanks, I'd rather stand. And what is with the serious tone? Look, if this is about Cass and Liam, don't worry, I have that handled. Wait, is this about Cass? He's okay, right?" Dammit, I should have checked on him last night like I planned to. Maybe I should call him.

"Skylar, *stop*. This isn't about Cass and Liam. Cass is fine. I mean, he's probably hungover as fuck and his face has seen better days, but he's fine. Look, there's something we need to talk about."

"So then just spit it out already." He's handling me with restraint and that has me edgy.

"Liam and I were down here making coffee, and I turned the L.A. morning news on like I always do, ya know?"

"Yeah, I know you love lusting after the anchor, William Elliot, more than you actually like watching the news."

"Skylar...shit...I don't know how to go about this."

"Just say it, Noah. And where the hell is Liam?" I slam my coffee cup on the kitchen counter. This is getting ridiculous, and my patience is wearing very thin. Whatever Noah has to tell me surely doesn't necessitate this kind of drama.

"Listen, there's a leaked video of you, Skylar. And it's everywhere."

My heart starts to pound in my chest. Realization dawns on me that this could be why my phone was blowing up this morning.

"What do you mean? What kind of video?"

My mind races through all the scenarios, the most damaging one being that I blew Liam in the car last night. It was reckless and stupid and hot as hell, but still dangerous. For me. For Liam. Shit, how could I be so stupid? I fucking know better. Noah gets up from the couch and walks over to me, grabbing my hand for comfort, I'm sure.

"Someone was filming you and Carl in the parking garage of Steve's office the day you met to talk about Jeff Roberts."

My heart stops. I forget to breathe, and my whole world turns black.

No.

No, no, no.

"Skylar!" Noah shakes my shoulders and I come back around.

"Oh my god. Oh my god, Noah. Please tell me the video is not what I think it is." I grab my hair in frustration with shaky hands, praying that the next words out of his mouth are the ones that were repeating in my head moments ago. Judging by the tears starting to pool in his eyes, I know they won't be.

"I'm so sorry, honey. Someone got a pretty good fucking video, complete with sound, of Carl abusing you at Steve's office, and it's all over the news. It's gone viral, and it does not look good. Why didn't you tell me that bastard started up with this shit again?" he whispers, pulling my trembling body into a hug.

I push away from Noah, creating some much-needed distance. I don't want to be touched right now. Not unless it's by—oh shit. "Noah, you said Liam was in the kitchen with you."

"He saw it, Skylar."

Bile rises in my throat and I quickly run to the sink, making it just in time as I empty what little contents I had in my stomach into it. Noah holds my hair back until I'm finished, then I grab a bottle of water from the fridge so I can rinse my mouth out. The events of that day play over and over in my head. I lied to Liam, straight to his face, and now he knows. He hated Carl before because he always suspected, and now he has a front row seat, the proof that he was right all along, the proof that I'm nothing but a liar.

"Where is he?"

"Listen, I think you should give Liam some time to himself. We need to come up with a game plan on how to deal with the media."

"Dammit, Noah! Where is he?" Given everything Liam has already been through, I know he shouldn't be alone right now. I can only pray he hasn't gone after Carl.

"Listen, he wanted to go after Carl, Skylar. Damn near tried to take me out when I wouldn't tell him where he lived. He needs time to cool off. I mean, Jesus, the guy punched a hole in your drywall!" He points to the wall near my bar, and sure enough, there's a fist-sized hole there. But I don't care. He won't hurt me, and I hurt him. I need to make this right.

"Noah, don't make me ask again."

Sighing, he finally relents. "He's down in the gym."

I should've known. "Stay here," I tell him, and I hurry down the stairs to the gym, hearing a faint "fuck" coming from Noah.

I practically run down the steps, already knowing that I'll see Liam hitting his bag, and I try and think of all the things I could say to make this better. What I see when I hit the last step creates a pain in my chest that I never knew was possible.

"LIAM, STOP! Christ, what are you doing?" I bolt over to him, wrapping my hands around his waist, pulling him from the heavy bag with a strength I didn't even know I possessed and slamming him against the wall. For as long as I live, I'll be haunted by the vision of him beating the bag mercilessly, with his bare, bloodied hands.

Silent seconds suspend in a slow wave around us as I hold him against the wall, our breathing frantic as I pull his bloodied, unprotected hands into my own. How long has he been hitting the bag? And why the fuck is he doing it without gloves or tape?

"God, Liam. Your hands. Jesus, what have you done?" Angry skin mars his knuckles, blood and open wounds visible. He doesn't even flinch when my salty tears hit his raw skin. I finally get the courage to look into his eyes, and I wish I had remained a coward a little longer, because the eyes staring back at me now are emoting a mixture of betrayal and an animalistic rage, but they refuse to look at me.

"Why didn't you tell me? Why didn't you say anything, Sky?" Liam asks, his eyes trained on the ceiling.

"I…"

"Fuck!" He slams his head against the back of the wall. "I let you walk out of this house with him. I fucking knew you shouldn't leave with that son of a bitch. Every fucking instinct told me to not leave you alone with him."

Liam grabs the wrist of my long-ago healed hand and brings it into his line of sight. "You came back here and your hand was bleeding. You said *you* hit your hand on a car. He did that to you, didn't he?" His gravelly tone sends a shiver down my spine. "And please don't fucking lie to me again." The pleading in his voice devastates me, and suddenly the guilt of that innocent lie starts tearing me apart. If he's seen the video, I don't even know why he's asking. I feel like he just wants to torture us both by having me say it.

"Liam. I don't know what you want me to say." That's not entirely true, I do know. But I just can't say it. Not while he's standing there looking like a tornado of rage and guilt ready to abolish everything in his path.

Finally, he looks at me before wrapping his trembling, bloodied hands around my upper arms, turning me so my back is now against the same wall he moments ago occupied. He's only wearing a pair of athletic shorts, his skin is beaded with sweat, and if this were any other situation I may have found myself slightly turned on.

"I want you to tell me the truth," he rasps. "I want you to tell me what he did to you. I want you tell me that he slammed you against that car. That he put his fucking hand around your throat." He rests his hand gently at the base of my throat. "I want you to tell me that he grabbed your already injured hand so hard that it opened your wound and caused you to bleed. I want…no, I *need* you to tell me how long this has been going on. How long has your father been abusing you, Skylar?"

That question, the one he asks in a whisper, feels like a verbal punch to my stomach.

"Liam, it isn't as bad as it seems."

"WHAT?" he roars, releasing me from the wall. "What the hell are you saying, Skylar? He was hurting you. You had a damn panic attack and fell to your knees when he left you in that garage. How is any of that not bad? If you start making excuses for that bastard, I'm going to lose it. Shit! I'm already fucking losing it!"

His jaw is clenched, his fists opening and closing at his side as he stares me down; he's clearly hanging on by a very thin thread.

"I wasn't going to make an excuse for Carl. What he did, what he's done, it's inexcusable." I step toward him cautiously, hoping that if I exude an excess of calm, Liam will soak up the vestiges.

"How long, Sky?"

"When I said it wasn't as bad as it seems, I just meant that…" I can't even say the words, the shame of it all weighing them down in my throat. "I meant that he hasn't *hurt* me like that in years. My father may as well have died when my mother did. After her death he changed, especially toward me. He was angry and drinking all the time, and because she killed herself, I think he blames me. He stopped when I got cast as Mandy Mayhem because he knew bruises would show on camera and the people that had to cover them up would be asking questions. This is the first time he has done anything physically to me in years."

Any idea I had that this explanation would calm him down quickly dissipates when he starts practically hyperventilating, pacing back and forth in front of me.

"I felt your fear," he mutters, refusing yet again to look at me. Liam did not appear present in this moment; he was somewhere else, he was someone else, becoming quickly unrecognizable.

"What?"

"I felt your fear. When he came to pick you up, I saw the fury in his eyes and I felt your fear, and I *knew* you shouldn't go with him. But you assured me he wouldn't hurt you, so I let you walk out that door."

Liam shoves his hands through his hair and crouches low to the ground, mumbling words under his breath that chill me: "*This is just like them.*"

Liam is blaming himself for this, comparing it to the loss of his family. To the woman he loved.

One second he's crouched on the ground, and the next his arms are wrapped around the heavy bag, ripping it from the ceiling. I cover my ears and head as pieces of drywall fall to the floor. When I look back up, Liam's hands are on his legs, his head bent as he attempts to suck air into his lungs. I walk to him cautiously, my fingers itching to touch him, to comfort him, but worried he may not want to be touched right now.

Hurried footsteps echo down the stairs. "Skylar, are you okay?" Noah is looking ready for battle, but also keeping his distance. I think he knows as well as I do that I'm safe with Liam, but he wants me to know that he's here for me.

My hand tentatively touches Liam's bare shoulder, and his muscles tense under my touch. Even his scars look angry—red and raised as if they are manifesting his rage for him.

"I need my phone, Skylar," he says between harsh breaths.

"What? Your phone?"

"Pants. In your room on the floor. I need it now."

"I got it, Skylar," Noah says before taking off, leaving me and Liam alone again. I fight my tears because I don't want to make this about me right now. I just want to fix this. To make this right with Liam, but I have no idea how.

"What can I do? Tell me what to say. Please. I can't lose you. Please just tell me what to do." I run my hand up his neck and into his hair, the strands soaked with sweat, but I don't care. I'm almost fooled that my touch relaxes him and he has calmed at least a little until he quickly pulls away, lacing his own hands on top of his head. He begins pacing back and forth, saying nothing.

"Liam, please. Will you just look at me? Say something, anything. Yell at me if you have to," I beg.

He looks at me, and I don't know if it's tears or sweat dripping down his face. His lips part slightly and I think he's about to speak, but then Noah is in the room, phone in hand, and whatever he was about to say is forgotten.

"I need to be alone right now," is all Liam says.

I just stand there like a fool, waiting, selfishly begging for something more.

"Come on, Skylar." Noah grabs my hand and leads me to the stairs.

The last thing I hear before I reach the kitchen is a tortured, *"Dad, I need help."*

Day 1 Post-Liam

I thought I would be devastated when he finally left me.

When he sat in front of me with the same bag he arrived with and told me he couldn't do this right now. That he needed a break.

But no, I'm not.

I knew my life would be too much for him.

I predicted it.

Fuck *him*.

Fuck Carl.

Fuck the media and the fucking tabloids.

I feel fine. Fantastic even.

Cass is taking me out tonight. We'll hit the clubs like old times. I don't need anyone.

Day 3 Post-Liam

I knew I could survive losing him. Maybe it's because I've been able to keep myself busy.

I don't even have time to sleep.

I don't need to anyway.

I can just party and forget. Dance and drink and have fun until the memories fade away.

I let them take pictures of me having a good time just to prove to the world I'm not what Carl says I am.

Day 5 Post-Liam

I hate him.

I love him.

I miss him.

I miss me. The old me. I want him back. I want me back.

I just want to stay in my bed. I want it all to go away.

Noah brought me my favorite Chinese takeout for dinner tonight. He says I need to eat. That three days without eating isn't healthy. Like I don't know that already. I just didn't realize it had been three days since I last ate because I don't care.

I took a bite of the orange chicken and it tasted like nothing.

I hate it.

I hate me for hating it. I want it to taste like how I remember.

I throw it away.

Then I look through all the photos of him and me just to torture myself more.

Day 6 Post-Liam

I actually thought about getting out of bed today.
    Noah and Winter keep demanding it.
    Maybe I'll go for a swim.
    It's quiet under the water. Sometimes I think about just sinking to

the bottom and staying there forever.

Day 9 Post-Liam

Noah won't leave me alone.

Winter won't leave me alone.

Cass won't leave me alone, all of them texting and just "dropping by" to check on me, trying to convince me they care.

They don't. I know it.

My agent won't leave me alone. She's pissed. Worried. Threatening to drop me because I missed a campaign shoot and two table reads for an upcoming project.

Carl won't leave me alone. He leaves me hateful texts and voice-mails, one after the other about how much of a disappointment I am. How I am destroying my career.

And the one person I wish wouldn't leave me alone is still radio silent. Because he finally realized what I knew all along:

I'm not worth it.

Day Who the Fuck Knows Post-Liam

I did it today. I sank to the bottom of the pool. It was quiet just like I knew it would be.

I stayed down there until my lungs burned, and I contemplated staying even longer.

Until they stopped burning at all.

But then I saw his face.

Liam's.

His rare and charming smile.

His charcoal eyes staring back at me.

I swear I even heard his voice telling me he loved me over and over.

So I pushed myself up and swam to the surface so I could breathe again.

Because somewhere deep down I know that if I was once worthy of Liam's love, I should be worthy of my own.

I just don't know how right now.

I miss him.

I love him.

I miss me.

CHAPTER 28

LIAM

I miss her. So fucking much. These last two weeks have been pure fucking torment.

I've run until my legs are numb. Punched my heavy bag until my hands are bloody and knuckles raw. I even caved on the third night without her and drank a fuck ton of whiskey until I passed out with the hope I wouldn't dream of her while I slept.

But none of it works, and it's all another reminder of why having a photographic memory fucking sucks. I'm completely consumed with memories of her. With thoughts of how she's doing. What she's doing.

Is she okay?

Is she safe?

Does she miss me?

The temptation to look her up online is strong, but I promised her I would never Google her, and even if we aren't together I plan to keep that promise. I put a moratorium on anyone even bringing up her name around me too. Shay has tried to bring it up but I shut her down. I haven't even gone back to work at the bar yet because everyone around this town looks at me with curiosity and pity and judgment, and I don't trust myself not to snap if any of those nosy fuckers decide to ask me questions about her.

Not to mention, for my own fucking sanity I need to stay blind to whatever media bullshit is surrounding her right now. If I see that video of Carl with his hand on her throat again, I will fucking snap and come for him.

And if I get to him, I will have no fucking problem putting him in the ground.

I want her back. I want to go back to her, but I know I can't. Skylar lied to me. She lied right to my face about something that affected her safety, and I gave her a pass even when I knew in my gut that something was off. But she made me weak, and I failed at protecting someone I love all over again.

The ringing of my cellphone breaks me out of my thoughts. I almost don't bother answering it because I know it's just Shay calling from the bar again, trying to get me out of the house, out of my room, out of my funk, but I grab it off the floor of my room anyway because I won't ignore her. Even if she has been annoying the hell out of me.

"Shayla, I'm not coming down to the bar today so if that's what you're calling for then hang up now," I tell her before she even has a chance to speak. I'm not in the fucking mood. I adore my sister enough to save her from my shitty fucking attitude in person.

"This isn't Shayla, ass," a familiar male voice says through the phone. Fucking Noah. "And who the hell is Shayla anyway? Two weeks away from Skylar and you already got a replacement? Shit. I obviously made a mistake calling you. Dick."

My blood starts to boil at his assumption, but quickly turns cold at the realization that Noah just called me. Why the hell is he calling me? Something must be wrong.

"Shayla is my sister. Where is she? How is she? Is everything okay?" I don't waste any time getting to the point, even ignoring his dick comment because I know he thinks he's defending Skylar.

"Oh. Sorry, man. Didn't even know you had a sister."

"It's fine. But why are you calling me? Is it about Sky?"

"Of course it's about Skylar. You know, I have to say you actually had me fooled. I thought you would be good for her, stick by her no matter what. The fact that you up and ditched her at a time like this—"

"Ditched her? Not that I need to explain myself to you or anyone else because this is between me and Skylar, but I fucking will anyway as a courtesy seeing as you're her family, but I didn't ditch her. She lied to me. Told me Carl wasn't an issue, that he had never hurt her. She put herself in danger and then looked me in the eyes and lied about it when I asked her a direct fucking question. Not to mention, I'm pretty fucking sure she has a drug problem that she lied about. I didn't ditch her. I took a break so I didn't say shit I would regret to the woman I love, and so I didn't end up in jail for murdering her father. I put distance between us in order to give her the opportunity to close it with the truth."

"Hold on a second. Drug problem? What the hell are you talking about, Liam? Skylar does *not* have a drug problem."

"Don't fucking treat me like an idiot, Noah. I'm not some naïve little hick over here. Sky was acting off. That girl was on ten for almost an entire week and she barely slept the whole time. She's been hyper as fuck. And don't even get me started on that night at Vacancy. You all can coddle her and kiss her ass and act like what's happening isn't actually happening, but I won't do that to her. I protect and look after what's mine. Even if I'm protecting them from themselves."

"Jesus, Liam. She isn't on drugs. Haven't you been watching the news? Seen a tabloid? Fucking turned on a television?" he says in a tone that sets me on edge.

"No. That's not my thing, and I've been busy."

Liar.

He takes a deep breath before speaking, and what he says causes my knees to give out until I'm sitting down on my bed.

"She's bipolar, Liam. She wasn't on drugs. She was racing. Hyperactive. She was on her upswing." Bipolar? Why the hell did she not tell me this? What the fuck is going on right now? "She was diagnosed over a year ago but refused treatment, pretended it wasn't real. *Shit,*" he curses under his breath. "I mean, I knew she hadn't told you yet, but I thought you would have at least heard it on the news. Carl outed her diagnosis a week ago at a fucking press conference, used it as his explanation as to why he treated her the way he did in that leaked video. Like he was somehow protecting himself from a violent outburst. Blamed it all on her. The fact that the lawsuit with Jeff leaked didn't help her at all either."

That fucking cocksucker. "Is she okay? How is she handling this right now?" I fucking left her. I left her and she is dealing with this shit on her own. I don't know much about what it means to be bipolar, but I do know the generic description. High highs. Low lows. I'm also starting to connect the dots in my head now, and her behavior is all starting to make sense.

"That's why I'm calling. Well, actually, I was calling to bitch your ass out, but seeing as you clearly had no damn clue, I will amend the original plan of this conversation."

"Does the amendment include you getting to the point fucking faster?" I don't mean to be a dick—well, maybe I do, but only because, seriously, he needs to get to the point.

"She's in a bad place, man. Barely left her bed in days. She won't leave the house, which I don't blame her for because the paparazzi have been swarming outside her place for days, waiting for her to come out. They won't leave her alone because she's worth more to them if she's having a mental breakdown, so they will push her to it if they can. She barely eats. She's at a low point biologically, but that coupled with los-ing you and Carl outing her...she's fucking bad, Liam. She needs help and I have no idea how to help her. She won't listen to me or Winter, and Cass is definitely in no place to help anyone else. He can't even help himself. But she might listen to you."

"She hasn't lost me," I mumble.

"What?"

"She hasn't lost me. We aren't over." We are *so* not fucking over. And while I appreciate Noah and Winter taking care of her the best way they know how, I know I can do better. I'm meant to do fucking better because she belongs with me. Not that I'm doing shit to prove that right now. I ran out on Sky when she needed me because I couldn't see past my anger, past my own hurt and need for control.

I'm a selfish asshole.

"Can you find a way to get her here?" I ask him.

"What?"

"Can you find a way to get her to Orcas Island without the

paparazzi or anyone else finding out about it?"

"I mean, yeah, I think so. I'm sure I can get her there without any-one finding out, I could use a friend's plane or something. That won't be the problem though."

"What's the problem, then?"

"I don't know if I can get her to agree to come. I'm not sure I can get her to go anywhere, let alone to you."

"Tell her I'm in the hospital."

"In the hospital?"

"Yes. Tell her I crashed my fucking bike and I'm in the ICU or something. That will get her here."

He sighs into the phone. "Yeah, that'll do it. But she will be pissed when she figures out we lied."

"Like I give a fuck. We can't get shit figured out there in L.A. I can't be there right now, and neither can she. Just get her here, yeah? And quick."

"Yeah, okay. I'll get her there by tomorrow. I'll text you the details."

"You're going to fly with her, right?"

"Of course I'm going to fly with her. I love her too, Liam. She's my family. I've been with her longer than you, don't forget that."

His unspoken message is clear, and I will never forget or ignore his role in her life.

"I won't. Thanks for bringing her to me."

"You got it. I'll send you the info in a few hours."

We don't say goodbye; there is no need. What I need to do is give my family a heads-up that we'll be having a houseguest. Then from now until Skylar lands, I'll be reading and researching every fucking thing I can about bipolar disorder so I'm prepared to help her.

※◈∽◯∾◈※

When the plane touches down on the tarmac I'm suddenly fucking nervous because Noah gave me a heads-up that Sky is pissed we lied in order to get her here. I'm also nervous because it's been weeks since I've seen her and I don't know what she will be like with what's been going on with her lately.

If she looks broken, I may fucking break with her, and that's not fair to her. I need to be there for her, not fall apart with her. I get out of my dad's truck when the door to the private plane opens. I see two figures standing at the top of the stairs, hugging, obviously Noah and Skylar. He is dropping her off and heading back to L.A. in order to somehow keep up the pretense that she is still there. I'm not sure how he can do that without her actually being there, but he seemed pretty confident about it so I didn't ask questions. Quite frankly, I'm glad he's going home. Not that I don't like the guy, but I need alone time with Skylar.

I shove my hands into my pockets, trying not to jump out of my fucking skin as it seems to take her a fucking week to finish up with Noah. When she descends the stairs and starts walking toward me, I let out a breath. Even in sweatpants and a hoodie she still looks gorgeous as ever. Tired and maybe thinner, but it's still her. She hasn't looked up from the ground yet, and I wish she fucking would. As she gets closer, I say her name and she stops. She can't be more than fifteen feet from me. I close the distance between us, careful to give her some space. When I hear her whisper "sorry," my heart cracks. I lift her chin so she finally looks at me, and when I see her tears, that crack spreads like a web.

"I'm so sorry, Liam." I waste no time pulling her into my arms. I pull so hard the bag she's holding drops to the ground, but she doesn't fight me. Her arms instinctively wrap around me as she buries her face deep into my chest, her tears seeping through my shirt and onto my skin. I let her cry until she has nothing left, until she's near exhaustion. I tell her it will all be okay and I tell her I'm sorry too.

So fucking sorry.

Sorry for leaving her when she needed me the most. Sorry for being too weak to help her. When she tries to shake her head in disagreement, I start stroking her hair until her breathing slows. Then I lift her into my arms and settle her in the cab of the truck. I grab her small duffle bag and throw it in the back. By the time we make it to my house, she is fast asleep. It's only afternoon, but I know she has to be exhausted. I can see it in her face. I don't bother to wake her. I just lay her down in my bed where she belongs, place a light kiss to her soft lips, climb in next to her, then I fall asleep.

"Are you watching me sleep?" Sky says, stretching her muscles out in my bed that she happens to look very fucking sexy in.

"Yep." No need to lie. I'm sitting in my office chair obviously staring at her. I woke up about an hour after we fell asleep. She slept two more.

"That's a little creepy." Her tone is happy, but her smile is a little sad.

"Whatever, you love it. You missed my creepy ass. Admit it." That gets me a bigger smile. Not a full-blown one, but I'll take it.

"I can't believe I'm here right now. In your room. It's kind of surreal."

"I like seeing you here in my room. But I am sorry for what I had to do to get you here."

"Oh yeah! I'm so fucking mad at you for that!" She throws one of my pillows at me.

"Hey, I said I was sorry." I throw it back at her.

"It was a shitty thing to do. I was devastated. I thought you were going to die! Noah didn't even tell me the truth until we were almost here."

"Probably self-preservation on his part. He knew you might be tempted to throw him out of the plane."

"The thought did cross my mind."

"Baby, we didn't know how else to get you here. That was the only thing I could think of. We both know you wouldn't have come if I just flat-out asked."

"You don't know that. You didn't even try to ask." I have to admit, her looking all sleepy and angry is fucking cute. I would tell her, but I'm sure that would piss her off even more.

"I do know that because you would've been too scared and felt too fucking ashamed and afraid to see me. Just like you've been the last two months."

Her face falls and we both know I've got her dead to rights.

"Noah told me he told you." She doesn't need to specify, we both know what she's talking about. "He told me you didn't know."

"I didn't."

"I thought that's why you weren't calling me. That you saw the press conference Carl did, read what the tabloids were saying."

"Sky, I promised you on that plane that I would never Google you, never pay attention to anything in the press about you, and I meant that. Even if I hadn't said that, I wouldn't have heard or seen a fucking thing about this. I've barely even left my house these last few weeks. Trust me, you have not been the only one hurting here. I've been like Howard fucking Hughes in the fortress of solitude."

"That's *Superman*."

"What?"

"*Superman* has the fortress of solitude. You somehow just managed to refer to yourself as a genius and a superhero all in one mixed-up analogy. That's a whole level of cocky I don't think anyone has ever reached before."

I laugh. Hard. "Fuck I missed you, baby." I go sit next to her on the bed, pulling her into my arms.

"I missed you too. So much." She starts to kiss me, and I let her pull away before it goes too far. My cock is hard enough—if it gets any harder, I'm going to fuck her into next week. And we can't do that. We need to talk first.

"Sky, as much as I want to do this, we need to talk first. I need you to tell me more about your bipolar diagnosis."

"Wow, so you are just getting right down to it, aren't you?"

I wink. "Pink T-Rex, baby."

"Touché." She laughs, shaking her head. "I don't know where to start."

"Start with when you think it started."

"I mean, I don't really know. I guess over a year ago. There may have been signs before, but I never noticed. Sometimes I would get a little depressed, but I would just always chalk it up to hormones or having a bad day. I never gave it much thought. Everyone seems to have days like that. Then I would be fine—better than fine—I would be feeling great. But two years ago is when I experienced the racing for the first time."

"Noah mentioned something about that. Racing. Explain it to me."

"I would just get hyper, for lack of a better word. Talking nonstop, moving nonstop, my mind felt like it needed to be constantly stimulated. I was like a shark. If I slowed down, if I stopped, I would die. It was like a damn adrenaline rush. That's when the tabloids first started reporting I was a drug addict. Hooked on coke or speed, whatever drug they could throw out there that fit my behavior. I was out partying for almost a week straight, all through the night until the next day, throwing back drinks like they were water just to try and slow my thoughts down. People just assumed I was high."

That's when it clicks. That fucking nickname. "Speedy."

She nods. "Yep. That was Cass. He bestowed me with that shitty fucking nickname because he was out with me every night the first time. He was impressed by my stamina, mostly because he was actually high on coke the whole time. He knew I wasn't doing it because he kept offering and I kept declining."

Just picturing her out clubbing with him, dancing with him, touching and fucking him is starting to piss me off. He should have been taking care of her, been paying attention, known something was wrong like I did. Hell, I had only known her two months and I knew something was wrong.

"Anyway, after about five days of that, I crashed. Hard. I was depressed, tired, angry. Mostly at myself because I was ashamed about my behavior. It kept playing through my head over and over, and I kept torturing myself by looking at the tabloids and reading the articles about what a screw-up I was. Then after a few weeks I just snapped out of it. I was better. I felt like me again, whatever that means." She scoots closer and I wrap my arm around her, willing her to keep going. "It wasn't until the second time, last year, that I knew something was wrong. I couldn't accept it then though any more than I could this last time."

"What happened?"

"Same thing as before. I was racing. Only this time it was different because my go-to club buddy happened to be on one of his sober kicks."

"Logue?"

She nods. "With him being sober, by day three he knew something wasn't right. He knew I wasn't using. Knew I wasn't sleeping, and he never flat-out said it, but I think he has some type of personal history that made him see my behavior wasn't normal. Day four he tried to convince me to see someone. To either get help, or at least just get peace of mind that nothing was wrong with me. I refused. Called him an asshole. He refused to leave my side as I continued to party, claimed he was looking out for me." Well, fuck. I'm starting to hate him a little less. "By day five I was so strung out from lack of sleep and alcohol that he was able to take topless photos of me without me even noticing, not that I would have cared if he had."

"What the fuck?!" I so take that fucking back. I'm going to knock his ass out the next time I see him.

"Calm down. He doesn't have them anymore."

"Why would he take them in the fucking first place, Skylar? He took advantage of you at the worst possible time! And for what purpose? So he had pictures of you to jack off to later? I swear, I'm going to finish what I started with him in that garage next time I see him!"

"Liam, stop. It wasn't like that. He didn't need naked photos of me to jack off to. We were sleeping together at the time."

"That is not fucking helping me calm down, Sky."

"Just listen. He took the photos to use them as blackmail." She must feel me tense under her because she hurries to explain. "Cass threatened to leak the nude photos if I didn't at least agree to a voluntary seventy-two-hour psych hold."

"What?"

"He made me check into a hospital. I tried to call his bluff, and not more than five minutes later he leaked to an outlet that he may have nude pictures of me. He wasn't bluffing. I think Cass knew I was going to crash again like before. That my high would become low and he wanted me to get help. So I checked myself into the hospital. I hated it. Hated him. Hated the drugs they made me take. Hated the doctor I had to see that diagnosed me as bipolar. I was paranoid that the media would get wind of it and destroy me, but luckily between Noah and Cass, they were able to keep it quiet. Not even Winter knows. I think she suspects something, but she won't press me on it. Anyway, I checked out on the third day and never looked back. Until now. It scared the hell out of me to accept something like this, Liam. I wanted to live in denial as long as possible, convinced myself it was all a fluke. I didn't want to believe that I could end up like my mother, so I refused to see a doctor again. That's why I couldn't tell you. It would make it finally real to me."

CHAPTER 29

Skylar

The silence seems to last a lifetime. Relief from finally telling him is invigorating, freeing even, but the fear of what he's going to say next is making time stand still.

"I can't decide if I want to kill Cassiel or just let him go with a slight beating."

"Seriously? That's all you have to say? You're pissed at Cass?"

"Kind of, yeah. I guess he was trying to help in his own dumbass way, but still, what a dick."

"Well, I think I'll take that over you being mad at me actually, so go forth, be pissed at Cass."

He chuckles in that manly way that makes me fall a little bit more in love with him. "I'm not mad at you, Sky. Well, let me correct myself. I'm not mad about *this*. I'm mad about you lying to me about Carl, but not this. I'm hurt you didn't think you could tell me, but Sky you obviously haven't even come to terms with it yourself, and that may take some time and some help, so I get it."

"I'm sorry I lied to you about Carl. I just didn't want you to do something bad, like go after him, or leave me. We had only known each another a few days, and you just got a crash course in paparazzi madness. I thought if I told you, you might decide I wasn't worth it and leave. I wasn't ready to lose you yet, I guess." I start to run my hands under his shirt, just wanting to feel his bare skin against mine.

"I know. And I can't honestly tell you that you wouldn't have had I known. I wanted to kill him, Skylar. When I saw that video, I wanted to end his fucking life. I don't know that I wouldn't have if you had told me that day. So I understand. It just...It can't happen again if you want this to work. You can't lie to me, okay?"

He places his hand on top of mine, stopping its movement as he waits for an answer. But all I can think to say is, "You still want this to work?" I can't believe after everything I just told him, he wants this to work. It almost feels too good to be true, and part of me thinks it is.

"Are you serious? Of course I fucking do. I wouldn't have asked you to come here if I didn't."

I feel put together, torn apart, secure and unsure all at the same time. I know we still have so much to work out, but all I want to do now is kiss him and make up for the weeks we've been apart. When I move to straddle him, he willingly accepts me, kissing me like he owns me.

I missed his lips.

His scent.

His groans when I suck his tongue into my mouth.

When I grind into his hard cock he grabs my hips. "Fuck. Baby, we need to stop."

"What? Why?" I suddenly feel self-conscious.

"Not for the reasons you're thinking, so don't even go there. Believe me when I tell you I want nothing more than to bend you over this bed and fuck you so hard the entire island hears you screaming my name."

"You're such a romantic."

"Thank you," he smirks. "But we can't because we're about to have dinner. And you're about to meet my parents."

"No. No way, Liam. I am not meeting your parents. I look like hell! I'm so not ready for this."

"You look great, so stop it. My parents will love you. Oh and Shayla, too. God knows she's been dying to see you again. I think she's been fangirling over you for a while now. Fuck, I think she's actually been fangirling over me just because I'm with you."

"Did you just say fangirling?" I bust out laughing. I can't help it. As pissed as I am that he's about to throw me into the lion's den, the fact that the word 'fangirling' just came out of his mouth has me forgetting it all.

"Knock it off, brat, and get up. Ma's made stew for dinner and they're all excited to meet you. Dad even brought out the expensive whiskey, and I think he may even be wearing a button-down shirt. So pull your shit together and let's go."

"Fine, I'll go. Under one condition."

He quirks a brow. "And what's that?"

"That I get to tell them you said 'fangirling' to me with a straight face."

He shoots forward, grabbing me around the waist, and throws me over his shoulder, making sure to land a hard slap to my ass. I'm equal parts turned on and still laughing as he drags me out to his family that way, who I realize are all standing in the kitchen smiling when he turns around and says, "Family this is Skylar, Skylar this is family." I give a small wave, not sure if I'm turning red from embarrassment or because I'm still upside down over his shoulder and all the blood is rushing to my head.

He finally sets me down on a chair and takes the seat next to me, resting his hand on my thigh. His dad, Sean, who looks exactly as I remember him from the bar the first night we met, smiles in appreciation. I hear him say "like father, like son" before kissing his smiling wife.

When Shayla informs Liam that he doesn't get out of setting the table just because he has a girlfriend over, and tosses a napkin at him, I know that I'm probably going to fall in love with his family just as much as I've fallen in love with him.

And probably turns into a definitely the more the night progresses. The more I see the love Lillian and Sean still have for one another after all these years. The more I see Shay smart off to Liam and him throwing it right back at her while still looking at her like she hung the moon. The love and affection they all have for one another after such a tragedy rocked their lives years ago is astounding. Exhausting even, or maybe I'm just exhausted. All that I've been through these last few weeks has finally caught up to me, and Liam must notice. When he excuses us from the table and tucks me into his bed, telling me he will be in later, I close my eyes and drift off with a smile on my face and the lasting feeling of a kiss on my forehead, and the idea that this could actually work between us lulling me into a deep sleep. It isn't until I wake up a few hours later to grab a glass a water, and I overhear a conversation I'm not meant to hear, that I realize my idea has some very real cracks in it.

"Do you love this girl, Liam?" his mother asks him.

"Ma, what the fuck?"

"Language, Liam."

"Well, damn, I haven't even had a chance to eat my pie yet and you're asking me about love."

"Liam, be serious."

"I am. You know how much I love your apple pie."

"Liam." She scolds him like she's probably done a million times before.

He sighs. *"I don't know, Mom. What do you want me to say? Why do you even want to know?"*

"I want you to be honest with me. I see the way you look at her, the way you are with Skylar, how you watch and worry and care over her. Reminds me of how you were with Ali."

I shake my head. *"She's not Ali. The way I feel for Sky is different than what I had with Ali. There is no comparison."*

"I know she's not like Ali, Liam. She's a bit more complicated and I want you to really recognize that." She places her hand on his. *"She has a mental disorder-"*

"I'm aware, and I don't fault her for that, and honestly I'm surprised you are, Mom."

"Liam, I'm not. That girl deserves to be happy just like you do, and if you truly love her I would be more than proud to one day call her a daughter-in-law. I just want you to be realistic before making this decision. What she's dealing with will never go away, she'll eventually make peace with that, but the person she spends the rest of her life with will have to make peace with that too and be ready to deal with whatever

obstacles are thrown their way."

That's the last I hear before I snap out of it and go back to bed. I don't want to hear any more. I don't even want my water.

❧❦❧

"Morning, sweetheart. Mind if I sit?" I may have to catalogue his husky *I just woke up voice* as my favorite.

"Pretty sure this is your house, therefore your cool swinging bench. I don't think you have to ask me if you can sit." I smile because it feels good to joke again. Last night, after I heard Liam and his mom speaking about Ali, I was devastated. To know I would never be like her, that I could never measure up, it hurt. But after the tears finally dried up, I realized something; I can set him free so he can find someone he feels that way about. I would never have to be a burden to him, and a certain kind of peace came over me in accepting that conclusion. I absolutely love him enough to give him a chance to find a love he deserves again.

"Smartass." He smiles back, sitting next to me. The bench swings a little under his weight, and I almost spill my tea. "You sleep good last night?" he asks.

"I did actually."

"I know." He starts playing with the ends of my hair, twisting it in his fingers.

"If you know, then why ask?"

"Because I wanted to hear you say it."

"How do you even know I slept good, mister know-it-all? Maybe I slept terribly. Maybe I didn't sleep at all."

"Nah. I slept like the dead. Which means you slept fucking great. You get antsy when you sleep like shit. Constantly kicking covers and changing positions. Smacking me with an arm to the face."

"What?! I do not smack you in the face."

"Baby, I promise you do."

Not wanting to argue about how wrong he is regarding my sleeping habits, I change the subject. "I forgot how gorgeous it is on this island. So calming." I rest my head on his shoulder, watching the early morning waves crash against the sand. His house is so close to the beach that I can feel the spray of the ocean on my face. "I honestly can't believe you ever left here to come with me to L.A."

"What can I say, something more gorgeous tempted me."

"Can I ask you something?"

"Despite the fact that I haven't seen you in three weeks, I remember one thing quite clearly. I'm more than positive I can't stop you from asking me something."

"Shut up." I elbow him playfully in the ribs. "Do you regret it?"

"Regret what? Coming to L.A. with you?" I nod, not really wanting to look at him when he answers. "Are you serious? Fuck no! Sky, of course I don't regret it. Hell, I would still be with you there now if this all hadn't gone down. How can you even ask me that?"

"Liam, you left. How could that not be something that crossed my mind? And I'm not blaming you for leaving, I get why you did, trust me I do, seeing as my mistakes and lies were the reason. Not to mention the fact I never informed you I was crazy."

"*Stop it.*" He jumps off the bench, sending it swinging. I place my feet on the wooden deck to still its movement before setting my mug on the ground. "Seriously, just stop. You are *not* crazy," he says.

"Liam, I'm bipolar." Saying it out loud once again makes me feel a little stronger in accepting it. "That's a life sentence of crazy. Listen, I didn't mean to eavesdrop, but I accidentally heard you and your mom last night. She's right, Liam. This is something I'll have to deal with the rest of my life, and anyone that decides to be with me will have to deal with it right along with me, and that isn't fair to ask of anyone. You had it so good and easy before with Ali." This is the first time I've ever had the nerve to say her name out loud, and I'm glad I did. He needs to be able to hear it, and I need to be able to get it out in the open, if only so we both can have some type of closure.

"You can have that again. You deserve easy and perfect, Liam. You deserve someone that gives back, not constantly takes from you. You've earned that. Don't let me rob you of it over some misguided need to protect me."

Liam says nothing, just stares at me quizzically for a second before scrubbing his hands down his face and groaning. Part of me feels a sense of relief that I finally set him free, said all the things that needed to be said, while another part of me is already mourning the loss of him.

"Don't move, okay. I'll be right back," he says before walking into his house. When he comes back out, he has a sweatshirt in his hand; I assume it's one of his.

"Stand up."

"Excuse me?"

"Stand up. Please." I stand, because like a love-struck fool I'll do whatever he tells me. "Arms up."

"You didn't say Simon Says," I joke.

"Fuck Simon. We'll be walking where I want to take you and it's going to get chilly."

When I put my arms up, he pulls the sweatshirt over me, and once I smell it I know it's definitely his. He holds out his hand and I take it without pause.

Apparently where he's taking me doesn't require a vehicle, though from what I remember about being in this town, nothing much does. We walk hand in hand in comfortable silence for the ten minutes it takes us to reach our destination. I never bothered to ask him where he was taking me, and he never offered to tell me. When we reach a small field with a weathered looking white church, he turns and walks toward it. I notice a few gravestones scattered around, and that's when I realize we are in a cemetery. I still don't speak, and neither does he, as we pass gravestone after gravestone.

It's not like any other cemetery that I've seen before. It's not perfectly manicured or filled with perfectly lined headstones. There's a certain chaotic personal quality to it. When he finally stops walking, I follow his line of sight. Two gravestones, wildflowers adorning the plot, names etched into them so clear and recognizable.

Trevor O'Connor. Isabel O'Connor.

"Liam?" I look up at him, tears threatening to fall. Why did he bring me here?

"I haven't been here since their funeral," he admits, taking something out of his pocket. When I look closer, I see they are four-leaf clovers. He sets one on each tombstone.

Tears begin to slide freely down my cheeks. "Why not?" I ask. I've only ever been to my mother's grave once, at her funeral, but only because there was never a need to go back. My time with her was short and filled with pain. It wasn't worth it to travel states over just to relive that. But Liam had happy memories with his brother, with his family. He lives ten minutes away; just on accident you'd think he would have ended up here at least once.

"Honestly, because I was fucking scared. And ashamed. I was so consumed with guilt over their deaths for so long that I never felt worthy enough to come back here. Never felt ready."

"But you came back now? Why?" I ask, turning to him.

"Because, Sky, *you* made me ready by making me feel fucking worthy, by assuaging me of my guilt." His hands rest on my shoulders as he looks deep into my eyes. "You gave that to me." His eyes glisten with the unshed tears pooling in them. "And let me tell you something. If Ali was buried here and not in North Carolina near her family, I would make sure you saw me be worthy enough to stand in front of hers too. You've only *ever* given to me, baby."

I shake my head; he's not looking at the big picture here. "Liam, that's only one thing. That's not enough for you to give—"

"Skylar, stop. Stop trying to cheapen your value to me. If one thing isn't enough to convince you, what about the fact that you make me laugh at least once a day, whether it's at you or with you? Because, let me tell you, that means a fucking lot to a guy who has barely managed to fake laugh in the last four years. Or that you calm me—your voice, your touch, your presence. Fuck, you don't even have to be there. Just the thought of you waiting for me somewhere is enough to keep me from completely losing my shit in a blind rage when I'm pushed."

His declaration overwhelms and consumes me, soaks into my soul and heart, and I have no idea what to do with it all. It scares the shit out of me because for some reason my heart doesn't want to accept what I'm hearing.

"But you said to your mom last night that I'm nothing like Ali. That what we have isn't the same thing."

"And?" I turn to walk away. I need a second. "Hey." He grabs my elbow, spinning me around to face him. "Sky, you aren't like Ali. What you and I have *is* completely different, but not in a bad way." He pulls my hands into his own. "Yes, Ali was my first love. She will always hold a place in my heart. I wouldn't be a man deserving of you if I didn't admit that. But the person I was when I loved Ali is gone, Skylar. He's fucking broken. I will never be the person I was before. But the man I am today, the one that is looking into your beautiful eyes, the version of me after the break, loves you. Ali may have been my first love, but you, Sky, you will be my last."

I am full on crying now. I want to stop the tears, but it seems impossible. Now that he's laid it out there, I know I have to. He can't take this risk without knowing the facts.

"But what if I decide not to go on any medication, Liam? Are you really prepared to deal with what you went through all over again, what I put you through?"

"Without question. It wasn't that terrible, Sky. I was just scared because I felt out of control. I wanted to help you, but didn't know how because I didn't know what was wrong. Now that I know, we'll proceed however you want as long as it's safe. I'll be there every step of the way for you. Your highs, your lows, your fucking mediums and unknowns."

"What if I get worse?"

"You won't," his thumb brushes against my cheek reassuringly. "This isn't a death sentence, sweetheart. We'll figure it out. We will get you the help you need in whatever form you need it."

"But what if I decide I never want children? I don't want to risk getting sicker like my mother did. That's no life for a child."

"We can look into all of that. You're a millionaire, baby. When the time comes you can use a surrogate or adopt fifteen kids, or if you decide you don't want any, I don't care. All I want is you, Sky, whichever way you come."

My smile grows bigger with every syllable he speaks until I start laughing through my tears. "Fifteen kids? I can tell you right now that I will *never* want fifteen kids."

He blows out a breath. "Thank fuck, baby, because I gotta be honest, I've always seen myself as a one and done kind of guy. I think I just got a little ahead of myself for a second." Throwing an arm around my neck, he starts to walk us back the way we came.

"For the record, I love you too."

"Yeah, I know."

"So cocky."

"No, confident."

"So, what happens now?"

"Whatever you want to happen. You want to go back to L.A. tonight, we can. You want to wait it out a few days and spend some time here, we can do that too. But one thing that absolutely must happen now is I take you to get some tacos."

"Tacos?"

"Yep. Best tacos you will ever eat. Come on, we just have to get Shayla first. She will disown me if she finds out I got Deeno's Tacos without her."

CHAPTER 30

Skylar

"SHAY! You want some tacos?" Liam yells from the bottom step.

"Liam, must you scream at your sister? You have two workable legs, use them to walk up the stairs and ask her," his mother scolds.

"HELL YEAH! I'm coming, give me a second!" Shayla's voice carries down to us.

"No time for travel, Ma. I gotta feed my hellcat. She gets fucking feisty when she doesn't eat regularly." He wraps an arm around my neck and pulls me into his side, kissing me on the forehead as if it's the most natural thing in the world.

Which for us, before my breakdown, it would have been. Liam never shies away from PDA. My biggest fear was that he wasn't going to look at me or treat me the same way he had before. That maybe I would embarrass him, or suddenly become unattractive to him, or he would treat me with kid gloves. But this, him showing me affection, in front of his mom no less, shows me we can still be us, even now that he truly knows the real me.

"Oh no. Don't you drag me into this, slugger." I duck under his arm and jump away when he tries to pull me back. I'm even laughing which feels nothing short of amazing. It's weird to think that something as simple as laughter can be taken for granted, but when you can't find the will to laugh no matter how hard you try, you learn really fast.

"Baby, the last time we were all late to go get lunch you told Noah to 'eat a dick' when he asked if you liked the shirt he was wearing before we left. Then, when you finally got a burrito, you almost bit your own finger off because you were scarfing it down too fucking fast."

"Oh my god." Yep, I can feel it. My face is turning red. I also feel an overwhelming need to slap that sexy smirk right off Liam's face.

"Liam, language," Lillian scolds, to which Liam simply rolls his eyes. "And don't worry, Skylar, I know how my boy can be, I'm sure you didn't actually tell someone to 'eat a dick.'"

"Ma she absolutely di—*umph*," Liam stumbles forward, and that's when I see Shayla attached to his back, her arms wrapped around his neck, her legs around his waist.

"Let's go!" Shayla says as Liam puts his arms under her legs to hoist her up further. "No time for idle chit-chat about dicks, Mom. Deeno's tacos wait for no one!"

Lillian shakes her head, Liam laughs, and I just stand there smiling and a little in awe at seeing how an actual family acts.

"All right, Ma. You heard the little monkey. We're outta here." Liam walks over and kisses his mom on the cheek.

"Why don't you take some tacos to your dad at work? You know how he loves them."

"You got it."

Shayla bends down slightly, still attached to Liam's back, and kisses her mother on the cheek before saying goodbye.

Liam starts to walk toward the front door and I know I need to follow him, but I can't seem to move. I'm just stuck here trying to comprehend what I've seen.

This is a family. An honest-to-god, loving family, the kind I always wished I had. And it's beautiful and sweet, and honestly a little weird to actually witness.

"Baby." Liam's voice breaks me from my trance.

"Huh? What?"

"Come on, let's go." His hand is outstretched, and I run over and grab it, but not before waving a quick goodbye to Lillian.

By the time we make it to the end of the driveway and onto the main road, Shayla has disengaged from Liam's back, walking next to me, while he has his arm thrown around my neck.

"So, Skylar, I have a very important question for you." Shayla starts walking backwards ahead of us.

"Okay."

"That Versace gown you wore to the Oscars last year, do you still own it, and if so can I come to L.A. and try it on?"

I laugh. She is so my type of girl.

"Jesus, Shay, what is it with you and her clothes?"

"It's not just clothes, Liam. It's fashion. It's wearable art! Tell him, Skylar." She throws both hands in the air as she continues to walk backwards, almost skipping. Her free-spirited nature and flair for the dramatic is completely endearing, and I find myself catching it like a virus.

"She's completely right, Liam. A Versace gown is art. Do not disparage the dress by referring to it simply as clothing. And of course I still have it. You are welcome to try it on anytime."

Shayla smiles huge and I swear the sun shines a little brighter. "You are the freaking best! You can never leave her, Liam. Keep her forever!"

He chuckles lightly before leaning in and whispering, "I plan on it," into my hair. "I missed this," he says quietly, brushing his thumb across my cheek.

"What?"

"Your smile. That laugh. Your spunk."

I'm hit with guilt at his confession because I hate that I've caused him any worry or stress. I hate that I can't always be the better version of me for him.

"Don't do that, Sky."

Jesus, he really can read my thoughts.

"Do what?" I ask, testing to see if he is some kind of weird Skylar specific clairvoyant.

"Just because I missed your fucking light doesn't mean I don't accept and worship your dark, too."

I'm stunned. Shocked into silence. Not only because he clearly *can* read my mind but also because he somehow managed to come up with the exact right words to say.

"Oh no! Run, bunny! Run for your life before it's too late!" I hear Shayla yell, interrupting my staring at Liam. Shayla's running in the middle of the street trying to shoo a little black bunny to the side of the road.

"Shay, get out of the street," Liam commands in that bossy tone he seems to love so much.

"Not before Thumper is safe!"

I'm pretty sure I hear him mutter "fucking Care Bear" under his breath, scowling until Shayla runs back to us.

"So, since we're speaking of fashion," she starts, and Liam groans, making me laugh. "I think I know what I want to do with my life." At that admission, Liam suddenly perks up, making it clear he really cares about her future plans. "I want to be a fashion designer!"

This doesn't surprise me at all. The girl has an eye for it. Even the way she's dressed now is cute—black shorts and designer tights matched with a funky vintage t-shirt and short boots. She has her own style, and that is important for any future designer.

"Can you sketch?" I ask her, suddenly curious.

She beams and I swear the sun shines brighter. What is it with this girl? "Yep. I have a few if you want to see them."

"I would love to. You know, if you're serious about it I can get you an internship with a few designers."

"Seriously?"

"Sure. Show me a few of your sketches, and if I think they'll fly I'll take some back to L.A. with me and get you in with someone. There's also a Fashion Institute in L.A. I could probably help get you into, but if you're good enough you could probably skip that step altogether."

"Oh my god, you're the freaking best!" She jumps up and hugs me. Hard. So hard I almost can't breathe and probably would have fallen to the ground if Liam wasn't holding my hand.

"All right, Shay, let up."

"Oh, back off, big bro. You're not the only one allowed to hug your woman."

"Jesus. Look, why don't you run ahead and place our order, Shayla. Work off some of that energy or something."

"On it, big brother!" She salutes Liam and takes off running down the street.

"You didn't even ask me what I want." I nudge him as we continue our steady pace.

"Because it doesn't matter. No menus. They just serve tacos. Whatever kind of tacos Deeno decides to serve today. But don't worry, you'll love them."

"I wasn't worried." I smile at him and he rewards me with a smile back.

"Thank you for that." He kisses me on my cheek, leaving me confused.

"For what?"

"For helping out Shay."

"Of course, she's your sister."

"Yeah, but she's also a nut."

"Whatever. You adore her and you know it. Plus, if she likes it and I can get her an internship, it may be good for her to live in L.A. It's a perfect spot for a fashionista, and I have all kinds of connections. And I think she wants to be near you. I also think it will give you peace of mind to have her close. With as much as you talked to her on the phone while you were in L.A. it makes sense to have her in the same city."

"Can't fucking disagree with you there. It drives me nuts some-times not being able to look after her. She's too fucking trusting, you know. Gets her into trouble."

"What about you?" I ask, because this is a question that has been haunting me since I got here.

"What about me, what?"

"What do you want to do with the rest of your life?"

"You firing me as your bodyguard already?"

"Come on, we both know this isn't for you, and I don't think it's particularly good for our relationship. Not that I don't love you looking after me—"

"I'll always look after you, Sky, whether you pay me or not. That will always be my fucking privilege. I love you."

I stop and kiss him. Kiss him until my lips are numb and he has lifted my feet off the ground by grabbing my ass. When he sets me back down, I grab his hand again and we continue walking like we didn't just full-on make out in the middle of the street.

"Well then, now that we have that settled, answer the question."

"I forgot what it was." He smirks at me.

"What do you want to do with the rest of your life?"

"To be honest, I don't know. I've never known anything but boxing and bartending, and I definitely don't want to be slinging drinks the rest of my life. And even if I was allowed to box professionally again, I wouldn't trust myself to. My mind isn't right for that anymore."

"Not competitively at least. But what about training other fighters? I'm sure there are gyms in L.A. you can work at. Or you could open your own."

The smile he gives me now almost matches the one his sister has mastered so easily. "That's not a half-bad idea, sweetheart. I'll have to think about it."

I like the idea of him staying in L.A. with me. Of his sister being there with us. I love the idea of a family, even if it wasn't mine to start with. By the time we reach Deeno's Tacos, which happens to be in a basement I'm pretty sure was once the home of a serial killer, Shayla has a huge plate of tacos ready for us, and despite the overall ambiance, these are the best fucking tacos I've ever had.

CHAPTER 31

Skylar

My stomach growls loud as Barry pulls up to my house, causing Liam to laugh. We just got back from the airport after having spent an extra two days on Orcas Island. We talked about our plans more, and my disorder, which I was surprised and extremely touched to learn he read up on. Thanks to his weird superpower of a photographic memory, he actually knows more medical facts about it than I do. I thought I'd feel embarrassed, but instead I just feel confident, secure, hopeful. Liam was right; this isn't a death sentence. This diagnosis doesn't stop my future.

"You hungry, baby?"

"Not for food." I creep my hand up his thigh in an effort to be flirty. It totally backfires when my stomach rumbles lightly again. Caught red-handed. "Okay, yes for food. I'm actually starving." He kisses me on the temple before getting out of the car. Barry already has our bags out of the trunk and on the driveway ready for us to take in. I give him a hug goodbye and Liam shakes his hand. Liam picks up both bags and we walk to the front door. When we get in, he disables the alarm and sets them down.

"Hey, why don't you take the bags upstairs and I'll make us

something to eat?" he suggests, knowing full well there is no way I can cook something edible. Only there's a small problem.

"Yeah, about that. I don't really have any food in here for you to cook." When he shakes his head I just shrug him off. "What? You were gone and we both know I wasn't going to cook anything."

"Well, how about I go pick us something up? What are you craving?"

"Hmmm. Chinese."

"Okay, Chinese it is." He heads toward the garage but I quickly stop him before the door closes.

"Wait! I changed my mind! I want In-N-Out."

"You want burgers?"

I nod excitedly.

"Are you sure?"

I nod again.

"Okay, burgers it is."

"See, this is why I love you."

"Good to know it doesn't take much. See you in a few." He gives me that sexy smirk before getting in the Mustang. Nothing is hotter than watching Liam O'Connor drive off in that car. Well, except, maybe having sex on the hood of it.

I run up the stairs to my room, our bags in hand, ready to unpack and shower off the plane ride. When I drop the bags and head into the bathroom, what I see has me freezing in place.

"What the hell are you doing here?" My entire body starts to tremble in fear when I see Carl sitting on the edge of my bathtub. I don't even wait for his answer before I start to back away. There's no good reason for him to be in my house right now, and my gut is screaming at me to get the hell out.

As if he can read my thoughts, he stops me. "I wouldn't if I were you." When he looks at me, his eyes are cold and vacant. Not even angry, just nothing. With his forearms resting casually on his legs, he is the picture-perfect version of relaxed, almost as if he is sitting in his own bathroom, in his own house, and he hasn't broken into mine. It's when I take him in fully that I notice what's in his hand, and my blood turns to ice.

"Carl, what are you doing in my house? How'd you even get in? You know Liam is here, right?"

"No he isn't. He went to go get you food. I must say though, him being here, back with you, kind of fucks up my plans a little."

"Plans? What are you talking about? Get the hell out of my house before I call the cops." I try and keep my tone steady and threatening, but I know it will do nothing.

He just laughs and shakes his head like I'm being a petulant child. "So here's what we're going to do."

Is he for real right now? "*We* are not going to do anything. I'm calling the cops." Is he going to try to shoot me in my own house? Carl may be a lot of things, but stupid is not one of them. Before I even get a chance to turn and run, he's got my hair in his hands, pulling me back and forcefully shoving me down on the side of the tub where he was just sitting.

"You are going nowhere, Skylar, and you will do exactly what I tell you to do for once in your fucking life." I don't know what the problem is between my brain and my mouth seeing as I currently have a gun pointed in my face, but apparently even the threat of a bullet isn't enough to make my filter kick in.

"For once in my life?! Are you for real right now, Carl? When have I ever not done exactly what you told me to do? I was your damn puppet for the first twenty years of my life, so fuck you!"

"You may have a point there, daughter. You were always a weak little bitch when it came to me, weren't you? If only it had stayed that way, at least you would be living until tomorrow."

He can't be serious. He has to be playing some type of twisted game with me. No way he's going to kill me. This is insane. I'm gripping the porcelain of the bathtub so hard my hand slips into the water.

Why is my bathtub filled with water?

"Carl, I don't know what game you're playing right now, but we both know you're not going to shoot me in my own home. You can't get away with something like that."

"You're right. I'm not going to shoot you. But I'm going to help you die."

He's severely unhinged.

"Here's how this is going to work." He reaches into his pocket and pulls out an orange bottle, tossing it to me, and instinct causes me to catch it. It's a bottle of Xanax. Noah's bottle of Xanax. "You are going to swallow that entire bottle. Then you're going to get undressed and get into the bathtub."

Normally some Xanax and a warm bath sounds like a relaxing time, but there has to be more than thirty pills in here, and that's when it clicks what his plan is. Doesn't take a genius to figure it out.

"You've lost your damn mind, Carl. You think you're going to get me to swallow a bottle of Xanax and drown myself in a bathtub? First, no one's going to believe I killed myself. Second, if you want me dead that bad you're going to have to do it yourself, asshole." I'm grasping the bottle so tight that it cracks slightly under my hand.

"Well now, that is where you are wrong. Suicide is completely believable. In fact, I'm sure some tabloids are even predicting it. I can see the headlines now. 'Troubled Hollywood Star Commits Suicide Amidst Former Bodyguard Scandal and Truth About Mental Illness.'" He uses the gun to swipe across the air; he's actually using a gun to pen an imaginary headline.

"That's a little wordy for a headline, don't you think?" Jesus, I need to shut up. And unfortunately, he's right. People will believe that.

"Always were a smartass, weren't you?"

"It's a gift," I deadpan. At this point I'm thinking if I can just keep him talking, Liam will get back, hear Carl, and call the cops. I just need to keep him talking long enough, which shouldn't be hard; he loves the sound of his own voice. "Maybe you're right. Maybe people will believe it. That doesn't mean I'm going to give you an out and do your dirty work for you, though. And what's the point of all this anyway? Why do you want me dead? Is it because I hurt your fragile ego by firing your worthless ass? Get over it, Carl! Move on, stop being a deadbeat and try finally working for a living!"

"You really think that's it? Give me a break. It's because you're worth more dead to me than alive, you stupid bitch! This would have happened eventually, just like it did with your mother. And if you had just settled with Jeff like I told you to, at least you would have bought yourself another few years of life."

Oh my god. "What does this have to do with Jeff? And what do you mean with my mother? Are you telling me that my mom didn't kill herself?" Bile rises in my throat as I try and process what he's just told me.

"Not that it matters now, but no she didn't. She probably would have eventually because, let's be honest, she was insane. On meds, off meds, it didn't matter. I just sped up the inevitable because I was sick of dealing with her shit. At least I was able to cash in on her life insurance policy."

"That's why you had your friend at the police department rule it an accidental drowning. Not to save her reputation, you did it to collect the money."

He crouches in front of me on the floor and lifts his hands to brush some hair behind my ear. I flinch away. "You always were smart, never told you as much because what's the point, but you certainly are."

I ignore that comment altogether, mostly because that seems like the least important thing right now, especially since he happens to be the sole beneficiary on my life insurance policy. He's forgetting one thing though.

"I don't understand how this plan will work for you. My life insurance policy doesn't pay out if I commit suicide, and that's how you want this to look."

"No, it won't. I won't make a dime off your policies, but your will on the other hand…"

My stomach drops. He's right. To him and only him I am absolutely worth more dead than alive because he gets it all. Every dime I have. Every investment. Every dollar I make from movies and merchandising, even after my death. He's set for life. My lower lip trembles as tears start to fall. My father actually wants me dead. For money.

"I don't understand. Why now? Why not do it years ago if all I am to you is a damn piggy bank!" I push him hard, not worrying about the consequences because I'm that mad. With any luck he'll beat me and leave bruises, so that at least if I do die today people will ask questions.

"Because you started to change the rules, Skylar! You started to take passion projects instead of ones that could make us money. You stopped listening to my decisions! Then you fired Jeff without talking to me first, refused to settle the lawsuit with him. Wouldn't let me hire your next bodyguard and hired that boy instead, then your slut-ass let him talk you into firing me! You were icing me out. This is your fault."

"What is it with you and the bodyguard thing?! What does Jeff have to do with any of this?" I'm somewhere between screaming and crying and in shock. How could I have missed all this? He's wrong. I was never smart.

"You really are naïve. I made money off of them. They fed me stories about what you were doing when you were out, when you were with your friends, when you were in your house and didn't even know they were there. They gave me the stories and I sold them to the tabloids. Then that idiot Jeff went and got caught sneaking into your room and ruined everything. You fired him and finally got fed up with my hires. Decided you needed to take matters into your own hands."

"That's why the lawsuit," I whisper, almost to myself as it all starts to fall into place.

"It was actually brilliant if you think about it. I figured you would settle just to make sure the story went away. Bullshit or not, you knew people would believe anything about you given your track record."

"But Jeff tried to warn me. Why would he even go along with this?"

"Because Jeff has a problem with hookers that I'm sure his wife and kids would have been none too happy about."

"You were blackmailing him. Jesus, you really *are* fucking insane. You know what? Fuck you, Carl! I made your whole life easy! You preyed on me and used me and degraded me, and if you think for one second I'm going to make this easy for you then you are sadly mistaken. You want me dead, man up and pull the trigger your fucking self!"

So much for buying time for Liam to get back. I may as well have dared him to kill me. I thought that would piss him off. His temper always got the better of him if I challenged him, but no. He slowly walks over to the bathroom counter, grabs an empty glass with his gloved hand, fills it with water, and sets it back down.

"You will swallow the pills, Skylar, and you will get in the water, and you need to speed it up."

"Fuck. You," I spit in his face. Literally.

He casually wipes my saliva away with his arm. "How ladylike."

"Go to hell."

"Skylar, if you don't take those pills I have to go to plan B."

"Go ahead then. Shoot me. You and I both know you'll get caught eventually."

"Not if I make it look like a murder-suicide."

"What? You're going to kill me and then yourself? Hell, that might even be worth getting shot for."

"Not me, Skylar. Your boyfriend. He should be here soon, right?" *No. No, no, no.* "I put a bullet in your head. Wait for him to get back, then put a bullet in his."

"That looks like murder, dipshit."

"You think I don't know where to aim on your head to make it look like you killed yourself. Or on his, for that matter? Let's see how these scenarios sound to you because I think to the police they will sound very believable. Liam comes back, sees you dead on the floor with a gun in your hand, and given this is the second love he's lost he is so consumed with grief that he shoots himself, not wanting to live through the pain again. Or maybe he decides to break up with you, and in your fragile state of mind following your mental breakdown, you kill him, and then take your own life."

"No way. You'll never be able to make the evidence match those bullshit stories. And Liam has a family, people that love and know him. They will *never* believe that's what happened."

"They know him, but they don't really know you, do they?" he cocks his head to the side surveying me. "Not to mention, I don't need them to believe or disbelieve it. I just need the cops to put the pieces and assumptions together. And given your behavior splattered all over the tabloids the last few years, or Liam's past and problems with anger, is it really that unbelievable? Are you willing to bet his life on it?"

I'm going to be sick. I run to the toilet and throw up. Carl is right. I have no choice. Either I die alone, or Carl kills Liam.

His voice is oddly soft when he speaks now, almost as if he's attempting to comfort me. "Skylar, you know this is the best way for you." He starts to rub a hand down my back and I almost throw up again. I push back from the toilet and step away from him.

"How do I know you won't kill him anyway? How do I know after

I swallow these pills and drown in the tub that you won't shoot him the second he walks in the door and make it look like he killed himself?"

"Well, I would say trust me, but we both know that means nothing. All I can tell you is I won't kill him because I don't need this to be messy. Like you pointed out, there are risks to my plan B, and while I'll do it if you leave me no choice, I can promise you I don't want to. There are too many variables if I kill Liam. Too many unknowns. Not to mention the unfortunate leak of that video of us in the parking garage. I think I explained it away enough, but you can never be too sure. I won't risk my future that way."

A sociopath through and through. But oddly enough, that is the most comforting answer he can give me.

"You need to make the decision fast though, Skylar," he says, looking down at his watch. "The longer you wait, the greater the risk for Liam."

This is my only choice. There is no way I will let him kill Liam, and whether or not I believe Carl will keep his word doesn't matter. This is the best option to keep him alive, even though my death may kill him anyway.

I nod in surrender; succumbing to defeat. I can't believe I'm about to die. I don't even want to buy time anymore knowing that if Liam walks in the door, Carl will kill him.

"Good girl. Now the faster you are, the better for Liam, Skylar."

"Wh-what do I do?"

"I need you take the pills." He takes the bottle from the ground where it fell after I threw up, and pops the top. He takes my wrist, flips my hand over, and dumps the entire bottle into my palm. My tears drop down onto some of the tiny orange pills, causing a few to start to dissolve. When he puts the glass of water into my other hand, I just stare.

"Skylar, you need to put the pills in your mouth now and drink."

"I don't know if I can swallow them all at once."

"Then take a few at a time, but the longer this takes the worse it gets for Liam." He's still speaking with a calm tone, as if I'm a sick child he's trying to help. It's disgusting and I start to cry harder.

But I suck it up, put my hand to my mouth, and throw all of them back. I quickly drink the water, trying to get them all down faster, but I start to gag. Carl slaps his palm over my mouth as I'm trying to swallow, working his fingers down my trachea.

"You have to get them all down, Skylar. They can't come back up or this won't work." I relax my throat as best I can and when I finally feel they are down, I push his hand off my mouth.

"See, you did good. Now I need you to get undressed."

"What?"

"You need to get undressed so you can get in the tub."

"Does it really matter if I kill myself naked or dressed?" I point out, not wanting to get naked in front of him. He's never made me feel uncomfortable in a sexual way, but it just feels like an added violation I don't want.

"Skylar, undressed and in the water. *Now*. The clock is ticking."

"I hate you."

"I don't care."

I start to strip, waiting for the impending feeling of the drugs I just ingested. "Is money really this important to you? You made millions off of me. How could that not be enough?"

"It's never enough for me. I owe creditors, I owe bookies. Had a gambling problem since before you were born. You were a convenient way to help fund my addiction. Money, spending, gambling, those were the only things I ever really loved."

Somehow, even with shaky hands, I'm able to get my clothes off and slip into the water in under ten seconds. It's actually pretty warm, thank god for small favors.

"You're pathetic, and eventually you'll run out again. Then what will you do, huh?"

"You won't be around, so you don't have to worry about it, do you?"

I shake my head. I don't know why I'm bothering. When he takes a seat on the side of bathtub, I try and scoot further away. He gives me a lingering look, not at my naked form, just at my face. Almost as if he's committing it to memory.

"You always were a beautiful girl, Skylar, I'll give you that. Just like your mother."

"Shut up! You don't get to talk about her *or* me."

Nodding once he says, "Fair enough. Now look, it can take half an hour for these pills to kick in and we can't risk Liam coming back and finding us. I also can't risk you throwing them up. So I'm going to need you to get under the water and I will hold you down until you stop breathing, okay?"

I start to cry harder. I can't believe this is happening. I can't believe I finally got my life together, fell in love even, only to have it all taken from me.

"I-I can't do this. I don't think I can do this," I choke on a sob.

"Skylar, yes you can. You are almost there. Drowning is supposed to be the most calming death there is. It won't even hurt. I promise. Your mother barely even thrashed. Now get under the water and make sure not to fight me. I can't leave any bruises on you. Remember, this is for Liam."

I hate that he says that. I hate that he dares to bring Liam up in that way, as if he's doing him some sort of favor, but I know he's right. And my last thought as I sink to the bottom, letting the water come over me, my last wish as Carl's hands press against my sternum to hold me down, is that Liam hates me. That he hates me for killing myself. Because at least if he hates me he can move on and forget he ever loved me.

CHAPTER 32

LIAM

I sense it the second I walk into the house.

It's the same unnerving feeling that took root when I got about a mile down the canyon road and noticed a black Escalade parked on the sidewalk near a neighbor's house. First, you don't typically see cars just parked on the sidewalk in this neighborhood. They pull into the gated houses. Second, something about that car was familiar. I know black Escalades are popular around here, around fucking anywhere really, but it still irritated me for some reason. When I hit mile five it finally clicked why it made me uneasy, and I turned right the hell around. The flashes of Skylar getting slammed into a similar black Escalade with a hand around her throat, her fucking father's hand, play through my mind. In the time it takes me to get back home, I've almost convinced myself I'm being paranoid. Fucking ridiculous. Sky will probably fucking laugh me right out of the house and send me back on my way to get that burger.

But when I make it to Sky's bathroom and see a man standing with his back to me, I realize it was not paranoia. I also realize I know who that man is.

"What the fuck do you think you're doing here, and where is

Skylar?" Most people that have a hand with a gun in it swing toward their face would be cowering or pissing their pants. I'm not most people though. Carl may as well be threatening me with a squirt gun right now for all I give a fuck.

Because my only concern is Skylar. And I want to know where the fuck she is.

Right fucking now.

"Shame you didn't come a little later," he says as if he hasn't a care in the world. "I would've at least been able to keep my promise to her not to kill you."

I walk up to him without breaking my stride. Right until the barrel of his gun is in my chest. "This is the last fucking time I ask. Where. Is. Skylar?" He finally has the courtesy to at least look nervous and my body begins to vibrate.

With rage.

Anxiety.

Sickness.

Fear.

I'm fucking terrified. Not because a whackjob holds a gun to my chest right now, but because there is no sign of Sky. And I fear I will kill him before he gets the chance to tell me where the fuck she is.

"I will shoot you, boy. Don't doubt it."

I push harder into the barrel.

He doesn't scare me. Because if she's dead, I'm dead. There is no other outcome.

So without wasting another second, I snatch the gun away from my chest and twist his body away, hearing the pleasurable crack of his wrist. He immediately crumples to the floor, holding his arm to his chest, screaming in pain.

"Motherfucker! You broke my fucking arm!" he wails.

When I pull him off the ground by the collar of his shirt and stick the barrel of his own gun to his forehead, he shuts the fuck up.

"I won't ask again. I'll just shoot you in individual fucking body parts until you tell me." Then I shoot him in the foot just so he knows I'm not fucking around. He screams again but this time I think he actually mumbles something I can't make out. When I aim the gun to his knee, his voice suddenly becomes clearer.

"Bathtub," he sputters out. The bathtub?

I pull him by his shirt collar, dragging this piece of shit further into the bathroom to make sure he doesn't get away in case he's lying to me. It's not until I reach the bathtub that I wish he fucking had been.

"*Oh, god no. FUCK!*" I drop Carl and shove the gun into the back of my pants before jumping into the tub and pulling Skylar out of the water. "Sky! Sky, baby, wake up!" I place her on the ground and lightly slap her face, trying to get her to open her eyes.

"I found her this way. I was about to call the cops before you got here."

"You're fucking lying, you sick fuck!"

Come on, baby. Come on. Wake up.

I put two fingers to the pulse point in her neck and get nothing. I don't know how long she's been in the water. It couldn't have been too long. I wasn't *gone* that long.

"Sky, you wake the fuck up right now!" I shout at her. This can't be fucking happening to me again.

"It's true. I swear," Carl groans, still trying to talk to me. I'm ten seconds away from kicking him in the face to shut him up.

Images of the CPR classes I took in high school start flashing through my head. I quickly put my palms to the middle of her chest and start pumping. I pump hard and fast until I count to thirty, plug her nose, tilt her head back, and blow into her mouth.

Her mouth that used to be warm but is cooling fast.

I do it again and again.

Still nothing.

I think about calling 911 but I'm too afraid that if I stop she will die, if she isn't dead already. When I blow for the fourth time into her mouth, I feel my tears start to wet her lips.

I pump again, hearing Carl's wailing in the background. I'm actually surprised he hasn't tried to run yet. He really should, shot foot and all.

"Sky, sweetheart, you have to wake up," I beg as I hit the thirtieth pump again, this time feeling the crack of her sternum under my hands. "FUCK!" I roar before tilting her head back again and blowing, practically sobbing into her mouth.

And that's when it happens. Water gushes onto my lips.

She's choking, barely sputtering, and I turn her to the side as water slowly pours from her mouth.

"Baby." I stroke her wet hair, trying to get her to look at me. "Sky, can you hear me? Fucking look at me dammit!" Grasping her face lightly in my hands I move her eyes to mine. Her eyes that are still fucking closed. I feel for a pulse; it's there but so fucking faint that I don't know if it's real or wishful thinking.

I quickly pull my phone from my pocket and dial 911. That's when Carl speaks yet again.

"I swear, Liam. I found her this way. She tried to kill herself."

I ignore him, waiting for the operator to pick up. He's fucking lucky I haven't decided to put a bullet in his head yet, especially since the gun tucked in my pants is a burning reminder that I could.

"911, what's your emergency?"

"My girlfriend. I found her in the bathtub. I think she drowned."

"You think she drowned, sir? Is she alive now?"

"Yes. I mean, I think so. I performed CPR. She's breathing, but barely."

"Okay, sir. We are sending an emergency vehicle your way now. Stay on the phone until they arrive, sir."

"Okay. Please send the cops too. The guy that tried to kill her is still here."

"Someone tried to kill her? Is the suspect armed, sir?"

"No, but I am, so you might want to fucking hurry."

I pull Skylar close to my chest, rocking her back and forth. I think the operator is still speaking, but I hear nothing. I start to turn my gaze upward, almost desperate enough to do something like fucking pray, and that's when I see it. An empty orange bottle sitting on top of the bathroom counter. One that I've never seen in her room before. I'm able to reach for it without moving her too much, and when I grab it I turn it so I can see the label.

Xanax.

Jesus.

That's why she's still not fucking breathing.

"I think she may have overdosed," I quickly interrupt the operator.

"Paramedics are close, just stay on the line."

"I told you," Carl whines. "I found her this way. She tried to kill herself. I was going to help her before you got here."

I know he's lying. The fact he thinks he could get away with this, that he thinks I would actually believe this is fucking insane.

I lift myself off the floor, Skylar cold and naked and cradled in my arms. Somehow he got her to take these drugs. I picture him putting a fucking gun to her head, forcing the pills down her throat. I picture him drowning her and her screaming and pleading for me to help her. When I start walking to the door, past his crippled body, I picture her telling me she loved me before I left. I kiss her on the forehead before I look down at Carl and give him something I've never granted anyone before. A fucking pardon.

"You're lucky I have my girl in my arms right now, motherfucker," I say, looking him right in the eyes. "Because if I didn't, I would shoot you in the fucking *face.*" Then I pull my foot back and land a kick so hard to his head that I feel his jawbone crack even through my shoe. He may not be dead, but I guarantee when he wakes up, if he wakes up, he will wish he was.

By the time I reach the bottom of the stairs, the paramedics have already entered with a stretcher. One of them takes her from me, I don't know which one. All their faces blur together—the only one I see is hers.

"Sir. Sir!" Fingers snap in front of my face and I snap the fuck out of it. "Sir, did she take anything?"

"No. I mean, yes. She took something, not willingly though."

"Do you know what it was?"

I hand him the empty bottle as they start to wheel her off. He's yelling something about an overdose. I follow close behind, not wanting to let her out of my sight. The EMT stops me before I follow them into the back.

"Please," I beg. "I want to ride with her. I can't leave her."

A hand on my shoulder startles me, and it's then that I notice the red and blue lights flashing. A cop stands next to me. "Sir, we're going to need to ask you a few questions."

"I need to go with her." I start to push against his hold, just wanting to get to Sky. When they close the ambulance doors, I almost flip out.

"Sir! I will take you to the hospital as soon as you answer some questions for me."

I look at him, and he must see the anguish in my eyes because he pats me on the shoulder and assures me she'll be all right. But he doesn't know shit. I follow him back into the house, ready to answer all their questions because the faster I do it the faster I can fucking get to her.

EPILOGUE

Skylar
6 months later

"**F**uck, I need a nap so fucking bad!" Liam pulls off his shirt and collapses onto the bed, my laptop bouncing under his weight. I close it because I know now that he's in here I will get nothing done, especially when he's not wearing a shirt.

"You just get back from the gym?" Liam decided a few months back that he wanted to try his hand at training boxers. He managed to hook up with a trainer he used to know from his boxing days that still worked the circuit, some guy named Ray, and has been working non-stop ever since attempting to learn and create a name for himself.

"Nah, I got back a few hours ago."

"Ah, so, you must have just finished helping Shay move into the pool house, I take it?"

I got Shay an internship with a fashion designer friend of mine about two months ago. He saw her sketches and, like I knew he would, immediately recognized her talent. Granted, she will have to work her ass off, but I think it's perfect for Shay. She was finally able to make the drive here yesterday, bringing all her stuff with her. Obviously I insisted she move into the pool house since it's now just sitting there vacant.

That way she doesn't have to worry about L.A. rent and she can be close to her brother. Which was Liam's only stipulation if she wanted to live in L.A.

He nods then grabs my hand off the laptop, kissing my palm. "I swear I had no idea she had that much fucking stuff. Who the hell needs twelve purses shaped like different fruits?"

"Aw man! Does she have that Betsey Johnson Strawberry one? If so, I have to borrow it."

"You're both ridiculous," he scolds, but I know he's smiling on the inside. "I still say we should have moved her into Noah's old room." Noah moved into Erik's house about a month ago. It was expected, and I'm going to miss him, but I'm happy for him.

"And I told *you* she's an adult and she needs her own space. She doesn't need her brother in the room right across the hall from her. What if she wants to have friends over or something? She needs her privacy. And sorry I couldn't help. I was just really in the zone." I scoot closer to him, and he wraps his arms around me, pulling me close. His arms are still my favorite place to be.

"It's cool, I said I didn't need your help. I want you to finish your script. If you're in the fucking zone, stay in it."

I started writing a script about my life after my psychiatrist suggested it. He said it may be therapeutic. A way to deal with all the things I've been through. The more I wrote the more I realized if I hadn't lived it, I never would believe it was a true story. Especially the part where my psycho father actually ended up getting sentenced to more prison for tax evasion than he did for my attempted murder.

Never fuck with the Government.

Luckily I never had to testify; he took a plea deal. Not that I would have minded facing him in court, but I was worried about Liam. When I had to give my statement to the police, Liam about lost his shit. For weeks he was racked with guilt thinking that if he hadn't left it never would have happened. Thinking that I chose his life over mine, not accepting that Carl wasn't leaving me with a choice. I was going to die either way.

The "what ifs" were choking us until finally I couldn't take it anymore and made him realize and accept that he was, that he is, my savior. That there were a whole lot of other "what ifs," all of which would have resulted in my death. He turned around on instinct. If he'd actually gone for that food, I wouldn't be here today. He gave me CPR; he made it possible for me to even have a fighting chance when they pumped my stomach to rid me of the drugs.

"Are you almost done with it?"

"Almost. I'm stuck on the ending though. I'm supposed to turn it into my agent at the end of the week so she can start pitching it to some studios."

I also plan on turning it into an actual movie. It's time I get to show my truth to the world instead of letting the media do it for me. Maybe people will believe it, maybe they won't. Maybe they'll think I'm full of shit and just trying to cover up my raging drug problem. All I know is I don't really fucking care; at least I get to tell it.

"Hmm, well I think I have a pretty good idea for an ending."

"Oh really?" I ask curiously, starting to trace his scars softly with my fingers.

"It's in my pants." He winks at me and I smack him on his stomach.

"Ouch!"

"You're so not romantic."

"What? I meant my pants pocket. What were you thinking, dirty girl?"

"Whatever. Which pocket?"

"My right one."

I reach into his right pocket, ignoring the growing bulge in his pants. *Yeah right, and I'm the dirty one.* When my hand touches what feels suspiciously like a ring box, I freeze.

"Aren't you going to take it out?" he asks softly, wrapping his fingers around my slender wrist, pulling until my hand is free.

I swallow hard when I see the green velvet box.

"Open it," Liam says.

"I-I don't think I can. My hands are shaking too much."

He opens it for me and my tears start to fall. Inside is a gorgeous ring, one unlike any other that I've seen before. A ruby heart is held together by two diamond encrusted hands, a diamond crown resting above the heart.

"It's called a Claddagh ring. The hands that hold the heart represent friendship. The crown on top," he points to the crown, "represents loyalty. And the heart, that represents love."

"It's so…I don't even have words, Liam. It's beautiful."

"Well, that is definitely a word."

"Smartass."

He laughs. "I have another word you can use. Yes."

I bite my lip, trying not smile or cry even harder. I know what he means, but I want to hear him say it anyway. "You didn't ask me a question though. I don't know what I'm saying yes to. Yes to pizza? Yes to a blowjob?"

"Did you really just say the words pizza and blowjob during a marriage proposal?"

"Technically no. You still haven't made it one."

"Cute." He pushes some loose hair behind my ear, causing me to shiver. "Okay, how's this? I love you, Skylar Barrett. I love every broken part of you, and I love even more how you love and accept every broken part of me. Marry me?"

When he slides the ring onto my left finger, I can do nothing but nod and cry and say yes between kisses. And when I'm finally able to move past my shock and form a cohesive sentence I will tell him that he's wrong.

We aren't broken people, we never were.

In fact we are far from it. We are fighters.

Survivors.

Apart we were always strong we just couldn't recognize it.

But together, together we are fucking lethal.

STAY TUNED FOR CASS & SHAYLA'S STORY

Coming 2017

Excerpt from: *Bound to Me* by Christy Pastore

The duo snogging didn't bother to make room for us, leaving me no choice but to stand on the same side of the lift with Alex. With our arms brushed against one another, heat spread across my skin like a raging wildfire. The two of us snuggled close in a compact space. My hand still tingled from his touch. It was impossible to concentrate on anything other than him. He was here. Right next to me, looking gorgeous and smelling perfectly divine. All sense I had retreated from my brain as I stood there fantasizing about pushing him up against the wall and allowing him to shag . . . *fuck* the hell out of me.

Shut up, Ella, you dirty bird.

When the car reached the fifth floor, and the couple playing slap and tickle walked out, I stifled a moan of relief. Unsure if I was comforted due to the fact that they left or that I had Alex all to myself. I glanced at him, trying to get a sense of his thoughts. His mouth was pressed into a hard line, and his eyes remained forward, fixed on the numeric panel.

The lift came to a halt at the lobby and Alex stepped out, his head turned left and back to the right. The unrehearsed movement was fluid. He motioned for me to walk in front of him, but I had no clue where we were going.

"You lead the way."

"All right, but keep your pace with mine," he instructed. His voice was firm not angry.

I nodded, and did as I was instructed, keeping my stride with his as we passed through the spacious lobby. Something had changed his demeanor during the ride in the lift . . . *elevator*. Mentally I noted that I needed to brush up on my American English. If I intended to do business here, I should at least make the effort to know the proper terms.

Once outside, his hand reached inside his jacket pocket, pulling out his sunglasses. As we approached the valent stand, he put them on, shielding me from seeing his gorgeous eyes that reminded me of glowing golden sunlight sifting through deep green leaves.

Snap out of it, Ella. He's your bodyguard.

Straightening my shoulders, I hauled my handbag higher onto my shoulder. I vowed to lock all my scandalous thoughts away.

ACKNOWLEDGMENTS

cracks knuckles

First and foremost, I must thank and praise The Husband. You make me laugh, you believe in me, you sacrifice for me; without question or hesitation. I swear the way you love me, turns love into something tangible. There will never be a book I write about love that has not, in some way, been inspired by you.

Christy Pastore, the Maximus to my William, my sounding board, my person. You have been there since the beginning with me. Literally the very, very super beginning, before I even had a Facebook and you had to constantly tell me it was a necessary evil if I wanted to be an author so I finally caved because as always, you were right. You had already finished and published your first book at this point (Fifteen Weekends in case you forgot, and FYI anyone reading this who has NOT read Fifteen Weekends you MUST immediately) and I just remember thinking how amazing it was that you took the time to answer any questions I may have had, give me advice I didn't even know I needed, or even read something for me I was unsure of. Our sprinting sessions were and still continue to be my favorite part of the writing process. I am so lucky that my first friend in the book and author community was you. Your loyalty, positivity and constant willingness to help, even when we barely knew one another, set the perfect example for me as I continued to meet new people in the book and author world. I am so proud to call you a friend. I love you bestie!

Jamie Mcguire. You yelled at me on a shuttle bus in L.A. to PICK A DAMN RELEASE DATE ALREADY! Okay, maybe not yelled so much as sternly scolded me. And to be fair it was much deserved seeing as I was two years into a book that should have taken half that time to write. That night I picked a release date and the day after that I announced it, and despite the fact that because of scheduling conflicts I had to move the date, I still hit my deadline. When you pushed me that day to pick a date something inside me changed. Knowing that you had my back, that you believed in me enough to take me to task, gave me that extra boost of confidence I didn't know was even lacking. If you hadn't done that I probably wouldn't have released this book until 2022, and we both know we can't have that seeing as we release our book that year ;). I look up to you and admire the woman are; especially knowing all the obstacles you have overcome and continue to overcome. You are a loving mother, a killer author, an amazing business woman, a giving and loyal friend, and girl you can hustle like no one's business. Seriously, it is impressive. You are my family and I can't thank you enough you feisty lil' ginge.

To my adulting guru, AKA The Wizard, AKA Jen Armentrout (I can already feel you side-eyeing me by the way), I thought long and hard as to how I could properly convey what your friendship and advice meant to me during this writing process, and honestly, I realized the few words I'm allowed to put in the acknowledgments probably won't do it justice. But I will say this, you saved me a million times mentally and you probably didn't even know it. If I was forced to choose between our phone calls and reality TV, I would give up reality TV, and you know how much I love my shows. You have become easily one of my best friends, and a mentor, and I am just so grateful you came into my life.

This is a very special thank you to my favorite Brit, Jodi Marie Maliszewski. We bonded over KC Lynn books and never looked back. You my love will never know how much your encouragement meant to me. I swear the first time you made me a teaser just because you liked a portion of the book I sent to you I almost cried because your opinion was incredibly important to me. Because, let's face it lady (and I think many, many, MANY people would agree with me); You are the heart of this book community. Your posts and commentaries make so many laugh, give recognition and praise to authors some may never have heard of, and your reviews are fucking epic every single time. You are a positive light in the book world and you better never leave us… because we will find you.

Someone once told me that a great editor will help the author learn, teach them how to be better through their notes. Because of Kara Malinczak I know that to be true. I lucked the hell out finding you as my first editor Kara (well actually not finding you so much as Jen recommending me to you. I owe you for that Jen by the way). You were patient, knowledgeable, and went above and beyond any expectations

I had about what an editor does for an author's manuscript. I am so excited for you to edit book two for me just so you can see how much I've learned and grown as an author. You are my hero woman!

KC Lynn, the fact that you were willing to be my friend after my super Facebook stalking of you and your books still amazes me to this day. Even though we voice message and chat on the regular I still fangirl out a little every time. And when I ask you to read something so I can get your opinion and you say yes, I get equally nervous and excited because, OMG KC LYNN IS ABOUT TO READ SOMETHING I WROTE!!!! Your books were my happy place, my wonderful escape when my mind needed that writing break (as you know I have read them all about a gazillion times). I was a fan from your first release, and now I get to be your friend through all the others. Thank you for being you!

To my KB Ritchie reading buddy and second BETA Jullie Anne, FINISH YOUR BOOK WOMAN I CAN'T STOP THINKING ABOUT IT! And also, thank you for all you did for me. Your amazingly hilarious and helpful notes, your opinions and your epic food videos on SnapChat. They almost make cooking seem easy. But seriously, please finish your book. The people need to see that natural talent on some pages yo.

A HUGE thank you to my Proofreader Kimberley Foster Holm. You took the job last minute and you freaking KILLED IT! Eyes of a freaking eagle. It scares me to even mention you here or sing your praises on Facebook as I want no one else to know of you. Well except KC Lynn of course since she was the one that sent me to you (THANK YOU KC!). You are amazing and I can't wait until next time.

Speaking of people who came through last minute for me. Kelly of For the Loves of Books and Alcohol (by the way if you have never seen that blog you should check it out, they have the COOLEST way of rating books), the fact that you agreed to BETA for me with a five-day deadline meant the world to me. You, my fellow Irish friend, are seriously the best. I thank you a million times over!

To my Aussie Nugget, Skyla Madi, you are my people. I love and adore you, and not just because you wrote Seth Marc into existence. But that is a huge reason. The rest of the reasons are because you make me laugh, you amaze me with all the things you've accomplished at such a young age, you are always willing to help when I need it, and also I'm still not entirely sure you know how Instagram works which amuses me to no end. I swear one day I'm going to kidnap you and bring you to the US and force you to be my neighbor! But until that day we always have Facebook messenger.

A much deserved thank you to my cousin and longtime bestie Whitney Edwards. Thank you for getting me out of the house for cocktails and sliders when I had been stuck in it too long writing. Also, thank you for understanding when I had to cancel last minute because I was in the writing zone. You just get me Whitters, and I love you for that.

Dad, nothing makes me prouder than to be able to tell people; I am my Father's daughter.

Mom, I would not be half the woman I am today without you in my life. Thank you for sacrificing all you did to make sure you would stay in it.

Sister, you are a unique one, and it has been awesome watching you grow into the woman you've become. I can't imagine what my life would be without you in it, and even though we aren't able to talk often (probably my fault by the way) don't think I'm not thinking about you every day. In fact, I wish I could awkward hug you right now Bubba.

AND FINALLY A MAJOR THANK YOU TO THE FOLLOWING PEOPLE

Alison Rian (Beneath The Covers Book Blog), Kelly Emery (Beneath The Covers Book Blog), Tiffany Riley, Millie Noonan, Ashley Erin, Fabiola Francisco, Rebecca Gates, Tiffany Robinson, Casey Decock, Jennifer Norman Corzine, Kat Maloney (Biblio Belles Book Blog), Danielle Rose Hernandez (For The Love of Books and Alcohol), Jessica Landers, Samien Newcomb, and Dannah Murray.

You guys have all been so vocal and supportive through this process, and it helped so much along the way knowing at least a few wanted to read it. You guys freaking rock!

And if I left anyone out on that list don't think I forgot about you. I probably just had a minor brain-dead type of moment. But don't worry, I will get you on the next book ;)